DEEP SILENCE

ALSO BY JONATHAN MABERRY

Kill Switch
Predator One
Fall of Night
Code Zero
Extinction Machine
Assassin's Code
The King of Plagues
The Dragon Factory
Patient Zero
Joe Ledger: Special Ops
Dead of Night
Fall of Night
The Wolfman
The Nightsiders: The Orphan Army
The Nightsiders: Vault of Shadows
Deadlands: Ghostwalkers
Bits & Pieces
Fire & Ash
Flesh & Bone
Dust & Decay
Rot & Ruin
Bad Moon Rising
Dead Man's Song
Ghost Road Blues
Glimpse
Mars One

ANTHOLOGIES (AS EDITOR)

Joe Ledger: Unstoppable
Nights of the Living Dead
V-Wars
V-Wars: Blood and Fire
V-Wars: Night Terrors
Out of Tune
The X-Files: Trust No One
The X-Files: The Truth Is Out There
Hardboiled Horror
V-Wars: Shockwaves
Aliens: Bug Hunt
The X-Files: Secret Agendas
Baker Street Irregulars
Scary Out There

JONATHAN MABERRY

DEEP SILENCE

ST. MARTIN'S GRIFFIN
NEW YORK

This is a work of fiction. All of the characters, organizations, and events portrayed in this novel are either products of the author's imagination or are used fictitiously.

 For information, address St. Martin's Press, 175 Fifth Avenue, New York, N.Y. 10010.

www.stmartins.com

The Library of Congress Cataloging-in-Publication Data is available upon request.

ISBN 978-1-250-09846-7 (trade paperback)
ISBN 978-1-250-09847-4 (ebook)

Our books may be purchased in bulk for promotional, educational, or business use. Please contact your local bookseller or the Macmillan Corporate and Premium Sales Department at 1-800-221-7945, extension 5442, or by email at MacmillanSpecialMarkets@macmillan.com.

First Edition: October 2018

10 9 8 7 6 5 4 3 2 1

This is for
Ted Adams and David Ozer.
For going to war for me and with me.
And, as always, for Sara Jo.

ACKNOWLEDGMENTS

As always, I owe a debt to several wonderful people. Thanks to my literary agent, Sara Crowe of Pippin Properties; my faithful and long-suffering editor at St. Martin's Griffin, Michael Homler; Robert Allen and the crew at Macmillan Audio; my film agent, Dana Spector of Paradigm; and my brilliant audiobook reader, Ray Porter.

Thanks to the winners of the Joe Ledger "Name the Character" contests: Francesco Tigninii, Dennis Crosby, Thom Erb, Johns D. Curtis, Dominic Oviedo, Geoff Brown, Jenny Robinson, Robert Thomas, and Kelly Littleton. Christopher Hitchcock, CEG, principal engineering geologist InfraTerra, Inc.; Scott M. Ausbrooks, assistant director and assistant state geologist, Arkansas Geological Survey; John Geissman, professor and department head, editor in chief of *Tectonics,* University of Texas at Dallas Geosciences; Dr. Wendy Bohon, geologist, Arizona State University; Dr. Blake P. Weissling, research assistant professor and senior lecturer in geophysics, University of Texas at San Antonio; Dr. David H. Salzberg, seismologist; Chris MacInnis, P.Geo, vice president (geology), Goldspot Discoveries Inc.; Marc Byrne, formerly of the School of Geosciences, University of South Florida.

Quote from *The Sandman: Endless Nights* by Neil Gaiman, used by permission of the author.

DEEP SILENCE

PROLOGUE

ABOARD THE *ANATOLY*
NINE NAUTICAL MILES SOUTHEAST OF HANAUMA BAY NATURE PRESERVE
OAHU, HAWAII
SEVEN YEARS AGO

"We're coming up on it," said the pilot. It was the third time he'd spoken, and this time he pitched it almost to a shout.

Valen Oruraka looked up this time, nodded, and put his satellite phone back into a pouch on his belt. The crew were used to having to say things to Valen several times. The man was deaf as a haddock, and either his hearing aid did not work well or he kept the volume turned down because of the annoying engine noise. Or, maybe it was that the strange man did not want to be bothered by chatter from the crew. He was quiet and the furthest thing from chatty. The captain did not think he was actually cold, like some of the Russians he'd worked with on jobs like this, but certainly not social. There were complex lights in Valen's eyes, and sometimes he looked hurt, and sometimes he looked scared. Once, in a moment when he was not aware the captain was looking at him, the Russian's eyes seemed filled with a bottomless despair. The captain knew absolutely nothing of substance about the man, though.

"I don't see anything," said Valen, and the captain gave the order for floodlights. All at once the empty and featureless black beyond the window revealed its secrets. A lumpy converted tug lay wallowing in the swell, but the pitch and yawl were distorted, out of time with the water. It was only when the pilot angled around to come up on the stern that it became clear the boat was lashed to another craft by lines fore and aft.

"Want me to lay her alongside?" asked the pilot, but Valen did not answer.

The captain pitched his voice a bit louder. "Sir, do you—?"

Valen smiled. "I heard you, Captain."

He was a tall, youthful, good-looking and well-built man in his midthirties. Although he seldom spoke and never raised his voice, people tended to defer to him. Oruraka was like many of the new breed of Russians—smart, educated, focused, and political. In the post-Soviet days someone like him would likely have been either a disillusioned officer now sucking on the tit of organized crime, or he would be a civilian son born to a Mafiya family. One of those bred to step into the cracks in the Berlin Wall that everyone who grew up during the Cold War knew were forming.

Not Oruraka. He was a different breed. Openly he was a businessman who did geological survey work for the Russian government. Privately—very privately indeed—he was part of the Novyy Sovetskiy, the New Soviet. Still an ideal, but one that was flourishing quite well in darkness, and tended lovingly by old and new power players who wanted to see a new Union of Soviet Socialist Republics that truly lived up to the vision of Karl Marx. Oruraka was a Party man in every way, even if that party existed in theory, in darkness. The captain and every man aboard this ship shared the same ideal, dreamed the same dreams.

The pilot slowed the boat but gave it just enough throttle for steerageway.

"Get some men on deck," ordered Valen from his vantage point on the rail. "Rifles. Do it now."

The captain growled an order and six crewmen with Kalashnikovs hurried to the rail, barrels raised, eyes staring at the two tethered craft.

"Mr. Oruraka, look there," said the captain, pointing to an intense green glow coming from the small submarine. "Maybe it's some kind of safety light . . . ?"

"No," said Valen. "I think the hatch is open. Damn."

"Interior running lights in subs are usually red. Why would they use a green light?"

Valen did not answer. Instead he frowned as he studied the two boats. The stark white lights revealed red splotches on the submarine's conning tower, on the sides of the gray hull, and also on the starboard rail of the converted tug. The red was not paint. Anyone could tell that. And it looked fresh, too. Still wet.

Suddenly a shadowy something rose up from behind the transom of the salvage boat.

"Christ, what's that?" gasped the captain. One of the deckhands swung a spotlight and there, frozen in the stark white beam, was a big, muscular young man with a Hawaiian face and torn clothes. His hair was wild and there were bright splashes of red blood on his face and chest and hands. He stared into the light with eyes that were filled with terror and madness, and a desperate species of hope.

"Hey," he cried, waving his arms, "help. God, help me. Please . . ."

The captain took up a megaphone out of metal clips on the outside of the pilothouse. "How many people are aboard?" he called.

"Me . . . just me . . . oh, God it got them," wailed the young man. "It came out of the sub and . . . and . . . and . . ." He collapsed into broken sobs, covering his face with his hands. Then he jerked erect and looked back at the sub as if he'd suddenly heard some new sound. "Please, for the love of God, get me off of here."

The captain licked his lips. "Do you . . . ah . . . want me to send some hands aboard?"

"No," cried Valen sharply. "No one sets foot on either of those boats."

"But . . . what about the survivor?" asked the captain. "What do you want to do, sir?"

Without turning to look at him, without taking his eyes off the submarine, Valen quietly said, "Kill him."

The captain stiffened for a moment, but he did not question the order. Instead he turned and nodded to the closest armed hand. Immediately six guns opened up. The bullets struck the Hawaiian and tore him to rags. Dozens of tiny geysers of blood leaped up like spurts of hot volcanic magma. The young man collapsed back and down out of sight.

The captain cut a sideways look at Valen and saw the man wince. But then Valen caught him looking and his face instantly turned to an emotionless mask. The guns fell silent and soon the only sound was the slap of water against the hulls of the three vessels. The freshening breeze out of the southeast whipped the smoke away.

Valen walked to the rail and the armed deckhands gave ground. "Captain, rig a towline without anyone setting foot on either boat."

The captain hesitated for a moment, poised to ask a question, thought better of it, and hurried away to give the orders. Valen Oruraka leaned on the rail and let out a breath that had burned hot and toxic in his chest.

One more, he thought. *One more ghost to haunt me.*

There were already too many, and it did not matter one bit that it was not his finger on the trigger. Would it ever get to the point where there were so many that they morphed into so large a crowd that no individual accusing voice could be heard above the others? Would their faces blur together over time? Did it ever happen that way?

Across the narrow gap, rising like a ghostly wail from within the submarine, a chorus of voices cried out together.

"Tekeli-li! Tekeli-li!" rose the cry. *"Tekeli-li! Tekeli-li!"*

All along the rails hardened soldiers blanched at the sound, which was strained and raw as if it rose from throats torn to ruin by screaming. Wet and ugly. Each voice cried out in perfect harmony to create an imperfect alien shriek. Not a prayer. Not as such, but there was a red and terrible reverence in it nonetheless.

"Tekeli-li! Tekeli-li!"

The green glow emanating from within the sub was not a steady light. It flickered as if something inside were capering and writhing, its movements casting goblin shapes.

Valen took the compact satellite phone from his pocket. His

fingers trembled so violently that he nearly dropped the device, and even when he got a firm grip he misdialed three times before finally getting the correct number. It rang only once.

"Gadyuka," he said in a tremulous voice, "I found it."

PART ONE
PATRIOT GAMES

Ask not what your country can do for you;
ask what you can do for your country.
—John Fitzgerald Kennedy

CHAPTER ONE

HOLY REDEEMER CEMETERY
BALTIMORE, MARYLAND

"Joe Ledger."

I looked up from the gravestone to see three big guys in the kind of dark suits Feds wear when they want to be intimidating.

I wasn't intimidated.

They weren't wearing topcoats because it was a chilly damn day in Baltimore. There was frost sparkling on the grass around Helen's grave. Winter birds huddled together in the bare trees and the sun was a white nothing behind a sheet of tinfoil-gray clouds.

"Who's asking?" I said.

"We need you to come with us," said the point man. He looked like Lurch from the *Addams Family* movies. Too tall, too pale, and with a ghoulish face. The other guys might as well have been wearing signs that said "Goon #1" and "Goon #2." I almost smiled. I'd been fronted like this before. Hell, I'd even been fronted *here* before. Didn't scare me then, didn't scare me now. Didn't like it either time, though.

"I didn't ask what you *needed,* chief," I said, giving Lurch a bright smile. "I asked who you *are.*"

"Doesn't matter who we are," he said, and he smiled, too.

"Yeah, pretty sure it does," I said, keeping it neutral.

"You need to come with us," Lurch repeated as he took a step toward me. He looked reasonably fit, but his weight was on his lead foot and he tended to gesticulate while he spoke. Whoever trained him to do this kind of stuff wasn't very good at it, or Lurch was simply dumb. He should have had his goons surround me in a wide three-point approach, with none of them directly in the others' lines of fire, and none of them close enough for me to hit or to use as a shield against the others. It always pissed me off when professionals acted like amateurs.

"Badge me or blow me," I suggested.

Goon #2 pulled back the flap of his jacket to expose the Glock he wore on his belt. The holster looked new; the gun looked like he'd never used it for anything except trying to overcompensate.

I ignored him. "Here's the thing, sparky," I said to Lurch in my best I'm-still-being-reasonable voice, "you either don't know who I am or you're operating with limited intelligence. And I mean that in every sense of the word."

"You're Joe Ledger," he said.

"*Captain* Joe Ledger," I corrected.

His sneer increased. "Not anymore, *Mister* Ledger."

"Says who?"

"Says the president of the United goddamn States."

They were standing in a kind of inverted vee, with Lurch at the point and the goons on either side. Goon #2 had his jacket open; Goon #1 did not. Nor did Lurch. If they were actually experienced agents, they could unbutton and draw in a little over one second. Goon #2 would beat them to the draw by maybe a quarter second.

That wasn't going to be enough time for them.

"Going to ask one more time," I said quietly, still smiling. "Show me your identification. Do it now and do it smart."

Lurch gave me a ninja death stare for three full seconds but then he reached into his jacket pocket and produced a leather identification wallet, flipped it open, and held it four inches from my nose. Secret Service.

"Someone could have made a phone call and gotten me in," I said.

"No," he said, without explaining. "Now, here's how it's going to play out. You're going to put your hands on your head, fingers laced, while we pat you down. If you behave, we won't have to cuff you. If you act out, we'll do a lot more than cuff you, understand, smart guy?"

"'Act out'?" I echoed. "That's adorable. Not sure I've ever heard a professional use that phrasing before."

"They said he'd be an asshole, Tony," said Goon #1.

Tony—Lurch—nodded and contrived to look sad. "Okay, then we do it the hard way."

All three of them went for their guns.

Like I said, they didn't have enough time for that.

CHAPTER TWO

HOLY REDEEMER CEMETERY
BALTIMORE, MARYLAND

I was close enough to kill him, but that wasn't my play.

So, instead I stepped fast into Lurch and hit him in the chest with a palm-heel shot, using all of my mass and sudden acceleration to put some real juice into it. He wasn't set for it at all and fell backward, hard and fast, into Goon #2. They both went down in a tangle. I kept moving forward and kicked Goon #1 in what my old jujitsu instructor used to call the "entertainment center." I wasn't trying to do permanent damage—and there are a lot of creative ways to do that—but I wanted to make a point. I made it with the reinforced rubber tip of my New Balance running shoe. He folded like a badly erected tent. I pivoted and chop-kicked Lurch across the mouth as he tried to simultaneously rise and draw his gun. The running shoes were new and the tread deep and hard. Ah well.

Lurch spun away, spitting blood and a tooth onto the grass. I stamped down on his hand while I took his gun away and tossed it behind me. Then I reached down and gave Goon #2 a double-tap of knuckle punches on either side of his nose. If he had sinus issues he would have a mother of a migraine for days. If he didn't, he'd only have the migraine for the rest of today. I took his gun away, too.

Then I pivoted back to Goon #1, who was wandering feebly on his hands and knees, drool hanging from slack lips, eyes goggling.

I gave him a nasty little Thai-boxing knee kick to flip him onto his back, drilled a corkscrew punch to his solar plexus, and took his gun for my collection.

In the movies, fight scenes take several minutes. There's a lot of flash and drama, and when either the good guy or bad guy knocks the other guy down, he lets him get up. As if fights are ever supposed to be fair. For me, fairness began and ended with me not killing them. Every other consideration centered on winning right here, right now, with zero seconds wasted. That's how real fights work.

This fight took maybe two seconds. Maybe less.

Not sure if these fucktards knew what they were getting into. They forced this game, though, which meant I got to set the rules. Sucks to be them. I stole their cuffs and, with a few additional love taps to encourage cooperation, cuffed them all together—wrists to ankles—and added a few zip ties from my pocket to keep it all interesting. The result is they looked like a piece of performance art sprawled there in the icy cemetery grass. None of them were able to talk yet, so I picked their pockets, taking IDs, wallets, key rings with car and handcuff keys. I ripped the curly wires out of their ears and patted them down to reveal small-caliber throwdown pieces strapped to their ankles. A glance showed me that the guns had their serial numbers filed off. The kind used during accidental or illegal killings and then planted on the deceased to build a case for resisting arrest. Wonder if that's what they'd had planned for me.

There was no one around, so I pulled out my cell phone and made a call. My boss, Mr. Church, answered on the second ring.

"I thought you were on vacation," he said by way of answering.

"Me too. Listen," I said, "remember a few years ago when some federal mooks braced me while I was visiting Helen's grave? Well, it must be rerun season, because three of them tried it again. Same place."

"What's the damage?" he asked.

"I think I tore a fingernail."

"Captain . . ."

"They'll recover," I said, and gave him the details, including reading off their names. "You have any idea why this happened?"

"Not yet. Get clear of the area and then find a quiet place where you can sweep your car with an Anteater. Then go to ground and wait for my call."

The line went dead. The Anteater was a state-of-the-art doohickey designed to find even the best active or passive listening system.

Speaking of my car, I could hear muffled barking in that direction. My big white combat shepherd, Ghost, was supposed to be sleeping in the car. He was up and clearly felt as cranky as I did. Lucky for the goon squad that I left the dog in the warm rental car or they'd need a lot more than ice packs and some career counseling.

I pocketed my phone, then dug an earbud out of my trouser pocket and pressed it to the inside of my outer ear. It looks like a freckle. I put the speaker dot on my upper lip by the corner of my mouth. Then I squatted beside Lurch, who was semiconscious and trying to muster the moral courage to give me another death stare. I patted his cheek as a warning, which he chose to ignore.

"You better like Gitmo, motherfu—" Lurch began, and I patted his cheek again, this time hard enough to dim the lights on Broadway.

"Whoever told you that you're good at this is not your friend," I said. "Whoever sent you made a mistake. You came at me here—*here*—which is an even bigger mistake. Be real careful that it doesn't cost you more than you can afford to pay, feel me?"

He almost said something else, but didn't. He was handcuffed to two guys who were probably supposed to be top-class muscle. I'd handed all of them their asses and hadn't worked up a sweat doing it, so my friend here was probably having a come-to-Jesus moment. His eyes looked wet and his gaze slid away. I picked up the tooth he'd lost, showed it to him, and tucked it into his shirt pocket.

"Now," I said calmly, "tell me why you were ordered to arrest me."

"Look, I—I mean they didn't . . . ," he stammered. Then he took a breath and tried it again. "The word came down to bring you in and not kiss your ass doing it."

"Who cut the order?"

"My supervisor said it came straight from the top," said Lurch. "Straight from the Oval Office."

"Listen to me," I said quietly. "I can give you a pass for fucking with me. You're following orders. Stupid orders, but orders. I don't hold grudges for that kind of thing. But you came here. You came to where someone very special to me is buried. Of all the places you could have come, you made it this place. That's on you. You're the crew chief here and you could have waited until I was done and walked out of the cemetery. You didn't. That crosses a line with me. I don't forgive that. So, listen very closely and believe me when I tell you that if I ever see you again—here, or anywhere; I don't care where it is or why—I'm going to kill you. I'll make it hurt, too, sparky, and I'll make it last. Now, look me in the eye and tell me that you understand."

I leaned back and let him take a look. He did.

"Tell me," I said.

He licked his lips. What he said was, "I'm sorry."

I punched two of his front teeth out. One fast hit. He fell back so hard his head bounced off the turf.

"I didn't ask for an apology," I said without raising my voice. "Your apology doesn't mean shit, because you already crossed the line. I asked you to tell me you understand."

He started to say something. Don't know what, but he bit down on it with the teeth he had left because it wasn't going to be what I wanted to hear. He was crying now; nose running and fat tears rolling down to mingle with the blood smeared around his mouth and on his chin.

"I . . ." He stopped, coughed, tried again. "You won't . . . see me again."

"Tell your dickhead friends, too." I straightened. "And tell whoever sent you that this isn't over. I'm going to pay someone a visit. Tell them that."

He nodded but did not dare say another word. There are times you can trash talk and times when you need to consider how comprehensive your healthcare plan really is.

The sun was trying to burn through the clouds and the birds were watching silently in the trees. I almost said something else to him, but left it. If he didn't get it now, then he was unteachable. So, I left him there with his buddies, cuffed in a tangle.

I took all of their personal belongings and weapons back to my car. As I got in, Ghost gave me a deeply reproachful look, as if to say that he couldn't leave me alone for five minutes without me stepping on my own dick.

"Not my fault, fuzzball," I said.

He seemed to read something in me that changed his attitude from high anxiety to wanting to comfort another member of his pack. He'd never known Helen, but he knew this place. He nuzzled me with a cold nose and whined softly until I bent and kissed his head. There were tears burning in my eyes.

They should never have come here. Those motherfuckers.

I started my car and drove over to where a big Crown Victoria with federal plates was parked. I got out and casually slashed the right front tire. I used Lurch's key to pop the locks, but a quick search showed that the vehicle was clean. No warrants, no nothing other than drive-through coffee. One cup was untouched and still hot, so I took it; but one sip revealed the awful truth that it was decaf. I poured it over the front seat and dropped the empty cardboard cup on the floor.

Ghost and I drove away at a casual speed. If anyone saw me they'd think I was calm, cool, and composed.

Was I scared? Yeah. I was absolutely terrified and, sadly, that was not a joke.

INTERLUDE ONE

FOUR SEASONS RESORT THE BILTMORE SANTA BARBARA
1260 CHANNEL DRIVE
SANTA BARBARA, CALIFORNIA
SEVEN YEARS AGO

Valen Oruraka was deep inside a dream of chase and escape.

He was aboard a smuggler's submarine, running from something unspeakable. The more he ran, the longer the hull was, stretching out before him like an endless road. Room to run, sure; but he could never seem to run fast enough. When he turned to look over his shoulder it was closer. Always closer.

"Tekeli-li! Tekeli-li!" rose the cry. *"Tekeli-li! Tekeli-li!"*

The thing had no real shape. It was a shadow that roiled and twisted, lunging out with amorphous pseudopods and whiskery feelers and clacking claws.

Valen screamed as he ran, and the scream filled the hotel room. No one came to investigate, though. He was aware of how bad and how loud his nightmares had become over the last year, and he often booked a corner suite and slept in whatever standard bed, fold-out, or couch was farthest from a connecting wall. Music blasted all night from his iPad, and that was directed at the door to the hallway.

He slept without his hearing aid, and so his own desperate cries never woke him. Nor did the shrieks of the ghosts he had created with every person he killed.

The night crawled on and he ran through his dreams and the sheets knotted like snakes around his naked thighs.

And then the dream ended with a touch. Bang. All of the horrors, gone. The submarine, the darkness, the capering shadows. Gone. He snapped awake, one hand darting blindly under the pillow for the small automatic he always slept with, the other whipping to block any attack. The pistol was not under his pillow; his scrabbling fingers felt nothing at all.

He froze and peered into the gloom. A figure stood above him, but as he turned it moved back. Valen blinked his eyes clear and the shadow shapes from his dream organized themselves into a human shape. A woman's shape, of that there was absolutely no doubt. There was also no doubt that she held a gun in one hand. His gun.

The woman leaned over and turned on the bedside light, and smiled. Then she dropped the magazine from the pistol, ejected the round from the chamber, caught it with a deft dart of her hand, and set the component parts on the bedside table. She did not speak because she knew he could not hear without his device. So, in silence she stood up and walked slowly, like a hunting cat, to the foot of the bed. She was very tall, with the strong shoulders and the muscle tone of the competitive skier she'd been twenty years ago.

Valen kept blinking until his eyes were clear as he fished for his hearing aid and put it on.

"Gadyuka," he murmured. "What are you doing here?"

Gadyuka—the viper—smiled as she slowly unbuttoned her sheer blouse. She was in no hurry, but the deliberate movement of her long fingers pulled Valen the rest of the way out of the dream and very much into the now. Beneath the blouse was a pink underwire bra with a subtle paisley print of pink, orange, and yellow with lace trim, a satin bow in the front, and rhinestones in the center of the bow. It was more persuasively feminine than anything Valen had assumed she would wear. But then again, what kind of bras do stone killers wear? She unclasped the bra and let it fall, revealing full breasts the color of snow. Then she slid down the zipper on the hip of her smoke-gray skirt and let it fall, too. Her underwear was a medium bubblegum pink, with lace trim on legs and waist.

"What are you doing?" he said, his words slurred with sleep, surprise, and confusion.

"Maybe you're dreaming," she said.

"But . . . ," he began, but she shook her head, and that was the last of the conversation between them.

Valen licked his lips. His pulse was still rapid from the nightmare, but now it beat even harder. Her nipples were a subtle shade of pink, and hard, with the areolas pebbled from the cool air in the room. She hooked her thumbs in the waistband of her panties and pulled them down, revealing a trimmed pubic bush only a shade darker than the white-blond of her long hair.

She was aggressively, unbearably, mercilessly female, and Valen felt himself grow hard while also physically diminishing in her presence. He was a tough man, a killer and a fighter, and was regarded as dangerous by nearly everyone, but he knew that he was not a match for this Russian viper. She was so completely in command of herself that she seemed to crackle with energy and vitality.

When she climbed into bed it was she who took him. And she took him as many times as she wanted.

Hours later, Valen Oruraka lay totally spent, which shook out to feeling fully alive and yet near death. He was greased with sweat and covered with scratches and bites and the heady scent of her. His breathing was bad and his heart felt like a nuclear reactor on overload. The bed was a wreck. Some of the room was a wreck. He was a disaster.

Gadyuka sat up in bed, the damp sheets across her lap, breasts bare in the morning light, as she rolled a joint with great care, licked it, smoothed it, and put it between her full lips. Then she lit it and took two deep hits, held them in her lungs for a long time, and exhaled high into the air.

"Why are you here?" he croaked.

"Do I need a reason?" she asked, speaking in Russian with a Pomor accent. He knew that she was from the north, but that was all. Valen once considered doing some research on her but gave it up as likely a suicidal hobby. People he feared were afraid of Gadyuka, so he feared her, too.

It was like that with the people they worked for, as well. All of the Novyy Sovetskiy senior committee members were inflexible and unforgiving when it came to matters of security. Errors simply could not be allowed and so there were ten times as many safeguards as with any other plan in the history of modern warfare. There was only one punishment for breaking the rules. One punishment with no hope of repeal, parole, or pardon. That was only common sense.

He struggled to sit up. "You don't walk across the street without a good damn reason. So what do you want?"

"I'm here to give you a job. Everyone is pleased with how you handled the recovery near Hawaii. That was as much a test as it was necessary to the goals of the Party. Now it's time for you to tackle a much bigger project, and you will do it well because I told the senior members that you would."

He looked at her naked body and cocked an eyebrow. "So . . . what? Are you my graduation present?"

"Hardly," she snorted. "No, it's a personal policy thing with me. I don't fuck minions."

"You lost me. . . ."

"Did you ever see that American movie *Meet the Parents*? Robert De Niro tells his daughter's boyfriend that he's now in the 'circle of trust.' Remember that? Well, welcome to my circle of trust."

"Um . . . thanks? And, what does that mean, exactly?"

"It means life is about to get more interesting, Valen. In *Star Wars*—the original one, I mean—Obi-Wan Kenobi tells Luke that he's just taken his first step in a larger world."

"I didn't know you were a movie buff."

"I am. And it's one of the things I'll miss most about America once it's gone."

Valen flinched. "Gone?"

"Well, when it is no longer the bloated whore that it is."

"Wishful thinking. Even after the election tampering and e-mail hacking and all that, they're still the biggest gorilla in the jungle."

Her smile was enigmatic. "That," she said, "is why I'm here, *lapochka*."

CHAPTER THREE

THE SITUATION ROOM
THE WHITE HOUSE
WASHINGTON, D.C.
TWENTY-TWO MONTHS AGO

The president of the United States sat at the head of the table and smiled at the men gathered around him. The Joint Chiefs; Admiral Lucas Murphy, the White House chief of staff; several top advisors; Jennifer VanOwen, the president's science advisor; and a few close friends to whom he had granted this highest level of security. Most of them looked attentive and mildly surprised since there was no active crisis.

The president turned to General Frank Ballard, chairman of the Joint Chiefs, and the ranking general of the U.S. Air Force. "Frank, I want to ask you a very important question. There was a program that was canceled by my predecessor. Majestic Three. M3, I believe it was called."

"Yes, Mr. President," said Ballard. "Majestic Three was shut down and all of its resources confiscated and assets reallotted."

"Tell me something, General, did the Majestic Three program do us any good?"

"Good?" The general shook his head. "Hardly, sir. The governors of Majestic Three very nearly caused World War Three."

"That isn't the question I asked, is it? Is it, General? No. I asked if the M3 project did us any measurable good over the years."

"Well, sir," said the general, clearly uncomfortable. He fidgeted and cut looks at the other officers around the table, but no one was willing to meet his eye.

"Do I need to phrase it in smaller words, General?" asked the president. "Or do I need to ask the next person to sit in your chair?"

"It is, um, fair to say that we have benefitted greatly from the various M3 projects," said the general. "New or improved metallurgy, polymers, fiber optics, aircraft design—"

"Correct me if I'm wrong, but didn't the entire stealth aircraft project come out of what they were doing?"

"Yes, Mr. President."

"And isn't the stealth program what's put us ahead in the arms race and kept us there?"

"To an, ah, degree, sir, but—"

"Then I'd say that the good it's done pretty well outweighs the bad, wouldn't you?"

"I'm not sure I can agree with that, sir. One of the T-craft developed by Howard Shelton very nearly destroyed Beijing. Others were being launched to destroy Shanghai, Moscow, Tehran, Pyongyang . . ."

"Which might have been a good damn thing," said the president, and every face around the table went pale. "No, don't look at me like that. Sure, it would have been a tragic loss of life, but overall, we'd have accomplished world peace. A lasting peace. We would have insured that American values were instituted around the globe."

The room was utterly silent. The president smiled as if all of the gaping officers and advisors had nodded in agreement.

Jennifer VanOwen spoke into the silence. Over the last few years the science advisor had hitched her star to the president's, even when he was only a candidate, and—even through staff cuts and public controversy—VanOwen had managed to stay out of the news and out of the limelight. A lot of the people in the president's inner circle were afraid of her because she always seemed to know something about them; things that no one else knew. She did; but because she seldom used her knowledge as anything other than an implied threat to support the president, they simply either deferred to her or steered clear. A surprising number of power players around her knelt to put their heads on the chopping block, but among the survivors it was generally believed VanOwen was the one keeping that blade sharp. When she spoke, the president listened.

"Mr. President," she said quietly, "the Majestic program, like all advanced and highly classified defense projects, was always potentially dangerous. The Manhattan Project was dangerous, and yet that ended World War Two and transformed the United States from a powerful nation into this world's first true global superpower. Howard Shelton had his faults, no doubt, but he and the other governors of M3 were working toward a goal of an unbeatable and indisputably powerful America. One that took the concept of 'superpower' to a new and unmatchable level. With firmer and more courageous guidance from your predecessor, we might now have ended all wars forever. Instead, he was killed. Perhaps 'executed' is not too strong a word."

"Now wait a minute, Jennifer," cried the general. "That's a pretty dangerous word to throw around. You weren't even here when the Department of Military Sciences went up against M3."

"No, General," she replied coldly. "*You* were. And now Howard Shelton is dead. He can neither explain his actions nor speak to his motives. There was no due process. There was not even the slightest attempt to allow him to offer any other version of what happened. Instead we have an after-action report written by the man who killed him. With other reports filed by that man's team. All biased, all of them in lockstep with an agreed-upon agenda."

"That's hardly—"

The president cut him off. "There were three people running Majestic Three?"

"Yes, Mr. President. Three governors," said VanOwen. "The second man, Alfred Bonetti, was also executed by Captain Ledger and his DMS goon squad. The third is a woman, Yuina Hoshino, and she's in prison serving thirty to life."

"Okay, okay," said the president, "so maybe the bad apples are out of the basket. That's fine, that's okay. We can discuss them another time. Let's see about putting some people we trust in charge of the program. We have people we can trust, right? We have the best people working for us. Get me a list of names, General. I want it on my desk this afternoon."

"In charge . . . ?" echoed the general, aghast. "Are you seriously considering restarting the Majestic program after everything that's happened?"

"It's my program now, General, or is someone else's name on my door? You know the door I mean, right? Nice big office, kind of oval shaped? That's mine. That's where I work. That means I get to do whatever I want to do. That means I have the power to do what I want. Me. My power." He placed his palms flat on the table and looked around, clearly quite happy with himself. "Ladies and gentlemen, to be perfectly clear, yes . . . we are going to restart the Majestic program. Only this time the president will be kept in the loop. This time the Majestic Three program will be my program. I am going to save this country. That's what the history books are going to say. Do I hear any arguments?"

No one spoke. No one dared.

The president leaned back in his chair and smiled. It was good to be the king.

INTERLUDE TWO

FOUR SEASONS RESORT THE BILTMORE SANTA BARBARA
1260 CHANNEL DRIVE
SANTA BARBARA, CALIFORNIA
SEVEN YEARS AGO

Gadyuka smoked, held, considered the curling wisp coming off the end of the joint, then exhaled with a smile. "In your file, there is a notation about a man you knew when you went to college in America. A Greek."

"Aristotle Kostas," Valen said. "Ari. Sure. What about him?"

"His family is involved with the Mediterranean black market?"

Valen grunted. "The Kostas family *is* the Mediterranean black market. And they are a big chunk of the Middle East and North African black markets. Actually, last time I spoke with Ari he had big plans on taking the family business global."

"Bigger than the Turk . . . what's his name? Ohan?"

"Parallel. They each have their specialties and they do some business together, but as Ari told me, it's a big world, and so far Ohan hasn't tried to take the wrong piece of it."

Gadyuka nodded as if she already knew it and was confirming that he did. "When's the last time you spoke with him?"

"Maybe eight years ago. There was a college reunion thing and we went to it. Kind of an ironic appearance because neither of us give much of a shit about Caltech. It was a school."

"He read business and archaeology, and you read geology and seismology," she said, amused. "What on earth inspired you to read those subjects?"

"Ari's choices were all about positioning himself to take over the family business, with maybe a small bias for the antiquities market, which he correctly predicted would go up. He's made his rich family richer."

"And you?" asked Gadyuka. "Why study those sciences?"

Valen absently reached out for the joint, took a hit, and held it while he thought of how to answer. He blew smoke up into the darkness gathered on the ceiling.

"When I was a boy," he said, "my family lived in Chelyabinsk. We were not wealthy by any stretch, but we had enough. And to spare, I suppose. My mother was the sister of Abram Golovin. When my parents were killed in a car accident, I was sent to Ukraine to live with my uncle and his family. This was in 1985. The wall was still up and we were still the Soviet Union. Forever ago." He sighed, took another hit, and then passed the joint back. "I loved my uncle. He was a good man, a decent man. He was a Communist and to him that meant something. To him, the Party was not the corrupt and decaying thing that they tell children in school nowadays. Back then it was a glorious ideal."

"You are lecturing," said Gadyuka mildly. "You are doing what the Americans call 'preaching to the choir.'"

He nodded. "Sorry. But I get that way when I think about Uncle Abram. When I think about Dr. Abram Golovin. Chief structural engineer at Chernobyl. A man whose books on building nuclear power plants were taught in the best universities. He taught me so much, you see. He explained the science of it. All of it, from A to Zed. From selecting the site and doing the geological surveys of the area, to working with architects to design and build a perfect facility, and to maintaining it despite the enormous pressures of cooling water, wastewater, nuclear waste management . . . the lot."

Gadyuka and Valen handed the joint back and forth. It was getting small now, so she pinched it out and rolled another while Valen talked about his uncle.

"And then," said Valen with a tightness in his voice, "on my eighth birthday, it all fell apart. 26 April, 1986. We woke to the sound of sirens. There were screams and explosions and people were fleeing like rats from a sinking ship. I stared out of my bedroom window and saw that the sky was on fire. Strange colors, too. Red and yellow and orange, but also a green hue. None of the papers ever mentioned that part, but I saw it clear as day. It was there for several minutes, and then it was gone. Everything was gone. My uncle was gone."

He took the joint from Gadyuka but thought better of it and handed it back.

"They blamed him, of course," said Valen. "Everyone did. They said that it was a structural fault, or a poor geological report. Oh, I know what you'll say—that some people have lobbied pretty heavily to say that it was operator error, but in the reports that mattered, they said the plant was not designed to safety standards, in effect, and incorporated unsafe features and that inadequate safety analysis was performed. A scapegoat was needed, and they picked Uncle Abram because he was from Ukraine, not from Russia. That mattered then. In the eyes of the world, it mattered. In terms of propaganda, it mattered. The family was disgraced. I was shipped back to Russia and my cousins, my mother's sisters, went into the system and I never heard from them again. Siberia, I suppose, though why they should be punished is beyond me. I was forbidden to even mention my uncle's name. My own surname, Sokolov, was changed to the absurd one I have now. Do you know that it has no actual meaning? I heard a joke once that it was something they made up in some ministry office, and saddled me with it because no one else would have the name and everyone who mattered would instantly know who I am and the shame I carry. Perhaps I'd have even vanished into a camp, except for the fact that my father's family had just enough pull to get me into a state school."

Gadyuka turned on her side and stroked his thigh. "But . . . ?" she prompted.

"But I don't believe that. My uncle was a brilliant and diligent man. He checked everything twice, three times. He never left the slightest thing to chance."

"You were a boy, Valen."

He shook his head. "I know, but I was observant, even then. Uncle Abram always joked that I had an insatiable mind. Like a shark, always looking for something new to eat. It's true. Always has been. So, when I was a little older, I managed to get hold of his research, his studies, as much of it as I could legally obtain. I've spent my life learning the things I needed to learn in order to understand it and then validate it."

"What if you'd found a flaw?"

"Then I'd have gotten a measure of peace from that," said Valen sharply. "I could have hated Uncle Abram like everyone else and been part of the crowd. But . . . no. I even went over those studies with my professors at Caltech. They all agreed that Chernobyl was sited correctly and built with great precision. Which left me with a puzzle. Why had it failed? What really caused it all to fall apart?" He sighed, then turned to her. "Why do you ask?"

"Because if you do what I want you to do, you may have the opportunity to clear your uncle's name. And you will be doing a great service to our people."

He gaped at her.

"Lovely *myshka*," she murmured, a smile curling the corners of her mouth. "When you read your uncle's research, did you read the report titled 'Anomalous and Incidental Minerals Recovered'?"

"Yes, of course. It was a list of various minerals found during excavation, but which had little or no significance."

"Did you, by any chance, take note of something called L. quartz?"

"I don't recall offhand."

"The *L* stands for a word. Lemurian, like the lost island in those stories. There is a white version, which is common. Not this, though. It is a vibrant green. It's exceptionally rare, and exceptionally important to your new project," she said. "Just like the quartz you were so clever to find for me in that submarine. I want you and your little black marketer friend, Ari Kostas, to find more of it. I want you to find all of it. Beg, borrow, or steal."

CHAPTER FOUR

DRIVING IN BALTIMORE, MARYLAND

We drove around for a while, watching to see if we picked up a tail. And we did. Ghost caught me glowering into the rearview mirror and turned to bare his titanium teeth through the window.

"It's smoked glass, Einstein," I told him. "They can't even see you."

He gave an eloquent fart and continued to snarl. I cracked a window.

The follow car was the same make and model of blue government Crown Victoria.

"Okay, kids," I said, "if you want to play, then let's have some jollies."

For the next ten minutes I made a whole bunch of random turns, U-turns, and even cut down a wide alley between factories. The driver of the follow car was good, but he was probably getting smug because he thought he was keeping up with someone who was attempting to flee. I was not in a fleeing mood, because the more I thought about the first bunch of assholes bracing me at Helen's grave, the madder I got.

Church was no help, because he was still making calls, and when

I got Aunt Sallie on the line, she told me to: "Stop bothering the grown-ups, stop whining like a girl, and grow a set."

The follow car kept up with me, and I began to wonder if I was making a mistake by judging them according to the three clown-shoes I roughed up at the cemetery. Maybe I was also letting my anger cloud my thinking.

Thunder suddenly boomed overhead and it began to rain. Kind of a dramatic bit of affirmation that my gloomy musings were correct, but that was fine. I tapped three digits into the keypad on the steering column to activate the MindReader Q1 artificial intelligence system.

"Calpurnia," I said, "can we use pigeon drones in this kind of weather?"

"Sure, as long as the wind doesn't pick up."

Bug, or some other maniac on his team, gave the AI a sexy, late-night-jazz-radio voice.

"Cool. Let's put a couple of them in the air."

"Of course, Joseph," she said, which made me feel all tingly. "What are they looking for?"

"Access traffic cams," I said. "Locate a dark blue Crown Victoria within three hundred feet of my location."

"Done."

"Track it. I want the license plate."

"On it," she promised.

There was a soft whir and a side panel opened near the left rear wheel and two small bundles fell out and rolled into the gutter. They were gray and unobtrusive in the steady rainfall. Luckily it wasn't a full-blown storm—for once Mother Nature was aiding and abetting me instead of the bad guys.

As soon as the follow car was past and there were no pedestrians close, the drones' proximity sensors activated the flight controls. The pigeon popped tiny propellers and rose straight up, then the wings deployed to hide the props. Once the bird was flying at sufficient speed, the propellers folded back into the body and the wings flapped like normal bird wings. It was very fast and the sensor software tracked possible line-of-sight observers to make sure none of this happened when anyone was watching. These are not the drones you buy at Target. These babies cost about four hundred thousand each, and if they were captured by anyone who did not have the right kind of RFID transponder chip, they would self-destruct.

The AI system that ran it was something new for us. It was the most sophisticated computer intelligence software in existence by something like an order of magnitude. Or maybe three. Freakishly intuitive, with natural conversational modes, various combat modes, and all sorts of other extras I barely understand. Bug—the über-geek head of the DMS computer sciences division—rebuilt the software after obtaining it from Zephyr Bain, the woman who'd designed it. Calpurnia's original program was to oversee a curated technological singularity. Meaning Bain and her crew were trying to bring about a controlled end of the world as we know it. She wanted to kill off the vast multitudes of poor who she considered to be a drain on the global system; but she also wanted to kill off any one percenters who controlled companies that polluted and exploited the planet. So, a little altruism and a whole lot of bugfuck insanity. Calpurnia was designed to be self-learning, but Bain had built it too well, because Calpurnia became self-aware in the bargain. That self-awareness did not lead to a Skynet scenario, which is why we don't have robot Arnold Schwarzeneggers stomping around shooting plasma rifles. No, Calpurnia went the other way and committed suicide rather than end the world. As acts of heroism go, it was really pretty goddamn touching. Lot of actual human beings I can name would never even consider that kind of selflessness.

While all that was happening, Bug put the new quantum upgrade of MindReader online. So, the suicidal self-aware artificial intelligence saw the birth of an almost godlike computer mind and begged it for salvation. Calpurnia downloaded every last one and zero of Bain's carefully constructed master plan into MindReader and then erased herself out of existence.

Or so Bug said. And he named the DMS AI system in honor of Calpurnia, to celebrate her sacrifice, because that gave us a much-needed win and—let's face it—saved the whole world. Personally, I have my doubts about some of that. I think maybe the best parts of Calpurnia are still alive within MindReader Q1. That scares me a little. Maybe more than a little. But it also gives us one hell of a weapon to bring into battle against other maniacs who want to burn it all down.

The data from the pigeon drones came in and Calpurnia processed it.

"The car is registered to the Secret Service motor pool," she told me. "It was checked out this morning by Agent Virginia Harrald. There are two heat signatures in the car."

"Thanks."

"Would you like me to kill their engine? I could override their drive systems and—"

"No, thanks."

"I could blow out the tires."

"Maybe later."

"Just let me know, Joseph. I'm happy to do whatever you need."

"Sure, sure. Monitor their radio and cell phones."

"On it. No current chatter."

"There is a second vehicle, a black SUV." As I made a random left, I gave her the plate numbers. "Find it."

A minute later, Calpurnia said, "The second vehicle is two blocks on a converging route, one block over and two blocks ahead. It just made a right turn. Probability of a pincer interception is high."

"Shit."

"Language, Joseph."

I made a mental note to kneecap Bug.

The next street was a one-way going the wrong way, but there was a public parking garage close to my end. No traffic heading in my direction, so I swung in and went into the garage. As I got my ticket from the machine I heard the squeal of tires and figured the Crown Vic was following after almost leaving it too late to make the turn.

I began moving up the levels.

"Calpurnia, call Top Sims's cell."

"It's ringing."

First Sergeant Bradley Sims—known as Top to everyone—was my number two, and he'd come to town with me to see an old friend. And by "old friend," I mean the smoking-hot anchorwoman on the six o'clock news. Dinah Trevor. She looks like a taller Kerry Washington and has a Pulitzer. Not sure when they'd become friends, but Top kept a lot of his private life to himself.

"Morning, Cap'n," he said, sounding more thoroughly relaxed than I think I've ever heard him.

"How much would you hate me if I asked you for a favor right now?"

There was a sound, maybe the rustle of sheets.

"Depends," he said cautiously. "You need me to be anywhere in the next half hour, you're likely to fall off my Christmas card list."

"Yeah, well, guess this will save you a stamp," I said, and told him what was happening.

"On my way," he said.

The line went dead before I could even thank him.

I kept busy entertaining the Secret Service while I waited to spring my own surprise.

CHAPTER FIVE

THE BASILICA OF THE NATIONAL SHRINE OF THE IMMACULATE CONCEPTION
WASHINGTON, D.C.
EIGHT DAYS AGO

It was the largest Roman Catholic church in the United States and was one of the largest churches in the world. Valen hoped it was large enough to let him get lost inside.

He spent two hours wandering through the collection of contemporary ecclesiastical art, and it might as well have been science fiction for all that he understood of it. Religion had formed no part of his life. Being aware of it was not the same as being part of it, and the various depictions of its strengths and weaknesses in movies, books, and TV gave him only a surface understanding.

He knew—or at least believed—that a priest was required to talk to someone in need. And he knew that many priests and ministers and other clerics were trained in psychology. They acted more like therapists than evangelists.

Even so, it took him five tries, five separate visits, before he worked up the courage to speak to any of the priests. It was as much a matter of timing as security. If he was too visible, or if there were too many people around, then either he couldn't speak with any frankness, or he would risk creating liabilities. Gadyuka was probably having him tailed, and he did not want to put anyone in the crosshairs of a cleanup team.

The priest working the confessional area that night was forty-ish, which meant he was probably not too much of a doctrinist and likely more college educated. Valen spent thirty minutes circling the man like a vulture before the priest noticed him. He was a thin man with an ascetic face and a hipster beard, but he wore a friendly smile as he came over to where Valen was standing.

"How can I help?" he asked. None of the "my son" crap. Good.

"I'm not a Catholic," said Valen.

"Not sure I care," said the priest. "I'm Father Steve. Steven Archer."

"Andy," lied Valen, and they shook hands. "Can we, um, talk for a minute?"

"Did you want to make a confession?"

"No," said Valen. "Just talk."

They sat at one end of a pew far away from the few other people there. Father Steve was patient and let Valen get to it on his own.

"This isn't a church thing," said Valen. "Not exactly."

The priest nodded.

Valen considered the cover story he'd prepared, and then gave it a try. "I'm in the military. JSOC. You know what that is?"

"Sure. Special operations. I was a chaplain in Afghanistan ten years ago."

Valen almost fled right then, but did not; instead he tweaked his approach.

"I can't tell you what unit I'm with. You understand?"

"I do."

"And I can't disclose any details of what I do."

"Sure. Nor would I ask."

"I want to continue with what I do," said Valen slowly. "I mean, I feel I have to. It's important work, and a lot of people are counting on me." He didn't need to fake being troubled. It all bubbled just below the surface. "But at the same time . . . the kind of work I do is bad. People get hurt. People die. You say you were a chaplain, then you've talked to guys like me. Guys who want to be good people, guys who don't want to be defined by the work they do, and yet because they're good at it, they have to keep doing it. Is any of this making sense?"

Father Steve exhaled through his nose and nodded. "Yes, it is, Andy. And you're right, I've talked with a lot of soldiers who are people of faith, often very strong faith, and yet who have to go against the precepts of that faith every day."

"How do they stay sane, Father?"

Valen heard the desperation in his own voice. There was too much of it, more than he wanted to share. But Father Steve leaned close.

"The pat answer is that ol' Fifth Commandment, 'Thou shalt not kill.' But the reality is that the Old Testament was filled wall to wall with incidences in which God ordered his chosen people to wage war, and there are all manner of crimes for which public execution is not only permitted but endorsed. It was the New Testament, the teachings of Jesus, where he taught nonviolence and turning the other cheek. This, of course, is often cited as contradictory because in those same teachings he said that he did not come to abolish the old laws, but to complete them. By inference, the traditional forms of public execution were upheld—even if he interceded at times in this, as with the attempted stoning of the prostitute—and by extension the wars in God's name waged by and for the people of His faith." He stopped and smiled. "From your face I don't think that's what you wanted to hear."

"Where does sin play into this?"

"Sin is something we have never fully defined. Not in any inarguable way, and yes, that sounds heretical to say. It's not." The priest smiled. "The laws of the church have changed and been interpreted more times than I can count. We can't stand fast and say that we adhere without fluctuation from the pacifistic teachings of Jesus. Especially not us Catholics. The Crusades alone fly in the face of that, and those were authorized by papal bull." Father Steve shook his head and offered a rueful grin. "The truth is that the commandment doesn't actually say 'Thou shalt not kill.' Most scholars agree that it says 'Thou shalt not murder.'"

"How is that different from what a soldier does? Innocent people are killed all the time in war."

"And that is unfortunate. The truth is that divine forgiveness is what we have to offer when a soldier pulls a trigger. We know there is no animus between the soldier and the enemy he kills. Not really. In basic training all soldiers are taught to step outside of their morality and civilized values and trust that the enemy they are ordered to kill is truly worthy of being killed. It is a kind of brainwashing, and all of us who have served have gone through some part of it."

The church seemed vast and dark and oppressive.

"So, you're saying that no matter how many people a soldier kills, as long as it's for the good of their country, then all they have to do is ask for forgiveness and that's it? The soul is whitewashed?"

Father Steve looked pained as he shook his head. "No, Andy, it isn't that easy, though quite a lot of people think it's like flipping a switch."

"What's the secret, then?"

"Faith," said the priest. "You have to believe that God will forgive you, and you have to genuinely repent of your sins."

Valen turned away and stared at the statues of dead prophets and martyrs. Then, without another word, he got heavily to his feet and walked out of the church.

CHAPTER SIX

THE SITUATION ROOM
THE WHITE HOUSE
WASHINGTON, D.C.
TWENTY-TWO MONTHS AGO

The generals and advisors left, singly or in pairs. The administration was still young enough that even old friends did not know where their colleagues' loyalties lay. It was an ugly and awkward part of any change in administration. They'd seen it in different ways during their individual paths upward through their own careers, and doubly so once those careers became more intensely political. Now there were wild cards in the old deck, and that skewed the odds and made card counting a failing proposition.

Jennifer VanOwen understood this and watched each of them as they left, noting who glanced at whom. Making mental tick marks when she saw small, hidden smiles or flicked glances; gauging the tightness of compressed lips, and assigning possible meaning to the degree of compression. Much of what she saw lined up nicely with her own assessments.

She lingered, as did the chief of staff, until they were the only ones left in the room, with even the military and Secret Service banished. Then the president tapped his chief of staff's wrist.

"Give us the room, Lucas."

Admiral Lucas Murphy's eyes clicked over to VanOwen and back. "Mr. President, I—"

"Now."

"Yes, sir." Admiral Murphy stood, back stiff, face wooden.

When the door was closed, VanOwen leaned toward the president. "First, sir, let me tell you how courageous and bold this decision is."

“Thank you. It’s what needs to be done to insure that this country is second to none.”

“And history will remember you for that.”

He smiled, pleased with the compliment. Thinking that it was a compliment. VanOwen was very happy that she had spent so much time with theater coaches over the years.

“There is something to consider, however, as we move forward,” she said. “We can’t ignore the possibility of pushback from the Department of Military Sciences.”

“Those clowns,” grumped the president.

“Yes,” she said, “those clowns. Despite their many flaws, they did manage to bring down the original Majestic Three program. They are reckless and dangerous, and it’s very uncertain as to where their loyalties lie. After all, they worked for the previous administrations, and there is a clear pattern of assuming control of matters without first clearing it with your office.”

The phrasing was precise, implying the failings of previous administrations to control the actions, and then reminding the president that it was now his office. VanOwen had practiced the right pace and inflection in her bathroom mirror that morning.

“No one has been able to keep them on a short enough leash,” she continued.

“Why not? And don’t give me that crap about Church having blackmail material on everyone, because I don’t believe it.”

“Church is a very large, very aggressive dog,” said VanOwen. “Not everyone who has sat in the Oval Office has had the physical strength or the strength of will to jerk back on his leash.”

“To hell with that. I’m not afraid of him.”

“No, sir, you are not.” She paused. “Mr. Church isn’t the only barking dog, though. There is Aunt Sallie.”

“Who? That black woman? The one that looks like Whoopi Goldberg? Who cares about her?”

“Exactly right, sir. She’s nothing,” lied VanOwen. “And there is Church’s number-one hotshot. Captain Joe Ledger. I gave you a briefing on him, too.”

"Right, right. He's the one who killed Howard Shelton. I liked Howard. Howard was a good guy. Golfer. Decent handicap."

"Howard Shelton was an American patriot. At most he should have been called to explain his actions. Instead Joe Ledger executed him and later claimed it was justified."

The president sipped his soda and seemed to stare through the middle of nowhere for a few moments.

VanOwen leaned a little closer. "Mr. Church, Aunt Sallie, and Joe Ledger destroyed M3. They prevented America from benefitting from these new advances in defense technologies. The DMS is still in operation and operates under a charter established by executive order."

"But not my order."

"No, Mr. President. Not your order."

He turned to meet her eyes. "Can we cancel their charter?"

"Not easily," she said. "And if we did, there's too good a chance it would draw congressional attention to your plan to rebuild the Majestic program."

"Can we defund them?"

"Not as such, sir."

"Then what?"

"Mr. President," she said, "there are other ways to handle this situation."

"Do I need to know what that means?" he asked.

"You know the phrase 'plausible deniability'?"

"Of course."

VanOwen gave him a radiant smile and said nothing else.

CHAPTER SEVEN

CITADEL OF SALAH ED-DIN
SEVEN KILOMETERS EAST OF AL-HAFFAH, SYRIA
TWO DAYS AGO

They hung like spiders from the ceiling. Both of them dressed all in black, armed with guns and knives, dangling from silk threads. Silent as the death they had brought with them.

The castle had stood for more than a thousand years, perched on a ridge between deep ravines and skirted by dense forests. Wars had raged around it and in it and past it, but the citadel endured and the memory of clashing steel and the screams of men seemed to be trapped like ghosts within its walls. Maybe more so down here, far below the grand halls. There were secrets built into the walls. Hidden rooms, concealed corridors and passages, vaults and tombs that even the historians and the UNESCO custodians had never found. Some were so skillfully built that it would take the outright destruction of the fortress for anyone to find them.

That had nearly happened, and still might. The fighters of ISIL had destroyed so many places like this. So had President Assad, who indiscriminately bombed historic sites with the same abandon with which he rained down death on rebel camps and civilian towns. The fact that Saladin's Castle survived for so long had nothing to do with any respect for history or the memory of the warrior of Allah who had fought back with such intelligence and ferocity against the Crusaders. No, this place survived because it was never important enough to destroy, and its position in this remote part of northwest Syria made it of little value to anyone in the current war. Some refugees found shelter there, thinking themselves safe within the partially collapsed walls.

They were wrong. They were not safe here.

"They're not coming," whispered one of the silent invaders. Although male, he was the shorter of the two.

"They're coming, Harry," soothed his companion. She spoke quietly rather than whispering, because whispers carried farther.

"This harness is cutting into my nuts," complained Harry Bolt.

"Stop squirming," suggested the woman, Violin, without much sympathy. "And be quiet. *Listen.*"

There was a sound; a clink of metal. Then the careful steps of rubber soles on stone. The soft whisk of clothing. More clinks and clanks. The sounds of people who thought they were alone.

Violin reached out a hand and gave her partner's arm a small, reassuring squeeze. *Be ready,* it said, and she felt Harry tense. He was often nervous, which made him clumsy despite the months of intense training she had given him. Training that was superior to what he had gotten during his years in the Central Intelligence Agency.

Since they'd begun traveling together, Harry Bolt—born Harcourt Bolton, Junior—had grown as a fighter, deepened his knowledge of espionage tradecraft, and gained in practical experience. Even so, he was a liability in almost every crisis situation. Violin accepted that and never took him into a situation where his shortcomings would tip the odds too far the wrong way. Until today. She'd intended to do this job with a full Arklight team, but the timing did not work and Harry was the only one available.

The intruders below were a mixed bag of ex-military working for the Turkish black marketer Ohan, and experts brought here to solve the mystery of this place. What unified them all was that they were thieves of time. Of antiquities. Of history. It was possible they were merely corrupt; but Violin's intelligence reports suggested they were looking for something truly and deeply dangerous. If that was the case, then this reconnaissance would have to turn into something else.

"Here," said a voice, speaking Arabic with an Iraqi accent. "Come on, give me some light."

Several flashlight beams flicked on, chasing the shadows back but a little. The light didn't illuminate very much, and certainly didn't reach all the way to the vaulted ceiling. A dozen men came hurrying through the darkness. She recognized their leader, a fierce man known as Ghul, who was Ohan's trusted lieutenant.

"I don't see anything," complained one of the experts, a geologist from Saudi Arabia.

Ghul laughed. "That's what you're supposed to see."

"We've scoured this place half a dozen times," said another of the research team, a structural engineer. He spoke bad Arabic with a heavy Irish accent. "There's nothing left to find, mate. Anything of value here is either already in museums or it's been destroyed by the ISIL madmen."

But Ghul shook his head. "No. This is something that was not meant to be found." He tapped the fourth researcher, a birdlike man with a pointed beard and professorial glasses perched on the end of a beaky nose. "It's time. Tell them."

Violin knew this man, too, and he was why she had been sent here. Professor Ali Nasser, formerly of the Hamad Bin Khalifa University in Qatar, where he had spearheaded several important research expeditions in the Middle East, including four in Syria. Before the war, Nasser had been one of the world's most respected scholars on the Crusades in general, and the related artifacts of this region in particular. His book on the relics of Antioch was still required reading in universities around the world, and it retained its validity even though Ali's personal reputation had crumbled when he was first arrested for selling artifacts to the black market. His fellow academics had banished him, treating him like a heretic for sins against scholarship. Violin thought it sad that such a man would have descended to this level. On the other hand, it might make what she had to do so much easier. Contempt was a weak barrier to violence and was more often a firm shove in the direction of action.

"Here," said Nasser, waving the others toward a spot by the base of the pillar. "Shine your lights there. No, *there*. Good. Do you see that writing?"

"Writing?" said the geologist. "It's nothing. Tool marks, maybe."

"No, no, no," insisted Nasser, his voice and face flushed with excitement, "it's been scuffed, but it is certainly writing."

Ghul placed a heavy hand on Nasser's shoulder. "Mr. Oruraka and Mr. Kostas said you could read it. Prove them right." The threat was unspoken, but eloquent.

Nasser unslung his pack and removed a few small vials and a sponge. As the others watched, he poured a little liquid from two of the vials into a plastic cup, used a coffee stirrer to blend them, and dabbed the corner of the sponge into the mixture. The geologist watched him do it and began to nod; however, Nasser explained his process to the others.

"Everything ages," he said, "even rock. And, as forensic science tells us, all contact leaves a trace. This solution will react only to microscopic trace elements of iron, and the older and more oxidized the iron, the more it will react to the solution."

"Brilliant," murmured the geologist.

Nasser used the sponge to dab the solution onto the marks in the rock. High above, Violin tapped the controls of the goggles she wore and the zoom function brought what the professor was doing into sharp focus. Beside her, Harry watched and repeated the action. On the pillar the rough scratches changed as the oxidized flecks of ancient iron turned to the color of blood, revealing the original markings made by some unknown hand many centuries ago. Violin felt her heart begin to hammer as she recognized the marks.

"What does it say?" asked Ghul, and the excitement was evident in his gruff voice. "That's not Arabic."

"No," said the professor, "nor is it the language of the Europeans who possessed this castle."

The Irishman grunted. "I saw something like this when I was doing a mining assessment in Greece near an old Minoan ruin. Is it Linear A?"

"Not exactly," said Nasser. "This is a very rare protolanguage used by a group within the Minoan culture. Linear A was their main language, and it has never been deciphered. This is older.

Incredibly ancient, actually. It was only used by a secret sect of Minoan priests."

"Then how can you translate it?" demanded the Irishman.

Nasser smiled and did not explain.

Ghul growled in irritation. "What the hell does it say?"

"It is both a warning and a set of instructions," said the professor. "Something I've seen before in a translation in *Von Unaussprechlichen Kulten* . . . a very rare book, gentlemen. Yes, very rare. One passage spoke of the writing in the oldest of languages on a stone believed to be a lintel from a forgotten temple excavated from off the shores of Santorini. The passage was a warning not to touch that which is untouchable, or attempt to learn what is unlearnable."

"Well, that's a bunch of shite," complained the Irishman.

Nasser ignored him. "The same warning is here, and it is meant for anyone except the priests whose job it is to protect what is hidden. Below the warning are instructions for those priests."

"Read them, damn you," snarled Ghul.

The professor nodded and bent close. "It says, 'Push high with four hands, push low with six, and four to bow before wisdom and pull. Left and right and back.'"

There was a beat.

"What the sodding hell does that mean?" demanded the Irishman.

Ghul chuckled. "It means the professor is about to earn his bonus."

Nasser straightened and ordered his colleagues back as he walked around the pillar, dabbing now and again with the mixture. A few more symbols appeared. Nasser instructed some of the guards to place their hands in very specific places. Two big men were positioned with hands on the central stone in the pillar, at about chest height. Three others were made to squat with their palms on the lowest stone. And then two more had to kneel and dig their fingers into the narrow crack between the base of the pillar and a rectangular flagstone.

"Put your backs into it," said the professor. "Ready? Go!"

The men pushing on the middle ring of the pillar pushed to the left, the lower three to the right, and the kneeling men pulled. They were big men, picked for this task. The pillar was heavy and ancient and held part of the ceiling. The other guards and scientists stood watching, their faces filled with equal parts confusion and skepticism.

There was a sudden harsh, deep, dusty, grating sound. Then the three pieces of ancient stone moved. The central stone rotated one way, the stone below it turned the other, and the flagstone slid away from the base. The men strained until some of them screamed with the effort.

"Stop," gasped Nasser, and the men staggered back, sweating, gasping, cursing, exhausted by their efforts. Then they all fell into a shocked silence. Violin felt her heart turn to ice and she heard a small, strangled sound from Harry.

A section of the floor began to move, folding downward with a grating rumble, revealing by slow degrees a set of stairs hidden for hundreds of years. And from below, from where those stairs vanished into swirling dust, there was a sudden ghostly green glow.

The men staggered back as gas and dust billowed up from below. Even from her lofty perch Violin caught a whiff that smelled like old, rotting fish.

"Perfect," breathed Nasser.

Violin turned, hooked a hand out, caught Harry by the sleeve, and pulled him close so she could whisper in his ear.

"It's time," she said.

Harry looked at her. "Wh-what?"

She did not answer. Instead she hit the release button on her tether and dropped down, drawing her knives as she fell.

CHAPTER EIGHT

WEST LAFAYETTE AVENUE
BALTIMORE, MARYLAND

I played follow the leader with the Secret Service agents as I worked my way over to the battlefield that is West Lafayette. Something like 16 percent of Baltimore buildings—homes and commercial properties—are abandoned. That makes for a large, spread-out, and very spooky ghost town within the thriving city. Lots and lots of ghosts there. Lots of bad things happening there. Crack houses, murder scenes, quiet places for all manner of horrific sexual abuse. Lonely places to hide, or be abandoned to die—or to be alive and hurt but left wondering if death was a useful doorway out.

Driving along West Lafayette is like driving into an Edgar Allan Poe opium dream, especially as you turn onto North Arlington and see the big, old, and sadly forgotten hulk of Sellers Mansion. It's a sprawling pile built in 1868 for Matthew Bacon Sellers, president of the Northern Central Railway. Once upon a time it was a showpiece, but those times are long gone. Three stories tall, sturdily built, and although long empty it never felt to me like it was actually dead.

Not saying it's a haunted house, but there is some kind of residual energy there, and we're not talking Casper the Friendly Ghost. More like something from a James Wan horror flick. The kind of place where if some weird haunted doll suddenly stepped out through the bare laths you'd be like—yeah, that fits.

So, that's where I led my entourage.

I put the pedal down to make some time and had Calpurnia hack into the traffic lights to slow the pursuit cars down. Did I mention that gadgets like this give me a woody? They do.

The rain had chased all the neighbors indoors. Good. I parked behind the mansion, took some goodies from a lockbox in the back of my car, told Calpurnia to secure the vehicle, then ran through slanting rain to the back door. Ghost's nails were padded with silicone tips that muffled the sound of him running with me.

The door was locked, but I was in a hurry and the place was a dump, so I kicked it in. I gave Ghost the order to range ahead to check and clear, while I made my way carefully through gloom and shadows and dust to the staircase. The place was by definition a death trap, with holes in the floor, exposed wiring, water damage, rat droppings, human waste, garbage, and refuse I did not want to even speculate about, and the skeleton of what looked like a raccoon. No idea how that got there, and don't really want to know.

Calpurnia whispered like a ghost into my ear. "The Secret Service vehicles have arrived at your location. Total five agents."

I smiled and faded into the shadows.

INTERLUDE THREE

SPETSES, CAVO SERENO
ATTICA ISLANDS, GREECE
SEVEN YEARS AGO

Valen hired a boat to take him to the Kostas mansion, which was a sprawling and vulgar piece of real estate so vast it nearly qualified as its own city.

It squatted on a kind of peninsula that thrust so aggressively into the sea that from the air it looked very much like the Kostas family was making a "fuck you" statement to anyone who could afford to see it. That was entirely in keeping with what Valen remembered of Ari. The man was a sexual animal. More goat than bull, with unsavory appetites that he could never quite assuage, but who had enough money to keep trying—and to handle any resulting legal or financial consequences. If he had not been very good at what he did for the family business, no doubt they would have shipped him off to some remote spot and then erased it off the map. But Ari, despite deep character flaws, was brilliant. He could find anything for anyone, and then get them to pay more than the market would bear to possess it. A dealer of antiquities, rarities, and art for the most discerning clientele, he'd made his first billion by age twenty-three. That was above what he inherited as the second son of a dynastic family of procurers.

Ari met him at the dock. Barefoot and smiling; a deep-water tan, generous belly, and sparkling white teeth. White trousers and an untucked white shirt that opened midway down a hairy chest. As they hugged and slapped each other's backs, Valen recalled the last time he'd seen his old college roommate. It had been a few days after graduation, when Valen helped Ari bury a body in an unmarked grave near San Gabriel Park. A college girl who had gone to the wrong party and whose body would never be found. Or, if it was found, would never be connected to Aristotle Kostas. Valen insured that by lining her grave with plastic tarps and dumping in ten gallons of bleach. There would be no forensics to collect and the bleach would ruin even the tissue samples. Ari, who'd sat on a tree stump trying out various just-in-case alibis, had done very little digging. He'd been too drunk.

Lunch was served on a private patio overlooking the flawless deep blue of the rippling waters of the Mediterranean. They ate grilled fish and vegetables and, being a good host, Ari had provided Old Rip Van Winkle twenty-five-year-old bourbon. The thirteen-thousand-dollars-a-bottle whiskey was very fine and went down exceptionally well.

"You never just come to visit," he said as honey-soaked dessert pastries were laid out. "So, why are we here getting drunk on a Tuesday afternoon?"

Valen nodded. "I am in the market for something that needs a delicate touch but a long reach to find. You once told me that you could get anything that can be gotten. That's how you phrased it."

The young Greek gave a small shrug. "I have had some luck in that department."

"Which is why I came to you first. I have been asked to find something."

"You are not the buyer?"

"You know better than that," said Valen. "I have no money, and you know that I haven't pursued a career in seismology. No, since college I've become something of a fixer. I help facilitate things for parties who, for various reasons, choose or need to remain anonymous. I'm the fellow who goes and fetches what they want."

Ari nodded, accepting it as something quite right and proper in the world as he knew it. "What is it you need to find, my friend?"

"Can I trust that our conversation is confidential?"

Ari pretended to be offended. "This is something you ask me? An old friend? A Kostas? I am wounded unto death, Valen. I am bleeding. See the cut all the way to my heart?"

"Yeah, yeah, cut it out. It's a serious question, because I am working with serious people and it's more than my life is worth to breach their trust. I ask because I am expected to ask."

Ari grinned and patted Valen's arm hard enough to nearly knock him out of his chair. Then the young Greek leaned forward and dropped his voice. "Tell me what you need and I will tell you how much it costs."

"You mean you'll tell me if you can procure it?"

Ari threw back his head and laughed. The guards glanced their way, but neither moved nor spoke. "No, Valen, you beautiful fool. If it is there, I can get it. Cost is the only factor."

They smiled at each other.

"It has many names, but among a certain community of—shall we say—credulous believers, it is called Lemurian quartz. The green variety, not the white."

"There's a lot of green quartz out there. How will I know I'm getting the right stuff for you? I don't want to waste a lot of my own time. No offense."

"None taken," said Valen. "Check your e-mail later. I sent a molecular profile to you. There are several kinds of quartz that are almost—but not quite—identical, and my employers are particular. To that end, I can provide a portable scanner to help you assess samples before you purchase. And, for any items you obtain that have been made from the Lemurian quartz—artworks, or whatever—we would like you to use luminescence dating to determine how long ago those minerals were last exposed to sunlight or sufficient heating. We are most interested in any green quartz objects older than 1000 B.C.E. Particularly any that are found on, or come from, Crete or neighboring Aegean islands."

Ari sipped his wine. "Are you looking for Minoan artifacts? You're confusing me. First you mention Lemurian quartz, but in the same breath you want stuff from where people thought Atlantis used to be. I mean, it's pretty well accepted these days that Plato created Atlantis as a way of explaining the wonders of the Minoan culture, and that an eruption on Thera—what is now Santorini—was what destroyed their civilization. The submergence of some areas is the basis for the myth of the so-called continent of Atlantis sinking. Basically, exaggeration by Plato based on indifferent reportage by scholars of previous eras."

Valen nodded, pleased at his friend's expertise. "And correct, insofar as what you know. However, as with all things, there is much more to the story."

Ari looked interested. "Tell me, then."

"The first significant artifact of this special kind of green quartz was found in a chamber beneath Minoan temple ruins in Gournia, in Crete. The site was first excavated in 1903. There were several small hexagonal pieces recovered. Three are in the British Museum, four are at the University of Pennsylvania, but nine others went missing at some point after they were described and stored away. These nine were very special, Ari, because they had the same molecular structure as what I want you to find for me."

"What makes them special?"

"That's something we can discuss later."

"Which means you don't know," said Ari, laying a finger beside his nose and nodding sagely. "You're working for someone and they haven't told you all of it. Or . . . maybe they don't know all of it yet. No, don't look so surprised. You're not the first person to come to me looking for something all tangled up in history and myth. Kind of a thing in the antiquities trade, my friend. So, tell me . . . how much of it do you need?"

Valen finished his glass of whiskey and held it out for a refill. "All of it."

CHAPTER NINE

SELLERS MANSION
BALTIMORE, MARYLAND

The back door opened with a creak and swung all the way in, spilling gray light and rain onto the dusty floor. There was a beat when the doorway stood empty, and then two figures came in fast, breaking right and left, pistols up and out. Then the front door burst inward, the lock torn roughly from the splintered frame by a breaching tool swung by a brute of an agent. He stepped aside, dropping the heavy tool, and drew his gun as two other agents ran quickly past him.

They moved through the downstairs with professional competence and speed, clearing each room, pointing guns into closets. There were four men and one woman. All were grim-faced, unsmiling, and efficient. The two who had entered through the rear went down into the vast, unlighted cellar, which was a warren of small storage and service rooms left over from when the mansion had been occupied. The other three moved quickly to the stairs and went up, making sure to check their corners and watch each other's backs. It was all done in a smooth and ghastly silence.

But they did not see the dark shape that waited for them beneath the stairs. It was not the natural place for them to look first. It wasn't where their flashlight beams fell as they came down to the concrete basement floor. The two agents did everything right.

It wasn't enough.

Upstairs, the three agents from the black SUV moved along the hallway in a three-point cover formation. One checked the hall behind and in front, moving in quick but smooth 180-degree turns. The second offered cover to the third, who pushed open doors to check and clear the rooms. For the larger rooms, they went in as a team, breaking to either side of the door while the first man watched their backs to prevent ambushers from coming from unchecked rooms.

They cleared four bedrooms and an old empty library and found nothing.

The second held up a fist to signal them to stop, then he pointed to the floor. There, in the dust, was a line of animal tracks. Heading toward the stairs to the third floor.

"He has a dog, doesn't he?" asked the first very quietly.

"Yes," said the third. "Big white combat dog."

The second agent touched a smudge near the baseboard. They all studied it; they all nodded. It was the kind of smudge someone made if they were walking on the edges of their shoes in an attempt to avoid leaving footprints. But there was too much dust in the old place. The agents looked down the hall, following the lines of animal and human tracks around the corner toward the stairs.

They smiled. There were three other rooms to check, but the tracks were an arrow pointing to their quarry. The first two agents began to move; the third agent hesitated for a moment, knowing that they were doing it wrong. They were tracking an expert, a senior covert operator. The others were almost to the foot of the stairs.

"Wait . . . ," he called.

One second too late.

The door to the second-to-last bedroom stood slightly ajar. They had less than one full second to register the fact that something was moving through the air toward them. Small. About the size of a soda can.

The agent behind them tried to yell, "Grenade!" But the flash-bang flashed and banged. Real damn bright, too damn loud.

The agents in the cellar heard the blast and turned toward it. Toward the stairs.

Toward the big man with the dark goggles and sound-suppressing headphones.

They never even glimpsed the stun grenade that blew them backward against the wall, burned their vision from white to blackness, and dropped them into huddled masses so shocked that they could not even hear their own screams.

Top Sims kicked their guns away from them and had both agents—male and female—belly down and cuffed in seconds. Only then did he remove his sound suppressors and nearly opaque dark glasses. He was grinning. It was not a nice grin.

He cocked his head and listened to the cries and groans from upstairs. And then the harsh, angry, triumphant barks of a very big dog.

It made his smile very bright in the dusty darkness.

CHAPTER TEN

SELLERS MANSION
BALTIMORE, MARYLAND

Five little agents all in a row.

They sat in the dust against a wall in the basement. Zip cuffs on wrists and ankles, pockets turned out, personal expectations and feelings of self-worth shattered. The effects of the flash-bangs had mostly worn off, though I think all five of them might need to see an ear, nose, and throat guy sometime soon. Maybe put Miracle-Ear on their birthday wish lists.

Top and I stood on either side of Ghost. All of their weapons and equipment were laid out on the floor. Top was examining their IDs and handing them off to me. The last person in the line was Agent Virginia Harrald, who was a snub-nosed woman with hate in her gray eyes and a stern slash of a thin-lipped mouth.

"You have no idea how much shit you just stepped in," she muttered. She spoke too loud, the way people do who can't hear all that well.

Top gave her a warm and fatherly smile. "Trouble? That's adorable. Isn't she being adorable, Cap'n? Making threats like a grown-up."

"Adorable," I agreed.

"Sitting there all tied up and shit."

"Yeah."

"Hair mussed up. Cuffed and scuffed and still full of stuff. Bet her parents would be so proud of her."

Harrald stared pure unfiltered death at him. "Fuck you."

"Such language. I'm shocked," said Top, looking aghast. "Shocked, I do declare."

Ghost made a sound that I swear to God was a doggy laugh.

I looked at Harrald's ID, then stuffed it in a pocket. The other agents were Kurt Krieg, Thomas Hurley, Christopher Jablonski, and John Smallwood. I pocketed all of their IDs. No need to call it in, because the American flag pin I wore on my lapel was a high-res video camera that was feeding everything to MindReader in real time. Calpurnia had run facial recognition on each of them and one of Bug's team was happily tearing through their entire lives via deep and unfiltered Net searches.

"Okay, kids," I said to the unsmiling faces glaring at us, "I know it's tough losing the big game, but we can take it as a learning experience. If you try real hard, make every practice, one day maybe—maybe—you'll be able to play with the big kids."

"Fuck you," repeated Harrald.

"Okay, that's a valid argument," I conceded. "Or . . . how about you five are already fucked. Deeply and comprehensively fucked. None of you are carrying warrants. No warrants have, in fact, been issued for me. I checked."

That put some doubt in the faces of the four men. They tried not to cut looks at Harrald, but mostly failed. Which confirmed that she was the foreman of this little crew.

"You guys know what happened to the three bozos who came at me at the cemetery this morning?"

"These pricks probably killed them," said one of the other agents. Krieg.

"Maybe they should have come after me with a warrant," I said, and for a moment I actually enjoyed the fear that flashed in their eyes. Then a second later I felt like a jackass and a bully. I caught Top looking at me, one eyebrow slightly raised in mild reproof. But he had a trace of a smile, too. Top is always the grown-up in the room. I seldom aspire to that role.

"We don't need a warrant," said Krieg.

"If you're going to try and play the 'national security' card, son," said Top, "maybe you'd better go reread the rules. We are national security. More than you know. More than you'll ever be. So, don't embarrass yourself here. Be a man, Agent Krieg."

I had to fight to keep the wince off my face. Krieg didn't. Ghost made that snarky sound again.

"Okay," I said, squatting down in front of Harrald, "let's cut right to it. Why were you following me? What were your orders? Who cut them?"

She tried to burn holes through me with her eyes.

"I didn't kill the first three agents," I said, "but they're having a bad day. You're having a bad day, too."

"What are you going to do?" she said. "Shoot us?"

"No, dumbass. I'm hoping to reason with you. One federal employee to another."

"Kiss my ass."

"That would be sexual harassment, and besides . . . ewww. No."

Harrald turned a very nice shade of tomato red.

"What I want here is for you to act like a professional. If you have a legal reason to attempt an arrest, then you need to tell me. And I don't want to hear 'Patriot Act,' because that is what I use to wipe my dog's ass. We both know that I'm with the Department of Military Sciences, which means I'm operating according to a precisely worded executive order. It is an irrevocable order, too. If you haven't read it, then maybe you should. Oh, that's right, it's about a zillion steps above your pay grade. Ask your boss's boss's boss to read it. We don't get arrested by the benchwarmers. If we somehow step on our own dicks, there are proper channels to address it and we would get spanked pretty damn hard. So, whatever you're doing is, literally, illegal. I can arrest all of you. I would, in fact, have been within my legal right to shoot the shit out of you when you came after me with guns drawn. Be real happy I didn't toss a fragmentation grenade in your face. I have some with me."

Her ferocity was showing cracks at the edges, and I knew that *she* knew I was telling the truth. Maybe if we were alone she might have opened up, but her crew was with her. From what I know about the current state of the Secret Service, there was a lot of backstabbing and cliquishness polluting an organization that used to be known for its deep integrity. That made me sad and, let's face it, a bit cranky.

But Harrald didn't say anything else. None of them did. They bit down on their humiliation, fear, and anger and sat like defeated lumps.

There was a huge temptation bubbling in my chest to threaten them with what I could do to their lives with MindReader. It would have felt good for about three seconds. It might even have crowbarred one of them open . . . but it would have been small. And I knew Top would disapprove. Adult in the room, blah blah blah. Moral decency can occasionally be a pain in the ass.

So instead, I straightened and said, "When you get back to the office, tell your boss to pass a message up the line. You've come at me twice today, and both times you fucked up. Both times you also got lucky. If I was some kind of bad guy, as you cats seem to think, then I'd put bullets in your heads and burn this building down on top of you. However, I think you're a bunch of misinformed idiots and not actual villains. Stay on that side of the line. Don't come after me again. Make sure no one else comes after me. I just used up the very last of my give-a-fuck. Got no fucks left to give."

"Hooah," breathed Top.

We turned to go. Ghost shot me a *seriously, no biting?* look, then snuffed and followed us up the stairs. Top paused at the top step and yelled over his shoulder.

"Sit tight," he said. "We'll call someone."

"Maybe," I said.

"Eventually," he amended.

We left.

CHAPTER ELEVEN

CITADEL OF SALAH ED-DIN
SEVEN KILOMETERS EAST OF AL-HAFFAH, SYRIA
TWO DAYS AGO

The men had no idea they were in danger.

They had no idea that death was falling toward them. They stood with their eyes fixed on the green glow that swirled up from below the castle floor. They stood transfixed. All of them.

And then Violin was among them.

The first hint any of them had of her presence was when one of the biggest men seemed to collapse beneath the improbable weight of shadow. Out of the corners of their eyes they saw a cloud of darkness strike him on the shoulders with such force that it bent him backward, broke him, crushed him down to the unforgiving stone. The scientists screamed in shock and sudden terror. The soldiers whirled, cursing, torn from one impossible thing to another.

And then the shadow rose from the twisted, dying man and coalesced into something else. Tall, slim, sheathed in black, with matched kukri knives in her gloved fists. Silver flashed and then the air was filled with rubies.

The closest man reeled backward, clutching at his throat, unable to process why it felt so hot and so wrong. Another soldier swung his Kalashnikov around with the speed of years of combat, but then it tilted and fell, held only by one hand. The other, still clutching the wooden handguard, no longer belonged to him. He gaped at it for a moment and then saw a line of silver moving toward him too fast for him to evade. He did not even have time to cry out.

Far above, Harry Bolt watched the carnage as he fought the release control on the silver wire that suspended him from the ceiling. It was supposed to operate with a gentle pressure of his thumb, but the goddamn thing would not move. He cursed and squeezed it with all his strength, hissing as his struggles made the harness cut even harder into his tortured scrotum.

"Come on, you goddamn cock-sucking son of a bitch," he snarled as he shook the stubborn release. "Come on . . . *please*!"

Below, Violin was in the center of a storm of violence. Guns fired but she was never there. Men lunged at her and grabbed nothing. But there were so many of them and she was alone. Harry had a sidearm, but he did not trust his accuracy enough to risk a shot. Even though he'd become more skilled under her tutelage, he seldom scored more than one shot in ten in the kill zone. Violin seemed to be everywhere, dancing like she did, performing a ballet of slaughter. He was absolutely certain that if he tried to shoot from up there he'd probably kill her.

So, in desperation, he held the release in one hand and punched it with the other.

It did, in fact, release.

But his blow bent the speed-belaying device out of alignment.

He did not descend.

He plummeted.

Violin heard the caterwauling wail as Harry Bolt dropped like a rock from the ceiling, but she could not do anything about it. Ghul and two of his men were chopping at her with knives and trying to bring pistols to bear, and she was forced to take the fight to ultraclose range, using speed and her natural athleticism to evade and engage at the same time.

Behind her there was a heavy, ugly *whump* as Harry crashed down, and an accompanying double scream of pain; proof that he'd landed on one of the invaders instead of the unyielding ground. Violin could not spare the time to look, because everything around her was blood and fury, rage and death.

She spun and twisted, danced and leapt, her heavy, curved blades cleaving through bone as easily as they parted flesh. The Kevlar body armor some of the men wore offered no defense. It was made to stop bullets but was of little use against the scalpel sharpness of her knives. A few shots rang out, but her first kills had been the men with the flashlights. The melee proceeded in a boiling darkness in which she could see very well, while they saw nothing that would help them.

Harry groaned and rolled over onto his knees. Pain exploded along his back and in his shoulders and legs. He heard a nearby rattling breath and he turned to see one of the guards crushed up against the base of the pillar, legs twisted and hanging over the edge of the stairway, gasping and trembling. The man's head was angled weirdly on his neck, and Harry realized with a sick jolt that his fall had broken the guard's neck but hadn't killed him.

"Sorry," mumbled Harry, which was an absurd thing to say in the middle of a bloodbath like this. He fumbled for his pistol, found it, drew it too fast, and instantly lost it. The gun went bumpity-bumping its way down the stone steps into the green glow.

"Shit," he growled, and cast around to see if he could find the AK-47 the guard had been carrying. It was ten feet away and he lunged for it, caught the stock, clawed it to him, sat up with it in his hands, looked for a target, and stared straight into the horrified, stricken face of Professor Nasser. The man was blind in the dark and nearly mad with fear. However, he had a gun in his hand.

"Drop it!" yelled Harry.

The professor flinched at the sound and his finger involuntarily twitched on the trigger. Harry felt himself falling backward as white-hot pain detonated in the exact center of his chest. As he fell, his hands both clenched and the rifle chattered out a ragged speech of death.

INTERLUDE FOUR

EMIRATES PALACE ABU DHABI
UNITED ARAB EMIRATES
SIX YEARS AGO

Gadyuka made another of her nighttime visits. What the Americans referred to as a booty call. Valen still hadn't decided if he was appalled or enchanted.

However, as before, the sex was a prelude to talking business. She came at it in a roundabout way, talking politics first and sharing a few exciting details about the New Soviet. Then she hit him with a very strange request and encouraged him to bring Ari Kostas in on it. The mad Greek's connections were crucial.

So, when he was alone, Valen called Ari.

"How are you at finding books?" asked Valen.

"What kind of books?" asked Ari, not particularly intrigued.

"These are books both sacred and profane. They are holy and unholy."

"Are you quoting her?"

"Yes," Valen admitted. "Though from what she's told me, if we were not trying to save our country, I would burn them all."

"Oh, please," laughed Ari, "you *must* tell me more. These sound like books I should read."

"Have you ever heard of the *Index Librorum Prohibitorum*?"

"Valen," said Ari slowly and with no lingering trace of humor, "you're talking about the Pauline Index, yes?"

"I am, yes." The Index was a list of books deemed heretical, lascivious, or anticlerical. The list had been created at the behest of Pope Paul IV in 1559, and many horrible and cruel things had been done in the name of the Church to suppress those works.

"Books of black magic," mused Ari. "I will say this for you, Valen, you are never ever boring. Now, let me think about this. Some of those books are supposed to have been destroyed. Some aren't even supposed to be real—they were added to the list because someone in the church thought they were real. I'm talking about books made up by horror writers. H. P. Lovecraft and that lot. Pulp writers. The *Necronomicon* and all that bullshit."

"Yes."

"And now Gadyuka wants us to *find* those books. Books that probably aren't real."

"Yes. Gadyuka believes they are real."

"How many of these books does she want?"

"All of them, Ari. Can you find them?"

"Me?" laughed Ari. "No. Not a chance. But . . . I may know a guy. . . ."

CHAPTER TWELVE

THE OVAL OFFICE
THE WHITE HOUSE
WASHINGTON, D.C.
TWENTY-ONE MONTHS AGO

"What do you have for me, General?" asked the president. "Do you have the list of names I told you to prepare?"

General Frank Ballard felt like a big green bug on a plain white wall. Easy to spot, easy to swat. He'd been called to the Oval Office without the support of the other Joint Chiefs. The only other person in the room was Jennifer VanOwen.

"Well, Mr. President," began Ballard, "let me first say that in terms of what Majestic Three accomplished . . . that all of the information related to the development, construction, and deployment of the T-craft has been destroyed."

"Destroyed?" asked VanOwen.

"Yes, ma'am," said Ballard. "Destroying all of that material was the agreement when the, um, situation involving the former president was resolved."

They sat with that. The situation in question was the abduction of the previous president by person or persons unknown. His safe return was conditional on the recovery of something called the Majestic Black Book, which was the repository for vast amounts of technical information supposedly reverse-engineered from a crashed vehicle of unknown origin.

"How can we recover that information?" demanded VanOwen.

"We can't," said Ballard. "And I think it would be a very dangerous thing to attempt."

"Why?" asked the president.

"Sir, it was all in the briefing I gave prior to your taking office."

"Little green men from outer space?" The president laughed. "My predecessor left a lot of that kind of stuff behind. Lies and misinformation left in the hopes of disrupting my presidency."

"Sir, I was there when this happened. I was in the Situation Room when—"

"When you were fooled, General. Don't embarrass yourself by saying that you believed that nonsense."

"With respect, Mr. President . . ."

But the president waved it away with an annoyed flap of his hand. To VanOwen he said, "Put someone on recovering the Majestic Black Book."

"Yes, sir," she said. "Tell me, General, who was specifically responsible for destroying the T-craft data?"

"The, ah, physical records were stored at Howard Shelton's estate—Van Meer Castle in Pennsylvania. The T-craft were also built and launched from there. After one T-craft was deployed, an order was given to have a flight of Thunderbolts destroy the launch site with missiles. The entire facility was incinerated and the mountains above the hangars collapsed. Shelton's mansion and labs were stripped of all remaining materials and everything was incinerated."

"That's a loss," said the president, "and typical of my predecessor. He had no real patriotism and no vision."

"The decision was made to protect the country from a threatened disaster."

"So, we're negotiating with terrorists, General?" asked VanOwen.

"Ms. VanOwen, excuse me, but you were not there."

"Then tell me this, General," said VanOwen, "what exactly happened to the computer records for the entire Majestic Three program? If they built T-craft, some of the information had to be in computers for the groups handling manufacture and assembly."

Ballard made his face show nothing. "The disposal of all such records was handled by the Department of Military Sciences."

VanOwen turned toward the president, whose lip curled as if he'd tasted something sour and foul.

"Then they probably still have them," said the president.

Ballard shook his head. "Mr. Church gave his word that the records would be destroyed. He ordered his computer people to use tapeworms to track down all records and references."

"Church gave his 'word'?" murmured VanOwen in a way that suggested only a complete damn fool would be gullible enough to accept that.

"Mr. Church is a patriot," said Ballard coldly. "He and his people have gone above and beyond more times than I can count. None of us would be here right now if—"

"Enough," interrupted the president. "Church has fooled a lot of people for a long time, believe me. Everyone knows that. If he took the M3 records, then he has those records. I am going to make sure he turns them over to us."

There was so much that Ballard wanted to say, but he forced himself to rely on forty years of military experience to simply reply, "Yes, sir."

"General," said the president, holding out a hand, "give me the list I asked for. The names of people who can serve as governors of my new Majestic Three."

It cost the general a lot to comply, and opening his briefcase felt like lifting an Abrams tank bare-handed. And yet he felt like a weakling in doing it. Forty years in the air force, combat missions in both Iraq wars and in Afghanistan, two Purple Hearts and a chestful of medals for actual courage, for defending his country from threats foreign and domestic. He had served with distinction no matter who was president, and he believed that true patriotism was putting the needs of the defense of America and all of its people ahead of any party's agenda. Now he felt like he was betraying the trust of everyone in the country.

Maybe everyone in the whole blessed world.

CHAPTER THIRTEEN

BROADWAY DINER
BALTIMORE, MARYLAND

We drove in separate cars to the Broadway Diner.

I ordered a Chesapeake burger, which comes topped with crabmeat and Old Bay sauce. Tomatoes if you want them, which I didn't. Lots of golden French fries. Top got his favorite from when we were both stationed here—a Juicy Lucy burger, which is stuffed with cheddar cheese and chopped bacon. I ordered two cheeseburgers without bread for Ghost, who looked properly docile in his service dog vest. The waitress knew he wasn't anyone's emotional support animal, but she was a dog person and brought him three patties. Her attitude toward my dog is reflected in the kind of tips I leave.

We had a corner booth and I placed an Anteater bug-detection gizmo on the table to make sure it was all clear. The device is designed to look like a clicker for my car. The lights popped green and stayed that way. The place was pretty empty, so there was no one to hear us when we leaned together for a chat.

"Called Bunny on the way over here," said Top. "He wants to come out."

"Tell him not to bother. We can handle—"

"He'll be here tonight."

I knew better than to argue. Top had a bit of mother hen in him.

If he was rattled enough on my behalf to want another set of eyes on me, then he was going to get his way.

"Thanks," I said.

Despite my parting words to Harrald, I made a call to some old friends in the Baltimore PD, and they sent a car. The five agents from the mansion and the three from the cemetery were all being treated at a local hospital. The goons from the graveyard were admitted for observation. I made a notation on my calendar to cry about it the day after hell freezes over.

I called Church and conferenced Top's cell in. "We anywhere with figuring this out?" I asked.

"We are not," said Church. "Bug has been poking around inside the Secret Service computers. E-mails, voicemails, procedural and case files. Whatever this is, no one is making a record of it. Or, put it another way, they are being very careful to make sure there's no record of it, which actually tells us a lot. It suggests that they know they are acting outside of the law. The Secret Service would not do that openly unless they had some offer of protection from higher up the food chain."

"How far up?" I asked. "The goon at the cemetery said it came from the Oval Office, but I figured he was lying."

"Maybe not."

"Damn," said Top.

"Yes," said Church.

We batted it back and forth for a bit but there was nowhere to go with it for now.

"What do you want us to do?" I asked.

"Nothing," said Church. "Sergeant Sims, you had some days off, I believe. Feel free to go back to doing what you were doing."

"Maybe I should loiter around and watch his back," suggested Top.

"No need. The captain can go to the Warehouse for a night or two and wait until we have something."

"That doesn't sound fun," I said.

"Life is full of little disappointments, Captain," said Church, and rang off.

The waitress brought our food and refilled our coffee cups. She started to say something, but then she caught the looks on our faces and retreated in hasty silence.

Top poured milk into his coffee, and without looking up at me, said, "And you got no idea why the G wants your head on a pike? You ain't pissed on anyone's shoes lately?"

"Not that I can recall," I said.

Top sipped his coffee and leaned back against the cushions. "Not that you can recall. And I guess you can recall every single time you pissed someone off who you shouldn't have? I mean, just this week?"

"You have a point, Top?"

"Me? Nah. I actually like you."

"But . . . ?"

"You been known to ruffle some feathers hither and yon."

"'Hither and yon'?"

"Being poetic." He sipped and set his cup down. "Not like you been making a secret about your feelings on how things are being run in D.C."

"I'm allowed to have an opinion."

"Sure. And people are allowed to get their noses out of joint about it."

"So, you think this is a proportional response to me mouthing off?"

He sighed and rubbed his eyes. "Nothing's proportional anymore, Cap'n."

"Yeah, damn it," I said.

We ate our burgers in a shared, troubled silence.

CHAPTER FOURTEEN

THE OVAL OFFICE
THE WHITE HOUSE
WASHINGTON, D.C.
TWENTY-ONE MONTHS AGO

Jennifer VanOwen spent an hour discussing the names on the list provided by General Ballard. "Well," she said, "no to the first four, right off the top. They're not political appointments and don't work in government, but they're outspoken about politics." She shook her blond head. "We need team players, not idealists."

VanOwen similarly eliminated most of the other scientists on the list. Some were cut because they were in the camp of climate change, which was politically inconvenient as long as petro-dollars ran the world. Others were axed because of their voting records or party affiliation; or for content on their social media pages.

"Well," said VanOwen again, this time almost as a sigh, "there's really only one good prospect. Donald Carpenter, CEO of Carpenter Systems out of Pasadena. His company has done extensive work with the guidance systems of the latest generations of stealth aircraft and drones, and he's built surveillance satellites for us. However . . . there is someone who knows the Majestic Black Book and all of its various technologies better than *anyone* else."

"Who?" asked the president then he stiffened. "No . . . wait a damn minute. You're not actually suggesting we hire Yuina Hoshino, are you? She's a convicted felon and a traitor."

"You can look at it like that, Mr. President," said VanOwen with a reptilian smile, "or you can look at it like she's one presidential pardon away from being the person who can put us so far out in front of the arms race that no one will ever catch us. The person who could make you—inarguably and without question—the most powerful man on Earth."

"Mr. Church won't like it," he said. "So, there can't be anything on the Net. No e-mails. Nothing."

"Of course, Mr. President, I know how to manage the DMS. Leave all the details to me."

CHAPTER FIFTEEN

THE WAREHOUSE
DMS FIELD OFFICE
BALTIMORE, MARYLAND
12:31 P.M.

I sat in what used to be my office, in a visitor's chair on the other side of the desk. The current head of this station was Sam Imura, who used to be the sniper on Echo Team. Sam and I were veterans of some of this world's more bizarre battlefields, and more or less friends. But after he got hurt during the Kill Switch affair, something had changed the dynamic between us. We stopped being friendly and operated with a kind of strained civility that I did not understand. I've seen that sort of thing happen sometimes when someone gets close to the edge of the big drop-off into the deep black. They turn sour on life, sometimes they pick someone to blame because every bullet needs a target.

Or, maybe that's me trying to carry someone else's emotional baggage. My best friend and therapist, Rudy Sanchez, says that it's likely me being a bit narcissistic while also making enormous assumptions about what's going on in someone else's head and heart. Whatever the reason, there is palpable distance between Sam and me these days. I can't reach him and he seems to only tolerate me as a necessary inconvenience.

We sat in our chairs, both of us with feet on the desk, both of us drinking coffee from oversized mugs. Top had gone back to his lady friend with a promise of joining me later on. Ghost was sprawled on the floor, dreaming doggy dreams.

"They're legit Secret Service," said Sam. The eight sets of identification were spread out on his desk along with the weapons and personal effects I'd confiscated. "All relatively new hires, though. Post Linden Brierley."

I nodded. Brierley was the former director of the Secret Service. He was the best example of the phrase "a good guy but not a nice guy." During his tenure on the job, the Service had been a tightly run department, with a zero-tolerance policy for screwups. Like a lot of us in this biz, Brierley was largely apolitical because political affiliations were a distraction, as the occupants of the White House tended to change with the whims of elections. Brierley was nobody's fawning toady, though, and the new POTUS didn't like that, and gave him the boot in favor of a spectacularly unqualified ass-kisser. The Service is in danger of becoming a circus act as a result, and that's a damn shame. Some of my oldest and most trusted friends have worked that job, and this feels like a deliberate slight to their integrity.

I said, "Knowing that they're legit doesn't tell us why they tried to arrest me and were willing to draw guns to do it."

Sam shrugged. "Maybe they know you."

"Ha," I said without emphasis. "Ha, ha."

"Bug's people hacked the Service's system," said Sam, "and there's no official order on file. So, figure VBO."

Verbal order only was becoming more common in D.C., especially in departments where people knew about MindReader. Fair enough. If I was going to try and kick the DMS in the wrinklies, I'd make sure there was no paper or digital trail. Mr. Church tends to get cranky about such things, and he is not the person you want to make cranky. Trust me on this.

"Shame we can't grill those agents," said Sam. He gave me a scowl of disapproval. "You know, you could have called in to have them arrested."

I sipped my coffee and manfully did not tell him to go stick it up his ass.

The clock on the wall above his desk ticked loudly for two full minutes.

When I'd been installed here it was a shrine to the Orioles, with balls, bats, gloves, and shirts signed by Cal Ripken, Jr., Frank Robinson, Jim Palmer, Eddie Murray, Boog Powell, Melvin Mora, and other gods of my personal pantheon.

Sam, however, was more culturally retro and had a matched pair of very old Japanese swords—katana and wakizashi—on a stand behind his desk, and photos of his parents in California and relatives back in Osaka on the walls. There were framed certificates from rifle competitions, and none of them were for second place. A shadow box on a stand had a deconstructed CheyTac M200 Intervention sniper rifle that I knew had been the one he'd used to win the International Sniper Competition at Fort Benning.

We drank coffee and the clock ticked. Then Church teleconferenced and Sam sent it to the big flat screen on the wall.

Church is a big man. Somewhere in his sixties; blocky, with dark hair streaked with gray, tinted glasses that hide his eyes, and black silk gloves over hands damaged by frostbite during the Predator One case. I don't know much about his life before he started the DMS. Rumors and strange tales, mostly. I am inclined to believe even the weirdest stories people tell about him, and I suspect they don't even scratch the surface. Anyone who could read power would immediately know that this was someone who was two or three levels above apex predator. He scares the people who scare me, and I'm pretty goddamn scary myownself.

"Gentlemen," Church said quietly, "it seems we have a problem."

"Well, gosh, boss, I kind of figured that," I said. "Who is it and when do we start kicking ass?"

Church gave a small shake of his head. "It's more complicated than that. The pickup order did indeed come from POTUS, or someone high up acting on his orders."

"Why?"

"Unknown at this time. POTUS has declined to take my call. Aunt Sallie is reaching out to her friends in Washington to see what she can find."

Sam gave a sour snort. "Do we even have any friends left in Washington?"

It was meant as a joke. Kind of. "Not many, I'm afraid," said Church. "Maybe not enough anymore."

"What's the call?" I asked. "How do you want me to go after this?"

"The call, Captain," said Church, "is to do nothing. Stay off the radar until further notice."

"Now wait just a goddamn minute," I roared. "The Secret Service just tried to arrest me. Twice. No way am I—"

Church hung up.

I said a lot of very loud, very ugly things. Ghost got to his feet and barked at the blank video screen. Behind his desk, Sam Imura turned his face away to hide the fact that he was laughing his ass off.

CHAPTER SIXTEEN

CITADEL OF SALAH ED-DIN
SEVEN KILOMETERS EAST OF AL-HAFFAH, SYRIA
TWO DAYS AGO

Harry Bolt lay at the entrance to hell and felt himself die.

The pain in his chest was astounding, almost beautiful in its purity. It allowed no other sensation to intrude, to interrupt the orchestra of agony that played through every single nerve ending. He opened his eyes and stared up at the deep shadows that clung to the lofty ceiling. Around him, outside of his peripheral vision, people fought and cursed and screamed. There were gunshots and the unmistakable and horrible sound of blades cleaving through meat and bone. The sounds were faint, though, as if the battle was happening far away.

He was going into the light. He was sure of it. What he did not understand, though, was why the light was green. Wasn't it supposed to be white? Purity of heaven and all that shit? Or, considering how many of the commandments he'd cheerfully and repeatedly broken over the years, hellfire red?

Then Harry took a breath and actually felt himself inhale and exhale. Felt the pain in his chest, in bone and flesh. Frowned. If he could still feel the pain, did that make sense? Did the dead and the damned have to feel the pain of the wounds that had killed them? Well . . . sure. Hell. Everything in hell is supposed to suck, so why not?

He tried to turn away from the light, to look at darkness. Tears leaked out from under his closed eyelids and it made him feel weak, small, stupid. Alone.

Lost.

"I'm sorry," he said in a tiny voice, directing it to God, to the Devil. Or to anyone or anything who could hear him. "I'm sorry. Please give me another chance. I swear I'll be a better person. I swear. No more drinking. No Internet porn. I'll give half my money to charity. Save the whales or trees or some shit. Whatever. I swear. Just don't let me burn."

Harry's whole face scrunched up and he began to sob.

Suddenly Violin slapped him so hard that his eyes popped wide and he stared up at her scowling face. "What the hell is wrong with you? Why are you just lying there?"

"Wait . . . What? I'm not dead?"

Violin pulled him roughly to his feet. "We're wasting time," she said sharply. "Ghul is getting away."

"I don't care," shouted Harry, then touched his body, feeling body armor instead of a sucking chest wound. "Oh," he said. "Shit."

Violin crouched at the top of the stairs, her face a mask of dark concern. "I was hoping Professor Nasser was wrong. I was hoping they wouldn't find any hidden doorway. I was hoping this would be nothing more than a training exercise for you. Truly, Harry . . . I never thought they would find . . ."

Her voice trailed off.

"Find what?"

A sound came from below. A hissing noise and then a rumble of guttural words and growls that Harry couldn't understand. If they were words, there weren't enough vowels. It was loud, too. As if blasted from massive speakers rather than from any human throat.

"Iä! Iä! F' nafl' fhtagn!"

"Goddess, no . . . ," gasped Violin, and she made a strange warding symbol in the air. The voice boomed out again and now dust fell from between the tightly pressed ceiling stones. The light streaming up from below changed in hue and intensity, becoming a luminescent green. It stung the eye to look at it, and the very sight of it made Harry's skin crawl.

"Y' ahor h' mgr' luh ahororr'e. H' nwngluii ah mgahnnn."

"Impossible," cried Violin. "They can't be that crazy. They'll kill us all. Come on, Harry, we have to hurry." She stepped down onto the top step, then—despite everything—threw him a wild grin. "What's wrong? Do you want to live forever?"

"Actually," he began, but Violin ran down the stairs before he could finish.

Harry licked his dry lips, tilted his head, and cut a sideways look heavenward. "Look," he said reasonably, "if I cut the porn stuff down but not out, you still let me live, right? Is that fair?"

There was no answer from the heavens. Harry saw his gun lying on the fourth step down, picked it up, and went down the stairs.

CHAPTER SEVENTEEN

THE HANGAR
DEPARTMENT OF MILITARY SCIENCES HEADQUARTERS
FLOYD BENNETT FIELD
BROOKLYN, NEW YORK

"He is a criminal and you will surrender him."

The words were not spoken, they were yelled. And the man yelling them was small, wrinkled, and livid. Red splotches bloomed on his cheeks and his eyes bugged out of his head. He seemed to lean out of the flat screen toward the two people seated at a table in the conference room.

Mr. Church, cool and comfortable in his Ermenegildo Zegna

bespoke suit, Stefano Ricci Formal Crystal silk satin tie, and hand-sewn Brunello Cucinelli leather shoes. Beside him, Aunt Sallie—a black woman in her late sixties—wore a Nigerian block-print dress and had colorful beads strung between her gray dreadlocks. A carafe of spring water stood between them and each had a glass. There was a large plate of assorted cookies near the carafe. Auntie had a smaller plate in front of her. Every few seconds she would take an animal cracker from the pile, bite the head off, and drop the rest into a growing mound. Church slowly nibbled at a vanilla wafer. Neither spoke.

When the man ranting at them wound down, there was an ugly silence broken only by faint crunching noises.

"Well," growled the little man on the screen, "did you hear me?"

"Yes," said Church mildly. His took his time finishing his cookie: chewing thoroughly, washing it down with a sip of water, dabbing at his lips with a linen napkin, then refolding the napkin and placing it neatly on the table.

"Damn it, Church, I asked you a question."

"My apologies, Mr. Spellman," said Church, "I believe that we are still waiting for an answer to *our* question. Why is there an arrest warrant out for Captain Ledger?"

"That's none of your business."

"I believe it *is* my business. If you would like to reread the DMS charter and get back to me, that would be fine."

Norris Spellman was the attorney general for the United States, but he was a man remarkably unsuited to his post. Nearly as unsuitable as the previous occupant of his office. A political appointee who did not have the kind of credentials appropriate to being the top law enforcement officer in the country. The press knew it, people on both sides of the aisle knew it, and he likely knew it himself. He had not been a very good attorney when he worked as a prosecutor in Arizona, and he had gained no ground at all in a series of escalating political bumps. His genius, if the word could be accurately applied, had always been in backing the right horse, even changing parties to make sure he was on the winning team.

"The reasons for the warrant are sealed by executive order," said Spellman.

"Captain Ledger works for me," said Church, unruffled. "The nature of the DMS charter expressly lays out the protocol of action if any of my people need to be detained or interviewed by any other government agency. That is also an executive order."

"Not signed by this president."

"Not rescinded, either," countered Church. "Which means it stands as policy. The actions of the agents today are in violation of that order, which means that they were committing crimes. They are, in fact, complicit in a conspiracy to violate an executive order. This discussion compounds that and calls into question your own level of involvement in these crimes." During the ensuing silence, he took another cookie and tapped crumbs from it on the edge of the plate.

"You think the president won't cancel your charter?" sneered Spellman.

"I want you to listen to me for a minute, Norris," said Aunt Sallie in a voice that would turn burning logs into icicles. "That pickup was illegal. We all know it, just as we know the pickup order is likely a whim or a mistake, and your boss would rather be eaten by rats than admit that he ever made a mistake. I know this puts you in a bind because you're not being given a choice. If POTUS says 'jump,' you have to jump or you're out like the last fool whose ass polished your chair. No . . . don't interrupt me, Norris; you know better than that. The pickup was bogus. If POTUS is going to rescind it, he has to notify us before doing so. That's the agreement. If he wants to amend it, ditto. Captain Ledger reacted to an illegal act and showed remarkable restraint. If they'd drawn on him, he was legally allowed to defend himself using any appropriate force. The fact that he chose to stay at the lowest possible rung on the force continuum ladder speaks to his integrity as an agent of this government. The fact that he hasn't filed federal charges against your goons also speaks to an admirable restraint and the best practices of the Department of Military Sciences. Push this, Norris, and he will file charges, and you know that we have judges who will back his play. And, if you don't know how scary our lawyers are, then you had better ask around, because we can out-lawyer you into the dirt. Now, either you tell us why POTUS issued the pickup order or we are going to start our own investigation. Ask what happens when we take a personal and particular interest in someone."

Spellman tried to tough it out, glaring and glowering, but his face had gone dead pale and he couldn't sell it.

Into the troubled silence, Mr. Church said, "I've placed several calls to the Oval Office, to the chief of staff, and to the director of the Secret Service. None of those calls were taken and none have been returned. Perhaps in the interest of cooperation and adherence to chartered protocols you might see what you can do about that."

Before the attorney general could organize a response, Church ended the call. He finished his cookie, sipped some water, and sighed.

Auntie kicked the desk. "What in the Technicolor hell is going on with that clown college in D.C.?"

Instead of addressing the question, Church said, "You spoke highly of Captain Ledger."

She scowled. "Well . . . he may be a mouth-breathing Neanderthal, but for something like this, he's one of us."

"Even so, Auntie, you were effusive in your praise. Did it hurt?"

"Bite me," she snarled.

INTERLUDE FIVE

ANTICA LOCANDA DI SESTO
LUCCA, ITALY
SIX YEARS AGO

Valen saw the woman and knew it was her right away. Dr. Marguerite Beaufort was a French national who had, according to her

Facebook page, "grown up all over the world." The daughter, granddaughter, and great-granddaughter of scholars, she had an air of bookishness and introspection that put a toe across the introversion line. She was a pretty and well-dressed thirty-something who sparkled with intelligence.

"Dr. Beaufort," he said, offering his hand as he approached the table.

"Mr. Oruraka," she said, "what a pleasure to meet you." Her hand was cool, strong, and dry.

"It's Valen," he said as he sat across from her. "May I call you Marguerite?"

"Oh, please do."

After the waiter came to take their order and brought wine for her and an Armorik French single malt for him, she said, "I was rather surprised to get your e-mail. How did you know about me? And how did you know I was here in Lucca?"

"You're an academic, Marguerite," he said, "and academics are always tethered to their universities. I played that game long enough to know how to find who I wanted."

She nodded. "I looked you up, of course. Geology and seismology, with a minor in structural engineering. Are you planning on building a dam?"

Archaeologists were often brought in during large-scale construction to assess the cultural or historical significance of items uncovered during excavation. However, Valen shook his head.

"No," he said. "I'm working on a very special project, and one that, I'm afraid, comes with a rather ponderous stack of nondisclosure agreements. Are . . . you familiar with NDAs?"

Marguerite sipped her wine and rolled her eyes. "I've written a mountain of grant proposals. So, yes."

"Yes. This is a little different than that." He sipped his whiskey. "There are a few things I can share with you before asking you to sign an NDA. Call them 'bait.' Tell me, have you ever heard of Lemurian crystal?"

That made her lean back, and she sipped more wine as she considered him. "That depends on what you mean."

"Tell me what you think I mean."

She smiled. "Well, first off, it's not Lemurian. Lemuria was part of a theory postulated by the nineteenth-century Darwinian taxonomist Ernst Haeckel, as a way of explaining some anomalies in biogeography—the natural spread of animal species. He theorized that Lemuria was a land bridge that connected existing land masses in the Indian Ocean but which has since been submerged. But that has been entirely discredited by modern theories of plate tectonics. Unfortunately, the Theosophists of his day grabbed onto the idea because that lot love the possibility of lost civilizations, especially those that leave no artifacts to prove or, more significantly, disprove their wild claims. It's no different than Atlantis or—"

"Okay, you can stop right there," said Valen. "Let me shift my question. Tell me something about the Roman festival of Lemuria."

Marguerite shrugged. "That was real. It was an important festival in which specific rites were performed to exorcise the lemures, the evil and restless dead who haunted their homes. During the rise of Christianity, Pope Boniface IV consecrated the Pantheon in Rome to the Virgin Mary and all of the Christian martyrs, effectively supplanting the old religious holiday with a new one."

Valen smiled. "Now tell me why I asked about that celebration?"

"Well, what most people do not know, Valen," she said, "is that the nickname of Lemurian quartz is not tied to a faux lost continent, but to that old Roman feast. At least when they refer to the green variety of Lemurian quartz. The white quartz is a label used by the New Age crowd, and actually *is* tied to their belief in an actual island nation of Lemuria." She waved her hand dismissively. "For what we're talking about, people in Rome would use pieces of rare green quartz to ward off the evil spirits. They made small fetishes from it in the shape of weapons—swords, knives, arrows, cudgels—and placed them in their homes for a full day, while gathering together in tents or lean-tos in the streets. On 13 May they would send the bravest and purest person from each town or village to go from house to house and collect the quartz weapons. These would be wrapped in blessed cloth and buried in a lead box in a place known only to the priests, safe until the following year."

Valen finished his whiskey and signaled the waiter for a refill. While he waited, he took the wine bottle from the table and poured more for Marguerite.

"What would you say if I told you that it is my belief that many of these fetish weapons were made from quartz mined, not in Rome, but elsewhere?"

She shrugged. "I read something to that effect. Some were found hidden in a mine near Santorini, which suggests that the Romans may have borrowed the practice of making such fetishes from an older culture, Greek or possibly Minoan ruins."

"I know. I've read that paper," said Valen. "But the mine I'm talking about is not in that region."

"Then where?"

Valen sat back, sipped his whiskey, and smiled. "That's where the nondisclosure agreement comes in."

CHAPTER EIGHTEEN

CITADEL OF SALAH ED-DIN
SEVEN KILOMETERS EAST OF AL-HAFFAH, SYRIA
TWO DAYS AGO

They descended into a green hell. Harry was three steps behind Violin, wishing he was ten thousand miles away from where they were going.

Once they were below the level of the floor it was immediately apparent that this was not some cramped hidden chamber, or even a roomy basement. No, the stairs zigzagged down out of sight, and Harry reckoned that it was forty or fifty feet to the floor.

The engineering skills of the ancient world always dazzled him. He understood a bit of structural engineering from a course he took in college—because of a very hot undergrad he wanted to impress.

While he had utterly failed to amaze the woman with his grasp of the science, he had nevertheless learned some things by simple exposure. He knew that many of the feats of building managed by cultures going back as far as the Sumerians were astonishing. Things that would be daunting undertakings with hundred-foot cranes, stonecutting machines, and all of the benefits of modern science were accomplished with simple tools, determination, and patience. From the Pyramid of the Sun in Teotihuacan to the Great Pyramid of Giza, from Angkor Wat in Cambodia to the Taj Mahal in India, those accomplishments made Harry feel particularly incompetent.

The source of the green glow was still not evident, but the illumination itself revealed a vast room supported by dozens of carved stone columns. There were hundreds of what looked like stone sarcophagi resting on bases of dark volcanic rock. As they reached the floor of the chamber Harry could see that none of those sarcophagi were normal. The ones he'd seen in museums and at other ancient sites with Violin were all roughly human, approximating some idealized version of the body entombed within. Not these. They were too big, for one thing: the smallest he saw was at least ten feet long, and some were twice that size. The figures were strange blends of human and fish, or human and octopus. Some with vast wings, others with too many heads to count.

"What are these?" he whispered.

"Children of the Deep Ones," she said.

"The hell's *that* supposed to mean?"

Violin paused and cocked an ear. "Listen."

He did. At first he heard nothing—and he was glad it wasn't more of that booming voice—but then, off in the direction where the green light was brightest, he could hear the fading sound of running feet.

"Hurry," said Violin as she sprinted toward the noise and the strange green light.

Harry lingered, and for a moment he almost did not follow. In that moment he thought about what in the world he was doing here. Sure, he was a former CIA operative, but not a good one. He was ten million miles away from being in the same league as Violin. Or his secret hero, Joe Ledger. He was a short, dumpy loser who sometimes got lucky. Luckier than he deserved.

What in the living hell was he doing here? What was he even thinking? That he was Indiana Jones? That he was Joe Ledger? He knew the real answer to those questions.

"Please," he said quietly, as if asking to be excused could get him out of this. He had a pistol in his hand and it felt like a prop from a bad TV movie. He ran to catch up but hadn't gotten fifty feet before the men they were chasing began to scream.

CHAPTER NINETEEN

THE WAREHOUSE
DMS FIELD OFFICE
BALTIMORE, MARYLAND

Waiting and doing nothing is a pain in the ass. I'm no good at it.

To keep from climbing the walls, I called home, but got the answering machine, then called Junie's cell. And got her voicemail. She was so busy with FreeTech that I had a closer and more meaningful relationship with her recording. I left a message for her to call, told her I loved her, and hung up feeling peevish and slighted, which I know is both immature and unfair.

Beneath my foul mood I was genuinely in love and deeply proud—possibly in awe—of what Junie Flynn had accomplished over the last few years. Church had offered her the role of CEO of a private company that took the deadly technologies the DMS forcibly appropriated from bad guys and repurposed them for humanitarian uses. New water filtration systems, new organic fertilizer enhancers, medical equipment, cybernetic implants for the physically challenged, and most recently a portable diagnostic device that was helping with the weaponized rabies plague spread by Zephyr

Bain during the Dogs of War case. She was saving lives every single day, and bringing light into a darkened world. She was one end of the evolutionary bell curve. I, a more primitive kind of creature, was way farther back.

The reason for my grumpiness was that we were both starting to feel the strain of being so deeply involved in our jobs that we were drifting from one another. It wasn't a lessening of love—at least not for me—but it was more like we were in danger of becoming strangers. Or worse, acquaintances. It was something we each promised to work on, and I prayed we still had time.

She didn't call back. I couldn't go home. So, I did what any tough-as-nails, battle-hardened, deeply skilled special operator would do. I sat in the mess hall and sulked.

Top was in there, too. Top knows how to make a sandwich. It's not about how many slices of pastrami or roast beef you add, it's about how they're placed. He makes sure there are irregular air pockets so that biting into the sandwich isn't like eating a slab of meat. He cuts his pickles lengthwise and uses the heart of a tomato so there's less skin and more juice. He also has a light hand with mustard or mayonnaise. He appreciates subtlety. Top is an artist and I am a devoted fan.

Like proper adult men, we ate the sandwiches over the big double sink.

Bunny arrived with a suitcase in one hand and a case of cold beer under his arm. He set the beer down on the counter, opened three, popped the caps, and handed them around. "Medical supplies."

"Hooah," said Top. We clinked bottles and drank.

That case of beer didn't stand a chance.

CHAPTER TWENTY

OFFICE OF JENNIFER VANOWEN
THE WHITE HOUSE
WASHINGTON, D.C.
TWENTY MONTHS AGO

The small Japanese-American woman perched on the edge of a leather guest chair. She was not wearing handcuffs, but a pair sat conspicuously on the desk. The woman who sat across from her smiled like a moray eel.

"Do you know why you're here?" asked Jennifer VanOwen.

Yuina Hoshino folded her hands in her lap and let nothing show on her face. "No," she said simply.

"Do you know who I am?"

A shake of the head.

"I am the special advisor to the president on all scientific matters," said VanOwen. She opened her desk and removed a crisp sheet of paper and placed it facedown on her desk. Then, after a moment's pause, removed a second and laid it next to the first. "You know that you will never live long enough to serve your entire sentence. You're lucky that you were not given the death penalty. A lot of people wanted that to happen. A lot of people wanted you to vanish into a black site where psychopaths on our payroll would make life a constant and intense hell for you."

Hoshino wanted to look away. She wanted to cry. But she did neither. Instead she looked into the middle of nowhere and let her expression go totally blank.

"The people who arrested you and wanted to end you belonged to a different administration," said VanOwen, then she corrected herself. "No, they belonged to a different view of what patriotism means. They subscribed to a view of America and its place in the world that is limited, skewed, and small." She paused. "I know that you have a different view of America's potential greatness. One that is built on ambition and courage, but which also prizes a shift away from globalism."

"I don't have any politics," said Hoshino. "I don't have any religion. Just science."

"And yet you worked with Howard Shelton to build the T-craft that almost destroyed Beijing and Moscow and the capitals of countries that have anti-American agendas."

"No," said Hoshino. "That was Howard's dream. He and his toady, Mr. Bones, closed me out of the T-craft program's real aims."

"So . . . you disapprove of what they tried to do?"

"Fear of a conqueror is one thing," Hoshino said carefully, "however, to conquer the world—this world—would be to make enemies or, worse, fearful slaves, of eight billion people. It would end open warfare, but it would not end war."

"Why not?"

"Because in the face of overwhelming military force, the weaker side will fight back using guerrilla tactics. These tactics are why we have not beaten ISIL, why America has failed to defeat the Taliban or al-Qaeda. It was hard enough in the pre-Internet days to beat a guerrilla resistance; now it is impossible. The army becomes a virtual one, connected through e-mails and the Internet. Their weapons become man-portable rocket launchers, drones, and other small but potent weapons. With a conquest of China and Russia, and the resulting de facto subjugation of all other military powers, you would create a network of nuclear states that also have access to advanced biological weaponry. You could not defeat that kind of opposition even with a fleet of T-craft. It would be the equivalent of fighting disease-carrying mosquitoes with carpet-bombing. The weapons you can bring to bear are too large for targets so small and maneuverable."

"Did you ever say as much to Howard Shelton?"

"I tried, but he was never interested."

"And yet you helped him build the T-craft . . . ," prompted VanOwen.

"We all wanted the craft built. We had different reasons, as it turned out."

VanOwen leaned forward. "What was your reason?"

"Power."

"Power?"

"Yes. To use the T-craft as this generation's ultra-advanced reconnaissance aircraft. Just as the Lockheed U-2 was the breakout technology of its day, and later supplanted by the Lockheed SR-71 Blackbird, and so on, the T-craft would give us another big jump forward."

"Only that?" asked VanOwen with a crafty smile.

"That, and to provide the next generation of stealth fighters and bombers. However, we were not the only country actively developing T-craft. Russia, China, North Korea, Japan, Great Britain, France, Brazil . . . there are—or maybe were—similar programs around the world. We were closer, though. We solved the problems they could not solve."

"The biomechanical interface?"

Hoshino nodded. "Without that, every engine exploded upon firing."

VanOwen's smile lingered. "In your estimation, how close were the other countries to solving that same problem?"

"I don't know."

"Guess."

"Maybe five years? Possibly less."

"A lot of that time burned off," observed VanOwen.

Hoshino said nothing.

VanOwen picked up the first of the two sheets of paper. "This is a presidential order, endorsed by the directors of Homeland Security and National Security, and countersigned by the attorney general. It effectively ends your status as a citizen and orders that you be sent to a special facility so remote that it has no name, appears on no map, and none of the prisoners who have gone there have ever returned. Not one."

The blood in Hoshino's veins turned to icy slush and she felt vomit burn in the back of her throat.

VanOwen picked up the second sheet. "This is a special executive order that includes a pardon for all past crimes and will effectively seal any legal matters involving you. Neither paper has yet been signed by the president."

"I . . . I . . . ," began Hoshino, but her mouth had gone too dry to speak.

VanOwen stood up and walked around her desk. She was tall and lithe and beautiful, and it made Hoshino feel small and breakable. The woman sat on the edge of the desk, one leg dangling as she swung it back and forth.

"The president of the United States is frequently referred to as the most powerful man on Earth," she said quietly. "He gets that nickname because of the financial and military power he wields. It's my job to make sure that he truly *is* the most powerful man. I want this to become clear to everyone else in the world. I want it to become clear to the people of this country. We are not looking to use T-craft to start a war. What we want is for the rest of the world to know that the age of nuclear weapons and mutually assured destruction is at an end, and a new age has begun. You, Dr. Hoshino, can help this president earn his place in history as the greatest American president since Washington. Tell me now . . . which of these papers should I send to the president for his signature, and which should I run through the shredder?"

INTERLUDE SIX

THE GREEN CAVES
BELOW TUVALU, POLYNESIA
SIX YEARS AGO

Dr. Marguerite Beaufort crouched in the dark and watched the snakes disappear, one by one, through a crack in the wall. Ten of them at least, and likely more that she had not seen. The soft rasp of their sinewy bodies was the only sound in the cave except for a distant slow drip of water. Work lights were strung on wires and she had a strong LED light on her metal hard hat, but the cavern was so vast that the darkness seemed to devour the illumination with rapacious hunger. The walls were slick with moisture and there was a faint rotten-egg stink of sulfur in the damp air.

"What the hell?" cried her assistant, Carlton Wrigley, known as Rig, a gnomelike graduate student who looked like he belonged on someone's lawn, or maybe in one of the lower-income Hobbit holes. "Hey, where are they going?"

At the sound of Rig's voice, the last of the snakes paused and turned its head toward them. There, frozen in the stark glow, Marguerite could see the glassy markings more clearly, and it startled her. Instead of true markings, they almost appeared to be flecks of Lemurian quartz embedded in its skin. That, of course, made no sense at all. Partly because the snakes all had them, and none of them looked to have been injured by some rockfall; and partly because the placement of the chips was orderly. Like something natural instead of accidental. And it would also be the greatest find so far in an otherwise disappointing dig, because the only green quartz they'd found were fragments left behind by some unknown miners in the distant past. For weeks now Marguerite had been trying to figure out the best way to tell Valen and his friend Ari that they were likely wasting their money. Wrangling snakes with shiny green markings was not what she was paid to do.

"What kind of snakes are they, Doc? Think they're poisonous?"

"I don't know, but don't touch them."

"As if."

The snake studied her with its dark eyes, and its tongue flicked out as if it could understand her through what it tasted on the still air. As if it took secrets from her that she did not want to share. Then it turned and slithered after the others and was gone.

"Jee-zus," breathed Rig. "Where do you think they went? You think there's a nest back there? I thought the walls down here were supposed to be solid. That's what Dr. Svoboda said, right?"

George Svoboda was a top geologist at the University of Chicago.

"That's what we were told," she replied, but there was as much doubt in her voice as his. She touched the wall. "This is strange, Rig. I don't remember seeing these cracks before. Do you?"

She told Rig to set up a portable light stand topped by a wide LED panel. He turned it on and angled the panel so that the light etched every bump and crack. Marguerite stepped toward the wall and used her fingertips to trace a crack that ran crookedly from the rocky ceiling to the stony floor. A dozen smaller cracks to her left were where the snakes had vanished; but this one was different. Not only because it was much longer, but because there the edges were crusted with some kind of plant life. A kind of moss with unusually long stalks and bulbous heads flecked with dots of red.

"Moss?" she murmured.

"That's weird," said Rig. "I didn't see any moss there yesterday."

He was right, but Marguerite didn't say so. The cracks and the vegetation were new. It was odd-looking, too. She'd seen all kinds of plant life in the various sites where her career had taken her. Weeds, fungi, molds, and thousands of other forms, but none exactly like this. In truth, this moss looked more like sea anemones, and when she touched it with her gloved fingertip the bulbous ends recoiled.

Marguerite snatched her hand back.

"Holy shit, Doc," gasped Rig, his voice jumping an octave in alarm. "Did that stuff just move?"

She cleared her throat and forced herself to sound calm. "Yes. Some plants are touch reactive."

"Yeah, sure, a Venus flytrap maybe, but . . . crap, Doc . . . *moss*? That's freaky stuff right there."

Yes, it is, she thought. Then she caught a brief glimpse of something inside the lichen. No, past it, deeper inside the cleft. She took a small but powerful penlight from her pocket and directed the beam inside.

She froze, staring, not believing what she was seeing. Sweat burst from her pores and ran down into her eyes, and her mouth, despite the humidity in the cave, went completely dry.

"Rig . . . ," she said very carefully, "go get Dr. Svoboda. Valen, too."

"What is it? What did you see?"

"Get them," she said. *"Right now."*

CHAPTER TWENTY-ONE

THE WAREHOUSE
DMS FIELD OFFICE
BALTIMORE, MARYLAND
8:12 P.M.

Church finally called twenty minutes shy of me actually climbing the goddamn wall. I'd long since said a tipsy goodnight to Top and Bunny, and was stretched out on a lumpy bed in one of the guest rooms used for visiting staff. I was uncomfortable, angry, drunk, confused, and scared in equal amounts. Ghost was hogging most of the square footage of the mattress. When my cell phone rang with the Darth Vader ring tone I'd set for calls from Church, I nearly jumped out of my skin.

I punched the button. "What do we know?"

"Not enough," said Church calmly. "Auntie is on her way to D.C. and will begin pushing at her network first thing in the morning. From what she's been able to determine through phone calls, though, if there is something official in the works against you, no one outside of the Oval Office seems to know what it is."

I sat on the edge of the bed, feet flat on the cold, polished concrete floor. "Well . . . shit. Do we have any guesses at least?"

"None that will make you happy, I'm afraid. There's been some talk about rescinding the DMS charter—"

I snorted. "Haven't they tried that like a dozen times?"

"Seven times," corrected Church. "However, Captain, I can't impress upon you enough that things are not 'politics as usual' in Washington, and they haven't been for some time. The old checks and balances are crumbling in what has become an increasingly obvious smash-and-grab phase. Trust, as a concept, is broken, and there is a lot of career anxiety because we've moved so far away from a merit-based hierarchy in the important departments."

"Was it ever an actual meritocracy?" I asked sourly.

"More than you might think. At least in the critical departments concerned with intelligence and national security."

"Not now, though," I suggested.

"Not now," he agreed. "Positions of power are being given out as payment for favors more than I've ever seen, and I have been involved in American politics for a very long time."

"Yeah, exactly how long?" I asked.

Church didn't take the bait. He never does. "It is entirely possible, according to Linden Brierley, that the arrest order was given as a test."

"To test *what*?"

"Us," he said. "Me. Brierley seems to think that this may have been done to see how I would react. To see how much power the DMS actually has."

Ghost shifted around and laid his head on my thigh in a "pet me now" move. I scratched his head and his eyes immediately began to drift shut. "Why play that game?" I asked.

"You know the rumors, Captain," said Church. "People think I have dirt on every power player, from junior senators all the way to the president. The knowledge that MindReader exists has fueled those beliefs, which is why there is such a mania to keep certain kinds of knowledge off of the Net, out of e-mails, and out of computer files."

"Well, yeah," I said, "guess I kind of believe that, too."

Church sighed, sounding unutterably weary. "Captain, if I was a master blackmailer, could anyone have betrayed us like they have?"

I said nothing and stared up at the uninformative wall across from the narrow bed. There was a framed painting of bulrushes along a riverbank. Pretty enough, in a bland and boring kind of way.

"It may surprise you," he said, "but I am not a sorcerer, nor am I omniscient. I'm a shooter turned upper management who is trying very hard to keep this country and this planet from burning down. Manipulating the government through blackmail would require far more time than I can spare from actually fighting the kinds of threats that come our way every day."

"Ah," I said, feeling a bit like an immature ass. "But what do we do if POTUS rescinds our charter? Or changes it? Or suddenly decides that we're all criminals or traitors or whatever? What then? Do we let them put black bags over our heads and waltz us off to some black site? Do we go into open rebellion?"

"None of those choices is acceptable," said Church.

"Then why not dig up dirt on these ass-clowns? Why not tear the whole thing down and . . ."

I trailed off because I heard what I was saying. Church knew that I'd gotten there, too. He was silent, waiting.

"No," I said at last. "I get it. Tear it down and we leave ourselves temporarily vulnerable. We'd be a big, tough gazelle with a limp. There are too many predators just waiting for that moment when we stumble."

"And if that happens . . . ?" he asked gently.

"The rest of the predators are free to take the whole herd."

We sat in silence for a few moments.

"So," I said, "now what? How do we respond to the arrest thing? Top and I kicked the shit out of a bunch of Secret Service agents—"

"—and no paperwork has been filed on it," said Church. "There are no witnesses and no official report. Brierley's people inside the Secret Service believe the pickup was ordered on a whim or as a test, but it was illegal. It was an attempt to make us do something actionable."

"Which I did."

"Not in a way useful to them. They needed you to resist and possibly cause some injuries while *also* being taken into custody. That latter part was the way they could reverse-engineer justification for the actual pickup. Without having you in custody, they had no play left, and now Aunt Sallie has spread the word to enough people that there's no way for them to fabricate a plausible chain of cause and effect that works for them. It's a fumble, and too many people know it. It's likely you would have gone to a black interrogation site and either been held as leverage over me, or been worked over until you gave them something they could use."

"Yeah, well, sorry to spoil their plans," I said.

"Quite frankly, I'm rather pleased with how it turned out. It's very informative."

"Okay," I said, "so what now? Shouldn't *we* be filing fifty kinds of formal charges?"

"That's one way to go, Captain," said Church, "but the fact that there are no records of this makes it the word of a covert group against that of the current administration. Remember, Captain, we don't officially exist, at least as far as the public knows. If we file formal charges, our useful anonymity ends, and there would be consequences to that."

He had a damn point. Because of betrayal from within, and hacking of the older generation of MindReader, the DMS had hit some serious heavy weather. The biggest problem was the Kill Switch case, where Harcourt Bolton, Sr. used a mind-control device to literally take over the actions of several DMS agents, including Top, Bunny, and me. While being suborned by this "mind-walking," we did some truly awful things. A lot of innocent people died and there was video footage of one bloodbath on the docks in Oceanside, California. Doesn't matter that we were all wearing balaclavas that hid most of our faces. Doesn't matter that Bug used MindReader to go in and mess with the images on those videos. There are people in the government who know, or at least suspect, that it was our fingers on the triggers.

"If we go after them," I said, "they bury us with Kill Switch."

"And other things, yes," said Church. "They don't need to prove anything. All they need to do is put us in the spotlight and wait for the public to demand our heads on pikes. If that happens, Captain, the DMS is effectively dead, which means that we will be cleared off the battlefield at a time when we are very much needed."

"Shit."

"It frequently astounds and disappoints me when I witness the lengths some people will go to to get in the way of their own conscience or sense of duty."

"So, do we just forgive and forget?"

"Did I say that?" When I did not answer, he said, "I seldom forgive, Captain; and I never forget."

"Then what's our play?"

I could hear him crunching on a cookie. If the world was actually burning and there were missiles inbound to where he sat, the man would pause for a vanilla wafer.

"Aunt Sallie will address matters in Washington," he said. "I want you to go back to San Diego. Take a week off. Maybe have your brother and his family come out for a visit."

"Why?" I asked suspiciously. "Are they in danger out here?"

"No. I'm recommending an actual vacation."

"A vacation? Who are you and what did you do with Mr. Church?"

"Good-bye, Captain," he said, and there was the slight chance he actually laughed. Or maybe that was just wishful thinking on my part. Hard to tell.

CHAPTER TWENTY-TWO

THE PRIORY
PRIVATE RESIDENCE OF MR. CHURCH
NEW YORK CITY, NEW YORK

Church set down his cell phone, leaned back against his pillows, and rubbed his tired eyes. For several moments, he did nothing but listen to one of his favorite albums, *Blue Moods* by Miles Davis. It seemed as apt now as when he'd first heard every cut played live at a club many years ago, while he was on a mission in Germany. Charlie Mingus had invited him to the gig, and Church—then known by the code name Der Rektor—had gone to hear a few songs but stayed for three sets. A good end to what had been a terrible day. He remembered standing in the bathroom at the club, washing blood off his face.

Church touched his face, remembering that night with awful clarity. He had done dreadful things and taken wounds that ran very deep. Not of flesh, but of soul.

How many times since had he been marked like that? he wondered. Even he'd lost count.

Then he recalled that it had been the same night he'd met Aunt Sallie, then a young African-American field operative working undercover with Interpol. Were the horrors of that night mitigated by meeting one of the most important people in his life? Auntie became an ally, a fellow warrior, and a trusted friend. Together they had saved the world from greater horrors even than those Church had faced in Germany. Now, of course, Aunt Sallie was getting old, and he knew that she did not understand why time touched her with a heavier and crueler hand than it did him.

It was so sad. Auntie was family to him. Kin.

Kin. That word had been stuck into him like a knife blade for months now. The mad trickster Nicodemus called him "kinsman," knowing that it would inflict a special kind of hurt. It did. Hurt and shame and a particularly dangerous frequency of nostalgia.

Kinsman. Not an accurate statement, but dangerous. It was tied to another of Church's names. One that he had left behind long ago, even before the affair in Germany. A name discarded like so many others. A name no one alive knew, and Church was content to let that aspect of him die and be forgotten.

In truth, "Mr. Church" was the latest identity into which he'd stepped when he formed the Department of Military Sciences. Shucking previous names had become easy for him. He was rarely sentimental about any of his former selves and had cast them off with the cold efficiency of a molting tarantula. He remembered each of them, though some only distantly. The Washington and U.S. military crowd still tended to call him Deacon. A few old friends and enemies in Eastern Europe, Lilith among them, called him St. Germaine. Here and there were key men and women who knew him as "Cardinal" or "Saishi" or "Epískopos." But most of those people were old and he knew he would outlive them. As he would outlive the memory of who he was when he wore those names. Other, older names were completely lost to time, and that was how it should be. Though once in a while—a very great while—a sadness crept into the edges of his day as he remembered old friends long gone. He even mourned some of his enemies.

Even Nicodemus.

Not that Church would ever admit that to the people who worked for him. And not that it stayed his hand when the two of them had fought last year during the Dogs of War matter. He closed his eyes and there, in his personal darkness, he could remember every moment of that battle. Nicodemus had worn as many names as had Church, and had shed them as easily. Church had flown from Brooklyn to the Pacific Northwest and tracked Nicodemus to the home of the brilliant and destructive psychopath Zephyr Bain. He'd arrived to find Nicodemus fighting—and beating—Top and Bunny. Church stepped between his men and Nicodemus, knowing that they could never have taken that man down. Not with the kinds of weapons they had—guns, knives, fists. He'd ordered his agents to flee, and Nicodemus, mindful of old rituals and etiquette, had allowed it.

That fight that took place had been a terrible ordeal. Church never let on to his people how close a battle it had been, or how much it cost him to win it. He never told them, or anyone, what happened in Zephyr Bain's house. It was a memory that haunted him, though, and he knew he would relive it for the rest of his life. And now, all these months later, alone in his quiet house, Church mourned Nicodemus. Not the man who wore that false name, though. No, Church's grief was older than that, ran deeper than that. Nicodemus had once been a different person, and Church mourned for that man.

There was a soft creak and he looked up to see Lilith standing in the bathroom doorway, drying her face with a hand towel. She wore a black silk camisole and matching slip. In the semidarkness shadows hid her eyes and hollowed her cheeks, transforming a beautiful face into a death mask. He hoped it wasn't an omen.

"Was that Ledger on the phone?" she asked.

"Yes."

Lilith nodded and reached into the bathroom to place the towel on the sink. Then she walked slowly over to the bed. He lifted the blanket and she climbed in. They held each other for a long time. Church buried his nose in her dark hair, closed his eyes, and wished that he was another person. In another life. In another world.

Beyond the window, above the sprawling city, the wheel of night turned.

CHAPTER TWENTY-THREE

THE RESIDENCE OF THE PRESIDENT
THE WHITE HOUSE
WASHINGTON, D.C.

They sat up late into the night. Jennifer VanOwen was in a deep armchair, a glass of brandy cradled between her palms. She wore a cream-colored blouse and a dark pencil skirt. Efficient heels that gave her enough of a lift to shape her calves—something that mattered to her as one of many tools with which she shaped the reactions of the people around her. Her hair was loose around her shoulders and her makeup was understated, suggesting power rather than sex. Very deliberate.

The president was slumped on the couch, dressed in an expensive satin bathrobe and hand-sewn silk slippers. The residence was quiet because the rest of his family was away.

"Well, that didn't work," said the president. He'd said something like that half a dozen different ways, each time with added acidity.

"I did advise against it," said VanOwen. "Ledger may be psychotic, but he is very dangerous. After all, he took down Howard Shelton and M3. He took down the Seven Kings, the Jakoby family, and other groups that should have been unbreakable. He broke them."

"He needs to be locked the hell up."

"He will be. If you let me handle it, we will neutralize any potential threat from him and the rest of the DMS."

"I should just go ahead and cancel their charter," growled the president.

"As I've explained," said VanOwen patiently, "that would almost certainly backfire. Church still has friends in Washington. It's much better if we leave him in place and see who steps up when he needs help. Then we have our list of targets. Then, once we remove his supporters, we can end the DMS."

The president sat up and studied her intently. "Today was a total disaster."

Of your making, she thought, but didn't say it. What she said was, "We have all the best cards, Mr. President."

He merely grunted.

"Besides, we have Majestic," she said, "and neither he nor Mr. Church know that it has been completely rebuilt. Stronger than ever."

"If Ledger is free, he'll find out."

"Not in time," she said with complete confidence. "Not in time."

INTERLUDE SEVEN

THE GREEN CAVES
BELOW TUVALU, POLYNESIA
SIX YEARS AGO

"It's not possible," said the chief geologist. "No way."

Dr. George Svoboda was a stooped, hatchet-faced man who seemed outraged by the crack in the wall. Valen Oruraka and Aristotle Kostas stood with him as they examined the fissure that ran from floor to ceiling. Svoboda fumed because he had done all of the principal work on this site and had a global reputation as the go-to person for this kind of work. Even those colleagues who competed with him for grants seldom offered opinions contrary to his, and for good reason. He had literally written the book, the definitive scholarly texts, on the geology of South Pacific island substrata.

Marguerite did not argue with him. She and Rig stood to one side of the crack and let Svoboda work his way through his denial and anger. She caught Valen and Ari exchanging covert looks several times as Svoboda ran through various frequencies of denial, outrage, and anger.

"Stop yelling, for the love of God," yelled Ari. "You're hurting my damn head."

The small, round Greek looked badly hungover and smelled of sweat, testosterone, wine, and sex. He looked like someone had dragged him down three flights of stairs. Marguerite had heard some sounds rolling over the surf from the expensive aluminum camper that had been airlifted in for him. Those sounds had been feminine, high-pitched, and it did not sound like anyone but Ari was having fun.

Valen stepped up and brushed the moss with his fingertips and peered close to watch how the stalks writhed. Rig offered him one end of a fiber-optic cable scope and fed the other end into the crack. When it was positioned, the scope sent high-definition video to Marguerite's laptop, which rested on a folding chair. They could see that the supposedly solid wall was anything but. A few meters beyond where they stood was a kind of pocket, about the size of an old-fashioned phone booth, and it was choked with more of the moss, and with other foliage—unusual ferns and flowers and the roots of large plants.

"How is there this much plant life inside a solid wall?" asked Valen. "How is it flourishing? How is there photosynthesis in there? I've seen cave plants before and I've never seen colors as vibrant as that down in the darkness."

"It's one of the reasons I called you down here," said Marguerite. "We can't explain it. Chu is on the other side of the island, but I sent her some pictures of it." Alice Chu was the team biologist. "She said that she couldn't identify the moss, or any of the plants or flowers. She's on her way here now."

Ari glowered at Svoboda. "The fuck, man? You're supposed to have checked every square inch of this place, and now someone else finds this?"

The geologist gave a stubborn shake of his head. "This section of rock is half a million years old. There are no vents to filter sunlight down into pockets like that. It doesn't make sense."

The two of them began yapping at each other until Valen roared at them to shut the fuck up. "Mistakes were made. It's not going to do any of us any good to dissect the past. Right now we need to understand this find and what it may, or may not, mean for our project. That means we need to reassess this entire area."

"It isn't the mining operations," insisted Svoboda. "It can't be. You're enough of a geologist to know that, surely."

"Valen, Ari, listen," Marguerite said quickly. "I didn't call you here to see the plants or the pocket. There's something a lot more important than that."

"What are you talking about?" demanded Ari. "Not interested in more bullshit."

Marguerite smiled. "Rig, show them what we found."

The grad student grinned and worked the fiber-optic tube so that the little camera turned and burrowed like a snake past the strange foliage.

Ari laughed, "You found some of the damned quartz. Why didn't you . . . ?"

His words trailed off and he stood staring. They all stared for a long, silent, astonished time.

"Dr. Svoboda," said Valen in a voice that was far calmer than the burning excitement in his eyes, "you say that this section of wall is at least five hundred thousand years old. I've read all of your reports, and I've seen the rest of the results, the radiocarbon dating, all of that." He touched the screen. "If that's the case, then tell me what I'm seeing. . . ."

Nobody spoke.

They did not have to. What the thing was . . . well, that was obvious. It was a piece of Lemurian quartz. Quite beautiful in color and luminosity.

What none of them could explain, or even dared to try and theorize about, was that the green quartz was shaped like a weapon, but not a sword or spear or cudgel. No. That would have painted the day in different and more predictable colors. This was not any weapon of the ancient world.

There was a mound of something green and organic-looking partially blocking it. A dead lizard, perhaps. But it was obvious even to the least perceptive of them gathered in the cavern that the weapon was a handgun made from green crystal.

CHAPTER TWENTY-FOUR

THE WAREHOUSE
DMS FIELD OFFICE
BALTIMORE, MARYLAND
2:33 A.M.

I slept badly and dreamed of monsters.

It was the kind of sleep where you know you're dreaming but you can't wake up. Sleep paralysis of a kind, but it feels worse than that. It feels wrong. As if the force that binds you into sleep is malicious, maybe even vampiric. It's feeding on something, some essence that's important to you. It's taking it against your will, and the violation is so subtle, so devious that you know that when you wake you'll be diminished but you'll never be able to prove the cause to anyone.

My body lay wrapped in the coils of some dark and shadowy thing, and it pulled me down into dreams. Fragments of dreams. Flash images. Parts of memories of things I've actually done, things I've seen in my waking life, but intercut with images from remembered nightmares and hallucinations.

I was fourteen and I never saw the punch that dropped me.

Sucker punch. There was a massive black explosion in the back of my head and then I was down. I would later learn that the blow cracked my skull. The resulting concussion was not the worst of it. Not by a mile. Not by a million miles.

Nor were the bones that snapped as four sets of sneakered feet kicked and stomped and broke me. Nor even the damage to kidney and liver and testicles and spleen. Not the broken jaw or broken teeth. None of that really mattered. What mattered—what hurt the most and what never healed—was what I saw. My eyes were swollen nearly shut, but not all the way. No. That would have been a mercy. Being beaten to death would have been a mercy. But there was no mercy at all in that shaded, remote corner of the park where I'd been walking with Helen. Two kids. Still virgins. Still innocent. Still optimistic and naïve enough to think the world was a place that treasured the innocent.

I lay there and watched them beat Helen. That wasn't the worst, either. I could hear the sounds of her clothes being torn. I could hear the sound of zippers being pulled down. I heard her muffled screams as she tried to shriek her outrage through the balled-up underwear they'd shoved into her mouth.

That was the worst thing that ever happened to me. Even though it wasn't happening to me. Lying there, broken and bleeding but not dead. Knowing that I wasn't going to die. Knowing that neither of us was going to die. Despite being killed like this.

Yeah. That was the worst.

Then it was later. *Being stopped by her sister at the front door. Being told that Helen didn't want to see me. Not anymore.*

This was years later. After surgeries. After therapy. After being told that there was nothing the cops could do. No witnesses. No DNA on file that matched anyone.

Cathy stopped me from going in. "It's killing her, Joe," she told me.

"You don't understand," I insisted. "Things are going good now. The new medicine, the therapy . . ."

She had a look in her eyes like someone at a funeral. The eyes of a mourner who had already accepted the reality of death.

"She can't stand to see you anymore, Joe. It's killing her."

This time I heard her. This time I got it. This time I felt the knife go deep and turn. Bleeding, I turned and left.

It was then that I felt the first fracture in my head. It was then that I knew that I was so far gone that there was never going to be a way home. Not for Helen. Not for me.

And that morphed into . . . *Me in the dojo, kneeling, my hands aching, bleeding. My eyes filled with sweat and tears while I watched my sensei apply compresses to the face of the kid with whom I'd been sparring. My friend Dino. So much blood on the floor where he'd fallen.*

Eyes looking at me. Not understanding. Hating me. Disappointed in me. Afraid of me. Sensei cutting me a look that was filled with pain and conflict. We'd only been sparring. It wasn't a real fight. Points only.

But the light coming through the windows had changed his face into someone else's. An older teenage face I'd seen in a park, grinning at me as he huffed and thrust and ruined something perfect.

I don't remember the actual fight with Dino. It wasn't me who hit him and hurt him. I know that. It was someone else inside my head. A stranger. Brutal and vicious and efficient in his cruelty.

Then later. Weeks, months, years telescoped together.

Learning about the people in my head. Thirty-four of them at one point. Not schizophrenia. Not true multiple personality disorder. Something else. A unique madness that was mine to own.

Rudy Sanchez came into my life. The memory of him was a light in the darkness of those dreams. Steady Rudy. Smart and kind Rudy. Doctor to Helen, doctor to me. Friend. Helping me hunt down the people in my head. Killing some, banishing others. Making hard deals with the ones who were left.

The Civilized Man. The tattered remnant of who I might have become if the world had not dealt those wicked cards.

The Cop. The person I was evolving into. Cool and precise, taking the discipline of martial arts and the analytical qualities of an investigator. Giving me a solid piece of ground on which to stand. Saving me.

And the Warrior. Or, as he prefers to be known, the Killer. The savage who had brutalized my friend Dino. The hunter who wanted to find those four teenagers—grown men by now—and hurt them in ugly ways. But who, denied that, was always ready to go to war under a black flag against anyone who hurt people like Helen.

There were other moments like that. None of them good. *Staring into my mother's eyes as she slipped over the edge of life and fell into the big black. That precise moment when, even through the cancer and the drugs, she found a moment of clarity and knew—knew—that she was dying. In that moment. Right then. The mixture of hope, regret, and doubt was unbearable. Hope that there would be something waiting. Regret that she was leaving her sons and her husband. Doubt that the fall would just go on and on and on.*

And the day Cathy called me to say that she hadn't been able to get in touch with Helen. Cathy asking me to go to Helen's apartment. Me going. At Helen's door. Smelling what there was to smell. Kicking the door in. Finding Helen days too late. Seeing the empty bottle of drain cleaner by her bloated hand.

Later still, holding Major Grace Courtland in my arms, inhaling her last breath as the assassin's bullet took her away from me. Feeling her begin to cool; believing in the moment that it was the black ice in my heart that was stealing away her heat.

On and on, all through the night.

Fighting monsters. The walkers created by the Seif al Din pathogen. Genetically engineered soldiers deep in the dark of a military research lab. Being hunted by genetic freaks beneath the Dragon Factory. Looking into the eyes of berserkers. Facing the Red Knights and their bloody appetites.

And on and on. Year after year.

Then the God Machine.

The device created by the young and tortured madman Prospero Bell. Getting caught in the energetic wave as the machine pulsed. Feeling myself being torn out of the now and into the nowhere. Fighting zombies after the world ended.

Walking on the beach of some other world, seeing alien spacecraft cut across the sky while some monstrous thing—a demon or god or something there isn't a name for—rose above me, wings spreading, eyes burning red above a beard of writhing tentacles.

So much. Too much.

I screamed myself awake. I could feel the scream coming from way down deep inside of me. Deeper than the pit of my stomach, deeper than my lungs. Maybe from the bottom of my soul. I don't know. It rose up, soared up, ripped its way up and burst from my mouth as I twisted free of whatever held me and the sound of it shattered the air as I fell to the cold floor.

I lay there, hearing the scream echo around me. It was not a wordless scream of pain or fear. No.

What I'd screamed was *"Ph'nglui mglw'nafh Cthulhu R'lyeh wgah'nagl fhtagn!"* It was the prayer to the dark god of that other world.

I sat there on the floor. Ghost stood five feet away from me. Invisible in the utter darkness. Growling.

At me.

INTERLUDE EIGHT

THE GREEN CAVES
BELOW TUVALU, POLYNESIA
SIX YEARS AGO

It took Svoboda's team, coordinating with Dr. Beaufort and Valen, two days to excavate the cavern wall. Most of that time was used in assembling timber-and-steel support beams for the ceiling. A separate team double-reinforced the exit tunnel in case the drilling caused a collapse. Once that was done, the jackhammers and pick-axes went to work.

The wall, even cracked, fought them. It was old stone, hard and stubborn, and they encountered anomalous veins of iron.

Valen and Svoboda tried to make sense of it, because as they cut their way into the wall, the cracks Marguerite had discovered made less and less sense. For one thing, they did not follow the standard irregularities and stress points in the stone. There were clearly preexisting fracture points and mineral weaknesses that should have been where some kind of tectonic shift would naturally create fissures. Those were untouched. Instead, the cracks were in what could best be described as random places. Svoboda kept urging Valen to stop, to allow him to do tests, take samples, document the phenomenon. Valen's answer each time was to order the diggers to up their game.

They broke through into the pocket near midnight on the second day.

"Mr. Valen," called the worker who broke through the wall, but Ari and Valen were there, pushing him aside, crowding past him. They froze in the ragged entrance, shocked to stillness by what they saw. Marguerite, Svoboda, and the others tried to crowd around them to get a look.

"No," cried Valen, though to Marguerite it wasn't clear if he was telling them to stop crowding him or making a statement of flat denial at what he saw in the pocket.

Then Valen sagged sideways against the edge and ran a trembling hand over his face. His knees buckled, and he would have fallen if Ari had not caught him. Valen grabbed his friend's arm and clawed his way up it like a drowning man coming over the edge of a lifeboat.

"Ari," whispered Valen in a hollow croak of a voice, "get them back. Get everyone back. Please, for God's sake."

Ari stood a moment, too shocked to move, then he blinked and whirled and roared at the others. "Get back. Get the fuck back. Everyone out of the tunnel. *Now!*"

They retreated with great reluctance. Everyone was scared, confused. Marguerite tried to linger but Valen shook his head and she finally backed away, turned, and followed the others out.

When they were alone, Valen went into the hole and stepped gingerly into the exposed pocket. He saw that, although the plants had looked fresh through the fiber-optic scope, it was clear that they were dying. At first, he thought it might be because of exposure to different air quality now that the pocket was opened, but it became apparent that this, like so many assumptions, was wrong. All of the plants, and the roots of others, were severed. Every single one of them seemed to have been sheared through as if the whole pocket had been carved out of a natural landscape and somehow transported into the center of a rock wall. Impossible as that was.

"Are you seeing this?" he asked Ari, who stood in the tunnel mouth.

"Jesus Christ . . ." was Ari's only reply.

Valen knelt by the crystal gun. It looked like something out of an old science fiction novel. Or a kid's toy. All knobs and bulbs and blunt barrel with no opening. Valen's eyes, though, were not fixed on the gun but on the thing that lay partly across the handle. Through the scope it had appeared to be some kind of dead animal. A lizard or something, but the foliage had blocked most of it. Now Valen and Ari could see the whole thing. It wasn't any kind of small animal.

No. It was a hand and part of a wrist. Neatly severed. It had a thumb and three long fingers, each of which ended in a thick dark nail, sharp as any claw.

And it was scaly and green.

CHAPTER TWENTY-FIVE

THE WAREHOUSE
DMS FIELD OFFICE
BALTIMORE, MARYLAND
2:33 A.M.

I held my hand out for Ghost to sniff but he hesitated a long time before he would even look at it. His dark eyes were filled with strange lights, but I knew that the strangeness was mine and he was merely reflecting it. Reacting to it. Fearing it.

"Please," I said, and reached another inch closer.

Ghost finally took the tiniest of steps forward, moving with a mincing delicacy for so large a dog. Like he was stepping onto thin ice. His wet nose twitched as he sniffed. All the hair along his spine still stood up, thick and stiff as brush bristles.

Then his tail moved. A wag. Half a wag. Enough of one.

I slid off the edge of the bed and onto the cold concrete floor. Ghost came to me and I wrapped my arms around him and pulled him against my chest. A sound, not quite a sob, broke from my chest and I really could not tell you why. The dreams. Something about those dreams.

I'm a grown man, a skilled fighter, a practiced killer, and a special operator. But not at that moment. In that moment I was very young, and very small, and there were monsters. Not in my closet or under my bed, but in my dreams. In my head.

I clung to Ghost and the night closed around us like a fist.

CHAPTER TWENTY-SIX

CITADEL OF SALAH ED-DIN
SEVEN KILOMETERS EAST OF AL-HAFFAH, SYRIA
TWO DAYS AGO

They ran toward the strange, booming voice. They ran toward the sound of men screaming in pain and terror. They ran toward the rattle of gunfire and the roar of something that was too alien, too weird, too big to exist down here. They ran.

Why the fuck are we running toward all this? That was the question pounding through Harry Bolt's head. He was positive that he was completely unprepared for whatever the hell this was. And yet he ran.

The pillars were so many and so thick that they blocked the view of whatever was happening. Green light flung impossible shadows on the walls. Men, their outlines distorted to capering goblin shapes, fighting something that writhed and twisted like a nest of giant snakes. Gunfire flashed and thunder boomed. Violin, running far ahead, rounded a corner and vanished into the green madness. Her shadow loomed like a giant warrior woman from some ancient myth.

Then Harry was there, rounding the same corner, seeing what Violin saw. He skidded to a stop, tripped, fell. Lay there staring, unable to do anything else. His heart punched the inside of his chest cavity over and over again.

The intense green light poured out through a doorway. Or a cleft. Or a hole. He could not understand what it was, because it seemed to hover in the air. It was not a door in the wall. It was not anchored to anything. It was merely *there* and it was open, and from the other side of that doorway stretched a dozen . . .

His mind tried hard to refuse the word.

Tentacles.

Gigantic tentacles were stretched through the doorway and they curled and thrashed and beat at Ghul. They curled around the shrieking tomb raiders. They crushed them and tore the men to pieces and dragged them, bleeding and dying, back through the doorway. Harry caught Ghul's eyes for a moment, and even though they were strangers, even though they would have otherwise murdered each other, there was a pleading and desperate appeal. Person to person. Human to human. But when Ghul opened his mouth to scream for help, he vomited a torrent of dark red blood.

However, it was not the tentacles, nor the impossible doorway that rooted Harry to where he lay and made him stare with eyes so wide they ached.

No. It was what he could see on the other side of the doorway. Beyond it was . . . daylight. Bright sun shone on hills and fields, and above them machines flew through the sky. He could see them quite clearly, silhouetted briefly as they flew in front of the moon.

The several moons that hung in a sky that was a luminous green instead of blue. The sky of another world.

That's when Harry Bolt screamed and screamed and screamed until he passed out.

INTERLUDE NINE

PARK HYATT SYDNEY
SYDNEY, AUSTRALIA
SIX YEARS AGO

Ari sat on one side of the table in the suite overlooking the bay. He was drunk, but Valen could not blame him. Neither of them had been entirely sober since the opening of the pocket in the Green Caves.

Valen sat across from him. There were wine and whiskey bottles everywhere. A thousand-dollar bottle of Pappy Van Winkle had fallen over and leaked a puddle onto the carpet, but neither of them cared.

The hand was wrapped in plastic and sitting in a cooler packed with dry ice. The green crystal gun lay on the table. Gadyuka was sending someone to collect them. All Valen told her via coded message was that there were unusual "artifacts" she needed to see.

Valen's cell phone rang, and he tensed when he saw the display. "It's the site."

"Valen," cried a breathless Marguerite, "you need to come back here right away."

"Whoa, wait . . . why? What's happened?"

"We found something else. God . . . how soon can you get here?"

CHAPTER TWENTY-SEVEN

MANDARIN ORIENTAL HOTEL
WASHINGTON, D.C.

DMS special agent D.J. Ming wrapped the blood-pressure cuff around Aunt Sallie's upper arm and began squeezing the rubber bulb.

"You're making it too damn tight," she complained, but D.J. ignored her. He had been her driver, bodyguard, and private nurse for two years now and had become so hardened to complaints and abuse that his friends joked that he was literally bulletproof. No one in the DMS was harder to work for than Aunt Sallie.

She was in a blue nightgown with little white flowers on it. It made her look like a senior citizen in a nursing home, and she knew it. Her dreadlocks hung limply down beside her rounded cheeks and the jewels in them caught little bits of lamplight. Dots of beauty around a sad, angry face.

D.J. finished pumping and then eased pressure as he looked at his watch. The digital meter told the story: 161 over 98.

"Jesus Christ," he breathed, appalled.

"It's better than it was this morning," Auntie said defensively.

"This morning I was going to drive you to the ER."

"You can't drive with my foot up your ass."

D.J. removed the cuff and stepped back. Not for perspective, but to be out of range. "Auntie, I'm just going to say this one more time—"

"Don't bother."

He ignored her. "Your blood pressure is off the charts and your blood sugar scares the hell out of me. Don't get me started on your balance. The fact that none of this scares you, scares me even more."

"It's fine. It'll go back down once I knock in a few heads to-morrow."

"And how long's that going to take?"

"A day, tops."

They both knew she was lying. Auntie was the queen of power phone calls. The fact that she couldn't unravel the mess involving Captain Ledger and thought coming here was a good next move told D.J. that the knots were tied way too tight. A day was a laughable estimate and they both knew it.

The agent-cum-nurse walked across the room and placed the cuff on the dresser next to her blood glucose monitor and insulin supplies. He turned, leaned back, and folded his thick arms. D.J. Ming was in his middle thirties and had been a Navy SEAL for seven years and a DMS operative for nine. He was one of the most highly qualified experts in small-arms and hand-to-hand combat in the agency, and would have had a chestful of medals if the DMS gave out any. Instead he had scars and memories. It was fair to say that there wasn't a whole lot that scared him.

Aunt Sallie did, but not for the reasons she scared everyone else. He knew the difference between bluster and real threat. He could take her barbs and insults and complaints without blinking. But he cared very deeply for her, and her declining health worried him more than any battlefield he'd ever been on. If he could put himself between her and her own self-destructive nature and somehow fight that enemy, he would do it without the slightest hesitation. Auntie, despite everything, inspired a level of loyalty that ran very deep in people like him. In soldiers. D.J. was a third-generation American citizen and a second-generation special operator. His mother and Auntie had run field ops together years ago. Now D.J. was watching her wither away. Maybe die. And it was killing him.

She was the deputy director of the Department of Military Sciences, second only to its founder, Mr. Church. No one crossed her. No one went behind her back. Ever. D.J. was giving it some real thought, though. It was a balancing act—betrayal or broken heart.

Before he could try another tack with her, Auntie heaved a sigh and held up a hand. "Look, kid, give me one more day. I promise to take better care of myself. Go fetch my pills and syringe and all that crap." When he didn't move, she smiled. It was a ghastly attempt at relaxed affability. "Trust me, this will all be fine."

He nodded and turned to begin sorting out her pills. And, mostly, to hide the tears that kept trying to form in the corners of his eyes.

CHAPTER TWENTY-EIGHT

THE WAREHOUSE
DMS FIELD OFFICE
BALTIMORE, MARYLAND

Something woke me from another round of bad dreams. I sprang awake, thinking it was an explosion or an attack. Ghost started barking. I grabbed my sidearm and whipped the door open, expecting to see flames and armed hostiles. Instead, a few other confused and sleepy DMS staff came out of bedrooms, peering around like confused turtles.

One of the science techs stood listening, then nodded to himself. "Minor earthquake."

"You sure that's all it was?" I asked.

"Positive."

We stood and listened to what a grumpy Mother Earth had to say, but apparently, she rolled over and went back to sleep.

Eventually everyone went to their rooms. I sat on the bed and stroked Ghost's fur. The following morning we'd be on a plane back to California, and leaving all this behind. The crap in Washington was going to be sorted out by Aunt Sallie, who would kick ass and take names.

"It's okay, Ghost," I said. "It's all okay."

Which neither of us believed.

CHAPTER TWENTY-NINE

THE BASILICA OF THE NATIONAL SHRINE OF THE IMMACULATE CONCEPTION WASHINGTON, D.C.

The priest was middle-aged and he'd seen it all. Desperate drunks looking to make a bargain with God. The broken heart who had no other lifeline to grab. The fallen and the falling. The displaced ones who came because the doors were open. Those sad ones who came in just to see if they were still welcome. People whose faith was cracking but who wanted to cling to belief.

So many kinds. Father Steve often mused that he could fill a book with the different types. Multiple volumes. He knew that only half of them still identified in some way as Catholic. The rest were a mixed bag of Christians, lapsed-somethings, agnostics, or atheists who were having a crisis of their own lack of faith. Why Immaculate Conception? Easy. It was in a part of town where the crime rate was low enough to risk keeping the doors open all night. A lot of cops came in here. People from the crisis centers took the Metro to come here.

It was all the same to him. Father Steve was a practical guy. He'd been a chaplain in the First Gulf War and had logged time as a missionary attached to crisis hospitals in five different African countries. Since then he'd been running Immaculate Conception, mostly doing counseling, taking confessions, and working the night shift. It was a big church and there were three priests, of which he had middle seniority and no ambition to run the whole shebang.

He preferred keeping the candles lit for the wanderers who came in for quiet reflection at odd hours. Right now, there were six people in the various pews. Each sitting as geographically far away from each other as was possible. He admired the desperate geometry of it.

The old woman closest to the front was a widow who had been in every three or four days since her husband of sixty-four years passed from cancer. She was one of the brokenhearted ones, because she'd outlived her husband, both daughters, and three grandchildren. She sat rocking in silence, and Father Steve knew that no words existed to offer comfort, and no advice—no psychology or scripture—could adequately explain to her why she survived while everyone else she loved died.

Then there was the guy who ran the NA meeting. Not using, earning his ten-year chip, and running a successful meeting was in no way a buffer against hearing the stories his fellow NA members told. He'd once admitted that he felt like he was carrying those stories around as surely as if they were tattooed on his skin.

The other four tonight were new, but there were always a lot of those.

Father Steve made just enough noise to ensure they all knew he was there in case they needed something more than the setting and the atmosphere.

Then he spotted a seventh visitor he hadn't noticed before, seated in the shadows to the left of the basin of holy water, just outside the circle of yellow light cast by the flickering candles. Late thirties, he judged; well dressed but with a kind of disheveled air about him. As if the man was rumpled rather than his suit.

He needs his soul dry-cleaned, mused Father Steve, then chewed for a moment on that thought. It was accurate, but he could not pinpoint why it was right.

There was a sound and everyone in the church looked up as a bass growl filled the air. It was not very loud and not sharp. Not like an explosion, and not quite thunder. Then Father Steve felt the floor vibrate beneath his feet. For a moment he thought it was a subway train rocketing along beneath the ground, but the sound was wrong, and the vibration was too strong.

The guy from Narcotics Anonymous said it out loud, putting a name to it. "Earthquake."

He was right and everyone knew it. They sat where they were. No one rushed for the protection of a doorway. The rumble was low, soft . . . and then it was gone.

"Thank God," said the NA guy.

"Yes, indeed," agreed Father Steve and, as all eyes were suddenly on him, he made the sign of the cross in the air and gave a blessing for the safety of one and all.

The others said amen.

Except the man in the shadows, who caved slowly forward, placed his face in his hands, and began to weep.

No one heard him whisper, "I'm sorry."

Not even Father Steve.

CHAPTER THIRTY

CITADEL OF SALAH ED-DIN
SEVEN KILOMETERS EAST OF AL-HAFFAH, SYRIA
TWO DAYS AGO

Harry woke up slowly. It hurt. His body ached, and there was a feeling like a splinter driven into his mind. He sat up, gasping, drool hanging from his rubbery lips. Understanding coalesced with slow reluctance. The citadel in Syria. The tomb raiders. The hidden chamber and the green glow and the . . .

His head whipped around but the strange doorway was gone. It was all gone. Ghul and his people, those damned tentacles, the glimpse of some alien sky. All that was left was a trace of the green glow. A fragment of something that gleamed like glass, or crystal, lying on the stone floor near the base of a pillar. It pulsed like a heartbeat, the light waxing and waning very slowly.

Violin stood over it, and by that bizarre light Harry could see her expression, and it froze the heart in his chest. He had never before seen a look of such profound and personal horror. It twisted her lovely face into an ugly mask of disgust and hate and fear.

"V-Violin . . . ?" he whispered, tripping over her name. His voice was hoarse and cracked.

She turned her head very slowly toward him. It was a strange movement that, in the strangeness of the moment, did not look at all human. It was more like a praying mantis swiveling its head. Her dark eyes looked like orbs of black onyx and he saw no warmth at all in them. However, the horror and fear slowly drained from her expression, like sand from a broken hourglass.

"Violin?" he asked again.

She blinked once. Slowly. Then again. And after a third blink there was a change. She was back.

"Harry?" Violin murmured in a voice stretched paper thin with tension. She took a step toward him, caught him under the arm, and jerked him to his feet with such shocking force that Harry went stumbling several paces forward. But he skidded to a stop when he realized that she'd accidently propelled him toward the piece of green crystal. Violin cried out, but Harry began backpedaling, pinwheeling his arms like a sloppy tightrope walker. Violin caught his shoulder and pulled him farther away. They stood for a moment, panting as if they'd run up ten flights of stairs, staring at the pulsing green object.

"What is that?" he asked in a church whisper.

Violin licked her lips. "Something that should not be here."

"'Here' where? In this frigging tomb?"

"No," said Violin. She shook her head as if trying to clear her thoughts, then pulled a compact satellite from a pouch on her belt. "No signal," she said after a moment.

"Violin, what is that thing? It makes me feel weird."

She turned and suddenly jerked to a stop, staring at him, her eyes wide but face wooden. "Harry," she said in a slow, calm, controlled voice, "put that down."

"Put what down?"

Then he felt the weight in his right hand and looked down to see, with total astonishment, that he was holding his pistol. "I . . . I . . ."

He had nowhere to go with that, because he hadn't been aware of drawing the pistol. Or wanting to.

"Give me the gun, Harry," said Violin.

"What?"

"Give it to me," she said. "Do it now."

"Oh . . . sure," he said vaguely, and offered it to her.

Except that's not what he did. His arm rose, but the barrel was pointing at a spot exactly between Violin's breasts. He could feel his finger moving along the curve of the trigger guard.

"Harry . . . give me the . . ."

Violin's voice melted into nothing. Into an absence of sound so profound that it was as if his ability to hear and perceive sound had been torn from him. As it happened, Harry felt totally detached from the motion of pointing the gun at her. In his head, it was as if a door every bit as strange and alien as the one they had seen a few moments ago had suddenly opened wide. He could not hear Violin's voice. It was gone. All sound was gone, and in its place a silence as vast and deep as forever yawned like the mouth of some great, hungry thing.

Harry looked into it. Hearing nothing, but seeing so far. So deep. Into forever. He never saw Violin move. He did not feel his finger pull the trigger; never heard the shot. He did not hear the scream. Nor did he feel the ground beneath him begin to rumble and growl.

INTERLUDE TEN

THE GREEN CAVES
BELOW TUVALU, POLYNESIA
SIX YEARS AGO

They gathered around a dark blue Tyvek tarp Rig stretched out on the floor of the cavern. The guards stood at the exit, but even they craned their necks to see the green objects brought with great care from new pockets discovered in the walls.

"I can't explain this," said Svoboda uselessly. He'd said it so many times that it was now as much background noise as the dripping water.

"What is it?" asked Rig. The whole thing was so riveting that Valen noticed that Rig and Ari stood shoulder to shoulder despite everything that had happened. This was bigger than that. Bigger than anything.

"What it is," said Marguerite, who knelt on the edge of the tarp, "is inarguably the greatest archaeological discovery in the history of the world. And I am not exaggerating. If the carbon and luminescence dating continues to come back with the numbers we've been seeing from the chips found in this cavern, then this will mean that history, as we know it, is wrong."

They all looked at each other. It was what they'd all been thinking, but somehow hearing it aloud made it somehow more real. That's how Valen took it, at least. More real.

He cleared his throat and knelt across from Marguerite. "First things first," he said. "The dating is going to take some time, so we can't let ourselves get caught up in wild speculations."

"But—" began Marguerite, but he caught her eye and gave a tiny shake of his head and she fell silent.

"First, we need to determine what this thing is."

They looked at the scattered pieces. Each one had been gently cleaned and placed on the tarp along with a small tag with a numerical code.

"It's a machine," said Rig. "What else *can* it be?"

There were more than three hundred pieces, ranging from some as large as a car battery to others that were clearly some kind of pin or fastener.

"What do we do, though?" asked Rig. His clothes were covered in rock dust and his eyes seemed to be filled with crazy lights. "I mean . . . can we put it back together?"

"No," said Svoboda and a few of the others in a chorus of alarm.

"We don't have a blueprint," said Marguerite, trying to be a voice of reason.

"I can figure it out," promised Rig. "I'm good at machines. My work-study job at MIT was repairing assistant engineer in the lab. I fixed everything from the processors on the electron microscope to the gears on that big industrial laser."

"Kid's telling the truth," said Ari. "When the generator in the other cave blew, he fixed it like nothing."

“Okay,” said Valen. “Kid, you just got a promotion. But every step gets documented. Marguerite will work with you on that. Pictures, video, complete notes. The works. Dot every i and cross every t.”

“History would never forgive us for making a mistake,” said Marguerite.

Valen nodded, though he was thinking of someone else who wouldn’t forgive him if there were any mistakes.

PART TWO
SHOCK WAVES

Hell is empty and all the devils are here.

—The Tempest

William Shakespeare

CHAPTER THIRTY-ONE

TORTILLA COAST RESTAURANT
WASHINGTON, D.C.

Linden Brierley looked like a man who wanted to be anywhere else and do anything else rather than be here to meet her. That made Aunt Sallie sad.

He saw her seated at a side table and angled her way, bent to kiss her offered cheek, and slid in across from her. He wore a medium gray suit and colorful Michael Kors tie, and Auntie figured that it was a deliberate attempt to look like anything else except a former Secret Service agent. It didn't work, though. He had too much of the Fed look, which was a less human and more anal-retentive version of the cop look. Anyone who saw him would mark him as what he used to be. Old habits died very hard.

"You look like shit," she said.

Brierley took off his glasses, pinched the bridge of his nose, winced, sighed, put on the glasses again. "Thanks. Heaps."

He looked down at her plate. "What in the hell is that?"

"Huevos rancheros. Four fried eggs topped with melted cheese and ranchero sauce, over crispy corn tortillas, rice, and black beans, served with breakfast potatoes."

"Good Christ." When the waitress came he ordered a decaf coffee, and gluten-free toast with a side of organic apple butter.

"Pussy," sneered Aunt Sallie.

They were alone in their corner of the restaurant. In a confidential voice, Brierley said, "Listen, Auntie, about this thing with Ledger, I think you're wasting your time coming down here. People talk about 'executive whim' as if it's funny, but it's not. It's scary as hell. This president is unhinged and unfit for the job. I'll take anyone of either party right now. Hell, I'll take a sock puppet. Just give me someone who understands how Washington is supposed to work."

"Corruption and all?"

"Corruption can be managed," said Brierley, buttering his toast with so much aggression it bent the bread and scattered crumbs everywhere. "We've been working with corrupt politicians since the invention of special interests, so figure . . . about when they built Mesopotamia? Incompetence is dangerous."

She toasted him with her Coke. Brierley frowned.

"Why are you drinking that? Especially this early in the morning. What happened to you being diabetic?"

"Everyone needs a day off."

"Did you tell your diabetes that?"

Auntie snorted. "Stop being a sissy, Linden."

They ate for a few moments in silence. Then Brierley pushed the plate of toast away. "Are you really planning on pushing this? No, don't answer that. You wouldn't have come all this way if you weren't hopping mad. So, let me say this, and please listen to me, okay?"

She sipped her Coke and waited.

"If you push this, you won't get anywhere. This isn't the Washington you used to know. You can't play cards with these people. You can't call in old markers, because everyone is in a state of mildly controlled panic. Those who still have their heads screwed on right are staying out of the line of fire and making no waves at all until this passes. They're afraid, and they're right to be afraid. Careers are being ruined right now. Good people—Republicans and Democrats, even some Independents—are losing everything they've spent years building. When the smoke clears, none of us know what Washington is going to look like."

"A nuclear wasteland . . . ?" suggested Auntie. "Sorry, bad joke."

Brierley leaned back and scowled. Not at her, but at everything. "I wish I could help you, Auntie. Hell, I wish I could actually advise you about how to profit from coming down here. But, if you're here to make sense of this, or to get someone to claim actual responsibility, then, frankly, I think you're wasting your time."

She was quiet for a moment. "Do you really think this was just POTUS playing with his toys? That he didn't mean anything, and that all he wanted to do was try and prove that he has power? Or, worse, that he simply doesn't understand due process and people are afraid to explain it to him?"

"That's what most people think here in the Beltway. Why? Don't you?"

"No," she said. "I think there's more to it. And why do I think that? Because there's always more to it. Every damn time."

Brierley shook his head. "That's old-world thinking, Auntie. The old rules don't apply."

Aunt Sallie sipped her Coke and said nothing.

INTERLUDE ELEVEN

THE GREEN CAVES
BELOW TUVALU, POLYNESIA
SIX YEARS AGO

Rig perched on a stool like the statue of *The Thinker,* chin resting on his fist, staring at the partially assembled machine.

"What's the problem, kid?" asked Valen as he came into the tent set aside for the assembly of the crystal machine.

"Problem? *Problem?*" whined Rig, kicking a foot toward the worktable. "It doesn't make sense, that's the problem."

"Then explain it to me. Walk me up to the edge of the problem."

Rig took a breath and slid off the stool. He began pointing to the various pieces, which he had assigned new numbers to according to a hypothetical blueprint he'd made of how the device should look when assembled.

"See that rod there?" he said, pointing to a piece about two inches long. "That pretty much has to go into the holes at the end of the main housing. It holds this other piece, which I think is a lever, in place."

"Okay. So . . . ?"

Rig put on a pair of polyethylene gloves and handed the box of them to Valen. Then he picked up the rod and offered it. "Try to put it into the hole. See what happens."

Valen shrugged and tried. The end of the rod fit through the opening with room to spare, but then it simply stopped moving.

"That's funny," said Valen, and tried again. Once more the rod stopped about a millimeter inside the hole. "Something's blocking it."

"Is there?" Rig handed him a large magnifying glass. Valen bent low to examine the hole, then the rod. Then he took a ruler and measured the rod's diameter and the hole's width. "It doesn't make sense. It's almost like the machine doesn't want to go back together."

"Which is impossible," said Valen.

"Tell that to the frigging machine, man. And, it's crazy, because some of the parts went together pretty easily, and some are like this. And some didn't want to go together until I put other pieces together first." He paused for a breath. "There are three hundred forty-six, and that's if we actually have all of them, which I can't tell until I finish building it. But, man, it's going to take forever to work out the order. And there's something kind of weird about the pieces that *do* fit together. Here, let me show you. It's kind of cool but also kind of freaky."

He went around to the far side of the table and very carefully removed a flat plate that fit on the main housing. Rig looked at him, and when Valen didn't react, he frowned.

"Didn't you hear that?"

"Hear what?"

"Um . . . look, I don't want to get fresh or anything, but maybe turn your hearing aid thingy up?"

Valen did.

"Okay," said Rig, "I'm going to remove another piece. Listen close, because it's not loud."

As Rig removed a circular pad that was near where the plate had been, Valen thought he heard a faint *hrooom* sound when the piece came free. "Did you hear it?"

"I did."

"It makes that sound anytime two previously connected pieces are detached. But what I really want you to see is what happens when I put them back."

Rig seemed to brace himself, and then placed the disk where it had been. There was no *hrooom* sound, but instead the whole unit flashed with intense light. It was there and gone, fast as a wink.

"How cool is that?" declared Rig.

"Give me the plate, kid." When Rig handed it to him, Valen attached it to the machine. Although his hearing was bad, his sense of touch was superb, and as he moved the plate into place he felt something. A pull, like a magnetic attraction. Very faint, but definitely there. There was also another flash of bright green light.

Without saying anything he picked up the rod again and tried once more to insert it into the hole, this time paying attention to the feel of the resistance. While the plate felt like it was being pulled into place, the rod felt like it was being pushed back. It was a subtle feeling, but he was sure it was there.

"What . . . ?" asked Rig.

"Magnetism," said Valen.

"Huh? There's no metal."

He handed the rod to the grad student and told him what to feel for. It took a moment, but then Rig's eyes popped wide.

"Holy crap," he said.

"Yes," agreed Valen. "And now I think we have a way of figuring out how to assemble this thing."

CHAPTER THIRTY-TWO

NEW DAY
CNN MORNING NEWS

Alisyn Camerota, the sharp-eyed blond co-anchor of *New Day*, was grilling an expert about the two Washington, D.C., quakes.

Geologist John Geissman, professor and department head of geosciences at the University of Texas at Dallas and editor in chief of *Tectonics,* was doing a workmanlike job of keeping his response down on the practical level. Mundanity for him to balance the needs of the seasoned journalist for something approaching apocalyptic hysteria.

"What is presently the Eastern Seaboard of North America," he said casually, "has experienced a geologically long and very complicated history. You see, earthquakes form when rocks are displaced against one another along what we call faults. These are planes of zero cohesion in the Earth's crust. So, there are 'cracks' along which displacement takes place. Once a fault forms, then there is a possibility, often a very good one, that subsequent displacement will take place over and over and over."

"Resulting in larger and larger earthquakes?" said Camerota, trying to lead him.

He stroked his thick, graying mustache. "Resulting in the possibility of additional shocks," he corrected.

"What can we do to predict these kinds of devastating events?"

Geissman suppressed a smile. "As advanced as geosciences have become, Alisyn, we still can't predict earthquakes. However, we have gotten much better at assessing the probability and likely level of ground shaking at any point from future earthquakes."

"Isn't that the same thing?"

"No, because it's based on statistical models. Looking at data from certain areas over a long period of time, we can build statistical models to say that an earthquake might happen there within a range of years."

Camerota looked crestfallen. "Years . . . ?"

"Years. We can't yet pin it down to specifics. Even the weathermen can't do that, and they have more indicators to work with. Maybe one day, but as of right now, we just can't determine when a specific fault may rupture, as the interaction between earthquake faults worldwide is so complex. . . ."

CHAPTER THIRTY-THREE

OFFICE OF THE ATTORNEY GENERAL OF THE UNITED STATES
WASHINGTON, D.C.

When United States Attorney General Norris Spellman heard that Aunt Sallie was in his outer office, he considered calling security. He also considered leaving by a side door. He even gave his window a long, appraising look. Worst-case scenario was that he'd break a leg on the jump down to the ground. That was better than the alternative.

"Send her in," he said to his secretary, and hated the quaver he heard in his own voice.

The door did not bang open, nor did it creak like something in a haunted house. Aunt Sallie was too dangerous to be that dramatic. He didn't know her very well, but he knew enough to be genuinely afraid of her. Not physically—although he was sure that as old and sick as she was, Auntie could beat him to a pulp—but because she represented something that he had no skills to confront. Power. She exuded it. It hung on her like armor and she wielded it like a sword. The very fact of her being here in his office felt like a statement about his own lack of power. He had never worn a uniform—not as a police officer or in the military. Not even a Cub Scout uniform. He had been a lawyer his whole life, mostly working as a prosecutor going after low-to-midlevel drug dealers because they were easy wins and it gave him good stats, at least on paper. That was a wave he rode for years, with pauses to back candidates whose political agendas suited his own. Law-and-order candidates, who knew how that played among lower-income blue-collar workers. The ones who thought their elected officials gave an actual damn about them. Whom Spellman and his friends called "rubes" when they laughed about it on the back nine.

"Sallie," said Spellman, pasting on a smile that showed his white-on-white caps to their best effect. "How lovely to see you."

He came around his desk and offered his hand and then waved her to a red leather guest chair. Aunt Sallie was dressed in a severe blue pantsuit and sensible shoes, along with her usual chunky jewelry. She walked with a cane that Spellman had heard rumors about. Some people said it had a sword inside; others said a gun. He didn't know or care either way, because it had a silver handle that could qualify as a lethal weapon in any jurisdiction.

"Lovely to see me," echoed Sallie as she lowered her bulk into the chair. "We both know that's not true, Norris."

"Oh, come on, Auntie," he said with a dismissive wave of his hand. Like it was nothing. "We know this is all politics."

Her smile stopped him. It was one of the less human things he'd ever seen on a person's face. "Norris, I'm too old and too sick at heart to play politics or any other kind of game. I've been at this since before your mama stuck her tit in your mouth, so don't lecture me on *what this is*."

"I—"

"Shhh, listen now. There's no one else here. Not the Deacon and not your boss. No one. Just us. You can even pat me down to make sure I'm not wearing a wire. Go on, I won't file any sexual harassment suits if you want to feel me up."

He flushed a deep red but did not dare comment.

"I want a straight answer about what happened with Ledger," continued Auntie. "No bullshit, no company line. If this is your boss just waving his dick around, tell me now. I need to know the truth in case he tries another stunt, because maybe next time someone will get killed. I don't want that to happen, not even to one of the short-bus types your side's been hiring. They're dumb as bags of hair, but they're probably not villains. So, if you have any influence at all over your boss, then tell him to check his ammo and pick his targets before going to war with us."

"Is that," Spellman began, but choked on it. He cleared his throat and tried it again. "Is that a threat?"

Aunt Sallie uncrossed and recrossed her legs. "Of *course,* Norris. It's a very serious threat, and if I were you, I'd take heed."

"I'm the attorney general of the—"

"Seriously, Norris . . . so fucking what? You know what I am? I'm an actual American patriot. In the service of this country I've killed more people than you've ever met. I've walked ankle-deep through blood on seven continents. So has Ledger. And so have a lot of the brave men and women who serve this country as operatives of the Department of Military Sciences. You want to measure dicks? Fine. You want to stack your service to this country against ours? You want to sit there and tell me that what you're doing is more righteous, more surely in the best interests of the American people, go on. Let's put all our cards on the table, faceup."

Spellman met her eyes for exactly as long as he could bear it. Maybe three seconds. Then he picked up some papers and tapped them into a neat stack and placed them on a corner of his blotter.

"You don't scare me," he said without looking at her.

Aunt Sallie stood up. "Norris, you are either truly stupid or you are insanely stupid. Everything I said here is true; you know it. That should scare you. That should terrify you."

"Good-bye, Aunt Sallie," he said. "Have a safe trip back to Brooklyn."

He turned his chair around and looked out the window, listening for the sounds of her leaving. There were none. Instead, something touched his shoulder and he flinched away from it, then looked along the length of her cane. The silver head had brushed his collarbone very lightly.

"You made your call, Norris," said Aunt Sallie. She withdrew the cane and leaned on it. "You made your bed."

She turned and limped out of his office.

Once she was gone, Spellman called down to the front security desk to make sure Auntie was out of the building. Then he used his cell phone to call Jennifer VanOwen.

INTERLUDE TWELVE

PARK HYATT SYDNEY
SYDNEY, AUSTRALIA
SIX YEARS AGO

Gadyuka stood looking down into the open cooler that had been delivered to her suite. The note from Valen was cryptic, with only sparse details about where it was found. He texted her to say that he and Ari were hurrying back to the site because other artifacts had been uncovered, but with no additional explanation.

Gadyuka backed away with a hand to her mouth as if stifling a shriek. She stared at the green, scaly hand and the crystal gun.

"Oh, God," she gasped. "They're back."

CHAPTER THIRTY-FOUR

U.S. SECRET SERVICE HEADQUARTERS
WASHINGTON, D.C.

Aunt Sallie saw the six agents standing in a defensive line before the security post in the entrance of the Secret Service headquarters. The agents were all large, impeccably dressed, unsmiling. A seventh agent pushed past them, an ID wallet with a blue-and-gold special agent's badge held out so she could see it.

"Please stop right there, ma'am," said the lead agent. "I am Special Agent Connor O'Hare."

She walked right up to him and stopped, inches away. "What's the play here, Agent?"

"Please turn around, exit the building, and return to your vehicle," said O'Hare in a nearly monotone voice. "If you need assistance, I will be happy to assign two agents to help you. If you prefer female agents, that can be arranged."

"So, this is a roust?"

He studied her for a moment, then took her by the elbow and exerted gentle pressure. Not toward the exit, but to one side, away from the others. She allowed it, interested to see what he wanted. O'Hare spoke very quietly. "Listen, ma'am, I used to work for Linden Brierley. I was on the presidential detail during the incident at the residence when POTUS went missing. I worked on his team during the whole Black Book project."

"And . . . ?"

"And I'm just about the last man standing from those days. Ask Brierley, he'll vouch for me. You need to back down. We got word that you harassed the AG. He is going to file charges."

Auntie snorted.

"Not saying they'll stick," said O'Hare, "but, like it or not, he is the attorney general. He has POTUS's ear. Word went out, and you're not going to get in to see anyone today. No one. Whatever you hoped to do here in D.C. is a wash. Best thing you can do is go back to your office and lawyer up. I wish I had something better to say. I wish it wasn't me saying this to you, but at least you're not in cuffs. If you push this, you will be."

Auntie could feel her pulse hammering, and heat was rising from her chest and up her neck. She didn't even want to think what her blood pressure was right now.

"This is horseshit, O'Hare."

"Yes it is, ma'am, and I wish it were otherwise. Please . . . you can't win this fight. Not here, and not today." His professional demeanor had cracked to reveal a fully human face. She could see the concern and pain in his eyes. It made her suddenly feel very old. And more than a little scared. "Please," he begged.

Aunt Sallie sighed and nodded. "Okay, O'Hare."

He looked incredibly relieved. "Thank you."

She lingered a moment longer, though. "Why do you stay in the middle of all this shit?"

O'Hare almost smiled. "Probably for the same reason you do, Aunt Sallie. Someone has to."

She studied him. "The war is the war," she said.

"Yes," he agreed. "The war is the war."

Aunt Sallie turned, feeling her years more than she had in a long time. Feeling the frustration and anger boiling inside of her. Feeling the humiliation as the six younger agents watched her go. Feeling the defeat.

O'Hare walked her to the door, and she let him help her down the steps and into the back of her car. D.J. Ming gave him very hard looks and started to say something, but Auntie shook her head. O'Hare leaned on the frame of the car. "Are you going to be okay, Auntie? You don't look . . ."

He trailed off because she shook her head. Then he stepped back and closed the door. When Auntie turned to look through the rear window of the DMS limo, he was standing on the curb watching, like a lone soldier lost in enemy country.

"You okay?" asked D.J.

"Don't start," she warned.

"Oooo-kay. Then where to, Auntie. Back to the hotel? Or the airport?"

"No," she said wearily. Her brown fists were clenched like a stranger's hands around the shaft of her cane. "The Capitol Building."

CHAPTER THIRTY-FIVE

THE WAREHOUSE
DMS FIELD OFFICE
BALTIMORE, MARYLAND

Sam Imura shook my hand without much warmth, gave me one of his uninformative kind of smiles, and told me to have a safe flight home. Which I took to mean, *Go away and don't hurry back.*

He gave Top and Bunny more comradely handshakes, complete with chest bumps and lots of back slapping. He patted Ghost's head, who seemed indifferent to whatever emotional dynamic was going on at the moment because no one was handing out Snausages. Our driver, one of Sam's people, pulled the car up, and Bunny loaded our bags. I literally had one foot in the car when my cell phone rang. The screen display told me it was D.J. Ming, Aunt Sallie's driver and bodyguard.

"Hey, D.J.," I said as I continued to slide into the front passenger seat.

"Joe, hey," said D.J., "are you still in Baltimore?"

"About to head to the airport now. Why?"

"Any chance I can talk you into coming down to D.C.?"

I snorted. "Pretty sure everyone with a badge there wants to arrest me."

"I know, but this is important."

"Yeah, well, so is not going to Gitmo."

"I'm serious, Joe," said D.J. "It's about Aunt Sallie."

The driver was about to turn the key, but I touched his wrist and shook my head. "Has something happened to her?"

"Not . . . exactly. And, man, she will absolutely kill me when she finds out I called you." He explained about Aunt Sallie's trip to D.C. to try and get to the truth about the pickup order on me. D.J. hadn't been in each of Auntie's meetings, but she'd told him the bones of it, including how she was ushered out of the Secret Service headquarters with an armed escort. "Frankly, Joe, I'm getting worried about her. She's been going way off her diet. Stress eating, I guess, though you couldn't force me to say that to her face if you put a gun to my head. Her BP's off the scale, she's always flushed and sweating, and I'm afraid she's going to have a heart attack or something."

"Okay, D.J.," I said, opening the car door, "text me her itinerary and I'll catch up. Can't promise she'll listen to me, but I'll see what I can do."

"Thanks, Joe. I just dropped her at the Capitol Building. She thinks I'm just parking the car. She's here to ambush some congressmen."

"Be there in an hour."

I got out and told the others about the call. Top never complains and he didn't wait for me to ask him if he was in. Instead he popped the trunk and grabbed his suitcase.

"Sam," I said, "you got some wheels for us?"

"Yeah," said Bunny, "something that a bunch of cranky Secret Service mooks can't shoot through."

Sam sighed. "Sure. Take a Betty Boop."

We turned to look where he was pointing. A line of black SUVs stood in a row. Two Escalades, two Land Rover Sport Diesels, and a Nissan Armada. They were the latest in a long series of gradually mutating urban transport. The first generation, known as Black Betty, was designed by the head of the Vehicles and Transportation Design Center, otherwise known as the Shop. Our chief mechanic, Mike Harnick, is—how should I put this nicely?—out of his damn mind. He watches all those scenes in James Bond movies where 007 gets tutored on the bizarre extras Q has built into his cars, and Mike thinks they're real. Point is, Mike tends to go a little beyond beyond when he builds a car for one of the field teams. My own car back home in San Diego has an ejector seat, which is something I once joked about wanting. Mike took me seriously. Very seriously. The demonstration of that ejector seat put four fifty-pound sacks of sand forty feet into the air. The ceiling in his garage is forty feet. You see where I'm going with that.

Anyway, roll forward until Mike meets the new head of the DMS Integrated Sciences Division, Dr. Joan Holliday, aka Doc Holliday. Doc is a Jedi Master of geeky weirdo gadgets. The two of them spent a week at the Shop and I swear dark clouds gathered overtop and there were peals of demonic laughter. Or so I've been told. The result is that the Black Betty model is yesterday's leftovers. The new line—improbably known as Betty Boops because . . . well, I really don't know why—look exactly like top-of-the-line SUVs. However, the only part of them that came out of the catalogs of Ford, Nissan, or other car companies is the silhouettes. The skin of each car is a polycarbon blend that infuses spider silk, Kevlar, and some kind of new polymer that will stop anything short of an RPG. And an RPG will dent but not penetrate. From gel-filled self-repairing tires to window glass that can shrug off fifty-caliber rounds, they are rolling tanks. The polymers and alloys keep the weight down so the supercharged engines aren't slowed at all.

Then we get to the hidden goodies. All sorts of compartments inside the cabin have guns, first-aid kits, plasma, and lots of electronic gizmos. And concealed external pods that open up to deploy drones, chain guns, rocket launchers, spike strips, and more. We can roll up to any kind of party and start the fun and games. They even have an autonomous drive option, though I couldn't begin to imagine any of us wanting to use it—although on reflection, it might be funny to have Ghost sit in the driver's seat and let the car roll through town for an hour or so. Church would be pissed. I'd have to think about it, because the idea was beginning to feel like a moral imperative.

We walked over to the Land Rover.

"Driving," said Top, not leaving it open to discussion.

"Shotgun," said Bunny, and I didn't argue.

"Not calling it Betty damn Boop, though," Top said under his breath as he popped the lock on the back. Ghost wagged his bushy white tail and climbed in and over the seats to claim the middle row as his domain. I climbed in beside him and he looked deeply imposed-upon.

Bunny leaned over and whispered in Top's ear. "Betty Boop."

We drove off.

INTERLUDE THIRTEEN

THE GREEN CAVES
BELOW TUVALU, POLYNESIA
SIX YEARS AGO

It was the screams that woke Valen. Even without his hearing aid they were so high and shrill that they stabbed at him all the way down deep inside his dreams.

He sprang awake, swinging a punch at the green and scaly monster he'd been fighting in the nightmare, but his fist hit nothing and the effort sent him toppling onto the cabin floor. But Valen had lived too long on the edge to let surprise or stupor own him, and he sprang up like a cat, froze, listened to the night, and then launched himself into motion. He was out the door dressed only in pajama bottoms but with a GSh-18 9mm in his fist.

Everyone else was erupting from cabins and tents all through the forested area near the cavern entrance. He saw Marguerite hurriedly belting a robe, and beyond her Svoboda, looking like a startled heron, blinking at the darkness and looking in the wrong direction. Then Valen turned and gaped at what loomed in the distance. Down the path, closest to the entrance, was the tent where Rig had been working.

It was on fire, totally engulfed and raging.

But the fire burned a fierce and ugly green.

"Out of my way," growled Valen, shoving people to one side as he ran. "Everyone get back to your quarters."

No one listened, of course. How could they when the world was being turned on its head?

Valen raced to the clearing with the tent and then jerked to a stop twenty feet away. The tent was not burning in any normal way. The top had ripped open and something like a beam of rippling green light shot hundreds of feet into the air. The fabric of the tent had become nearly transparent because of the sheer intensity of whatever was going on inside. Ari Kostas was sprawled like a starfish on the ground with his clothes shredded and every inch of exposed skin flash-burned. His eyes were open and he was panting, but there was no trace of intelligence or recognition to be seen. Ari's mouth worked like a fish's, speaking words that made no sense at all. Without his hearing aid, Valen could barely make out the sounds, but none of them sounded like they were in any language he knew.

"Ph'nglui mglw'nafh . . . Cthulhu R'lyeh . . . wgah'nagl . . . fhtagn . . ."

Bloody drool ran from the corners of Ari's mouth and he was weeping red tears.

Inside the tent, silhouetted by the green light, was Rig. He stood with his head thrown back and his body gone impossibly rigid.

And he was floating inches above the floor, surrounded by the fiery glow.

"Oh my God, no!" Valen turned just in time to intercept Marguerite as she ran for the fluttering tent flap. He grabbed her in a bear hug and had to pick her up to drag her back, and he was not a second too soon, because there was a massive explosion—not of fire but of air. It flattened trees, tore plants from their roots, ripped all of the surrounding tents to shreds, and flung the dig team into the air. Valen and Marguerite were already turning, falling, when the blast hit them.

The wave of air swept outward across the entire island, carrying with it the intense green light. The blast was so powerful that it went far beyond their remote camp and swept across the entire ten square miles of the island of Tuvalu. All ten thousand people living and vacationing on the island were shocked awake by the force of the blast.

Back at the dig site, Valen and Marguerite lay bruised and bleeding and dazed. Valen hung on the very edge of consciousness, while Marguerite was out, her forehead swelling from where a heavy branch had struck her.

The tent was nothing but rags fluttering on twisted poles. The guards stationed there were dead, half their skin ripped away. Of

Rig, no sign at all was ever found. The table on which he'd been assembling the machine was slag.

The machine itself, though, sat whole and complete, glowing with some inexplicable power, humming with energy. Valen stared at it, seeing that it was whole and untouched and bizarre and alien.

"Wh-what . . . ?" stammered Valen.

It was then that the earthquake began.

CHAPTER THIRTY-SIX

MARYLAND STATE ROUTE 295 SOUTH
NEAR HANOVER, MARYLAND

It was still raining all across the Eastern Seaboard. A steady downpour that fell in straight lines because there was no wind to push it. Morning looked like twilight, and even with the heater on there was a sense of deep cold. Not the numbing cold of an icy winter day, but the kind of soaking cold that keeps all of your nerve endings completely awake. Ghost snuggled in against me and leached my body heat away.

While Top drove, I made a bunch of calls. The first was to Junie, and I got her answering service again. A moment later a text popped up:

> In a meeting. Will call later
> XOXOXOXO

And a bunch of emojis. Hearts and palm trees and kissy faces. I think those things are totally ridiculous; a sign that, as a culture, our collective emotional maturity was approximately that of pre-K kids using precut shapes to make pictures for Mom and Dad. Absurd. So, I made sure my guys didn't see me send twice as many back.

Then I called the Hangar, but was told Church was in but not available except for missiles inbound or a zombie apocalypse. I left a message for a callback at his convenience.

"Cap'n," said Top quietly. "We got company. Black Lincoln Navigator three cars back."

I turned in my seat and studied the moderate traffic behind us. Top changed lanes a couple of times so I could see how the Lincoln adjusted.

"Yup," I said, "that would be an actual tail."

"Since when does the Secret Service drive Navigators?" asked Bunny.

We hadn't yet gotten onto Maryland 295 South, so I suggested Top take a side route. The Lincoln followed, keeping well back.

"Does this boat have Calpurnia?" I asked.

"Yes," said the sexy voice of the AI. "I'm here, Joseph."

Bunny snorted. "Not sure where that falls. Somewhere between cool and I want to put a bullet into the dashboard."

"I don't bite, Bunny," purred the computer.

Top shook his head. He hated gadgets.

"Calpurnia," I said, "Lincoln Navigator on our six. Deploy a drone. I want details."

"Done."

There was a soft click as the pigeon drone rolled out of a concealed compartment near the front fender. It waited until the Lincoln passed and then shot into the air. Half a mile rolled past.

"Plates are federal," said Calpurnia. "Registered to the Department of Homeland Security motor pool. However, there is a sixty-three percent possibility that the registration was the result of a hack into the motor pool server."

"Then they're not friendlies," said Bunny as he opened the glovebox to reveal a thumbprint scanner, pressed it, and was rewarded when a second door hissed up out of sight. "Nice."

"What've we got, Farm Boy?" asked Top.

"Two choices. Heckler & Koch .45s with sound suppressors or a couple good ol' Glock 19s."

"No Sigs?"

"No Sigs. You want 9mm or a .45?"

"Nine," said Top. Bunny selected one, checked the magazine, and handed it to Top, who nodded and rested it on his lap, tucked in between thigh and belt. Bunny also handed him three magazines, which Top pocketed. He handed me the H&K and took the remaining Glock for himself. Our own handguns were in locked travel boxes in their suitcases, with additional trigger locks in place. We hadn't come to Baltimore on business and were scheduled to take a commercial flight back home. But Mike Harnick would never leave us high and dry. According to the brief tour of the Betty Boop, there were enough handguns, long guns, and other weapons to start a war with a moderate-sized country. And likely win it. There were also some of what we call our "exotics." Weapons based on tech we'd taken from the bad guys over the years. Hey, not everything went to FreeTech.

"If we're going to do something," mused Top, "I don't want to get into a fuss in Beltway traffic, feel me? How 'bout we take this to neutral ground? Cash Creek Lake? Sound good?"

"Yup," I said.

A few minutes later we were on a smaller road, cutting between Pheasant Run Community Park and South Laurel Neighborhood Park. Top didn't slow down because those were residential areas. He headed south and east, leading the follow car and shedding incidental traffic like leaves.

Soon it was just the two SUVs rolling along a country road. Then Top made a hard right down Powder Mill Road, which cut through dense forestland. The follow car began to speed up because, hey, nobody was fooling anybody by then. Top cut left onto the narrow Scarlet Tanager Loop and looked for the first major bend in the road.

"Get ready," he told Bunny, who already had a panel open on the center console. As soon as Top rounded the bend and the other car vanished momentarily from sight, Bunny punched the button. There was a metallic thump and rattle. Top made another hard turn, but this time he hit the brakes and steered through a hissing, screeching turn and then jammed the brakes to stop us facing the way we'd come.

The driver of the other car was moving at about sixty when his tires hit the spike net Bunny had deployed. All four tires blew and the SUV went into a nasty, crunchy, turning, glass-shattering and metal-rending series of rolls until it dropped back onto wheels wrapped in rubber shreds. Smoke curled from under the buckled hood and was punched back down to the steaming asphalt by the rain.

By then we were moving. Bunny ran along the right-hand side of the road; I was on the left. Top was still in the driver's seat, but he'd hit the controls to drop the headlights down and allow an ugly pair of M230 chain guns to roll out.

I yelled, "Federal agents! Step out of the vehicle with your hands on your heads. Do it right now."

Bunny roared, "Hands only, motherfuckers. If I see a gun I will kill you."

The two front doors opened as we approached. One fell off into the road; the other had to be kicked open. The driver stepped out and stood looking at us. His clothes were torn and he had bruises on his face, but he was smiling. The passenger got out and actually wiped window glass from his lapels like this was some kind of movie. He was smiling, too, and this was not a smiling moment.

"Captain Ledger," said the driver, "you are making a mistake here."

I pointed my gun at his face. "Then I'll cry a little later. Hands on your head. Do it right now."

"We are not your enemy."

There was something weird about the way he spoke. His lips didn't really move even though his words were clearly enunciated. It was like watching a ventriloquist. Neither of them looked anything at all like they'd just been bounced around a Maryland highway in a metal box. Ghost began to growl very softly.

"Hands on your head," I said, feeling my heart begin to hammer harder than I wanted it to. "I won't tell you again."

"We are not your enemy," said the passenger. In exactly the same way. Identical words, identical voice. It was like listening to a recording. And it sounded vaguely familiar, but I could not place from where.

Then they both said it. Exactly at the same time.

"We are not your enemy."

"Cowboy," warned Top, using my combat call sign. Ghost gave a single savage bark. A warning of his own.

Faster than the eye could see, the two agents crouched, spun, and came up with guns.

Bunny and I fired at the same time, hitting each agent with round after round. The agents straightened, still smiling, and returned fire, filling the air with a sound louder than our shots. Both of their guns made loud, hollow *tok* sounds.

And suddenly the world turned a bright green and caught fire. I felt myself rising into the air, punched off my feet by a fist of pure heat. Then I was falling as the green fires burned the world into a black cinder.

INTERLUDE FOURTEEN

THE GREEN CAVES
BELOW TUVALU, POLYNESIA
SIX YEARS AGO

Valen walked through the camp like a drunken man.

His pajama bottoms were torn to rags and blood ran in lines down his body. He was missing two teeth on the upper left side, and one eye was puffed shut. There were corpses everywhere. Dr. Svoboda sat with his back to a portable generator, eyes wide, mouth agape, hands clutched around a split stomach from which everything of importance had slid out into the dirt. He called for his mother in a high, plaintive voice.

Dr. Chu was missing her head and left arm. The senior staff officer was impaled on a tent pole. Several of the miners had been caught in the jaws of the hungry earth as the quake sent the land into a feeding frenzy.

Valen had no idea what time it was. Dawn, or a little after, perhaps; though the pale light could have just as easily been midday viewed through a curtain of dust. There were helicopters in the air, but closer to the towns. Not here.

All that he saw here was death and destruction.

The machine.

The machine.

The fucking machine.

It sat there. Without a scratch. Silent now, though. Even as the whole island seemed to tear itself apart, the machine sat there. Unmoving except for a slight vibration. The ground rumbled and churned beneath it, but the machine simply stayed there, as if it was governed by a different set of physical laws than the rest of reality.

Ten minutes ago, Valen staggered through waves of green pulsing energy to tear one of the plates away, and that seemed to stop it. The green glow vanished as surely as if a light switch had been thrown. There was a faint *whoomph* sound, something that Valen felt more than he heard, and the machine died.

The earthquake stopped at that precise moment.

Valen stood for long minutes, looking at the plate he held, at the machine, and at the incredible devastation around him.

"What . . . ?" he asked aloud, but there was no one alive or awake to hear him. Ari Kostas was alive, but he had two broken legs, a broken jaw, and was unconscious. And Marguerite seemed to linger at the edge of the big fall into blackness with a concussion and possibly a skull fracture.

Valen was awake, mostly whole, and alone. The earthquake had torn the island apart. The cave system had collapsed, burying their dig under a million tons of broken rock. Everywhere he looked were the jagged stumps of broken trees, and far away, on the populated side of the island, towers of smoke from fires smudged the sky.

He wandered back to the machine and found the plate he'd torn loose. He picked it up and for a moment considered hurling it into the jungle. With all of the uprooted trees and torn earth no one would ever find it again. Maybe that was what he should do. And then dismantle the rest and carry the pieces to the roiling surf, smash the quartz on the rocks. End whatever ancient or alien madness this thing was.

That was what he should have done. Valen knew it. The human heart inside his chest warred with the colder exigencies of political agenda and patriotism. Gadyuka and her superiors had selected him for a reason. Did they know this might happen? It seemed likely. Or, if not this specific thing, then something equally unnatural.

He stared at the machine as he bent and picked up a piece of twisted tent pole.

Smash it and be done with it, he told himself. *No one will know. No one can see.*

He could claim it was destroyed along with everything else. Whatever it was, this thing was too powerful. What if it had been activated in a city? What if it had been assembled in Moscow? What kind of devastation would it do?

And then something occurred to him. Something Gadyuka had alluded to but not really explained. He spoke a name aloud and knew that it, all those years ago, and this right here, were part of the same new skewed reality.

"Chernobyl . . . ," he whispered.

CHAPTER THIRTY-SEVEN

THE CAPITOL BUILDING
WASHINGTON, D.C.

There were no Secret Service agents waiting in ambush for Aunt Sallie when she entered the Capitol Building. She made her way to the chamber where the House of Representatives was gathering. She made it in time to see the Speaker call the House to order, then yield to the chaplain to offer a brief prayer. It was nondescript and the *amens* were perfunctory, even among the more devout representatives. If the bill on tap this morning had been one dealing with a hot-button topic, there would have been the usual grandstanders needing to be seen as openly devout, especially those up for reelection. Then the Speaker offered up the legislative journal from the previous business day, which was approved by all. After that they stood to recite the Pledge of Allegiance. It was all rote, and done without passion or fuss, clearing the decks for that day's legislative business.

Auntie stood watching, scanning for familiar faces among the Republicans on the right side of the center aisle and Democrats on the left. Found a few, caught no one's eye. Everyone was focused on the Speaker of the House, Andrew Jackson Howell. The bill was read and the debate was waived because this was a bipartisan agreement that had already been worked over so that it was palatable to both sides. Even so, there were steps to follow and rituals to be honored, so Aunt Sallie leaned against a wall and waited, expecting this to be tedious and probably a waste of her time.

It was neither.

Speaker Andrew Jackson Howell sat with his head bowed during the reading of the bill and through some points of order. He did not say anything when the voting began. It was not until the eleventh member of the House was asked to cast her vote that Speaker Howell abruptly stood up and screamed out eleven words that shocked the whole chamber to silence.

"My God, my God, why is it so quiet in here?"

His scream was so loud, so high, so raw that bloody spit flecked his desk.

Everyone froze, staring at him. Gaping. No one knew how to react to a moment like this. Even Aunt Sallie was shocked to gaping stillness.

Howell glared around, turning this way and that like a trapped animal. His eyes were huge, unblinking. Filled with madness. He suddenly snatched up the fountain pen and shook that fist at the representatives and the staff and the press.

"They can walk through walls, you know!" he roared, and then Howell rammed the pen into his own throat.

He tore it free and arterial blood shot from the wound like spray from a hose.

And he stabbed himself again. This time in the right eye.

His knees buckled and he collapsed face-forward, and the impact drove the nib of the pen all the way through his eye socket and into his brain.

Andrew Jackson Howell was dead before anyone could reach him.

CHAPTER THIRTY-EIGHT

SCARLET TANAGER LOOP
MARYLAND CITY, MARYLAND

I flew through the air, propelled by a cloud of green fire. *This isn't too bad,* I thought. Then I hit a tree, crashed through a mass of pine needles, feeling the sharp ends of twigs slash at me. A moment later I was falling the other way. Down. Hitting every fucking tree branch on the way to the grassy ground. The grass did nothing to cushion the impact. I lay there, flattened and gasping.

Something else crashed down beside me. It yelped and howled. Ghost. Alive. Hurt, but alive.

Raising my head was next to impossible, but the Killer within me roared. Pain drives him. He eats it and lives off it. I found myself on my knees, blinking to clear my eyes. I couldn't see Bunny. No way to tell if he rode the wave of superheated air, like Ghost and I had, or if he'd been burned to nothing. The agents were hiding behind their wrecked car, no longer bold, because Top had opened up with the chain guns. The agents were clearly wearing some kind of shock-dampening body armor under their suits, but a heavy-caliber machine gun doesn't give much of a shit about that. Both agents were, weirdly, splashed with luminous green paint. I had no idea why, how, or where it came from.

They each held pistols that were very familiar to me. Not firearms in the conventional sense. They had round, blunt barrels, but instead of an opening, the flat end of each gun was ringed by three curved metal spikes that ended in tiny steel balls. The guns didn't fire bullets or even Taser flechettes. No, these weapons discharged short and intense bursts of superheated microwave energy, except that the green color was a new touch. I'd fought against men armed with microwave pulse pistols before. Those killers had also been dressed like this. Black suits, white shirts, black ties. Men in black. The name they went by was "Closers." The first ones we'd met had worked for a group called Majestic Three. The DMS had shut down M3, wiped out the Closers, and acquired several of the MPP weapons.

I wished I had one right then, because the SUV had soaked up the machine-gun fire and the agents were still alive.

I tapped my earbud for Top. "Sergeant Rock, ram the vehicle. Do it now."

If he responded, I couldn't hear it over the gunfire, but a moment later the engine roared and he hit the gas, sending the Betty Boop forward like a battering ram. Mike Harnick built the frame to be able to take a head-on collision with an armored personnel carrier. The beat-up SUV belonging to the Closers had no chance at all. Top smashed into it with a horrendous shriek of metal on metal. The smaller SUV jumped backward and I saw both agents vanish beneath its bulk.

Then I was up and running. My handgun was lost but I grabbed my Wilson folding knife from its pocket sheath, flicked the small, wicked blade into place, and ran to the far end of the wreck.

There was a loud *Tok!* and the SUV suddenly lifted into the air, rising ass-first as if it had been punched by a giant. It turned over in midair and smashed down on the hood and windshield of Betty Boop.

There, getting to his knees, was one of the Closers, an MPP gripped in both hands. His face was painted with the luminous green. The other Closer lay facedown on the ground in a pool of the weird paint. I saw him move, though. He was alive.

Somehow, impossibly, they were both alive.

In the crushing silence I heard sounds. Ghost gave a single uncertain bark. A foot crunched on the roadside to my right as Bunny staggered into view. A car door opened and Top came hurrying up.

I heard the agent speak the same words as he rose. "We are not your enemy."

I had my knife but my legs did not want to move. The uninjured agent studied me.

"You were warned, Captain Ledger. We thought you understood."

"What . . . ?"

"We are not your enemy."

He reached down and pulled his companion to his feet. The second agent was hurt, that much was obvious. His face was torn up and I could see the gleam of teeth through a cheek that had been totally ripped open.

Bunny said, "What . . . ?"

An existential question. Him needing someone to explain the shape of the day to him—or the shape of the world—because the terrible wounds on the agent's face were bleeding *green*. There was not a drop of red to be seen. Not on either of them. Not on their clothes or the ground. Nowhere except on Top and Ghost and Me.

The agents were bleeding, though. Intensely, profusely.

A sound suddenly filled the air and we all looked up.

And then there was darkness.

CHAPTER THIRTY-NINE

THE CAPITOL BUILDING
WASHINGTON, D.C.

Speaker of the House Andrew Jackson Howell gave no warning. No one saw this coming. Not his colleagues in the House of Representatives. Not his family or friends. Not the press. Not even his political enemies.

Until that morning he had been viewed as a fit, active man of middle years. Lean from his free-time hobby of playing soccer with classmates from law school. He was not ill; at least not that anyone knew. He rarely drank, his marriage was in good shape, and his two daughters were both successful young women who were making their way toward good careers, one in law and one in medicine.

So, no one saw it coming.

His chief of staff, Amanda Grel, briefed him that morning, and later, when interviewed by the Secret Service, police detectives, and others, said that the Speaker looked a little tired. That was all. A little tired.

Video security footage of the Speaker as he entered the Capitol, walked the hallways, and entered the House showed him moving slowly, but if the day ended in any other way there would be nothing on those tapes to suggest a problem. He moved slowly, but that was not a red flag. The House was voting on a bill to fund an aid package for Ukraine, which was reeling from the third major earthquake in as many months. The representatives had been split because most of them would rather have seen the bulk of that money go to their own states, but common sense had won out. The earthquakes had done extensive damage to key Ukrainian military bases, including those where American and United Nations advisors were situated. Without that funding, Ukraine would have been weak against strategic incursion by the Russians. The Speaker and key representatives he trusted had wrangled for weeks, so a case might have been made that he was tired from long nights and political lobbying.

The only unusual blip in the Speaker's actions before entering the lower house, and it was completely overlooked at the time, was that he skipped a meeting with the majority whip. But since the last count showed the odds in favor of passing the bill, the whip—at the time—figured the Speaker felt that any last-minute strategizing was a time-waster.

It was truly a surprise. A shock.

Aunt Sallie stood staring. She had no authority here. And even if she did, there was nothing she could do. The man was dead. It was over. There were screams and shouts and voices raised in anger, in fear, giving orders, yelling for EMTs. Someone kept shouting for someone to call 911. As if that would help.

"What . . . ?" asked a voice, and Auntie turned to see a congressional aide standing there, white-faced, horrified, irreparably marked by what just happened. The aide was a girl, a child. Twenty, perhaps. Still in college. Too young for this.

But then Auntie realized that she had been twenty when the CIA had recruited her. She'd been only twenty-five the day she met Mr. Church. Still a child, but one who had walked knee-deep through a stream of blood. Innocent and guilty. Much of it spilled by her.

She reached out and took the aide's hand and held it. The girl turned toward Auntie, buried her face in the hollow between chin and shoulder, and began to weep like a broken thing. Asking the same question over and over again.

What?

Auntie had no answers at all.

CHAPTER FORTY

SCARLET TANAGER LOOP
MARYLAND CITY, MARYLAND

I blinked and it was suddenly pitch black. Like the middle of the night, only darker. A total absence of light.

I blinked again and it was daytime. A gray day, with drizzle falling around me and on me. I was no longer standing by the side of the road. I was in the rear seat of the Betty Boop. Ghost was there, asleep, his head on my lap. Top was behind the wheel, Bunny was in the shotgun seat. The engine was off and rain pinged on the roof and popped on the windshield. My clothes were damp but not soaked. My face was dry, but I could see a grittiness as if rain had dried only recently. Top suddenly jerked and it was clear he just woke up. As I had. As Bunny did a few seconds later. Then Ghost. We woke up, but we sat there, oddly still. Staring.

Bunny said, "What . . . ?"

Fair question. Impossible to answer. Top turned very slowly, as if his body was still more asleep than awake. He wiped rainwater from his eyes and looked at Bunny, then turned more to look at me.

The engine was running and the heat was on. I realized that now. Had it been on when I woke? Maybe. No way to tell. Top certainly hadn't turned it on. Ghost whined and cowered against me.

We got out of the car. It took a lot of doing. I felt clumsy and sick and strangely stiff, as if I'd been sitting too long without moving. Top moved like he was old and riddled with arthritis. We tottered around to the far side of our car. I had to help Ghost down, and he stood on trembling legs with his tail curled under.

Bunny slid down to the ground, his back to the front wheel, eyes staring and half vacant.

"They're gone," said Top, looking around.

Bunny shook his head, and, without saying a word, raised a shaky finger and pointed to the near woods. There, lying crumpled like a toy thrown away by a bored child, was the SUV. Riddled with pocked bullet holes from the chain guns. It was on its side with the smashed windshield toward us. Empty.

When I managed to shamble over to examine it, I saw that there were no smudges of the green . . . blood? Did I want to call it that? Was that how this day was going to go? My mind rebelled. The Cop told me I was wrong, that trauma made my memory faulty. The Modern Man was hiding under the bed. Only the Killer part of me seemed able to accept it on its own terms. He was much more practical about such things. Things are what they are. The green stuff was gone. That was a fact.

There was none of it on the road, either. In fact, the whole road looked like it had been steam cleaned. The shell casings were all in the weeds on either side, as if the same force that had scoured the blood had swept everything to the sides. Even our spike net was over in a drainage ditch.

"Who came and cleaned this up?" asked Top.

I shook my head. A shiver whipped through me and then I rubbed my face vigorously with my hands and then clapped in front of my face. Hard and loud.

"Okay," I said, forcing my voice to sound normal. Or, normal-ish. "We don't know what happened, but we have the vehicle and we have a forensics field kit. Let's start acting like professionals instead of Victorian ingénues with the vapors."

"I think that's sexist, boss," muttered Bunny.

"Fuck it," I said.

"Yeah, that's a good point." He held out a hand and allowed Top to haul him to his feet. Then he blew out his cheeks and nodded, turned, and went to fetch the forensics kit that is built into every DMS vehicle. I checked the time on my watch and froze.

"Hey, Top . . . what time do you have?"

He studied his watch, frowned, tapped the crystal face, and shook his head. "It stopped. Must have happened when I fell."

We compared our watches. They'd all stopped at the same time. To the second. I checked my cell phone, and then the dashboard clock. They'd all stopped at exactly the same time. Calpurnia was offline, too.

"Okay," said Bunny, "this is freaking me out a little."

"A little?" Top hit the reset button on the AI system and the digital clock was one of the first systems to come online. We looked at the time. Then we looked around at the road, at the day. The sky was too overcast to see the sun, but we knew that the online time was telling the truth. We'd lost time.

We'd lost two whole hours of our lives.

CHAPTER FORTY-ONE

SCARLET TANAGER LOOP
MARYLAND CITY, MARYLAND

I called it in. Or tried to. My cell phone was acting funky, so I turned it off and back on again. While it rebooted I tapped my earbud, but it gave me a lot of painful static. So I took the booster pack out of my pocket and hit Reset on that, too.

I slid into the driver's seat and said, "Calpurnia, open a line to the TOC."

Calpurnia did not do that. Instead she began singing a Barry Manilow song. Not playing one—singing one. Top and Bunny stared at the car as if expecting it to suddenly break out into a dance routine.

"Cancel," I growled.

Silence.

"Calpurnia," I said with great patience, "open a line to the TOC."

She said, "Playing Top Forty hits of the week ending May 26, 1973." Immediately the song "Frankenstein" by the Edgar Winter Group blasted out with the volume turned to 11.

"Cancel!" I roared.

"I think Calpurnia's having a moment," murmured Top.

"I love working for the DMS," said Bunny, not meaning it.

My cell finished rebooting and that worked fine, so I called the DMS and got Doc Holliday on the line. She listened while I went over everything.

"That's amazing," she cried. "Ever since I signed on to this rodeo I've been waiting for something fun to happen. I'm happier than a tornado in a trailer park."

"Yeah, well, Doc, you wouldn't have enjoyed it all that much if you just had your ass handed to you by guys who I'm pretty sure aren't from a local zip code."

"Point taken," she said, but the excitement was still in her voice. Even a hint of a giggle. "You said they bled green? Could the green fluid have been gel from their body armor?"

"Well, I sure as hell hope so."

"But you don't think so?"

"Ah, jeez, Doc, I really don't know. I mean, this is weird, even by my standards. I saw facial lacerations and did not see red blood. I don't know what that means. Maybe they're taking some kind of drug, maybe a compound that gives them enhanced strength or something like that. Maybe they're men from Mars. I don't know. If I did know I'd call to tell you what's going on instead of calling to ask for help."

Top shifted fully into my line of sight and made a small patting gesture in the air, and it was only then that I heard, like an afterthought, the rising panic in my own voice. I took a breath, let it out slowly, nodded acknowledgement to him.

"We're collecting evidence now," I said more calmly, "and then there's a good chance we're going to find a bar and get drunk. And, no, that's not a true statement but can I get an amen from my team?"

"Amen," said Bunny under his breath. Top merely nodded.

"So, please get a forensics team rolling ASAP. It's raining on the scene and we don't have the right supplies to maintain integrity."

"I'll have a team there faster than the babysitter's boyfriend when the grown-ups drive away," promised Doc.

"And we still have to get to Washington," I said. "Auntie was heading to the Capitol Building to ambush some congressmen, and if she's still there I'll—"

"Well, damn," said Doc, "you haven't heard?"

"Heard what? Far as I know I've been nowhere for two hours. I think those men in black hit us with one of those flashy-forgetty things."

"Well, then . . . buckle up, Cowboy," Doc said, and told me about the dramatic suicide of the Speaker of the House. I exchanged a look with my guys.

"What's the bottom line?" I asked. "Are we thinking this is something else? A murder, or—?"

"So far, no," said Doc. "Local law's coordinating with the Secret Service and other agencies. The wheels are turning, but no one's talking about this being anything but a tragedy. But . . . Aunt Sallie was there. She saw it. D.J. thinks it really rattled her, too. Pretty horrible thing to see, though I expect she's seen worse, from what I've heard."

"I'll check her out when I get there," I said, "and give you an update."

Top leaned into the cab and nodded for me to mute the call. "You might as well go, Cap'n," he said. "The Farm Boy and me'll stay here and secure the scene until the techs get here. Take the Betty Boop and get on your way."

Bunny snorted. "Thought you weren't going to call it Betty Boop."

"Why don't you keep your mouth shut when grown folks is talking?"

Bunny flipped him the bird.

I unmuted Doc Holliday and put her on speaker. "Okay, I'm heading out now."

"You fit to drive?" she asked.

"Far as I know. Got some scratches and burns, but nothing major. But, listen, Doc . . . Church gave us a big speech about how outside the box you are when it comes to this kind of stuff. So, if you have any insights, maybe now might be a good time to start."

She gave that a beat. "Fair enough. Okay, what do we have? Green blood, MPP pistols, and missing time. That builds a certain kind of case. Tell me, Joe, did you see anything in the sky before you blanked out?"

"No . . ."

"Really? Because you don't sound like you're sure."

"I'm not sure," I admitted. "Actually, I'm nowhere near sure."

"Then do me a favor," said Doc. "Don't ask questions, just do it, okay?"

"Sure. Whatever. Call it."

"Close your eyes. Don't ask why, just do it." I sighed and closed my eyes and she immediately asked, "What color was the aircraft?"

"It was black," I said. And then stopped. I opened my eyes and looked at Top, then Bunny. They wore expressions of astonishment that were probably a mirror of my own. We all glanced up at the sky. "I never said we saw an aircraft."

"No," she giggled. "Now, sweet cheeks, tell me what shape it was."

I swallowed a lump the size of a regulation softball. "It was a triangle."

I heard her give a gasp of pure delight. "Well, jumping june bugs, boys, you got yourself a *gen-ewe-ine* T-craft. Now how about that?"

Top closed his eyes. "Son of a bitch."

INTERLUDE FIFTEEN

ROYAL PRINCE ALFRED HOSPITAL
CAMPERDOWN, AUSTRALIA
SIX YEARS AGO

Ari Kostas was in a coma for days, but gradually swam back to consciousness. Valen visited him every day, even when Ari was in a coma. He did not know why he did it, and wrestled with the questions through long bedside hours. He certainly did not like or trust Ari—the man was a psychopath and criminal devoid of any loyalties beyond his bankbook and his cock. And yet, Valen knew that if he were to sit down and make a list of his "friends," there would be a few names, but most would be lies.

Valen kept in touch with some friends from Russia—the few who had been educated by Gadyuka on how to communicate with the man now officially known as Valen Oruraka. The fact that they had known him by his birth name, Oleg Sokolov, was something they had to erase from their minds. Access to certain jobs and other perks greased this process. And the e-mails that went back and forth were mostly coded messages about various aspects of work for the New Soviet.

The truth was, he had no actual friends. The closest thing to that definition was Ari Kostas. That was an ugly, disfiguring truth. Sometimes, as Valen sat beside the comatose man, he wept. Passing nurses were touched by the depth of feeling this nice-looking young man had for his injured friend.

Gadyuka was back in Russia, and Valen was under orders to sit tight and wait for further instructions. She'd taken the crystal gun and the hand with her, and refused to discuss them with Valen. It left him torn and confused and lost.

One bad evening at the hospital, Valen took a notepad and actually wrote down the names of everyone he had killed. In cases where he didn't know the name, he assigned a unique nickname. When he got to eighteen names, he staggered to his feet and barely made it to the bathroom in time to throw up in the toilet. He washed his mouth out with handfuls of water, and then tore up the list and flushed the pieces. The following night he wrote the list again, this time adding the names of everyone who died at the dig site. And again the next night. Each time he flushed the ripped pieces away.

He closed his eyes as he sat beside Ari's bed, but there was no escape even in personal darkness. It took him straight back to his hotel suite with Gadyuka and the cooler and those four dreadful, impossible words.

Oh, God. They're back.

"Who are they?" he asked aloud. "Jesus Christ, who the hell are they?"

Gadyuka had refused to answer and quickly left, taking the gun and the hand with her.

"Valen . . . ," whispered a ghostly voice. His eyes snapped open to see Ari Kostas looking at him. Small, wasted, pale, and terrified.

CHAPTER FORTY-TWO

EN ROUTE IN MARYLAND

Ghost was happy enough to leave that freaky stretch of road, but he wasn't actually happy. I sure as hell wasn't laughing and singing all the way, either. My tension level dropped a small notch with every mile, but all that did was free my mind up to ask about ten million damn questions.

Like . . . T-craft? Holy shit. Far as I knew, all of those damn things had been reduced to rubble when the air force hit Howard Shelton's secret base with a whole wave of AGM-65H/K Maverick air-to-ground missiles. DMS teams tore the rubble apart to make sure everything Majestic 3 built was destroyed. It was. We made damn sure of that. And yet . . .

That's what had flown over the road in the microsecond before me and my guys blanked out. A T-craft. Now that I'd found that fragment of a memory, it was very clear and very real. However, I'd only gotten so brief a glimpse that I could never be sure if it was the Shelton model, the Chinese version that buzzed the Seventh Fleet, or one belonging to someone else. And by "someone else" I mean the holders of the original patent. My imagination kept trying to fill in the blanks, and I had to fight that. All I knew for sure was that it was big—maybe fifty feet per side, and perfectly triangular, with glowing white lights in each of its three symmetrical wings.

So, I had nowhere to go with that, but it opened up so many doors of speculation. Nothing coming through those doors made me a particularly happy guy. On one hand, if another country had managed to develop working T-craft, then we were back to the brink of another arms race, especially if they wanted to follow Shelton's insane plan of using them as suicide bombers. On the other hand, if that ship came from somewhere else—off-planet, say, or sideways through a hole in dimensional reality—then how seriously screwed were we? Rhetorical question. We were bent over a barrel and the universe was about to have its way with us.

So, who was in the ship we saw?

The Cop and Modern Man in my head kept spinning theories, but the Killer wasn't looking north or south, east or west. He was crouched in the tall grass watching the skies.

Green blood. Damn. I reached over to pet Ghost, telling myself *I* was comforting *him*. I lie to myself like that a lot. Ghost lets me.

INTERLUDE SIXTEEN

ROYAL PRINCE ALFRED HOSPITAL
CAMPERDOWN, AUSTRALIA
SIX YEARS AGO

"So, what are we talking about here," croaked Ari a few nights later. He was getting stronger, but not yet able to leave the hospital. "Little green men from outer space?"

Valen, worn and unshaven, shook his head. "I . . . don't know."

Ari snorted. "Don't give me that bullshit. You can lie to your scary little girlfriend, but I've known you too well and too long. You know something, don't you?"

"Know? No, I don't know. All I have are some theories, and some stuff I found on the Net, but before you tell me it's all bullshit, I—"

"Valen," said Ari in his raspy voice, "we found a lizard-man's hand in a rock wall and then a machine made out of half-a-million-year-old quartz blew us up. Not sure about you, my friend, but I find that I'm open to all sorts of possibilities."

Valen nodded. He went out into the hall and returned with two cold cans of Coke, opened them, and handed one to Ari. "Before all this," he said slowly, "I believed I knew the shape of the world. Since we found that damn gun and that double-damned machine, I've been reassessing a lot of my long-standing beliefs. Maybe we've been looking at this wrong, Ari. I'm beginning to wonder if my uncle was talking about doorways between here and somewhere else."

"Like where? Outer space?"

"No," said Valen. "Within the UFO and ancient alien communities there's one viewpoint that the distances between star systems is so great that it's improbable to suggest that aliens were able to cross those light-years to come to Earth. Why would they? If they were somehow able to see our world and recognize it as habitable or interesting enough to want to visit, by the time they actually arrived, the world they viewed would have changed. Even if they were relatively close, the distances are too great and there is no workable theory for exceeding the speed of light."

"Even if you build a big enough engine? Maybe that's what the green machine was, have you thought about that?"

"Not a chance, Ari. Particles that have mass require energy to accelerate them. The closer to the speed of light you get a particle, the more energy is required to go faster. This is because the particles themselves get more massive in proportion to the increased velocity."

"I have no idea what that means."

"It means that a spaceship can't fly faster than the speed of light, and the exoplanets we've discovered in what they call the 'Goldilocks Zone,' meaning the habitable zone for life as we know it, are too far away. The closest one is Proxima Centauri, which is four light-years away."

"That's close."

"No, it's not. Look, if you break a light-year down to smaller units, the distance between the Earth and our sun is eight light-minutes away. It would take our fastest spacecraft months to travel that distance. Now do the math on a light-year. There are over five hundred thousand light minutes in each year. Now multiply that by four, and that's just Proxima Centauri. Try to grasp how big space is."

Ari nodded. "Okay, okay, so it would take a long time."

"Centuries. Unless what people call aliens aren't coming from other planets."

"What's the alternative?"

"Look, Ari, maybe the artifacts we've found don't come from outer space but from there." He pointed to the wall.

Ari looked confused and then understanding blossomed in his eyes.

"Doors?" he asked in a hushed voice.

"Doors," agreed Valen.

CHAPTER FORTY-THREE

THE HOWELL RESIDENCE
ALDIE, VIRGINIA

When no one could reach the Speaker's wife by phone, text, or e-mail, Holly Bellmeyer, a senior aide from his office, had two local police officers meet her outside of the Howell residence. No one answered the bell. No one answered when they knocked, nor even when the police loudly announced that they were on the doorstep.

"No one's home," suggested one of the officers.

Bellmeyer went and peered in through the small windows on the garage door. "Mrs. Howell's car is still there. And her daughter's rental." She turned and pointed to a five-year-old Toyota parked in the shade under a maple tree. "That's the cleaning lady's car."

"Tony," said the older officer, "take a look at this."

"Whatcha got, Al?" asked Tony, hurrying over.

Officer Al Costas was kneeling to peer at the welcome mat. The mat was made from indoor-outdoor carpet and had a pattern of fluttering birds. There were various colored dots woven into the pattern, but a few of them were very dark and glistened as if wet.

His partner, Tony Shapley, slowed to a walk and stared.

"Oh, God," said Bellmeyer, taking a half step back. "Is that . . . ?"

She didn't finish the statement. The looks on the officers' faces gave her the answer. Tony called it in, explaining that they had found what appeared to be bloodstains, and about the cars. He was advised to determine the status of the Speaker's family.

The officers verified that their body cameras were on, then made Bellmeyer go stand behind their cruiser. They hammered on the door again and got the same empty response. Careful not to smudge any prints, Al tried the handle and found that it turned. The door wasn't locked and it swung inward with an illusion of quiet invitation.

The officers stepped inside.

"Holy mother of God," murmured Tony.

What they found was unspeakable. The bodycams recorded it all. The lake of blood that covered the expensive tiled floor and soaked the imported area rugs. The ragged islands that rose, large and small, throughout that crimson expanse. A piece of shoulder. A hand. Legs. Heads arranged in a row on the couch, with mouths opened as if screaming.

Screaming.

Screaming.

Without sound.

Above the heads, above the couch, painted in sloppy letters across the living room wall, were two words. Analysis would later show that the letters were written in mingled blood from all of the victims. The message was:

DEEP SILENCE

CHAPTER FORTY-FOUR

BALTIMORE—WASHINGTON PARKWAY
MARYLAND

Church finally called me, and the first thing he said to me was, "Can you confirm that the men who attacked you were Closers?"

Not "Hey, Joe, you okay?" Not "Sorry you had such a shitty day." No. Not him. If I had a crowbar stuck through my head he wouldn't even express sympathy that my favorite Orioles cap would no longer fit. Mr. Warmth he is not.

"They were dressed in black suits," I said, "wore some kind of bullet-resistant body armor under their clothes, they shot at us with MMPs, and I'm pretty sure their escape car was a T-craft. So, on the whole . . . ? Yeah, there was a pretty good chance they were freaking Closers."

He was quiet for a moment. "And the green blood . . . ?"

"Was blood."

"How sure are you?"

"Pretty damn."

"Then go over it from the beginning. Omit no detail."

His coldness and precision, and the demands those placed on his subordinates, often had a specific effect. You don't want to disappoint Church. You want his approval, because that approval means something. He isn't just our boss, he's the kind of person whose personal standards are so high that his evaluation of you often helps define you. I know, that sounds a little needy on my part, but it's not. He's been in the fight longer than I have, and probably longer than I've been alive. He's won the fights he's been in, and the fact that the world still has its wheels on the rails has a lot to do with his being there to set things right. Do I exaggerate? No. I really don't.

So, as I drove, I went over it all. Everything since Top picked up the follow car. Church listened without comment until I was done. Then he made me go over certain portions of it again, focusing on the things the agents said, to how they said them.

"Bug accessed the Calpurnia-MindReader Q1 substation in your vehicle, Captain," he said. "The onboard cameras and mics did not record the incident. Apparently, from the moment the follow car crossed your spike net all onboard surveillance and telemetric systems in your car blanked out. We lost the signals from the drones, too."

The drizzle had slowed to random spitting, so I adjusted the wipers to intermittent as I headed toward Washington.

"What kind of jammer can knock out everything including Calpurnia and the link to MindReader?"

"If there's something on the market like that, Captain, let me know and I'll buy out their warehouse. However, I seriously doubt we're going to be able to order it from anyone's catalog."

Traffic was heavy and it slowed to a crawl. That was fine.

"Meaning?" I asked.

"Let me ask this first," Church said. "Is it your professional opinion that the agents you dealt with at the cemetery and at Sellers Mansion were the same kind of Closers you encountered on the road?"

I had been expecting that question.

"No," I said. "I thought so at first, but now . . . ? No. They were completely different."

"Do you believe these Closers were working toward the same goal as the Secret Service agents?"

"Hunh," I said, and thought about it, trying to play it all back in widescreen and high definition. "They both tried to arrest me and—"

"Did they, Captain?" interrupted Church. "Did they say or do anything to validate that assumption? Can you say with certainty that this was an attempt to arrest you?"

I tried not to wince because Ghost was watching and I didn't want him to lose confidence in the basic intelligence of his pack leader. That was already shaky ground.

"No," I said.

"Tell me the difference," said Church, as pedantic as a patient schoolteacher.

It was a measure of how rattled I was that I needed him to do this. Doc Holliday had done her trick with visualizing the T-craft, but this was a step deeper. Inside my head, the Cop squared his shoulders, cleared his throat, and came back to work.

"They identified our vehicle and followed at a practical distance," I said slowly. "They didn't attempt to close on us until we made it clear we were aware of them and attempting to elude. Calpurnia established that they were driving a government car obtained through illegal means using sophisticated computer hacking."

"*Ultra*sophisticated," corrected Church. "Bug has been studying the hack of the motor pool servers and he says that whoever did it used superior skills."

"Superior to his?"

"He wouldn't admit to that under torture, but yes."

"Boss," I said, "we're talking about details here, but I think there's a conversation neither of us wants to have."

"Agreed."

"Are these the same—what's the word? Aliens? Beings? E.T.s?—who made us give them the Majestic Black Book?"

"We have to consider that possibility," he conceded. "Just as we have to consider that the Majestic program is not as dead as we thought."

"We pretty much drove a stake through its heart."

"We've been wrong before, Captain."

We talked for a few minutes longer, but it was clear to both of us that we didn't have enough information. For now. He said he was going to make sure all of the right wheels were in motion.

Before he signed off, he said something off-topic. "I appreciate your going to D.C. to see to Aunt Sallie. She won't like you for it, but you have my gratitude."

"She's family," I said.

"Yes," said Church, "and it may amuse you to know that she said the same about you."

The line went dead as I crossed into the nation's capital.

INTERLUDE SEVENTEEN

MOTU RAUORO ISLAND, SOCIETY ISLANDS
FRENCH POLYNESIA
FOUR YEARS AGO

The lab did not look like a lab. It looked like a hedonistic retreat for people with too much money and too few clothes. That's how Valen saw it.

However, there were no greased tourists sprawled on the sugar-white beaches. There were no bikini women or Speedo men romping in the blue-green perfection of the water. Not a single drink with a paper umbrella to be seen.

Valen stood with Ari, who leaned heavily on a cane, watching as a silent army of men sweated and grunted as they unloaded crate after crate of equipment. Stone-faced and flint-hearted sentries with automatic weapons stood in the shelter of camouflaged tarps. Another group—men and women in white lab coats—milled like ants, going in and out of a row of Quonset huts built beneath half an acre of netting.

Ari leaned close. "You must be a wizard in the sheets, brother."

"What?"

"This must be costing millions. Tens of millions. You must have screwed Gadyuka's brains loose to fund all of this. She gave us everything we asked for. The high-tech lab, the security systems. All of it."

"Believe me, Ari," said Valen, "the fact that I'm sleeping with her had nothing to do with this. After she saw the gun and that hand, she couldn't get her checkbook out fast enough."

"And she said 'They're back'? But didn't tell you what she meant by that?"

"No. She tried to laugh it off, tried to say I misheard her because of my hearing aid."

They watched as crate after crate of equipment was carried up the beach.

"Look, man," said Ari, "what the hell are we into here?" Since the explosion of the green machine, the Greek was much less bombastic and arrogant. He merely looked scared and uncertain. "We are so far into the dark with this shit even I don't know what we're trying to accomplish. Do they want us to figure out who or what left that hand behind? Do they want to use those crystals for something? Or is it the machine? Do they want to blow themselves up? She gives us all this money, hires all these people, spends years sending us around the world to find green stones and ancient books, and I mean, what the actual fuck is the point?"

"All of it."

Valen took a pack of cigarettes from his pocket and lit one. He was aware of how badly his hands shook these days.

"Since when do you smoke?" asked Ari.

"Since when do you wear a religious medal?"

Ari's hand reflexively touched the small gold likeness of Saint Nicholas that had the words "Pray For Us" engraved below it.

"You didn't answer my question, brother," he said. "What does Gadyuka want?"

"She wants what happened at the dig site. She wants us to figure out the science."

Ari laughed, then gaped. "Wait, you're *serious*? Is she out of her mind? That was a fucking accident. A side effect. I nearly died, for Christ's sake. Who in the fuck would want that? Why?"

Valen took a long drag and let the smoke leak out of his nostrils.

"She wants the earthquakes."

CHAPTER FORTY-FIVE

THE CAPITOL BUILDING
WASHINGTON, D.C.

There was nowhere to park anywhere near the Capitol Building, even when I flashed my very realistic but totally fake DHS identification. The place was already ass-deep in actual guys from Homeland, as well as every other agency that has badges and buys off-the-rack dark suits. So, I parked about four blocks away and hoofed it, with Ghost trotting dutifully by my side wearing an official-looking vest.

Once inside, I saw Aunt Sallie and D.J. standing in the back, leaning against the wall, and I immediately understood why D.J. had called me. I did a quick calculation of how long since I'd last seen her. Eight months? Could it really be that long? It jolted me to see how that amount of time had changed her. Aunt Sallie was heavier, with a more pronounced osteoarthritic hump to her back, and skin that hung in loose folds. I always figured her for late sixties, but if I didn't know her I would have pegged her as mideighties. She looked like a frail old woman. That scared me. I may not like Aunt Sallie, but I admired the living hell out of her. She was one of those legendary agents whose reality exceeded even the wild tales people told.

D.J. saw me and bent to whisper in her ear. Her head shot up and swiveled toward me, and even though her body was sickly, the eyes she fixed on me glowed with nuclear heat.

"What in the living hell are you doing here, you jackass?" she growled as I approached. "I'm here trying to keep your sorry white ass out of jail and you come strolling in, bold as brass?"

"Nice to see you, too, Auntie," I said, dialing up the wattage on my smile. I shook hands with D.J. but did not want to risk amputation and so did not offer my hand to Aunt Sallie. Ghost wagged his tail at her and her scowl softened by maybe one-millionth of a degree.

All around us were huge crowds of people who did not seem willing or able to respect the police demands to clear the room. The space around the spot where the Speaker of the House died was clear of rubberneckers, though. Instead, a bunch of forensic technicians were scouring every single inch of each table, chair, and the various items particular to the House of Representatives. I recognized the faces of several congressmen, including senators, clustered together in worried knots. I felt like making a snide comment about how those clusters were composed of members of both parties, but it didn't seem to be the time for jokes. In the moment, having witnessed a horror that was on a human level, they were just being frightened, confused, sickened people.

"Why are you here?" she demanded again.

All the way here I'd been rehearsing how to answer that question. Came up with a few good ones, too, but when I looked in Auntie's wise, fierce old eyes, I knew that the truth was my only play. Dangerous as that was.

"I'm here to take you back home," I said.

"Why?" She wasn't going to make it easy for me, and I could see something flicker in her eyes. A kind of fear? The specter of mortality? Sounds dramatic, but it wasn't—it was merely sad.

"Because no one who cares about you wants you to die," I said. "Because as much as I appreciate you coming down here to try and save my neck, it's not worth you making yourself sick over it. Not on my account."

"This ain't about you, sonny boy," she snapped. "This is about the DMS not getting pissed on."

"Shakes out to the same thing," I said. "The White House has it in for us, and they came after me to make a point. We've got lawyers, Auntie. Good ones. Literally the best that money can buy. Let them rack up billable hours with this. Big Tobacco and Big Pharma aren't the only ones who can play that game. Let the sharks be sharks and let's us get the hell out of here. Neither of us needs to get shit on our shoes."

D.J. edged a little closer to Aunt Sallie. "Joe has a point, Auntie. You rattled some cages. You made your point. Let's go home."

He and I were both braced for a tirade, maybe for actual physical violence. And, sick as she was, I didn't like our odds if she made a fight of this.

But then something happened that truly broke my heart.

I saw two tears grow into jewels in the corners of her eyes and then fall down her brown cheeks. She slumped against a pillar and I swear to God I could see the fight go out of her. It was like watching a ghost leave a body. It was at that moment that Aunt Sallie realized that she had no fight left in her. That the war had passed her by and she was no longer able to take up her sword and shield. It was one of the saddest things I've ever seen. I wanted to hug her. Not kidding. I wanted to take her in my arms and tell her how much I admired her, how much I . . .

Loved her?

Yeah.

Fuck. That's where I was going.

And thinking that opened up a door of insight inside my head. When I first met her I'd been scouted by Church to be the new top gunslinger for the DMS. I represented the power and potential that used to be hers. And it meant that if I was this year's model, then she was past her use-by date. Being the one who sends other fighters into battle is mighty damn hard on the soldiers who used to be on the front line. She knew it at that first moment, and she hated me for being what she no longer could be.

When I held out my hands to her, I could see that Aunt Sallie knew I knew it. That I understood. There was a moment, a flicker of a smile that held no animosity, no resentment. It was a smile shared from one soldier to another. Accepting the reality, acknowledging that the war was bigger than either of us, than all of us, and sometimes we best serve by stepping out of the way so the shooter behind us can take better aim. It also said that we both knew my day would come, as it inevitably does for all warriors. The war was the war, and in the grand scheme of things, we were day players in an endless drama.

But then Aunt Sallie slapped my hand away, screwed on a familiar scowl, and said, "I can walk on my own two legs, damn it."

She marched past me and I stood for a moment, watching her. At that moment I would have walked through fire for her. Maybe that was always true.

INTERLUDE EIGHTEEN

MOTU RAUORO ISLAND, SOCIETY ISLANDS
FRENCH POLYNESIA
THREE YEARS AGO

Valen stood in the open doorway to Ari's cottage. He held a flashlight in one hand and a pistol in the other.

The room was a wreck. The lamp overturned, bulb smashed; the laptop stomped into useless debris; the bed soaked with blood.

And the girl.

"Ari," breathed Valen, "what have you done?"

Ari Kostas knelt naked on the floor. His thighs and cock were smeared with blood and his hands were so thoroughly drenched they looked like red gloves. It was clear Ari had been masturbating there, using the girl's blood as a lubricant.

"Leave me alone," snarled the burly Greek. "Get the fuck out. Can't a man have some privacy?"

Drool hung from his lower lip and there was a cocaine glaze in his eyes. Empty bottles of wine and vodka were everywhere.

And the girl.

The girl.

The things he had done to her.

Worse this time than before. Worse than back in college. Worse than the secretary four months ago. At least she had died whole.

"What have you done?" whispered Valen, stepping inside and closing the door so that no one in the camp could see.

"Go away, you fucker," growled Ari. "Go away. I'm not done here."

"Not . . . done . . . ? Ari, what in God's name are you talking about?"

"God?" Ari spat on the floor between them. There was red in the spittle. "You don't believe in God. Not in my God or any god. You fucking Communist atheist prick. You don't believe in anything."

Valen came and crouched down in front of Ari. The man stunk of booze, sex, blood, and piss. Valen took him by the shoulders and shook him. "Ari . . . Ari . . . listen to me, you idiot. This girl isn't some college bimbo to use and throw away. She's part of our team. People will know she was in here. Are you out of your mind?"

Ari grinned at him.

"Of course I'm out of my mind. We all are, Valen. The world is mad." He began to laugh. A hitch-pitched cackle like a witch from some old production of *Macbeth*.

Valen slapped him across the face. Hard. It rocked Ari so violently that the Greek fell onto his side. Valen grabbed him by the hair and jerked him back onto his knees and struck him again. And again.

And again.

He could not stop hitting him.

Valen became suddenly and acutely aware that he could not stop hitting Ari. His hand moved as if it no longer belonged to him. The blows came harder and harder. So hard Valen felt the muscles in his hand bruising and tearing. He felt a bone break in his hand. One of the carpals. The pain was explosive but he could not stop. Ari's head rocked back and sideways and up and down with the erratic angles of the blows. His nose disintegrated into red pulp, his eyebrows split, his lips tore against his teeth. Two big caps broke from his gums and flew over Valen's shoulder. Ari vomited and still Valen hit him.

Outside, in the camp, Dr. Marguerite Beaufort stood in her own cabin. The door was locked and her iPad was running through her playlist of Puccini arias. Marguerite took great care in laying out all of her many combs and brushes, making sure they were in a perfectly straight line, like cutlery on a dining table of a great manor house. When she was satisfied, she picked up the large hand mirror, considered her reflection, turning this way and that to study her complexion, the orientation of her freckles, the way in which her blond hair accentuated her cheekbones.

"Beautiful," she told the face in the mirror. Then she began humming along to the aria. "Vissi d'arte," from *Tosca*. She listened to the words, able to understand the Italian. Floria Tosca sings about how she and her lover were at the mercy of the vile Baron Scarpia. Tosca begs God to tell her why He has abandoned her. Sad as the song was, its beauty always made her smile.

Marguerite was still smiling and humming when she shattered the mirror against the edge of her bureau, selected the largest piece, and began cutting her wrists.

In the security booth, the senior guard was removing bullets from a magazine and lining them up on the counter. Then he reloaded the magazine and slapped it into place. Then removed and unloaded it again. Over and over again.

In the largest of the Quonset huts used for the team's work, the machine crouched on its reinforced table. There were six staff members in the hut. A bottle of champagne lay smashed where it had fallen. Each of them had taken a swig to celebrate the completion of the machine. They had followed every instruction to the letter, making sure that all of the settings on the device were at their lowest. No one wanted another earthquake. No one wanted another explosion. The thing was barely even on.

Two of the lab techs copulated with brutal frenzy on the floor. The woman was on top, and with each buck of the man's hips she punched him in the chest, or stomach, or face. Which made him thrust harder. Both of them were bleeding. If their eyes saw anything, it was nothing in that room.

Three other techs were on the floor, crawling toward the wall, which was smeared with blood and bits of scalp. None was able to run headlong into the wall anymore. All they could do now was crawl toward it over and over again. Strike their foreheads. Fall back. Reorient themselves. Repeat.

The last of the techs stood by the table and stared at the glowing crystal machine, his face bathed in the green light. He did not see the machine at all. Or anything in that room. Instead he saw a vast creature that only vaguely looked like a human. It had arms, legs, and a torso, but all other similarities failed into obscenity. Its head was as bulbous as an octopus's, and dozens of small tentacles hung like a beard from its gash of a mouth. The thing stood on a mountain slope that ran down to a beach that ran for miles and against which lapped the waters of a nameless ocean. Smaller creatures writhed and squirmed in the froth, and scuttling things ran along the gray sands. The tentacled monster dominated them all, rising impossibly high, immeasurably vast and powerful. Wings, stunted and leathery and ugly, spread out from its back, but were too small to lift the ponderous bulk. The monster turned toward the tech, as if able to see from its world to this one. It threw back its head and laughed. If laughter it was. The sound was like thunder and instantly all thought, all interior sound in the tech's head was blasted to utter silence. Not even the whisper of a thought remained; only the awareness of their total absence. The room around him went equally silent. As did the world; and that silence was bottomless.

The technician screamed—a sound even he could not hear.

The other five in the room could not hear it either.

If anyone could, the scream would have sounded unlike any scream but rather a prayer shouted in a language never spoken by a people living on our world. The words were utterly meaningless on this side of the wall separating the machine and the monster.

"Ph'nglui mglw'nafh Cthulhu R'lyeh wgah'nagl fhtagn!" he shrieked.

And although the technicians in the lab could not hear him with their ears, they nevertheless responded, screaming out in one unified voice.

"Tekeli-li! Tekeli-li!"

CHAPTER FORTY-SIX

THE CAPITOL BUILDING
WASHINGTON, D.C.

Secret Service Agent Marilyn Kang was assigned the task of liaising with the local police who were investigating the death of the Speaker of the House. She was tasked with observing everything, documenting the scene, and taking notes so that the Service could provide their own information to the administration and the senior members of Congress. It was a tedious job, and there were other investigative bodies involved in doing essentially the same thing.

Kang did not mind the tedium, though. She had been on shore patrol in the navy and had accompanied investigators on dozens of crime scenes. She'd also helped with gathering details following suicides of active military. That experience was what helped her get hired by the Service and be picked for this assignment. She was patient, alert, intuitive, and thorough. Several times she made useful suggestions to the police, which were accepted with varying degrees of good or bad grace.

When it came time to process all of the evidence, she took photos of every item placed into the sterile bags, and kept a copy of her own evidence log. Later her bosses would want to match it against the one kept by the police.

The fountain pen that the Speaker had used to stab himself in the eye lay on the floor in a pool of blood. After stabbing himself with it, the Speaker had been clutching the instrument in his hand, and it was torn free when he fell. It landed on the floor, shattering the green crystal into a dozen little chunks. The forensic evidence collectors had taken the pen and the larger chunks, but there were still some left, standing like tiny islands in small lakes of drying blood. An orange evidence marker cone stood beside the blood and the green chips. The number on that cone was nine.

Kang looked at the cone and kept hearing the Beatles song "Revolution 9." John Lennon's voice droned "Number nine, number nine, number nine," and it echoed through her head.

The pieces of crystal were small, and most were completely covered by blood, but the bits that weren't seemed to glow with an inner light. Had that been the case all along? she wondered. Or was it a reflection from the panel of ultrabright LEDs the police had erected to help the forensics team? She wasn't sure, but she began to have the impression that it was the stones themselves. Lit from within.

Suddenly one of the chips, the largest piece, seemed to move all by itself. And the small pool of blood around it rippled. Kang flinched.

Number nine, number nine, number nine.

That kept playing in her mind despite what was happening on the floor.

Someone somewhere off to one side said, "Holy shit."

It surprised her because no one else was close enough to see the chip. Well, chips, because now they were all trembling. Shivering. And there were tidy, sluggish ripples in the viscous blood.

Then another voice, equally distant, said, "What the hell's going on?"

Kang didn't look at them. They were far away. At the other end of the room, or down a hall, or maybe up in the air. She didn't know and didn't care.

Number nine, number nine, number nine.

The chips were all moving, turning in place like the hands of tiny clocks. Not fast. But turning. They seemed to vibrate, to dance.

Number nine, number nine, number nine.

"Everyone get out," yelled a voice. "Get into the doorways. That's where it's safe."

Something fell over and broke. Someone screamed. Kang did not look. She was absolutely fascinated by the chips. The green crystal fragments were so pretty and they seemed to want her to bend closer, to listen, to know something.

"Agent Kang," yelled a voice. "Come on—move! We have to get—"

She stopped listening as surely as if there was a mute switch in her mind that she was able to locate and flip.

Number nine, number nine, number nine.

She began reaching for the closest chip.

"What the hell are you doing?" yelled another voice. Or maybe the same voice. Kang neither knew nor cared. "Don't bother with that stuff. We need to get out of here."

Number nine, number nine, number nine.

The words were muted and made no real sense to her. It was as if whoever was speaking was underwater.

Then a hand grabbed her, caught her by the arm, pulled her back, spun her. She stared into the face of a man in a police uniform. He was screaming at her. She could feel the heat of his breath. She could feel spit on her face. His eyes were wide with panic.

"It's okay," she said.

Then the man's face seemed to blossom like a red flower. No. It came apart like a rose in a windstorm. Red petals flew everywhere. Something—was it a body?—fell backward and down. Dropping out of her awareness.

Number nine, number nine, number nine.

Marilyn Kang did not look at the gun in her hand. She did not feel the recoil as she fired the shot into the face of the police evidence collection technician. She did not feel any of the shots she fired. She did not hear the bangs or the screams. Or anything. Except for the song lyric repeating in her head, there was nothing at all, no sound. The silence gaped around her, vast and deep. Bottomless.

Number nine, number nine, number nine.

She thought about the lovely green crystal chips.

"So pretty," she said.

She was unaware of the slide locking back on her gun. She did not feel her hands move as they ejected the spent magazine and slapped in a new one. None of that was part of who she was or where she was or what she saw or what was happening.

Number nine, number nine, number nine.

When she killed the people crouching in the doorway as pieces of debris fell from the ceiling, Kang saw none of it. When she walked into the hall and began firing at screaming staff members, it was all happening to someone else in some other place.

She never heard the ceiling above her crack.

All she could see were the crystal chips. They seemed to rise into the air on tiny red wings as they soared toward . . .

Toward what?

Where?

They didn't fly through stone halls or inside a building at all. What Kang saw was an opening in the whole world, and beyond . . .

A rocky slope edged by plants and flowers of extraordinary beauty. Ferns towered a hundred feet above her, and there was a rose growing up from a crack in the ground; at the end of each stem three bright red flowers spread their petals. Far above her, at the top of the slope, was a slender tower made from red stones. Behind the top of the tower was the moon. One of the moons. There were many others hanging in the sky like pale balloons. Triangular-shaped craft shot past at incredible speeds. And in the distance, there was a vast and terrible thing. Beautiful in its way, like a giant or a god. An impossibly large body that was vaguely human but which had a head like a giant octopus and a beard made entirely of writhing tentacles. Long, dark wings unfolded from its broad back and it reached for her with a scaly hand tipped with claws as long as—

Sixty pounds of plaster and stone from the ceiling struck her on the crown of her head, crushing all thoughts from Marilyn Kang's mind.

CHAPTER FORTY-SEVEN

THE CAPITOL BUILDING
WASHINGTON, D.C.

The earthquake hit the Capitol Building with the fists of giants.

D.J., Aunt Sallie, and I were on the steps outside, and we could all tell right away that this was no tremor. This was a monster waking up beneath our feet. Ghost crouched down, barking furiously. The whole world seemed to suddenly go out of focus, because every wall, every street pole, every parked car began to vibrate at the same time. It was surreal in the worst possible way.

Auntie twisted as the steps beneath her feet cracked, and she spun, arms reaching for D.J., but he was toppling backward. I lunged forward and caught her. She was a heavy woman, too much fat over her muscle, and I was falling, too. I spun with her in my arms, tucked my head, and took the impact across my hip and shoulders. It was like getting simultaneously kicked in the lower back while being hit across the upper back with a two-by-four. Auntie cried out in pain as she landed atop me.

She rolled off and I could see that despite my best efforts, she'd struck her shins against the edge of the stone step. Intense pain shot through my hip and spine, telling me that I was more badly hurt than I thought. I ground my teeth and fought my way to my knees. All around me people were screaming and running, and I stared in abject horror as a deep black crack opened like a mouth right in front of where I knelt. A police car canted sideways into it. Gas and water shot upward from different parts of the torn street. The growl of the tortured earth was a horrible, deafening thing. The earthquake was intensifying. People ran, collided, fell. Some vanished into the cracks that fed on them.

"D.J.," I yelled as I fought my way through pain and lights that burst in my eyes to where Auntie lay, "help me."

When he didn't answer I turned to see if he was okay. He was. But he stood stock-still, not looking at Aunt Sallie or me. Or anything. His eyes were as empty as a store mannequin's and his lips hung rubbery and slack. Ghost began growling at him, baring his titanium teeth, no longer recognizing D.J. as one of us. Turning on him the way he'd nearly turned on me last night at the Warehouse.

I heard Auntie speak, her confusion more evident than her pain. "D.J. . . . ?"

D.J. turned to her and smiled.

Then he drew his sidearm in a smooth movement that was all reflex, the kind of thing agents are trained to do. His hand brushed his jacket flap back, reached up to the Sig Sauer he wore in a nylon shoulder holster, drew it, pressed the barrel under his chin, and pulled the trigger. The bullet blew off the top of his head and blew one eye out of its socket and blew all the sanity out of the day.

Aunt Sallie screamed. Ghost yelped. I gaped at the body of my friend as he fell like a boneless rag doll.

The world shook itself to pieces around us. People screamed as they ran. Auntie and I looked around, trying to find some answer to what had just happened. There were none. The world was not going to help us out of this. No. Because everywhere we looked we saw madness.

People running.

People standing still as if they had turned to stone.

People *attacking* each other. Beating, biting, tearing at clothes and skin and hair and eyes. Two police officers stood twenty feet apart and shot each other over and over until they both fell dead.

A woman picked up her infant child and threw her into the closest crack. Then, with a shriek, leaped in after her. They both vanished from sight. A man in a business suit was slowly undressing, folding each garment and placing them on the rattling ground. When he was naked he sat down and began punching himself in the face with slow, hard, measured blows. A pair of Secret Service agents were trying to break up a fight between reporters and civilians. Finally, one of the agents staggered back, his face streaming with blood, drew his gun, and fired. He aimed every single shot at a fireplug, hitting it every time.

A fat woman went running past us, screaming at the top of her lungs. She said, "Why can't I hear my own head?" Those words, clear and loud, over and over again.

A young woman was fighting with a much larger man who was trying to grab an older woman. The young woman seemed quite sane and was fighting well, obviously having had a little karate training. The old woman was one of the silent and unmoving ones. The big man was much stronger, but he seemed to have forgotten everything about how to fight.

Most of the people in the street still looked sane, but they were terrified and ran with blind panic away from toppling walls and exploding streets and from those who had gone insane. I heard more gunshots and glass shattering and gas hissing. Suddenly a car burst into flame and half a dozen news reporters flung themselves into the blaze. They all screamed as they burned, but there were words twisted into the screams.

And, because this is the fucked-up twenty-first century, some of them stood there with their cell phones, recording it all. For what? Their Facebook pages? Snapchat or Instagram?

"Quiet! Quiet! Quiet!" shrieked a cameraman near us as he clapped his hands violently in front of his face.

"Can't you fucking hear me?" demanded a blond reporter I recognized from a cable station. "Can't you fucking hear me?"

The earthquake tore through Washington, and pieces of stone crashed down around us. I forced myself to move, grabbed Auntie, and dragged her away from the building. We clung together as we staggered down the juddering stairs and then there was a massive sound and we turned to see three of the massive marble columns crack and break apart. They toppled over us and crashed on the lower steps, forcing us back.

"Silence!" shouted a man in a bloody sweatshirt. He pointed at Aunt Sallie. "Silence! Silence! Silence!"

And then he ran forward, howling like a demon, slashing at the air with his fingers. Other people followed, screaming equally meaningless things. I forced myself up, put myself in their path. There were at least a dozen of them. None of them were armed. None of them looked sane as they rushed forward, seeming to focus on the sick woman lying behind me. The Killer in me seemed to understand it. She was hurt, weak, vulnerable, and they were acting on an instinct deep in the lizard brain. Some of them even snapped their jaws as if promising what they wanted to do.

They were civilians, sure. They were also a mob. They were coming for one of mine. For a member of my family.

The Cop, the Modern Man, and the Killer all stood up inside of me. Shoulder to shoulder for the first time I could ever remember. In a twisted way they were all my family, which made them all family with Aunt Sallie.

I almost drew my gun. *Almost*. And I almost drew the rapid-release folding knife clipped to the inside of my trouser pocket. With either of those I could have killed the whole bunch of the people.

Could have.

Didn't.

Maybe after I'd first joined the DMS I'd have reacted differently. Killed more easily, made assumptions that this was a plague like Seif al Din. Part of me even wondered if this was the genetically engineered rabies we'd encountered during the Dogs of War affair last year. But for once I think the Modern Man in my head won out. He, of all of us, knew that this wasn't anything I'd ever faced before. He begged for mercy.

Mercy, though, is relative.

This whole thought process took maybe a tenth of a second, and then the man with the bloody sweatshirt reached for Aunt Sallie.

And all of the broken parts of me went to war.

CHAPTER FORTY-EIGHT

THE WHITE HOUSE
WASHINGTON, D.C.

Jennifer VanOwen was stepping out of the elevator when she felt the tremor ripple up through her leg muscles. It was not fierce, not frightening. If anything it felt rather nice. Like the higher jets in a Jacuzzi. Even so, she frowned.

People up and down the hall stopped and looked around. After last night's rumbles they had to know what this was, and yet they all had that deer-in-the-headlights look. VanOwen found it equal parts amusing and disappointing. She worked with these people; they could at least pretend to be intelligent.

The rumbling ended and there was a moment of silent stillness, after which some people laughed. Some began telling each other what had just happened. While still others whispered as if speaking in a normal voice would invoke and anger the gods of the earth. VanOwen pasted on a mildly concerned half smile and made her way to her office. Her assistant was jabbering in the hall with one of the junior assistants to some nobody from the next floor. VanOwen locked herself in, ran a scanner over the walls to make sure there were no bugs. There never were. Then she settled in her chair and used her cell to make a call, waiting through eight rings until it was answered.

"Why are you calling early?" asked the voice on the other end.

"I wanted to get something straight between us," said VanOwen.

A pause. "Okay."

"You'd better be right about this," said VanOwen.

"About which part?"

"Don't screw with me. I'm warning you, and you had better listen."

"I am listening."

"If I get killed today, then lawyers you don't know about are going to open documents that are going to make life very damn ugly for you. Don't even think I'm joking."

The second pause was much longer. "Just do your job, Jennifer. Let us do ours."

The line went dead.

CHAPTER FORTY-NINE

WASHINGTON, D.C.

There had been earthquakes in the nation's capital before. In 2011 an interpolate quake with a magnitude of 5.8 rocked the region and was one of the largest of its kind east of the Rocky Mountains. That quake was felt across more than a dozen states and even up into parts of Canada. It was estimated that the quake was felt by more people than any other quake in United States history, owing to the dense East Coast population. That event did a lot of damage, but none of the damage was individually very intense. Cracked walls, broken windows, street disruption. The price tag was hefty, though, costing insurance companies, businesses, and individuals nearly three hundred million dollars. No one died, and there were very few injuries.

That was 2011.

That was not today.

The epicenter of the quake that struck Washington, D.C., on that February morning was within blocks of the Capitol Building. At its peak, it rocked the region as a monstrous 7.8.

Five hundred thousand car alarms went off almost at once. It was as if all the banshees in the world had gathered for a convention and were trying to outdo each other in tearing the air apart.

Building alarms jangled, too. Then police cars, fire engines, and ambulances screamed their way through the writhing streets. And, almost as an afterthought, alert sirens began caterwauling.

The Washington Monument did not collapse, but massive chunks of it broke off and fell. The very first fatalities in the disaster were three teenagers who stood in its shadow, ignoring the massive spike in favor of the texts they were sending about the fact that there was an earthquake. They were part of a group of tourists from San Jose. Earthquakes were nothing to them. Until this one became everything.

They never heard the screams of their teacher, who was four feet away and did not get a scratch on her skin. Her heart and mind, though, were deeply and irrevocably scarred.

Two police cars collided at the intersection where New York Avenue Northwest crosses Thirteenth Street. Both patrol cars were tearing along with lights flashing and sirens wailing and buildings shivering themselves apart on both sides of the street. When the National Museum of Women in the Arts building collapsed, it shot a huge cloud of dust and debris into the intersection at exactly the wrong moment. The two cars punched into the cloud from opposite sides. Visibility was three feet in front of the windshields. They never saw each other until after they collided. Airbags and seat belts can only do so much, and they had not been designed for this.

Not for this.

Zach Jonas was doing a standup on the steps of the Capitol Building, updating the reports he had been filing all day. His tie was askew because his producer thought that looked good. In fact, before each new segment the producer messed his hair a little more, jerked the tie a little this way or that, and had the makeup woman touch him up to look more flushed, suggesting urgency and passionate involvement. Zach figured that he'd have been in shirtsleeves if it wasn't so damn cold, and the producer absolutely would not let him shoot while wearing his parka. He could snug into it for a few minutes at a time, gulping coffee to keep the wind from leeching the last bits of warmth from him, but then the producer was badgering him to take it off and get ready.

Get ready.

That was always the thing. Prior to the last couple of years, nothing in Washington ever happened fast. For a while the network could have put a cardboard cutout of him on the steps without affecting the ratings. That ship sailed, hit an iceberg, caught fire, and sank. Now, instead of having to pad the twenty-four-hour news cycle, there was no damn way to keep up with all of the shit that rained down here every hour or every day. It was Zach's personal opinion that everyone currently holding office in modern politics was certifiably insane. Didn't matter which party. Didn't matter what their job. They were, collectively, a basket of rabid hamsters.

The producer loved that because of the ratings. Zach figured that somewhere in all of that was his first Pulitzer. Oh hell yes.

So, he didn't complain about the cold or the stage managing of his gradual dishevelment. That was the same process Anderson Cooper used during Hurricane Katrina, and that worked out.

No, Zach was good with it, and he waited for the cameraman to adjust the lighting and the producer to give him a nod.

"The story here in the nation's capital continues to unfold," began Zach, "with shocking and tragic new elements being uncovered following the discovery of—"

And then the first shock wave hit.

The first tremblers had been in Virginia, but the real shock punched its way out of the ground before the news of that reached D.C. No one knew it was coming. It did not start small and build. It happened very fast and very big, and lines of force shot along the avenues, up the sides of buildings, across fields, and collectively stabbed the city through the heart.

Suddenly people were running and screaming and . . . fighting?

Zach stared in dumb horror as the crowds all around him erupted into a mad brawl. The logical part of his mind tried to choreograph it, trying to turn what he saw into a saner flight to safety from the devastation. That worked, too, for maybe three seconds. But the truth won out, even though the truth made no sense of any kind.

People were fighting. Screaming. Smashing their own faces against cars and biting each other and swinging wild punches.

Behind him, Zach heard his cameraman yell, "Say something, you fucker. Why don't you say something?"

Zach whirled in time to see the cameraman swing his bulky shoulder-cam at Zach's head. There was one split second where the reporter saw his own horrified reflection in the curved lens, and then the heavy device smashed into him. Zach fell, stunned and bleeding, and lay there while his longtime friend and colleague raised the camera and brought it down again and again.

In one of those perverse twists of probability, the camera still functioned. It caught every last moment. Every newsworthy detail of the utter destruction of Zach Jonas.

The president of the United States was at his desk when the shock waves slammed into the White House. He looked up from the trade briefing and stared in blank incomprehension at what was happening around him. Flowers danced in their vases, paintings rattled against the walls, the carpet writhed, and even the couches juddered against the carpet.

He said, "What . . . ?"

Then the door burst open and two Secret Service agents came rushing into the room, yelling at him. Telling him to move. Ordering him to comply. In his confusion the president slapped their hands away, bellowing with outrage. They overpowered him, though, and began half walking, half dragging him toward the door.

It was only when the wall behind his desk cracked apart with a huge snap and pieces of masonry struck his abandoned chair and desk did he understand.

"Is it an attack?" he demanded as he began running with the agents. "Are we under attack?"

* * *

The first fires didn't start until a few minutes after the first shock wave hit the city. Broken gas lines, wrecked cars, crushed homes—all of these conspired to spill flammable chemicals everywhere. It was inevitable that the worst would happen.

It did.

Then the second shock hit.

CHAPTER FIFTY

THE CAPITOL BUILDING
WASHINGTON, D.C.

"Ghost," I roared, "shield Auntie."

The command stopped Ghost as he was about to leap forward to kill. Instead, the dog would stand his ground in the gap between me and Aunt Sallie. Anyone who got past me would be savaged and likely crippled, but not killed. It wasn't nice, but it was what we had. If I'd turned Ghost on the crowd he would keep killing until they dragged him down.

The guy in the bloody sweatshirt lunged at me, and I bashed his arms aside with a chop of my left hand and hit him very hard in the temple with my right palm. I put a lot of thrust into it, not going for a skull fracture but instead wanting to scramble his brains while shoving him at the people behind him. He took four people down with him, and I stepped to my right and front-kicked a fifty-something woman who tried to bite me. She flew backward and bumped down the stone steps.

I pivoted to evade a punch and hit the next person with a reverse elbow shot to the nose, then shoved him, too.

Hands closed on my shoulders, so I ducked, spun, and came completely out of my sports coat, then kicked the grabber in the stomach. Someone else tried to rush past me and I almost kicked her—but then to my absolute horror saw that it was a pregnant woman. Maybe eight months along, and she made a dive for Aunt Sallie.

I am known for never hesitating in a fight, but let's face it, some things give anyone pause. I froze for maybe a microsecond as my combat mind ran through ten thousand possible responses. If we'd been alone, just the two of us, stopping her without injury would be no problem. If it had been two or three attackers, I could have figured something out.

That wasn't this. My back and shoulders were hurt. Aunt Sallie was down, and if the woman slipped past me, then things Ghost might do to stop her were appalling. If I punched her, she might fall and hurt the baby. If I broke her leg, ditto. If I grabbed her and tried to quiet her, we'd both probably get swarmed. If I grabbed her hair to try and sprain her neck—and, yes, I can do that with some degree of control—again, she'd fall. My options were insanely limited.

The microsecond ticked slower than the wheels of eternity.

Then time caught up and I was moving. My body turned, and as her foot came down on the step just below Auntie, I lunged and stamped down on her instep. I could feel the bones break. There was no way to tell if she could even feel pain, but broken bones are broken bones. The structural integrity of the foot is part of the overall scaffolding of the body. Gravity is constantly trying to force us down, and the bones have to be intact to fight the pull.

She screamed—more in hate than in pain—but buckled, falling toward me. I caught her and turned, lowering her down as gently as I could while stabbing backward with a mule kick that caught someone else in the crotch.

Once the pregnant woman was down I said, "Sorry!" And punched her in the nose. She fell back, gagging on blood in her Eustachian tubes and feeling the swirl of a light dose of whiplash. She was done for the moment, and although she was alive and the baby safe, there was no way I was ever going to be okay about beating up a pregnant woman. Mr. Hero. Pretty sure I'd book some vacation time in one of the hotter pits of hell for what I just did.

Ghost was snarling and snapping, and when I flicked a look at him I could see badly injured people all around him, and his white fur was splashed with bright red.

Christ.

Then two new people came at me like defensive tackles, driving low with their shoulders like they'd practiced this a hundred times. I stepped into them and palm-smashed their heads together. There was a loud melon-smack sound and they went right down. I ran over them and jump-kicked a Pulitzer Prize–winning news anchor, dropped a DCPD cop with a forearm smash across the face, broke the leg of a Secret Service guy I recognized from the old Linden Brierley days, swept the legs out from under a skinny teenage girl with magenta hair, and clocked the junior senator from Idaho with an overhand right that knocked the lights from his eyes.

All of this happened in fragments of seconds. So fast. Insanely fast. While all around us Washington, D.C., tore itself apart.

My back was white-hot fire and I couldn't get a good breath. Sweat stung my eyes and I knew that I could not win this fight. Ghost yelped in pain, but I wasn't able to help him.

But then I felt movement behind me and I whirled, ready to hurt someone else.

It was Aunt Sallie. Somehow she'd gotten to her feet. Blood ran down her legs from where she'd hit the edges of the steps, and her clothes were torn. She had something in her hand that looked like a roll of quarters, but then she gave her arm a whiplike shake and a dense polycarbonate telescoping rod snapped into place. With a growl, Auntie stepped past me and began attacking the crowd, breaking knees and ribs and hands and elbows with savage force and ruthless precision. Ghost jumped forward to fight beside her, with me on her left.

Together we met the charge of the last eight attackers.

In all the years I've known Auntie, I've never seen her fight. She was old, sick, injured, but goddamn if she wasn't one of the best fighters I'd ever seen. Like . . . ever. If this was how she fought now, I knew full well that I would never have wanted to face her back when she was in her prime. Church hadn't partnered with her for her charm.

There were three of us, and we were injured. There were eight of them and they were driven by insane fury and evident madness.

It lasted maybe three full seconds and we fought our way down to the bottom step.

Then it was over.

We stood panting, exhausted, nearly feral as we crouched there, ready for more, almost wanting more. I could see four or five people in the street with cell cameras aimed at us. Capturing it all.

A moment later an awful sound filled the air, and we looked up in horror to see the Statue of Freedom, the nineteen-and-a-half-foot-tall bronze colossus that has stood on the cupola above the Capitol Building since 1863, lean outward. She seemed to bow her head as if admitting defeat, and then the fifteen thousand pounds of her mass crashed down on the edge of the dome, cracking it like glass. The statue turned as it struck, and went rolling and tumbling down onto the upper structure and then falling outward and down to the steps. The crested military helmet punched through the flat stone and broke the statue's neck. The rest of the massive body crashed down onto D.J.'s body and came to rest where Auntie and I had been mere seconds before.

Auntie leaned against me as a sob broke deep in her chest. I caught her and held her. The earthquake, as if satisfied with this dramatic finale, abated, and everything faded out into screams and weeping, to sirens and despairing cries. I held Auntie as the tears ran like cold mercury down our cheeks.

"It's okay," I said, "we're safe."

She said my name, but it came out wrong.

So wrong. Garbled and wet and slack.

I looked down and saw her staring up at me with mad, desperate eyes, and for a moment I thought that she had fallen victim to whatever insanity had made D.J. kill himself and some of the people erupt into violence.

No.

It wasn't that.

Her eyes were glazed and staring. Her lips tried to speak, tried to form words. My name. Any words. But they couldn't. I could see them fail in the attempt. The skin on the right side of her face looked like melting wax, losing its natural shape, sliding, turning to rubber. Her right arm and leg twitched once and then lay slack as if half of her had died there in my arms. Her eyes looked through me and if they saw or recognized me, I couldn't tell. Drool ran from the corners of her mouth. I knew the symptoms because I'd seen the effect before. In my grandfather. In a neighbor's uncle.

Aunt Sallie had just suffered a massive stroke. She lay dying in my arms. The world was broken and there was no help coming.

CHAPTER FIFTY-ONE

THE OVAL OFFICE
THE WHITE HOUSE
WASHINGTON, D.C.

The shelter beneath the White House was so heavily reinforced that even the earthquake could not destroy it. The shock waves tried, though. Chunks of concrete had broken loose from the walls, exposing sheets of steel that were buckled but not ruptured. Cracks ran along the ceiling, but the concrete up there was veined with wire netting to prevent falling debris.

The president sat on a sofa which was innocuously ornate, a leftover from some previous administration and moved down here for want of something better to do with it. He sat in the corner of the couch, fists balled on his thighs, eyes blinking too often, lips parted and rubbery with shock. Eight other members of his staff were there, but not the chief of staff, who had gone over to the Capitol Building after Howell's suicide. Eight Secret Service agents. Eleven military officers. Aides and advisors. Jennifer VanOwen sat beside him. The president's wife and children were elsewhere. Safe, he was told.

The air filtration was working perfectly, as were the lights. The sounds of the troubled earth had faded now, followed by a long, expectant, dreadful silence.

"I think it's over," someone said, but no one acknowledged the statement. The earthquake had been big. Way too big. Too furious. The TV screens showed feeds from news services, and the stories unfolding made no sense. People had turned on each other. That was as big a story as the quake itself. So much violence. So much blood. Some of the video footage came from cameras that stood on unattended tripods or lay abandoned on the ground where they'd fallen, and God only knew what happened to the film crews.

"Is it over?" asked the president after another few moments.

One of the generals was on his phone and turned toward him. "I . . . I think so, Mr. President. But we should stay down here a little longer just in case."

"Yes," agreed the president quickly. "As long as we're safe down here."

"This bunker was built to withstand a direct nuclear hit on the White House, Mr. President. We're quite safe."

The president licked his lips and nodded. Then he fished his cell phone out of his pocket and composed a tweet.

It's okay. I'm fine.

One of his senior advisors, his director of communications, asked if he could see the text. The president shook his head and sent it.

The tweet hit social media with the same unstoppable force as the earthquake had struck D.C. And did nearly as much damage.

It's okay. I'm fine.

I.

Those words would haunt the president for the rest of his time in office.

As the others in the room checked their Twitter feeds, which had become automatic actions for them, they saw those words. Many stared in horror, or shock. A few turned away to hide more telling expressions.

Only Jennifer VanOwen smiled, but she hid that, too.

CHAPTER FIFTY-TWO

BUSBOYS AND POETS VEGETARIAN RESTAURANT
WASHINGTON, D.C.

Valen and Ari sat at a corner table of the restaurant, watching the drama on the big-screen TV, checking news feeds on their smartphones, listening to the people all around them talk about it.

When it started, the building had rattled, but that was all. Valen knew that sometime soon the staff and patrons would talk about how lucky they were. They'd tell all their friends about what a miracle it was that that whole block, and a few blocks on either side of the restaurant, were virtually unscathed, while everywhere else seemed to get the full brunt. Fires were already raging out of control because the firefighters were unable to fight through streets choked with debris, crashed cars, or rioting people. All that happened to the restaurant was a single jagged crack in one corner of the plate-glass window. Only that.

It was a different world there than what was on TV, like watching a big-budget disaster film.

The patrons began asking questions and buzzing with theories. Was this an earthquake? Was it a bomb? Did someone drop a nuke? It wasn't until the news crawl declared that it was an earthquake that everyone accepted it, though with some reluctance. Earthquakes were rare on the East Coast of America, but in an age of global terrorism, bombs were not. As the chatter shifted, the self-appointed experts who manage to be in any given crowd began holding court. It was an earthquake, they pronounced, and when the majority of the crowd began to nod in agreement, the experts started throwing numbers around—5.4, 6.1, 7.6. They mostly got it wrong, Valen noted, citing the Richter scale, which nobody used anymore. Then one black man with a grizzled white goatee and a Shakespearean brow took it upon himself to correct the error.

"It's the moment magnitude scale," he said, pitching his voice to be heard over the car alarms outside. There was such authority in his voice that others turned to listen. "That's what they're using now."

The black man actually launched into a lecture on the subject. Valen listened for a few moments and found himself mildly impressed, even nodding when terms like "body-wave magnitude, logarithmic scale," and "shear modulus" floated to the top. But soon he tuned it out and cut a look at Ari, who was trying hard not to grin. The little Greek was actually biting his lip so hard his eyes were watering. If anyone else noticed, though, they probably thought the man was fighting tears of shock or horror.

As if.

The crowd watched dumbstruck as video footage from a few minutes ago was played back to show the collapsing dome, the cracking White House walls, and other kinds of structural devastation, but also the wild fighting in the streets. The anchors and reporters were chattering and interrupting each other and throwing around wild theories. Valen stared at the struggling figures and at the bodies lying dead or dying in the street.

Valen's cell vibrated in his pocket and he tapped Ari on the arm, showed him the phone, and walked into the empty men's room to take the call.

"You promised me this would be, at very least, a six point five," said Gadyuka without preamble.

"I assure you, Gadyuka, it—"

"It's a *seven point eight,*" she interrupted, then laughed as sweetly as a songbird. "I am very, very happy with you, *lapochka,*" she said. "When I see you I'll show you exactly how happy."

A shiver swept through Valen. There was no "love" in their lovemaking. It was all about need and greed and control, and he always lost to her. Every single time. To have sex after this was appalling.

"Can't . . . wait," he lied.

She caught it, though, quick as she always was. "What's wrong?"

"Nothing."

"Something, I think."

He leaned his head against the cool stone wall. "I just wonder if there was another way. . . ."

It was out before he could stop the words.

"Ah, my dear," said Gadyuka, "we've been over this and over this. Stalin did much worse to his own people. Our own people. We are at war, but we are not cutting throats with clumsy bayonets. We have delicate scalpels in our hands. We are the surgeons who are removing the cancers so the world can grow healthy again."

"I know the rhetoric," he said wearily, "but now's not the time. I'm not like you, Gadyuka. I'm not a monster."

She actually laughed at that. "Oh, my dear, you underestimate yourself. In my entire career I have ordered the deaths of not quite two dozen people and personally executed another eleven. I consider myself a monster for doing that. A monster, but a patriotic one. However, you, sweet Valen, have killed a hundred for every one of mine. And soon you will be responsible for killing more people than any one person ever has. More than Stalin or Hitler or the leaders of the Mongol conquests. More than in World War One and Two combined. You are indeed a monster."

"Jesus Christ, what are you doing to me?" he begged. "You're *killing* me. . . ."

Gadyuka laughed again, though not as sweetly. "Shhh, listen. There is nothing wrong, and everything right in being a monster, my sweet. Nations require us to be more than ordinary men. Three thousand years ago they would have called you a demigod, like Prometheus. He was a Titan who stole the heavenly fire for humanity, enabling the progress of civilization. If we read between the lines and strip away the primitive theology, what that means is that a man, a visionary, defied terrible odds to bring truth to the people so that they may have agency over their own lives. Karl Marx was such a man. Lenin was such a man. Stalin, for all his flaws, was such a man. They were all monsters, too, because they spilled rivers of blood. Without their actions, without their willingness to *become* monsters, America would have swept us out of history after the Second World War. They would have dropped the next atomic bombs on us, and you know I'm telling the truth."

"Please," he begged.

"Listen to me, Valen. Hear me. You are a brave and glorious monster. A hero. A Titan. And history will remember you as the man who saved the world."

"How?" he demanded. "By cracking it open?"

"Yes," she said in a voice filled with love. "By exposing the cancer to the scalpel."

The first of the aftershocks rumbled beneath his feet. Much smaller than the big strike. He prayed it wouldn't do more damage, but knew that it would.

"They'll never recover from this," he murmured, forgetting in the moment that he was still on a call.

"America is hurt, yes," she said fiercely. "It is shocked, yes. But this is not the blow that will drive it to its knees, and you know it. They can rebuild this. They can rise from this. And we simply cannot allow that.

"Do you know how to win a knife fight, Valen?" she asked, and now there was a cold pragmatism in her voice that crusted his breaking heart with ice. "You don't deliver a bad cut and then step back and hope your enemy loses heart and gives up, or limps from the field. No. If you do that you find that they can eat their own pain and they can—what's the American expression? Man up? If you let them catch their breath and regain their footing, then they are stronger in those broken places. Nietzsche was right about that. No, *lapochka,* when you have inflicted an injury on your opponent, when his blood is on your knife and you can smell it in the air, then that's the time to cut again, and cut deeper. Cut all the way to the bone. Cut all the way to the heart."

"God . . . ," he whispered.

"It's time to deliver the killing cut, Valen," said Gadyuka. "It's time for America as a nation, as a power, as a concept, to end. This is a war. Go be a soldier. Be a hero. Save us all."

Valen closed his eyes and felt as if the ground were tilting under him, but in ways that had nothing to do with the earthquake he and Ari had inflicted on this city. He knew what was coming.

CHAPTER FIFTY-THREE

THE CAPITOL BUILDING
WASHINGTON, D.C.

"Auntie," I called, "stay awake. Stay with me."

Those words are so cliché. You hear them in every movie or TV show where someone is shot or concussed. It sounds like a kind of ego, telling someone to stay awake so they can stay alive. As if any of us have that power.

Because I was a cop and a soldier and now a special operator, I have first-aid training that's a few cuts above the ordinary. I can set a bone, stitch a wound, deliver a baby, treat for shock, immobilize a broken neck, can take vitals and give injections. All of which is great if you have even a basic medical kit. Which I did not. I had a dying woman, a dog, and a cell phone. My car was four blocks away and my back was injured. At the very least I had a muscle tear, but it felt worse than that. I didn't want to kill her by dropping her. Calling 9-1-1 was definitely going to be a waste of time because there was no chance at all they weren't swamped.

Instead I called the Hangar. Weak, confused, or inexperienced people will react with shock when you tell them this kind of news. They will waste precious seconds reacting rather than responding. The DMS doesn't hire those kinds of people. I told Bug what happened and what I needed and he said help was on its way. I believed him.

I told Doc Holliday about Auntie, and she talked me through the steps that might help until EMTs arrived.

"Ask her to smile," ordered Doc. I did. And it stabbed me through the fucking heart. Only part of one half of her face moved. I will never forget the ghastly grimace and the horrified realization in Auntie's eyes. She knew.

Then Doc had me ask Auntie to raise both arms. One moved. One twitched.

"Can she say anything?" asked Doc. "See if you can get her to talk."

I asked Auntie to tell me how she was feeling. She made a lot of sounds but none of them were words in any language I could understand. And then one single word came through—broken, half-formed, melting, but coherent.

". . . scared . . ."

I swear to God I would rather have taken a bullet than have Aunt Sallie tell me how scared she was.

"Listen to me, Ledger," said Doc, speaking slowly and clearly in order to ground me. "She's had a stroke. She's aphasic, which means she can't talk. Keep her awake. That's crucial, because it sounds like a bad one. You cannot let her go to sleep. Don't try to give her anything. No food or water or anything. Not even her meds. Nothing. She won't be able to swallow and would choke. We can't yet tell if this is a hemorrhagic or ischemic stroke. If it's ischemic, aspirin could kill her. The reports about D.C. are coming in and it's bad, Cowboy. It's really bad. We can't give you a reliable ETA on when someone's going to get to you. Maybe there's not even enough time. I pray so, but . . . you need to be there for her. Make her as comfortable as you can. Keep talking to her. Reassure her. Lie to her, if you have to. Tell her that help is coming. Tell her everything is going to be fine. Make her believe it."

I swallowed something that felt like a rock. "Yes," I said. "Roger that."

"Emergency services are going to be slow arriving, but do not move her. You don't want to make it worse."

I wanted to ask how this could be worse. Just like I wanted to ask how long I could risk staying there. Luckily, Doc Holliday is sharp as a knife.

"Bug is working on a timetable for soonest possibility of help to your location. The sooner she gets treatment, the better her chances and the less you need to take the risk of moving her. That said, Cowboy, if it looks like we can't get an ambulance to you, then you may have to get her out yourself. What condition are you in?"

"Back," I said. One word, trusting again that she was quick.

"Pain or serious damage?"

"Both."

"Scale of one to ten, ten being you're totally unable to try."

"Seven."

"Shit. Is there anyone around who can help?"

There were people around me. They weren't fighting anymore, but they weren't going to be of much help. Some were kneeling over people more visibly injured, doing what they could to stanch bleeding and provide help. Others wandered in shock, their eyes filled with a more recognizable kind of vacuity than before. Victims whose injuries were inflicted on their psyches. I've seen that before, after terrorist bombings or natural disasters. Some were awake and alert but overwhelmed by how many people screamed for help and how few resources they had to work with. Behind me, the main entrance to the Capitol Building was blocked by rubble, so the cops, Secret Service, politicians, and reporters who'd crowded the chamber must either be still inside—alive or dead—or they had exited through another route.

"No," I said. "Just me."

"Let me talk to Bug," Doc said. "We'll figure something out."

Then Mr. Church came on the line. He didn't ask for details, so I assumed he'd been listening. He did not ask to speak to Auntie.

"I'm talking to you because she'd be embarrassed to speak with me," Church said, and there was so much awareness and pain in his voice that it hurt me to hear it. "She will see this as some kind of failure on her part to be the same young, strong, effective field operator she pretends to be. I understand that, as much as it hurts to admit it. Do you understand, Captain?"

"Yes," I said, and it felt like my throat was filled with glass splinters.

"Be strong for her and with her," said Church. "If it is within your power, then keep her here. Keep her with us."

"Yes."

"Captain . . . do you have any idea why people began attacking one another? Is this a disease?"

"I don't know," I said. "It started right before the first tremor and stopped when the ground stopped shaking. Does that make any kind of sense?"

He didn't reply to that, but instead said, "Help is coming."

I looked around at the ruined city. At slack bodies and blood-streaked faces, at the ruptured streets and broken buildings. At the fires and the smoke that reached like the arms of dying giants to the uncaring gray sky. Then I looked down at Aunt Sallie. There was so little of her left.

"Help is coming," I said, repeating Church's words so Aunt Sallie could hear.

Her hand, the one that wasn't already dead, squeezed two of my fingers. Telling me that she believed what I said. Trusting. I wanted to bow my head and weep as first responder sirens filled the air. Too few and too far away. Aunt Sallie smiled up at me with a quarter of a mouth and gave my fingers another squeeze.

Reassuring *me,* for fuck's sake.

The world was mad and it was broken. This wasn't a fight and I was the wrong damn man for the job of offering comfort. I held her close and talked to her. Sometimes she talked back. As best she could. We waited.

As best we could.

CHAPTER FIFTY-FOUR

THE HANGAR
FLOYD BENNETT FIELD
BROOKLYN, NEW YORK

Church looked at Doc Holliday, at Bug, at the staff in the Hangar who were all scrambling to put the right machinery into action. No one in the world was better suited to the job.

Beside him, Brick Anderson touched Church on the shoulder. "She'll be okay."

They exchanged a look and both nodded at the lie. Accepting it for what it was. Then, without waiting to be told, Brick pulled his own cell phone and began making calls. The first one was to the flight deck to order Church's chopper, and the second was to the private airfield to tell the pilot to have the Lear smoking when they got there.

"Doc," began Church, but the tall, gangly scientist shook her head.

"We got this. *Go.*"

He whirled and ran for the door, with Brick right beside him.

INTERLUDE NINETEEN

THE *SUICIDE KINGS*
MOTU RAUORO ISLAND, SOCIETY ISLANDS
FRENCH POLYNESIA
THREE YEARS AGO

Valen and Ari sat in the matched leather pilot's chairs and studied the island. They both held powerful binoculars and had them trained on the camp.

Ari's face was swathed in bandages and one eye was swollen shut. He had tissue plugs in his nose and he hovered on the narcotic edge of being awake. Hours had passed since Valen dragged him off the island, and the drugs and booze in the Greek's system were fading, leaving Ari more or less awake and aware.

The *Suicide Kings* bobbed in the swells a hundred yards from the shoreline. The research camp was surrounded by a new fence of sturdy pipes and chain link, and the silver finish glittered in the morning sun. The guard booth was painted a pale green to allow it to fade somewhat into the background. The booth was empty and its glass window was painted a different color. Red, in an artless splash pattern.

"What the hell happened to us?" mumbled Ari slowly. "I mean, what the actual hell?"

Valen shook his head, but in truth he thought he knew. Last night, when everyone was killing each other or themselves, when he was beating Ari, something happened. The violence caused his hearing aid to come loose, and suddenly the madness that had overtaken him ended. Just like that. As if a switch had been thrown. The utter silence inside his head was replaced by his own confused and terrified thoughts; but they were his thoughts. He could hear them even if he could hear nothing else, deaf as he was without the aid.

He'd staggered to his feet and blundered out into the camp. Into carnage and wholesale slaughter. Into rape and sodomy and self-mutilation and suicide. When he reached the lab, it was immediately clear to him that the fool technicians had not only completed assembling the new machine, but they'd turned it on as well. The device squatted like a conjured demon while all around it the air seemed to shimmer and shift as if it was a sheer curtain hanging between this world and some hellish *otherwhere.*

Valen saw that the dials on the device were positioned on their lowest settings. Beneath his feet a tremble troubled the ground.

"No," he breathed as understanding flooded into him. He shut the machine off, staggered back, fetched Ari, and dragged him to a Zodiac and from there out to the boat. There was no one else left to save.

"We have to call Gadyuka," said Ari thickly. His words were softened to a lisp because of his missing front teeth. "We have to tell her what happened."

Tell her it failed, whispered a voice inside his head. Or maybe it was the fading voice from his breaking heart. *It will be so easy. Shoot Ari. He's a monster anyway. Shoot him and then take the machine far out to sea and throw it overboard. Do the same with the hard drives and the research and all of the spare parts and extra crystals. This is the only chance to end it all right here and now. Do it. Do it!*

He closed his eyes as he made the call to Gadyuka. She answered right away.

"The device works," he said in a voice he did not even recognize. "It works perfectly."

If Ari noticed the tears running down Valen's cheeks, he did not comment on them.

CHAPTER FIFTY-FIVE

THE CAPITOL BUILDING
WASHINGTON, D.C.

Doc Holliday came on the line.

"Cowboy, listen to me," she said, "there's no help coming. Not from the locals and not in time. There are already three hundred dead and five thousand injured, with new reports coming in every second. Emergency response networks are swamped. How close is your car?"

"Four blocks away," I said, and heard her hiss like she'd been scalded.

"I know you're hurt, but can you carry her?"

I ground my teeth together. There was no way I was going to be able to pick up a badly injured 220-pound woman and carry her—carefully—all that distance and across those obstacles. No way in hell.

"I'll try," I said.

"When you get her there," said Doc, "hook her up to Calpurnia so I can assess remotely. We'll try to arrange a medevac chopper to meet you once you get out of the city and—"

Bug suddenly cut in. "Cowboy, listen, I think we can shorten the distance you'll have to carry her. Betty Boop has autonomous drive. I'll have Calpurnia bring it as close as possible. We have drone pictures, so we can see you and see the street. There's a lot of damage and some of it's going to mean we have to come to you the long way, but I think we can get the car as close as one block. You're looking straight down East Capitol Street Northeast. It's totally blocked, and First Street Southeast is not happening. Between street damage and parked vehicles, the closest we can get your car is across the grounds to the Southeast Drive loop closest to the corner of First Street and Independence Avenue."

"Understood."

"Cowboy," said Doc, "don't move her until you see the car. We need to reduce the amount of additional trauma and shorten the time between moving her and getting her to the chopper."

"Understood," I said again. "Do it. And don't stop for coffee, Bug."

"Rolling. ETA seven minutes."

I told Auntie that help was on the way. Maybe she understood. Hard to tell with stroke victims. Sometimes the body dies by degrees while the mind remains alert and aware of the burning building in which it's trapped.

Seven minutes. We huddled together and waited for hope. I talked to her, got her to grunt. Even got her to laugh, kind of. Telling stupid stories about the weird stuff that happens on field ops. It did not take seven minutes. It took thirteen. I tried so hard not to take that as an ill omen.

Then a voice in my ear said, "Cowboy, on your six."

I turned and saw Betty Boop come thumping over the cracked asphalt sixty yards away. The windshield was white with spiderweb cracks, the armored shell was streaked with dust and blood. It rolled as far as possible and stopped on the other side of an overturned news van.

"Your carriage awaits, princess," I said.

Auntie looked confused, and I explained that I needed to carry her to the car. I padded that with too much technical information and a lot of preloaded apologies for how much it might hurt. Auntie's fingers twitched, pointing to her slack mouth, so I bent and listened to what she was trying to tell me.

"Stop . . . ," she gasped, slurring the word so that I had to reconstruct it phonetically, "being . . . such a . . . pussy . . . and just . . . f-f-fucking . . . *do it*."

I straightened and grinned down at her. There was a glitter of her old edge in one eye. Even then.

"Yes, Auntie," I said, and did not let her see my own tears.

CHAPTER FIFTY-SIX

THE BUNKER
THE WHITE HOUSE
WASHINGTON D.C.

"They don't understand," growled the president, shaking his cell phone at VanOwen. "How can they not understand? What are they? Stupid?"

It's okay. I'm fine.

"A lot of them are," agreed VanOwen. "A towering vision is hard for most people to grasp. History will explain it to them. That's what is important."

The bunker was empty except for them and two agents. Everyone else had left to dive into crisis management. Most to the devastation, and a few to spin control.

"My tweet was simple," groused the president. "After all, I am the country and I wanted to reassure them that this will be business as usual, despite setbacks."

VanOwen did not even blink at the word "setbacks." Her smile was pretty and accommodating and unbreakable. It was exactly the right wattage for him and it drew him like he were a moth.

"The people will understand once they're over their initial shock," she said. "That's why I think it would be best if you stayed off of social media for the rest of the day."

"No way, I—"

"Please, Mr. President," she said patiently, "it's the best way to play this. If you dominate the conversation now, then you draw attention away from the rescue efforts. Even the corrupt news services are helping with relief efforts, posting locations of rescue stations, and sending out information. The best thing we can do is sit back and let the professionals do their jobs. Believe me, you'll be thanked for your restraint and for the trust you show in the emergency responders. And then once the first responders have done their job, then you can step forward and show them the strength and presence that the public will need for comfort and optimism."

The president frowned and cast a longing look at his phone, then he nodded and put it away. "I should suspend trading, though. Have you seen the numbers?"

Again VanOwen smiled and shook her head. "Surely you don't want to blink now, Mr. President. You know how this works. Who better? The stock market goes up, it goes down, but it always levels off. If you suspend trading, then you validate the flight-to-safety fear that causes such swings. The most commanding play is to stand firm and make a visible statement that you believe in the enduring power of the American economy."

The president got up from the couch and walked across the bunker floor. His frown was deep, but he was nodding again.

"Okay," he said. "I've decided to keep the stock market open."

CHAPTER FIFTY-SEVEN

OVER BROOKLYN AIRSPACE

The cabin of the AgustaWestland AW101 was so thoroughly soundproofed Church could hear the beating of his own heart. Faster than he wanted, but understandable. As the bird flew toward the airfield, he wondered at what speed his heart would need to beat for it to break. It was poetic music, which usually annoyed him, but he let it go without self-excoriation.

Aunt Sallie, he mused, and felt the deep ache.

If she died, then she would become another of the ghosts that haunted him. She should have retired years ago. Definitely after that time assassins nearly killed her at her condo during the Predator One affair. Church had allowed her to bully him into keeping her active; he'd agreed to it out of compassion, but also because he was selfish. The war required him to be selfish, to keep in play those assets that gave him the best chance of winning. It would take ten people to replace Aunt Sallie. Her insight, her judgment, her experience . . . those things made her invaluable.

Now she was going away.

Brick poured tea for both of them and handed Church a cup. His dark, wise eyes scanned Church's face.

"She's going to be a tough act to follow," he said.

If it was anyone else, those words might have sounded insensitive. Burying the body before it stopped breathing. But Brick got a pass because Brick understood. The war was the war. Soldiers fell. The war did not allow time to stop and mourn, because a pause is also a moment of inattention. His comment had nothing at all to do with whether she would live or die. It was all about the needs of the moment.

When Church did not comment, Brick said, "Body count is rising. No word at all from POTUS. Not directly. He wasn't hurt and they got him to safety, but he hasn't made a statement yet beyond that one tweet. Kind of weird. Seems like a good time for a hand at the wheel."

"Yes," said Church. The chopper flew on.

They both put on headsets and plugged into the MindReader Q1 communications network. There were a lot of calls to be made. Brick coordinated with the Hangar and the Warehouse to make sure that the DMS field teams were putting the right resources into play. Church made calls to friends in various industries, arranging for the highest-quality medical experts to begin heading to D.C. Cost was no object, and any logistical issue was dealt with.

He called Junie Flynn, who had returned that morning from one of her many trips to field test or implement the technologies entrusted to her by the DMS.

"Miss Flynn," began Church.

"Call me Junie, for God's sake," she pleaded. "We're practically family."

"Junie," he conceded, "you're right. We are family. Captain Ledger—Joe—has had a challenging day. Details are unfolding and some can't be shared at the moment. He has some minor injuries, but that's all we know. He is taking care of Aunt Sallie and I will make sure he calls you at the first opportunity."

There was a pause and Church let her process things. Then she said, "I want to ask you a question. You may not be able to answer me. I understand that there are some things you can't talk about."

"Ask anyway," he said quietly.

"I'm watching the news right now. They're showing people fighting in the streets during the earthquake. Killing each other."

"Yes."

"That's not normal, even during a crisis like this. People attacking each other, I mean. Killing themselves."

"It's unusual."

"It's not normal," she repeated. "And right before the earthquake, the Speaker of the House killed himself. Tell me . . . is this a DMS case? One of your, um, *special* cases?"

"Why would you ask that?"

"Because for the last five nights I've been having strange dreams."

"What kind of dreams?" asked Church.

"Before I tell you," said Junie, "I want you to remember my background. My history. I want you to remember who and, more to the point, what I am."

"I remember," said Church. Junie Flynn had come into his life, and that of Captain Ledger, during the Extinction Machine case. She was a woman with exceptional abilities, including an exceptional intelligence as well as eidetic memory and hyperthymesia—a superior autobiographic memory. These were not gifts from random genetics but actual features designed into Junie and hundreds of children like her as part of a breeding program run by Majestic Three. The goal was to create potential pilots for T-craft. People who were mostly human but who had a small percentage of DNA harvested from the pilots of crashed vehicles of unknown origin. "What were your dreams?"

"I dreamed I was standing in a field of wildflowers somewhere. It was in the States. Don't know how I knew that, but I was sure of it. The sky was on fire and dark clouds covered the sun. The whole landscape was shaking. It was an earthquake, but not exactly like one. It was more like there was a thunderstorm beneath my feet, inside the ground on which I stood. People were screaming and running and dying, catching fire or choking, and the sky above me was filled with T-craft." Junie stopped, and when Church said nothing, she continued. "It was a very vivid dream, though also surreal. Now, I know you're going to tell me that it's just a dream, but . . ."

"No," said Church, "that's not what I'm going to say."

"I know that M3 is gone and all the T-craft destroyed."

Church said nothing.

"But," continued Junie, "as soon as I heard about the earthquake, the dream came right back to me. It's like a punch in the brain. It reminded me of the dreams I had when Joe was sick after he got back from Antarctica. During the Kill Switch thing. I told Rudy about my dreams. And Joe. I dreamed that he was running on a beach on some alien world and a gigantic monster was hovering in the sky. You know what monster I'm talking about. With stubby wings and a beard of writhing tentacles. You know. The one the pulp fiction writers called Cthulhu."

"Yes," said Church faintly.

"Joe had dreams of it, too, and in his dream there were T-craft in the sky. Not ships made by Majestic Three. Original design. Now I'm dreaming of those ships in our world, and the sky is burning. There's an earthquake. Now we have an earthquake in Washington while Joe's there. I . . . I can't believe it's a coincidence."

There was a soft tone and the pilot's voice filled the air. "Coming up on it."

Church leaned over to look out of the windows. Below, the Gulfstream G650 that had once belonged to Hugo Vox sat waiting on an airstrip. A fuel truck was trundling away from it and a signal was waving the chopper to a spot on the grass nearby.

To Junie, he said, "We need to have a longer conversation about this. Take Joe's jet and fly to Brooklyn. I want you to tell Doc Holliday every detail you can remember about your dream."

"Why? Am I right? Is there something about the T-craft and the earthquake?"

"Every detail," repeated Church. "I'll be in touch as soon as I can."

He ended the call, aware that Brick was staring at him.

CHAPTER FIFTY-EIGHT

THE CAPITOL BUILDING
WASHINGTON, D.C.

There is a concept of "exquisite pain," which is a level of agony coupled with an absolute precision of awareness in every nerve ending that transcends discomfort. It has a kind of perfection to it, a beauty for those who appreciate things at their absolute best. This is not a masochistic thing. No, it's closer to an understanding of the techniques of how a great painting was rendered or a beautiful clock constructed. If you feel it and do not pass out, or pass into the bluntness of screaming, then you truly grasp the precise mechanics of pain.

That was what I felt as I squatted to pick Aunt Sallie up.

She tried to help, tried to loop her good arm around my neck in order to transfer some of her weight to my frame. She tried to stiffen her body to give me better leverage. She tried. There was simply not enough of her left *to* help.

I raised her improbably heavy body and felt the swords of agony strike deep. The first step was the worst because the level of intensity was unexpected. And I immediately knew that my assessment was wrong. The second step was worse. And the third.

The car was a million miles away and receding. I felt a sob break in my chest before I was half the way there. Felt Auntie begin to slip.

"I'm sorry," I said, but there was no breath for making those words audible.

She clung to me with failing strength, and as her muscular strength ebbed, her body seemed to become heavier. Holding her was going to be impossible long before I reached Betty Boop. We both knew it.

My knees tried to buckle with each step. Blood boiled in my ears and there was a feeling in my muscles like violin strings being played to the breaking point. I could almost hear them. My lower back was a ball of fiery heat. Black and red flowers blossomed in the air in front of my eyes.

And then a shadow passed in front of me. I blinked through tears and saw a man there. Young, black, dressed in jeans and a white T-shirt under a red-and-blue Washington Wizards jacket. Maybe twenty years old, but with a hard face that was much older. Some scars on his skin and in his eyes. The kind of guy that my white upscale urban genes wanted to categorize, because even with people of good intentions there is often a latent xenophobia, a hardwired racism.

He looked at me and at the burden I carried. His face was without expression, telling me nothing at all.

"I got her, yo," he said.

I studied him. "She had a stroke."

"Yeah," he said. "Her face."

"My car is over there." He looked where I nodded.

"Yeah. I got you."

He said that to her, not to me. Same thing, though. He reached out and took Aunt Sallie from me. Her weight surprised him. He hissed and groaned and gasped, but he took her.

I sagged down to my knees.

"You hurt?"

"Tore my . . . back . . . ," I wheezed.

"That's fucked up."

That was all he said. He turned away and staggered with her to my car. The doors opened for him, and if he was surprised he didn't say a word. I struggled up and followed and caught up in time to help him put her in the backseat. Aunt Sallie was nearly gone now and could not even speak. That one eye still saw me. Saw him.

With trembling fingers, I reached for my wallet, and immediately saw a look of utter contempt and profound disappointment on the young man's face.

"Shit," he breathed, but I shook my head, removed a business card, and offered it to him. "Fuck's this? I didn't ask for shit."

"Take it," I said. "Please."

He hesitated and then did. There was my name and a phone number.

"You ever need anything, I don't care what it is, call me. Day or night. Someone will always answer that call."

"You Five-Oh?"

"I'm grateful to meet a friend," I said, and offered my hand. He looked at it for a moment, shrugged, shook it, and stepped back. I struggled behind the wheel and he closed the doors. Calpurnia started the engine and drove us away.

I turned a few times to see if he was there, but the young man was gone.

CHAPTER FIFTY-NINE

FORT RENO PARK
WASHINGTON, D.C.

The two agents in black suits stood side by side near their vehicle and watched the burning city.

One of them held a small device, and he held it up as if scanning the devastation. They leaned close to study the details that scrolled sideways on the screen, running from left to right in a stream of symbols.

Both of them frowned.

They looked at each other.

They both flinched as something exploded half a block away. They whirled to see the trunk lid of a parked Toyota Camry go flying into the air, twisted and scorched, pushed into the air by a fist of burning smoke. For a moment there seemed to be a crackle of bright lightning within the cloud, but then it paled to ordinary grayness. The trunk lid thumped down and lay on the debris from shattered car windows and collapsed walls.

The agents glanced at each other for a moment, and then ran toward the car. The one with the scanner raised it again. They skidded to a stop and looked into the ruined trunk to see a heap of slag that ran like mercury until it slowed and cooled into a shapeless nothing.

Their frowns deepened. The lightning had been as intense as thermite, but it had not been white or even blue-white. The glow had been a lambent green.

"Fahf ah cr'azath," said the taller of the two. He had a network of fading pink scars on his face.

"H' ah og or'azath," agreed his companion. *"Ahf' ah cahff apes ah?"*

The one with the scanner lowered it and looked out across the city. There was a second small explosion accompanied by a flash of green. Far away to their left. And then another. And another.

"C' mgep l' ah," he said.

CHAPTER SIXTY

COURTYARD BY MARRIOTT—NEW CARROLLTON
LANDOVER, MARYLAND

Valen and Ari met with a small group of agents provided by Gadyuka. Nondescript but capable-looking people who'd long ago been seeded into American society. They had jobs, friends, lives, and secrets.

They were the kind of people who, Valen was sure, could probably laugh and love and appear totally plausible to anyone who knew them; but now they were on the job. None of them smiled. None of them showed a thing.

Valen walked over to the dresser under the TV, opened a door, and knelt in front of the small room safe. He punched in the code and removed a stack of disposable cell phones. Each of the agents accepted one, and Valen gave one to Ari and kept the last.

"As soon as you're all in position," he said, "I've sent the cleanup code, but we haven't got confirmations from all the devices. There's a chance that the quake might have damaged some or buried them under so much debris that the signal can't get through. I want each of you to go through your sectors, locate those devices, and either detonate them from a safe distance, or if that doesn't work, then transmit the deactivation code and retrieve the faulty device. Bring any remaining devices back here." He paused. "If you are cornered or caught, you know what you have to do."

They nodded. All of them wore leather motorcycle jackets that were laced with special explosive compounds. No one was to be taken alive. Even Valen and Ari had identical jackets.

"If all of your devices are clear, then follow your orders. Park your bikes, place the jackets over the gas tank, and once you're at a safe distance and are sure you're not being observed, activate the detonation sequence. After that, go back into the crowds near any crisis site. Be visible. Make sure you're seen helping friends and neighbors. Volunteer at shelters."

They nodded. None of them asked a question or made a comment as they turned to file out.

"Christ on the cross," said Ari once they all left. "Remind me never to play poker with those sons of bitches. You can't read a thing on their faces. Worse than freaking robots."

"They're soldiers," said Valen weakly.

Ari answered that with a derisive snort. "They better do their damn jobs," he groused. Since getting back from the restaurant, Ari had become increasingly moody and uneasy. Visibly nervous.

"What's wrong with you?" asked Valen.

Ari flinched at the question and even shivered. "Oh, hell . . . I don't know, brother. I think we should cut and run, you know? We did our bit. Hell, they said on the news that the president was nearly crushed to death in the Oval Office. Kind of a shame if he was. I love that motherfucker." He went to the window and looked out as if expecting to see a squad of Secret Service agents about to storm the hotel. "I want to get the hell out of here."

"So do I," said Valen, and for a moment they studied each other. A whole conversation seemed to be taking place without words.

"We had a run of good cards," said Ari, "but luck doesn't always hold."

A good run of cards. That made Valen think about sitting aboard the *Suicide Kings* offshore from where everyone they worked with lay dead. Murdered, or by their own hands. All because of them. Because of their "good luck."

Aloud he said, "We have to oversee the cleanup."

"Let those robots do it." He went over to the bed and picked up his motorcycle jacket. "We're the executive level. Why are we putting our asses on the line like this?"

"Because those are all the agents Gadyuka had in the area," said Valen. "And because I told her we'd oversee the cleanup."

Ari shook his head. "You really have been drinking the Kool-Aid, haven't you? Are you really that willing to die for the cause?"

Valen shook his head and took the jacket from Ari. He opened it and showed him the lining. "I deactivated the switches and removed the thermite. Unless you blow yourself up trying to retrieve a broken machine, you'll be fine." He handed the jacket back to Ari.

"Well," said the Greek, a slow smile forming on his face, "it's nice to know that you're not completely out of your mind."

Valen turned away and began changing his clothes. He did not reply to Ari's comments. He'd told enough lies already.

CHAPTER SIXTY-ONE

ON THE ROAD
WASHINGTON, D.C.

I tried to take Aunt Sallie to a local hospital, but everything was crowded. Even though she was critical, there was a flood of others with massive wounds from the earthquake or from fighting. I could have pulled rank, flashed credentials, and gotten her a bed ahead of a mutilated five-year-old girl, or a pregnant woman who was in danger of losing her baby and her life, or . . .

Well, you get it. And Calpurnia estimated the quickest triage and treatment time, based on the hundreds being brought in to all ERs, was two hours and sixteen minutes. So, I made a judgment call and prayed Aunt Sallie and Mr. Church would understand.

"Calpurnia," I yelled, "what is the closest hospital that can handle a stroke victim?"

"Johns Hopkins University Hospital."

My heart sank. That was in Baltimore. It was a hundred miles away.

"What are my chances of getting Aunt Sallie there in time?"

"I'm monitoring her vitals, Cowboy," said the computer. "She has a forty-six percent chance of survival if you leave now."

"Shit."

"She has a twenty-one percent chance if you take her to a local hospital under the current conditions."

"Shit, shit, shit," I said, and punched the steering wheel. "Plot me the best route."

I threw the car into gear and hit the gas.

"Route is computed," said the AI. "I will adjust streetlights as we go to allow for maximum posted road speed."

I did not drive at the maximum posted road speed. By the time I was on the highway I was punching along at 140.

CHAPTER SIXTY-TWO

JOHNS HOPKINS UNIVERSITY HOSPITAL
BALTIMORE, MARYLAND

Doctors were waiting with a gurney before I had the engine off. Calpurnia made all the right calls, and the right specialists were on deck. Maybe Church had been on the phone, too. It would be like him.

I handed Auntie off to the experts and told them what I could and explained that my vehicle had an onboard medical triage system and that all details were being uploaded to the Johns Hopkins servers. That got me some strange looks, but the doctors and nurses there are too professional to blink, and they are always out on the cutting edge of technology, so they accepted it and thanked me and took her away. She was still alive.

Still alive.

My back suddenly flared, and I canted sideways against the intake nurse's desk, hissing with pain. Ghost gave a single bark of alarm.

"Sir," said the nurse sharply, "are you hurt?"

It took a lot of effort not to yap at her like a cranky shih tzu. Five or six different caustic expressions warred to be the first one out of my mouth.

"I'm fine," I said in a voice that sounded so false that it was like bad comedy. "Just lost my balance."

Her wise eyes scanned me but then read something in my expression and did not pursue. Instead she nodded toward Ghost. "Is he the patient's service dog?"

"No," I said through gritted teeth as I pulled an ID wallet out of my pocket and showed her a badge. "I'm with the Department of Homeland Security and he's my dog."

Despite the badge she looked skeptical, but her phone rang before she could say anything. She answered, listened for almost fifteen seconds, then frowned and looked at me again.

"Are you Captain Ledger?"

"Yes. Why?"

The nurse held out the phone. "It's for you."

I took the receiver, expecting it to be Bug, but it was Church.

"Captain," he said, "this will be quick. First, thank you for getting Auntie to the hospital. I have specialists on the way."

"I figured."

"Right now, though, I need you back in the field. I know you're injured, but we are resource poor. Can you manage it?"

"Yes," I said without even asking what it was first.

"Something is happening back in D.C.," he said. "A series of small but unusual explosions. We've been tracking them via drones and by hacking into feeds from news helicopters and other aerial surveillance. No one else has pegged them as anything more than additional damage from ruptured gas lines or other damage related to the earthquake."

"But you don't think so?"

"Nikki has been running pattern recognition on them and she's seeing a clear pattern. The explosions have been occurring in a wide ring around the Capitol. Too perfect a circle around the epicenter of the quake. Police and firefighters are too badly stretched to be able to check it out. And Sam has virtually emptied the Warehouse. Everyone down to the janitorial staff is on the streets helping with the rescue operations. I've sent him in, too, because there are curious gaps in the ring of blasts. It may be that the devices, whatever they are, have been disrupted by the quake. Some may have misfired."

"What do you need from me?"

"Go back to D.C. Sam can't check out all of the unexploded bombs, if they are indeed bombs, and if they are there at all. We can give you probable locations of two of them. Sam is checking out three others. If these things are somehow tied to what's happened—either the earthquakes themselves or the violent behavior of the people, then we need to identify what kind of technology this is. My guess is that they are involved and the explosions are part of a post-event cleanup. We don't want a clean sweep. All of the details will be sent to Calpurnia. Go."

"I'm gone," I said, and ran for my car. As best I could, with Ghost having to slow down to keep from outrunning me.

CHAPTER SIXTY-THREE

DRIVING IN MARYLAND

When I got to the car there was a pigeon drone sitting on the hood. It had a small package attached to its metal legs that, once opened, proved to be a new earbud kit, complete with booster pack. A gift from Sam. Nice. I put it on.

I let Calpurnia do some of the driving while I dug out the first-aid kit and shot myself up with enough painkillers to keep me from crying like a newborn, but not so much that I fell asleep at the wheel.

Ghost gave me a subtle *whuff,* reminding me that, why yes—food would be most appreciated. I had nothing. He sat there looking wistfully out the window as we passed McDonald's and Burger King.

Calpurnia is a learning computer, so she adjusted her driving to the way I'd driven from D.C. Meaning, she became reckless and drove too fast. I thoroughly approved.

En route, I caught up on the intel about Washington, D.C. The miles melted past and yet somehow it felt as if I wasn't traveling fast enough. When I looked out at the cars on either side of the road, they seemed to be traveling from normal places to normal places as if the world wasn't falling apart. How is that even possible? I've seen it in a thousand places around the world. People going through a Starbucks drive-through half a block from a fatal shooting. Happy kids on swings in a playground near where Echo Team had stopped drones filled with weaponized Ebola. A couple old guys playing chess in the park half an hour after EMTs took a stabbing victim away. There is a reset that happens, and I suppose it needs to happen. When something horrible happens, it really physically only happens in that spot; the rest of the world still turns, still goes on with its day.

Along the way I got a briefing. When you're not driving, the inside of the windshield turns into a computer monitor with an intense high-def 3-D screen. The first face to pop up was that of Doc Holliday.

Doc also brings with her some geeky-cool heritage. She is the great-granddaughter of the actual John Henry "Doc" Holliday, the noted gunslinger, dentist, and gambler who accompanied the Earp brothers to the shootout at the O.K. Corral. Apparently, the historical Doc Holliday had an affair with Mary Katherine Horony-Cummings, a prostitute known as Big Nose Kate.

Doc's a character. She is the actual definition of larger than life. She's a six-foot-one-inch natural blond—I think—whose raw energy and obvious intelligence dominate nearly any room into which she strides. She doesn't walk—she strides. Doc walks forward with such purpose and confidence that people get out of her way and walls cringe for fear that she will plow through them. She has big hands, big eyes, big hair, big boobs, and big lips that part for frequent big smiles. Think of Dolly Parton on growth hormones. A borderline cartoon character who loves playing it up. She flirts with everyone—male, female, potted plants. It doesn't matter to her. Not sure I've ever heard of her going out with anyone, but she goes after life with an enormous and infectious passion and a tongue firmly in cheek. However, it was the fact that she has a mighty damn big brain that Church hired her away from DARPA to run the Integrated Sciences Division of the DMS. She was brought in to replace the supergenius Dr. William Hu, and from the talk around the watercooler, she's exceeded expectations. The catchphrase that's begun to circulate is telling: "Glad she's on our side."

Doc brought a bunch of her own science with her and has used the apparently limitless finances and resources provided by Church to go further. Like Hu, Doc is a multidiscipline scientist. Her background is in physics and engineering, but she knows enough about medicine, genetics, chemistry, and other fields to be a forward-thinking—and, let's face it, devious—manager for our team of top experts. When she popped onto the screen, she was smiling as if it was a sunny day and all was right with the world.

"Howdy, Cowboy," she said. "Boy, do I have some fun stuff to tell you."

INTERLUDE TWENTY

THE *SUICIDE KINGS*
THE PACIFIC OCEAN
TWO NAUTICAL MILES WEST OF VALPARAISO, CHILE
TWO YEARS AGO

They sat on deck chairs and watched a city die.

Ari thought about the money they were going to make after today. Buyers would be lining up to kiss his ass. Valen was thinking about how much damage he was going to do to his soul if this all worked. If the machine did what he and Ari thought it would do.

Gadyuka had pressed them for a practical demonstration in a place where there was no possible connection to the politics of the United States or Russia. Other players within the new party were already at work with different tools. Computers, the Internet, and social media. None of them were likely to draw blood. He couldn't contribute to the New Soviet *without* bloodshed.

Ari looked at his watch. "Any second now." When Valen did not respond, Ari sighed and shouted, "Turn your fucking hearing aid on, you deaf son of a whore."

Valen winced. "No need to yell. It's on."

"This is going to be beautiful," Ari murmured. He wore a shit-eating grin and his eyes were glazed from drink, pot, and some small pills he popped when he thought Valen wasn't looking. "Any . . . second . . . now . . ."

There was a sudden flash of green.

It was not the green flash of the kind seen at sunset in Key West and other resort spots, and it was not a firework burst. This was soft, deeper, and it seemed to pulse upward from beneath the rolling waters, as if a great light bulb was turned quickly on and off, there and gone.

"Beautiful . . . ," breathed Ari as he grabbed his crotch and gave it a squeeze.

"Here it comes," said Valen. His own emotions were hovering between dread and excitement. They had never tried the machine out like this before. Gadyuka and the senior party members needed proof that the millions of dollars invested were going to pay off. They wanted proof. They wanted headlines. Valen was sure they would get at least that much.

The sea suddenly changed. It wasn't another flash of green. Instead, the sea seemed to darken as if tons of octopus ink had been discharged into the waters, and there was a strange stillness that lasted nearly a full minute. Then the seabirds all launched themselves off the gently rolling waves and into the air, crying out in alarm as they rose high, fleeing from sea and land for the protection of the empty air.

Valen picked up a pair of binoculars, adjusted the focus, and studied the water and the beach. The same agitation as on the surface of his champagne was stirring the waters between their boat and the shoreline, except everything was on a massive scale. The rollers disintegrated into tens of thousands of spiky wavelets which grew and grew, spitting seawater up at the flawless blue sky. On the beach the sand rippled, too. Slowly at first, and then in shivering waves that seemed to march from the waterline up the beach to the rows of trees and shrubs that separated the tourist beaches from the rocks. People were getting to their feet, standing by their beach chairs or on their blankets. Dozens stood in the shallows, with the water dancing erratically around them.

"This is going to be big," said Ari, and despite his growing horror at what they were doing, Valen felt his pulse jump.

Suddenly the sandy beach seemed to explode as geysers of water and sand leapt up and showered the tourists. It was impossible to hear the screams two miles out, but he could see the open mouths, the panic in body language. People running or caught in frozen moments of shocked indecision.

"Ni-i-i-ice," said Ari, drawing it out.

"The computer models were right," said Valen. "Right to the damn minute."

Valen turned the gain on his hearing aid to full. The sound was there, rolling over the waves toward them. A soft, deep, growing growl, as if the earth itself was being awakened from a long sleep and was not at all happy about it.

"It's beautiful, isn't it?" asked Ari. "Look at the frigging hotel. You can hear it come apart."

It was true. The façade of the big building looked for a moment like an image painted on a screen that was rippling in a variable breeze. Then the big picture windows on the first floor exploded as the frames twisted out of shape. Glass blew outward in glittering clouds. Valen flinched as people fell, slashed to red ribbons. Others staggered awkwardly away, clutching at faces, covering their blinded eyes, trying to slap at their bodies as if the stings they felt were nothing more than biting insects. One woman carrying a baby suddenly caved over it as if she could protect it, but a chunk of masonry leaned out from the cracked wall and crushed her flat.

Valen closed his eyes. Distance was the only buffer for him. He could not hear their cries, or the crunch of their bones. He could not smell their blood. He had no animus toward the people of Valparaiso, and he hoped mother and child had died quickly. He gagged and tasted bile burning the back of his throat. More deaths. More ghosts. So many more this time. Dozens, maybe hundreds. Dead because of him.

They are not my people, he told himself. *They're not Russian. They're not Communists. They were not . . .*

The word "human" floated to the top of his mind, and he gagged. They were innocents, caught in the unforgiving gears of politics and war. Bad things happen even to good people, and Valen tried to convince himself of the reality of Hobbes's eloquent quote that life outside of society was solitary, poor, nasty, brutish, and short. This destruction was a patriotic choice. This was war, even if the lunkheads in the West thought the war had ended with the fall of the Berlin Wall. As if. No, the war had never ended, and these people were unfortunate casualties of that conflict. Collateral damage.

The rationalization worked for nearly five seconds. But it, too, crumbled.

I am a monster. He opened his eyes and forced himself to witness his own crimes. The rumbling continued as balconies broke from other hotels and collapsed onto the patios. Valen reached up and turned his hearing aid down.

"Fuuuuuuck," howled Ari, drawing it out, pointing at the catastrophe. "Did you see that? Did you see that?"

"Yes," said Valen weakly, "I saw it."

"Christ, I want to take this moment, bend it over the rail, and fuck it up the ass. That's what I want to do." Ari was rubbing his crotch and it was clear he had an enormous erection. Then he grabbed for the bottle and refilled their glasses as if more booze would help the moment hurry along. "Come on, come on, come on . . ."

The rumble became a deeper growl and finally a full-throated roar. The whole hotel seemed to leap upward as if the entire structure, all 240 rooms, had abandoned its reliance on gravity, was trying to escape the moment and fly into the safety of the blue sky. Then it broke apart. Bang. Just like that. Masses of it jumped away from the central structure and collapsed across the beach. Dozens of people vanished beneath it, and the rest were swallowed by clouds of smoke, dust, and sand. The guts of the hotel were visible and Valen caught one moment of a woman standing naked beside her bed, one leg raised to step into a floral bathing suit, her eyes wide, mouth open in a silent *Oh.* And then the floor beneath her simply disintegrated into nothing and she was sucked down into the hungry teeth of concrete and structural steel. Valen was glad he could not hear screams at this distance.

The trees began falling then, because by now the earthquake was in full fury. They watched shock waves ripple through the hotel and along the cliffs, tearing it all apart. On either side of this hotel the competing resorts flew apart, and the mountain against which they were set shook itself like a wet dog. A massive avalanche of dirt, rocks, trees, and people hammered down onto the crumbling buildings. Valen wished he had Superman's X-ray vision so he could look into the earth and see the process as the subduction zone interface between the Nazca and Pacific plates went to war with each other. He wanted to see the science so that he did not have to see the pain.

"Start the engine," said Valen, and then had to shout it to jolt Ari out of whatever daydream of carnal carnage was playing out in his thoughts. "Hey! Are *you* deaf now? We need to get away from here."

The Greek snapped out of it. "What? Oh, shit. Yes."

Within a few short minutes they were far out to sea, chased by the echoes of the devastation.

CHAPTER SIXTY-FOUR

EN ROUTE

"Tell me fast, Doc," I said. "Getting close to D.C."

Ghost sat up beside me, staring at the lifelike 3-D image but unable to sniff anything. I dared not suggest a scratch-and-sniff upgrade to the Betty Boops, or Mike Harnick would install them.

"Okay," said Doc, "we've been gathering intel since the Secret Service first ambushed you. Whoever sent them with the thought of hauling you in against your will was one fry short of a Happy Meal."

"No argument."

"Those other two, though," she said, "now that's a horse of a different color. I spoke with Top and Bunny and had them go through the whole thing, and something weird popped up."

"Um, Doc . . . ? There's not one part of this that isn't weird."

"No, something weird*er*. I've read through a lot of your cases, and son, either you're crazier than a dog in a cat factory, or you're plum unlucky."

"Both," I suggested.

"That's the consensus around here, too. Point is, I need to ask you a question. Those two Closers on the road . . . did they look at all familiar?"

"You mean generally, in the fact that they were Closers, or personally?"

"Personally," she said. "Have you ever seen those two men before?"

"Maybe. There was something vaguely familiar about them, but no . . . I don't think we ever had a conversation. I have a good head for faces."

"Weird. I asked Top and Bunny that same question, and they said more or less the same thing."

"So what?" I asked.

"So," she said, "you may not recall their faces, but MindReader pinged their fingerprints, and you *have* met them before. In fact, you were in a hell of a fight with them a couple of years ago."

"I don't think so," I said, but even I could hear the uncertainty in my voice. There really was something about them.

"Let me nudge your memory. It was a case before my time. You and the boys were at Shelton Aeronautics in Wolf Trap, Virginia. You got into a tussle with two men who showed you FBI badges. Do the names Henckhouser and Spinlicker tickle you at all?"

"Sure," I said. That was early on in the Extinction Machine case. We were running down some leads on a case and stumbled onto the first two Closers we ever met. What we didn't know at the time was that they'd just slaughtered everyone who worked for Howard Shelton, who we later learned was one of the governors of Majestic Three. Agents Henckhouser and Spinlicker put up an incredible fight, nearly beating the three of us to a pulp, and then nearly frying us with microwave pulse pistols. First of those we'd seen, too. "But the guys we fought on the road didn't look like the agents from Wolf Trap. No way it was them. Not unless they had some serious cosmetic surgery."

"Or something," she said.

"What's that supposed to mean?"

"It means, Captain, that they may have some technology for changing their appearances. The fingerprints Bunny lifted from their vehicle are a perfect match, however. No question at all."

"That doesn't make sense. Those Closers in Wolf Trap worked for M3. They killed the staff at Shelton's lab as a way of hiding his involvement."

"Can you be certain of that?" asked Doc. "Meaning, can you be certain the two men you encountered at Shelton's lab were the ones who actually committed those murders?"

"The staff were killed by MPP blasts."

"Yes, but you later determined that Howard Shelton and the M3 scientists had developed their own versions of microwave guns. Just as Bill Hu developed his versions. Can you say for sure that the guns the agents had in the loading bay were the same kind? Exactly the same? Can you say for sure that the weapons they fired at you on the road in Maryland were the same as Shelton's?"

I looked at her, then at Ghost, who had nothing to say but contrived to cock an eyebrow.

Into the silence, Doc said, "From the reports, it was three days from the time the Closers met you and your guys in Virginia to when they abducted the president. Plenty of time to have evaluated your efficiency, maybe checked you out—however they do that sort of thing—and opted to orchestrate things so that it would be handed off to the organization you worked for. After all, the DMS is designed to handle the weird stuff, and it doesn't get weirder than that."

"Doc," I said, "that's a hell of a jump."

"It's an intuitive leap," she corrected, "and one I wouldn't have made if it hadn't been for those fingerprints."

"Yeah, okay, but we gave the Black Book back. We shut down M3. All that's over with."

"Tell that to the Closers, hoss. Makes me wonder what they would have said had you had an actual conversation with them instead of setting an ambush."

"Seemed reasonable at the time."

"No doubt," she said with a sigh, clearly not agreeing. "And that brings me to the second thing. As soon as we started getting reliable intel on the explosions around D.C. I had Nikki begin running random pattern searches to look for any common element. I admit it was reaching, but that's why we do pattern searches. If you don't look, you can't find."

"And did you find anything?"

Doc grinned at me like a happy cat in a canary store. In the short time I've known her I've learned that she does that when she has something juicy and nasty. She grooves on the grimmer aspects of the job.

"Although there was a lot of violence throughout the city, both aggressive to others and self-inflicted, in areas where bombs went off there was a greater concentration."

"Which tells us what? That the bombs drove people crazy?"

"No," she said. "The aberrant behavior stopped *after* the explosions. What I think is that whatever caused that behavior is tied to the bombs. I think those bombs were there to hide evidence. Maybe destroy whatever *was* affecting behavior."

I turned off the video and took the controls back from Calpurnia. I needed to feel a measure of control. The drugs were helping my back, but the pain was still there.

"What kind of device could do that?" I asked.

"I have no dadgum idea, sweet cheeks," she said. "I want you to find whatever they were blowing up. Maybe some of them malfunctioned—it was an earthquake, after all—and if so, I want you or Sam to make me a happy girl and deliver one to me with a big red bow on it."

"I'll see what I can do," I said, and ended the call.

CHAPTER SIXTY-FIVE

CITADEL OF SALAH ED-DIN
SEVEN KILOMETERS EAST OF AL-HAFFAH, SYRIA
ONE DAY AGO

The team of women moved like ghosts through the shadows, and everywhere they looked they saw death, destruction, and mystery.

The citadel had stood for over a thousand years, and had endured battles, sieges, takeovers, and atrocities. Yet somehow it had endured, even if partially ruined. Now it was a completely dead thing. The earthquake that rocked the region did what no armies ever managed to do. The walls were heaps of shattered stone, exposing framing timbers like broken bones. Tiles and windows were smashed to fragments as fine as powder.

Qadira, the team leader, stood by the stump of a massive pillar and shone a flashlight down into an opening that was too regular to have been caused by the vagaries of a shivering landscape. She fanned the dust away and saw the top of a stair, and below that another. Cracked and treacherous, like everything else, but still there.

"Over here," Qadira called in a language that only a few hundred people on Earth knew, a language used exclusively by them. By the Mothers of the Fallen, and by their Arklight field teams. "The signal came from here. We must be quick. The United Nations peacekeepers will be here soon to evaluate the disaster."

The other women picked their way through the rubble. The youngest of them, Adina, a girl of seventeen but whose face was pinched and scarred and stern, said, "Violin can't be alive down there."

"Hush, Adina," scolded Qadira, then she paused and touched the girl's arm. "If she is dead, then she's dead. We can at least bring her body back to her mother. Either way, Lilith wants to know what happened."

The team leader stepped down into darkness and the others followed.

CHAPTER SIXTY-SIX

CORNER OF WISCONSIN AVENUE NW AND SOUTH STREET NW
WASHINGTON, D.C.

Sam Imura rolled to a stop, killed his lights and sirens, and studied the area.

Wisconsin Avenue was not as badly damaged as some of the streets he'd fought through. The asphalt was cracked but drivable, and there were no cars or buildings on fire. There was damage, though.

The entire face of a building—a restaurant by the look of it—had broken free and collapsed across the pavement. Chunks of brick, shattered neon tubing, and shards of decorative metal molding lay like a blanket over the hood of one car—a five-year-old Honda Accord—and the trunk of the vehicle in front of it, a late-model Ford Focus. The weight of the impact had blown out the front tires of the second car and crumpled the dark blue skin.

People wandered like ghosts, most of them dusted with ash or smudged with smoke. Nearly all of them were bleeding from cuts, large or small; many had burns. Every face Sam saw was filled with that special awareness of having lived through something they would never and could never forget. It was all still too new, too real, to be a shared experience, and there was no crisis work to snap them out of it. No one was caught beneath wreckage or needing critical first aid. Everyone was caught in a kind of homogenized level of injury—not serious, but of a kind that would leave scars. These people were not only going to remember this moment forever, they would be deeply marked by it. Sam understood that. He had seen it in the eyes of his grandfather and great-aunt, both of whom had lived in a village near enough to Hiroshima to have gotten flash-burned, but not so close that the radiation killed them. Instead they became lifelong witnesses to an event that was always intensely real and intensely current in their minds.

Now D.C. was going to be that for hundreds of thousands of people. It would be something different to the families of those whose loved ones had died. Different still for people who had been caught up in the strange fits of madness and now had to reconcile their actions with what they knew of themselves. For all of them, the world had changed, and there was no reset button to make it normal again. Ask anyone who'd been in New York on 9/11. Sam knew a lot of those people, too.

He took a breath and tapped his earbud. "I'm here."

"Any sign of a device?" asked the voice of Doc Holliday.

"Not yet." To the vehicle, Sam said, "Calpurnia, deploy drones. Scan the area. I want a full-picture three-D."

Four hummingbird-sized drones shot from concealed compartments and rose into the air, circling the scene. Only one person noticed, but the tiny machines looked like birds, and even if they didn't, they were not the strangest part of the day.

A ghostly image overlaid the inside of Sam's windshield, turning everything he saw into a kind of blueprint, complete with small identifier tags. Every car was labeled for make, model, and year; and when license plates were visible the name and basic information for the driver was given. Stores and buildings were named. Even people on the street were quickly identified through facial recognition. Sam, who was impressed by very little, nodded in appreciation.

"Search for chemical signatures," ordered Sam.

"Searching," Calpurnia assured him. "Detecting no traces of particulate matter consistent with nitroglycerin, pentaerythritol tetranitrate, trinitrotoluene, or triacetone triperoxide."

"What about Semtex? Scan for ammonium nitrate and fuel oil."

"No evidence of Semtex or its components. Fuel oil is present, but consistent with admixtures in fuel tanks. No trace of cyclomethylene trinitramine."

Sam frowned. "Expand scan. Search for timing devices, clocks, anything."

A series of yellow circles popped up on the display. "Forty-eight cell phones have been tagged," Calpurnia said. "Forty-four on the persons of people within the scanning area. Three are on the street."

These items were highlighted, but the drones sent pictures of three phones lying where they'd fallen from the hands or pockets of fleeing people.

"Where's the last one?" asked Sam, then he stiffened. "Wait. I think I have it."

A motorcycle came weaving through the debris and stopped near the Ford Focus. The bike was a new black Kawasaki Z650 with green trim, ridden by a driver dressed head to toe in black leather. His helmet had no logo and a smoked visor. The driver leaned over and steadied the bike on one foot and drew a cell from his pocket. He pointed it at the Focus and appeared to be pressing a button as if he was aiming a TV remote.

"Calpurnia . . . ?"

"The driver of the motorcycle is sending a call to a number registered to a Virgin Mobile ZTE Temple X 4G LTE disposable phone."

"A burner," said Sam. "Hack it."

"The call has not been answered."

The driver looked around and did not see Sam behind his dark security windows. He punched in a number and pointed it at the Ford Focus again. Nothing appeared to happen.

"The other cell phone is in the trunk of that car," said Calpurnia. "It is operational but appears to be damaged. I pinged it to verify that it is the number the driver is attempting to reach, but the phone is not ringing. Ronin," she continued, using Sam's combat call sign, "I am detecting other electronic equipment inside the trunk but cannot verify what kind."

"This is our guy," decided Sam. He touched his earbud. "Do I have backup?"

"No backup is available at this time, Ronin," said Doc.

"Fuck it."

He tapped the dashboard display to clear it and hit another key to slide out the tray of handguns. Then he opened the door of his car, stood up from the driver's seat, leaned his arm across the hood, and pointed his pistol at the man on the bike.

"Federal agent," he yelled. "Drop the cell phone and put both of your hands on top of your head. Do it now or I will shoot."

The motorcycle driver froze, clearly startled.

But not startled enough. He dropped the cell phone, but with a smooth move that was as fast as it was elegant, his hand flashed toward the unzipped vee of his leather jacket and closed around a holstered pistol. It was so fast that it might have worked on nearly anyone. A regular street cop for sure, and maybe even some top-quality federal agents or marshals.

Sam was faster than that.

He fired three shots, catching the man in each shoulder and the middle of the thigh. Most professionals would have fired center mass to guarantee a kill; but Sam wanted the man alive, and the former sniper was a superb shot with any firearm. The man cried out in a foreign language and collapsed. And it should have ended there, except for a bit of bad luck. The cell phone landed facedown on a pile of debris and one sharp stone hit a key. Not the one to resend the deactivation code. The other one. The wrong one.

Sam saw a huge and intensely bright flash of green, and then he felt himself being lifted on a ball of glowing green gas. It burned like fire and the flames punched him into the air and across the street and through the window of a restaurant. In the movies, windows break easily and people are rarely hurt.

In real life they are made from thick, tempered glass, and smashing through them is akin to flying through a cutlery store. Those big, wickedly sharp pieces of glass did not break easily, and they punished Sam—oh yes, they punished him—for his rude passage through. They slashed at him like knives, like spears, like swords. Seeding the air with his blood.

Pieces of the Ford Focus, the debris that lay atop it, the Kawasaki, and the biker also chased Sam through the window. All along the street, windows shattered and car alarms blared and people screamed because they thought it was all starting up again.

CHAPTER SIXTY-SEVEN

CORNER OF WHITTIER STREET NW AND HARLAN PLACE NW
WASHINGTON, D.C.

Calpurnia called the turns and I fought the traffic. D.C. looked like a war zone. I was hoping that it actually wasn't, that we were wrong about what was going on.

I also hope that politicians are honest and Santa Claus is real.

The sky was filled with helicopters of every stripe, and there was blood on the sidewalks.

The street Doc thought might be a location for another bomb was impossible to access because of damage and emergency vehicles. So I parked, put on a vest that could stop shrapnel, fished a tool kit from the back, clicked my tongue for Ghost, and told Calpurnia to lock up. Walking was painful as all hell. I said fuck it and jogged.

That was fun. Every nerve ending from my shoulder blades to the tops of my thighs was sending me hate mail. Ghost ranged ahead and glared people out of our way. I had a DHS badge hung around my neck on a lanyard, but nobody stopped to look, and no one asked to see the badge up close. Everyone was dealing with their own stuff, and they had a lot on their plates. I saw two Latino boys, both dressed like they were either in a gang or wanted to be seen that way, doing first aid on an old white man with a leg injury. I saw a young Asian man sitting cross-legged in the middle of the street, face in his hands, weeping. He looked untouched, but that was a relative concept. I saw a heavyset black woman whose face was covered with ash walking slowly across the street, eyes seeing nothing. She had pieces of burned newspaper sticking to her clothes. A dead cat lay on the hood of a crushed Volvo. There were two houses on the corner where I parked. One had collapsed into a sinkhole and smoke curled up from the splinters of the room; the other was absolutely untouched.

Flash images of hell.

Or maybe purgatory. Not sure of the difference. Ask a priest, or maybe a surrealist filmmaker.

We ran.

The target was on Second Street, Northwest, just off of Whittier. The through street was ruptured and water shot upward from a broken main. I had to circle wide to keep from being drenched. Cars on both sides of the street had been upended and lay on their sides, or on lawns, or atop one another like copulating metal turtles. A few people were with the cars, removing stuff, or maybe stealing it. Looks the same in a crisis. Three teens were huddled together, laughing at something inside one of the cars. It annoyed me so I told them to fuck off. Then I saw that the windshield was cracked and splashed red, and they weren't laughing. They were crying. A figure sat belted into the car, but from the slack way the head lolled on the neck I could read the story. It did not matter that the kids hadn't heard me yell at them, but I knew I'd just bought myself some evil karma for my quick and stupid judgment.

Damn.

I moved on quickly, coward that I am, and I applied a thin veneer of salve to my conscience by calling it in to the TOC. Someone would come, I told myself. Sure. And that would make it all better, right?

There was a Harley-Davidson parked near four cars that were heaped like discarded toys, and to the left of that a man stood on the end of the soaked lawn. He looked ordinary enough. About my height, with sandy blond hair and sunglasses, jeans, and a heavy leather jacket. There was tension and frustration in his body language, but that seemed to fit, especially if one of the cars was his. But as I got closer my brain began picking out details that did not really fit with the moment. Two things really stood out. First, he was absolutely unmarked by blood, dirt, ash, or trauma. And the second thing was that he held a crowbar in his hands.

I slowed as I approached from his blind side, and signaled Ghost to be ready. The man was unaware of us. When we were fifty feet away I heard a cell phone ring. It was surprisingly loud, as if the ringer was turned all the way up. The man shifted the crowbar to one hand and removed a sleek cell with the other. I couldn't hear what the caller said, but the man stiffened into a posture of animal alertness.

He began looking around as if suddenly expecting to find someone creeping up on him.

Which is when he saw me. At that same moment, Bug's voice was in my ear telling me bad things about Sam Imura. I went for my gun. The man dropped the crowbar and ran, vanishing around the end of the pile of wrecked cars.

"Ghost—*own*!"

The big white shepherd, tired as he had to be, exploded into motion, transforming into a pale blur as he raced across the lawn and around the cars. I broke into a run, too, but it was slower, spoiled by pain and limping legs and a fatigue that had not yet been overwhelmed by adrenaline.

Then I heard Ghost utter a high, sharp cry of terrible pain.

CHAPTER SIXTY-EIGHT

CORNER OF WHITTIER STREET NW AND HARLAN PLACE NW
WASHINGTON, D.C.

I ran. Pain or not, I ran.

As I rounded the mound of dead cars, I saw Ghost first. He lay on the wet grass, twitching with terrible spasms, foam and spit flying from his gaping mouth, eyes wide, legs straight and rigid. It took my brain a microsecond longer to see and understand the two silver wires that ran from my dog's shoulder to a tiny power pack that lay next to him. I knew that kind of gun. A multishot Taser that discharged the power pack of each round and automatically loaded the next.

I shot the man in the chest but he shot me almost at the same time. My brain processed the fact that my rounds should have knocked him way back, but didn't. In the too-little time I had to understand it, it was obvious that he had some high-end body armor that absorbed impact as well as protected against penetration. But before I could adjust and park the next round in his brainpan, the flechettes of his Taser hit me in the shoulder.

He stayed on his feet and I went down.

If you have never been hit with a Taser, try it sometime. It's almost exactly as much fun as being punted in the balls by an enthusiastic NFL placekicker, but there are no crowds to cheer. The power can range all the way up to a molar-melting million volts, and most shots will drop even a supermax prison yard monster for a minimum of thirty seconds. The one he used on me was a son of a bitch. You can feel it start, and for a split second you think, *I got this. I can do this.*

You can't.

The electricity opens up your nerve endings and commandeers your nerve conduction and you go the hell down. Your entire body contracts into one massive cramp and even though you can scream, all that you manage is a prolonged and inarticulate howl.

Sure, there are stories of people shaking them off. I've even done it with some of the lower-wattage versions they use in training and demonstrations. This wasn't one of those. This was military grade, and on the higher end of that scale. These are designed to put anyone down. It did not help one damn bit that I was twitching around on wet grass.

The power pack had a thirty-second charge, but the aftereffect of that level of stunner was going to leave me about as spry as a Gumby left out in the sun, and it would last for maybe five minutes. The man bent and picked up my pistol, and stuck it in the back of his belt. He did not shoot me with it. He glanced at my Department of Homeland Security badge and nodded to himself.

Then he went and fetched his dropped crowbar.

I twitched and thrashed and screamed and could not do a single useful thing. Voices in my ear—Bug and Doc—sounded like they were a hundred miles away, on the other side of a vast thunderstorm. I caught words, but each of them cracked open like fortune cookies in which no one had thought to include fortunes.

The man returned, and for a moment I thought he was going to strike me with the crowbar. Or worse, Ghost. He didn't. Instead he went immediately to work on the trunk of one of the smashed cars. It took him maybe ten seconds to break the lock. It went up with a creak of protest. The man dropped the crowbar between Ghost and me, then bent to lift something out of the trunk. It was a device about the size of an old-fashioned boom box, but not shaped like that.

No. This was built like a small generator but with a large circular opening wrapped in coils of silver and copper wires.

My heart stopped beating for a moment. I was sure of it.

I knew that machine.

I'd seen two of them. Big ones. Much bigger than this. One was down in Antarctica. The other was in the basement of a mansion on the West Coast. I knew what those machines could do, and nothing I'd ever seen in life scared me as much as seeing one now, in the hands of some stranger.

He began walking toward the parked Harley, then stopped at the edge of the lawn, and looked down the street toward burning houses and the endless sound of sirens. Then he turned back to me.

"I'm sorry," he said. "If you were me, you'd do the same. The war never ends, does it?"

I was incapable of speech. I wanted to ask what he meant. I wanted to tell him that he was a murderous bastard. All I could do was scream.

He nodded, though, as if I had agreed with his words. He went over to his bike and put the device into the cargo rack behind the saddle, wrapping it in a blue tarp and securing it with bungee cords. Then he put on a plain black helmet and swung his leg over. He started the engine, turned once more toward me, though now his face was nothing but a wall of curved, impenetrable plastic. He nodded to me.

Then he drove away.

The battery sputtered out and died in a puddle. I fought against the lingering pain and disorientation and rolled over onto hands and knees. Ghost was whimpering and trying to stand; and failing.

I lifted a trembling hand to tap my earbud. The ones we use are hardened against most kinds of power surges or shocks, but even so I was surprised that it still worked.

"C-Cowboy to T-T-TOC."

Doc Holliday was right there, clear as a bell and urgent as a heart attack. "Cowboy, your telemetry is spiking. Are you all right?"

"No," I gasped as I crawled over to Ghost and pulled him into my arms. "Nothing's all right, goddamn it."

"Did you locate the bomb?"

Ghost gave my face a feeble, desperate lick.

"It's not a bomb," I wheezed.

"You're not making sense. . . ."

"It was a God Machine. . . ."

Ghost shivered and I bent and pressed my forehead against his and waited for the pain to stop.

Knowing it would not.

CHAPTER SIXTY-NINE

CITADEL OF SALAH ED-DIN
SEVEN KILOMETERS EAST OF AL-HAFFAH, SYRIA
ONE DAY AGO

The Arklight team moved through dusty shadows, following old maps and instinct. The leader was wise and older than she looked, and the others trusted her intuition when it came to missions like this. The older members of the team had walked through worse shadows than these with her and come out on the other side. Only the youngest of the team, Adina, Qadira's grandniece, was new to field missions of this kind. She tried not to let her fear and apprehension show, but her words betrayed her nervousness.

"Won't there be aftershocks?"

"Probably," said her great-aunt.

"These walls are all broken," said Adina. "Most of the ceiling has collapsed. What if—?"

Qadira stopped and turned to her, holding the flashlight so that they each leaned into a cone of its glow. "Listen to me," she said. "There are always dangers. There will always be dangers. You know this. You were born into horror, and every day of your life until you were five was filled with dangers worse than anything down here. The walls may collapse, the rest of the roof may fall, and Gaia might swallow us whole. All of that could happen, but if so . . . then what?"

"We would die."

"Yes. We would, as so many of our sisters and mothers and daughters have died. So, tell me then, Adina . . . what is death? What is it to women such as us?"

Adina straightened and took a breath. "Death is a doorway," she recited. It was part of a very old catechism the Mothers of the Fallen had written for themselves during their centuries of captivity in the breeding pits of the Red Knights.

"What is beyond the doorway?" asked the older woman.

"There is life beyond life beyond life."

Qadira smiled and touched Adina's face and hair and shoulders.

"Men fear death," said one of them. "But we are women. We give birth to ourselves."

"Death is a doorway to life," said Qadira. Then she grinned, and the lines on her face creased like a playful monkey's. "But let's not wait for death to catch us. He is slow and we are . . . what . . . ?"

"We are fast," said Adina, smiling in spite of herself.

"Yes, we are."

And, true to their litany, the women, old and young, moved off quickly through the darkness beneath the broken earth.

Ten minutes later they found a man sitting with his back to a wall. He was covered with dust and blood, and his eyes were filled with madness. A woman lay on the ground with her head on his lap. She, too, was bloody. A pistol, with the slide locked back, was on the ground near them.

Both the man and the woman were as pale as ghosts.

CHAPTER SEVENTY

CORNER OF WHITTIER STREET NW AND HARLAN PLACE NW
WASHINGTON, D.C.

It took a long time to get back to the car.

Ghost limped along on wobbly legs and we both had to stop and rest. Whatever kind of stun gun was used had more kick than anything I'd ever even heard of. Nearly lethal, but not actually.

When I reached the Betty Boop, I collapsed against it and stood there on macaroni legs, trembling and weak and stupid. The locks clicked open and I helped Ghost inside.

"Calpurnia," I wheezed, "get a forensics team here. I want that car taken to the Warehouse. And find that motorcycle. Retask any drones you need and access all pertinent traffic cams. This guy doesn't slip away, understood?"

"Of course, Cowboy," she said briskly, then added, "You appear ill. According to the RFID chip, there is a ninety-two percent possibility that you have been Tased."

"Well, no shit, Sherlock."

"Don't be snotty," scolded the computer. "And watch your—"

"If you tell me one more time to watch my fucking language I'm going to open up your CPU and let Ghost take a piss in it."

There was a beat. "Initiating a full medical diagnostic, Joseph."

"Do that," I said, and called Doc Holliday. "Tell me if Sam is alive."

"He is," Doc said, "but he's in bad shape. Shrapnel, shock, and blood loss. An evac team is flying him out of D.C. and when I know more you'll know. He was wearing a bodycam but it was damaged and the video feed is distorted. Our people are running all kinds of filters and we should have something soon. One thing I can tell you, though, is the blast that took him down was weird. Not orange or yellow flame. It was bright green. That jibes with witness reports from the other explosions."

"What the hell blows up green?"

"For fireworks," she said, "they use barium chloride. People throw copper wire into campfires to make the flames burn green, but there's a longer answer about color spectrums, heat, and gas that you don't want to hear."

I gave myself another jab of painkillers. "No," I hissed. "I don't."

"So, short answer is we don't know why the explosions are green. Or, why they're so hot. Teams that have managed to examine blast sites report a great degree of melting, indicating intensely high temperatures. We don't know what it means, but it's weird and I don't like weird unless I'm in bed with someone."

"Is Sam going to be okay?"

"Honey, he's a mess and the only people who've seen him are EMTs. I hope so, but right now I can't put good money on any bets."

"What about Auntie . . . ?" I asked, afraid of almost any answer.

"Alive and holding on," said Doc, "but she's critical and, trite as it is to say this, they're doing everything they can. Seriously."

"Will she make it?"

"Cowboy, you're asking me to read the future, and I left my tarot cards at home. If I was still a church lady I'd pray to one of them saints, but far as I know nobody up there's taking calls from this Texas gal."

Right about then, Church joined the call from his jet, which was nearing D.C., and asked for a full report. I didn't omit a single detail.

When I was done there was a solid two-count, and Church said, "A God Machine?"

"A small one, but, yeah, that's what it looked like, boss," I said. "So, any of you geniuses want to tell me what the hell's going on? Earthquakes, insanity, mass suicides and murder, and now this.

And, if this thing was the same as all the others, the ones that exploded, then why? What's the point of *any* of this?"

"We can draw a few conclusions," said Doc. "These devices, whether they're actually the same technology that Prospero Bell created or not, were positioned around the epicenter of this quake. They have to be involved, but we don't know how. I read all of the reports obtained during the Kill Switch matter and there is absolutely nothing in there about effects on plate tectonics. Nothing."

"I—" I began, but she cut me off.

"There is quite a lot," she continued, "about psychic disturbances. We know from that case that when a large God Machine was idling at the lowest power settings, it caused a number of effects. The Gateway Project, which was the ugly stepsister of the larger and better-funded Majestic program, was experimenting with those machines, and there were a number of suicides reported at their base in the Antarctic. Which, I believe, you blew into orbit, Cowboy."

"Seemed like the thing to do at the time," I said.

"Ain't arguing, sugar," she conceded, "given what they were working on. Remote-viewing, mind control, psychic spying, and—the big enchilada—trying to open an interdimensional gateway without actually knowing what was on the other side of it. As stupid goes, that's the prize hog. They could as easily have opened a doorway to a toxic environment, the airless vacuum of space, or a dadburn black hole. I'm frequently forced to push back the limits of my understanding of human stupidity, and that goes triple when the Department of Defense is involved."

"Not always," I said lamely.

"You've just had your tight white ass handed to you, Cowboy," said Doc, "so we'll all pretend you didn't just hashtag-NotAllMen the DoD."

"Shutting up now," I said.

"The takeaway here," said Church, "is that we have a bead on the technology used to cause the mass suicides and other violence. How many explosions have you tracked?"

"A total of forty-six devices were detonated," she said. "The one taken away by the bad boy with the Taser makes forty-seven, unless that is somehow different. Considering the situation—a bunch of cars wrecked by the earthquake—we can postulate that that device was damaged and not able to detonate according to plan. The telemetry from Sam's RFID and his car tell us that the first biker was also there to retrieve a faulty device that was in a car partly buried by debris. So, of the known machines we had eyes on, two faulted out, and in both cases someone was sent to retrieve them when they failed to detonate."

"Why would the first biker blow himself up?"

Calpurnia played the video on the screen inside the car but Doc narrated the key points. "It's likely he was trying to use his cell to deactivate the detonator and was unable to do so. When Sam confronted him, the biker dropped the cell, and the resulting jolt to the burner somehow made the firing sequence work. I believe that's what you military boys call a clusterfuck. Unfortunate for him and for Sam. Before you ask, Cowboy, the biker was blown to rags. We can run DNA and dental, if they find enough of his face, but that's going to take time. His body will be collected and hopefully there will be papers or some other kind of ID."

"Calpurnia's drones are hunting for the second biker," I said. "And her dashboard cam should have—"

"Yes," she said, cutting me off again, "we got the license plate of the Kawasaki. It's stolen, as was the other bike. Both thefts were done after the earthquake started, which is a narrow time frame, so it's likely they had eyes on possible vehicles to steal, and they certainly weren't worried about being chased by the cops. Not today."

I rubbed Ghost's soggy neck. He was looking a little better.

"Okay," I said, "someone has the God Machine technology and they're using it to drive people batshit crazy. Are they using it to cause earthquakes, too?"

There was silence on the line.

"Kind of like an actual answer to that one," I said.

Doc sighed. It was so long and hard that it sounded like a hot-air balloon deflating. "Your little sweetheart seems to think so."

"Junie?"

"She's here. In the computer room with Bug, and they're jabbering on about this and that. Aliens and reptilians and all sorts of New Age weirdness. I think they've both lost their damn minds."

"I've found," said Church very dryly, "that Junie Flynn speaks from great experience and insight. She has been correct far more often than she's been wrong. Wouldn't you agree, Captain?"

"Yeah, damn it."

Doc sighed again. "That," she said, "is what I'm afraid of. So, the short and less facetious answer to your question is that we're working on it."

"Which leaves me where?" I demanded.

"Sam Imura is on his way to Johns Hopkins," said Church. "Aunt Sallie is already there. I'll be there shortly. Why don't we make that the center of our operations for now? We can get you and Ghost some treatment as well. We'll close ranks and be family with our injured until we have our next move planned. Meanwhile Doc Holliday, Bug, and Miss Flynn will continue to work the problem from their end."

So, I drove the hell back to Maryland. Thinking bad, confused, alarming thoughts as the miles fell away behind me.

INTERLUDE TWENTY-ONE

THE *SUICIDE KINGS*
THE PACIFIC OCEAN
TWENTY NAUTICAL MILES WEST OF VALPARAISO, CHILE
TWO YEARS AGO

Gadyuka called while the coastline of Chile was dwindling over the horizon. "You promised a six point five at least."

"I did," he said, and there was a small flicker of doubt in his chest. Gadyuka purred when she was angry as often as when she was happy.

"Early reports are calling it a six point nine," said Gadyuka. "That is very, very impressive."

If she had been there and stabbed him in the stomach it would not have hurt as much. Being thanked for this.

"Now," she said, "let's talk about the next phase. Now that we know it works, how quickly can you orchestrate another one? Something inland this time."

Valen cleared his throat. The boat was cutting through the water at high speed. Ari was below and Valen tried not to hear the screams of pain and horror that came up from the cabin. He forced himself to focus on the science. "It depends on how far inland," he said, "and on what kind of terrain. It depends on existing geology. We'd have to get precise seismographic information and then look for a stress point we can exploit."

"What if there are no stress points?"

"There always are," Valen assured her. "Even if they're old and haven't had any appreciable activity in ten thousand years. The Earth is a big cracked egg and the pieces are always in motion. Always."

"Very well," said Gadyuka, "that's fair enough. Crunch some numbers for me. And a related question—what can you do with a dormant, or semidormant, volcano?"

"Volcano . . . ," mused Valen. "We never even considered it because, let's face it, that's pretty dangerous."

"More than an earthquake?" asked Gadyuka.

"Different. A lot harder to control. There's more than damage to surface structures; there's lava and, more critically, all that ash. A volcano has a bigger overall environmental impact. Besides . . . if we hit a volcano with our gear, it would not just blow, it would blow big."

"How big?"

"You know that famous one, Krakatoa? It's in Indonesia, in the Sunda Strait. It blew in 1883 with a force that was thirteen thousand times more powerful than the bomb the Americans dropped on Hiroshima. They say it was the loudest sound ever heard. People reported hearing it in Australia. It hit six on the VEI, the Volcano

Explosivity Index. It kicked out over twenty-one cubic kilometers of rock, ash, and pumice. It caused tsunamis that killed something like thirty-seven thousand people. More, if you consider the effect on air quality and damage to crops and livestock. If we'd used our tech to ignite Krakatoa it would have been worse. A lot worse. So, yes . . . big."

"Big," said Gadyuka slowly, like a cat licking a trapped and trembling mouse. "Big is exactly the right word."

CHAPTER SEVENTY-ONE

JOHNS HOPKINS UNIVERSITY HOSPITAL
BALTIMORE, MARYLAND

They treated me at the hospital and wanted to keep me for observation. I told one doctor that he could observe me putting my foot up his ass, so the rest of that conversation got shelved. Instead they jabbed me with a bunch of needles, shoved some pills into my hand, and told me to take it easy.

Yeah. Top of my to-do list.

Sam and Auntie were both still clinging to the edge of life's cliff, and from the looks the staff gave me—or turned away to avoid giving me—I was feeling pretty scared. And really angry, but still had no one to paint a target on.

Who were the damn bad guys?

I paced the hallways, drank too much coffee, told people to fuck off when they tried to tell me Ghost wasn't allowed in there, and was close to going out of my damn mind, when a voice called my name.

"Joe!"

I whirled and saw Dr. Rudy Sanchez walking toward me, arms out to take me in a brother's embrace. We hugged and slapped and when I winced, he recoiled.

"*Ay dios mío*, Joe," he cried. "Are you hurt?"

Rudy sounds exactly like Raul Julia from those old *Addams Family* movies. A rich Puerto Rican baritone that carries gravity and sobriety and comfort, which are all weapons he brings to bear in his version of the war. Rudy is a top-notch psychiatrist who specializes in trauma and PTSD. He joined the DMS when I did, and without him most of us shooters would have been crippled by the scar tissue on our souls.

He is also my best friend. One of those rare ones you can tell any damn thing to. No filters at all. And, although Church is usually the adult in any given room, Rudy is the adult you *like* in those rooms.

We went into a small solarium and I explained about my injuries and how I got them. He sat, with Ghost's head on his thigh, and listened without interruption.

"This has been a terrible day, Cowboy," he said. "For us and for everyone in Washington. Have you heard the latest numbers? More than eleven hundred dead and almost eight thousand still missing. And now you tell me that God Machines may be involved? What are we into here?"

It is a sign of Rudy's empathy and compassion that he said "we" and not "you." He may not go into battle, but he doesn't stand on the sanitary edges of the swamp of emotional involvement.

"You now know as much as I do, brother," I said. "Which is somewhere between jack and shit."

He pursed his lips and stared into the middle of nowhere for a few silent moments, then began shaking his head. "No, I don't think that is true at all."

"What's that supposed to mean?"

Rudy leaned back and crossed his legs. "Joe, the Kill Switch and Extinction Machine cases were two of the most traumatic of your career since joining the DMS. The possibility of alien life, psychic invasion, threats so big that they forced all of us to reevaluate what we believe about the world. No, about the universe. Listen, as we grow from childhood into adolescence and then adulthood, our worldview is forced to change. The simpler things that comforted us at each stage are torn down and replaced by new structures that are no longer built as shelters for us but as inarguable truths that force us to accept that we are not the center of the universe. We are parts of a greater universe that is always going to be too large to grasp in any one lifetime. As we mature we try to build structures around us that help us contain the infinite into something easier to grasp. If we are careless, then we once more come to see ourselves as the centers of finite worlds whose rules we understand and whose structures we accept."

Ghost began sniffing at Rudy's pockets, and he smiled and produced a few liver treats he'd brought with him. Rudy's like that. Ghost ate them with his peculiar delicacy.

"When the former president was abducted out of the White House at the beginning of the Extinction Machine case," continued Rudy, smiling at Ghost, "we had a choice. Accept that some kind of alien intelligence exists, or bury our heads in the sand. I am a psychiatrist and my profession is always about seeking the truth. And you are a special operator, and if you refuse to accept facts—what you call 'intelligence'—then people will die and so will you."

I nodded.

"The DMS was built around a kind of martial pragmatism. We have to look for the truth in any given situation, otherwise our actions will be questionable, and people will die. If we had not had to accept hard and occasionally dangerous truths, then billions of people would have died. The Jakoby ethnic cleansing project, the weaponized Ebola the Seven Kings tried to deploy . . . sadly, many other examples come to mind . . . all of these required that we accept the truth for what it is."

"You're going to quote Marcus Aurelius at me, aren't you?"

"I am. Two quotes come to mind," said Rudy, nodding at me like I was an attentive schoolboy. "First, this is one I was thinking while you were telling me about what happened. Aurelius wrote, 'Never let the future disturb you. You will meet it, if you have to, with the same weapons of reason which today arm you against the present.' And do you know what 'weapons' he was referring to?"

"Logic, analysis, perception, and practicality."

He offered me a dog treat and I smacked his hand away.

"The other quote," he said, "is one misquoted by Hannibal Lecter in *Silence of the Lambs*. The actual quote is more apt anyway. When confronted by things we do not understand but truly want or need to understand, Aurelius suggests, 'This, what is it in itself, and by itself, according to its proper constitution? What is the substance of it? What is the matter, or proper use? What is the form, or efficient cause? What is it for in this world, and how long will it abide? Thus must thou examine all things that present themselves unto thee.' And later, in that same book, Aurelius writes, 'As every fancy and imagination presents itself unto thee, consider (if it be possible) the true nature, and the proper qualities of it, and reason with thyself about it.'" He studied me. "Do you understand what that means?"

"I do," I said, "but I don't want to."

"But you must."

"I must," I agreed.

"There is no such thing as an alternative fact," said Rudy. "The truth is only ever the truth. What changes is whether we accept it, even if it is inconvenient and contrary to the truth we'd prefer."

I sighed and rubbed my face with my callused hands. "Yeah, damn it."

He put his hand on my shoulder. "What then, is the truth? Or, what is the likely truth. Construct a workable theory to explain recent events. If you go outside of your mental comfort zone, what then is probable?"

I gave him a sour look. "Is this how you comfort all of your traumatized patients?"

"You're not on my couch, Cowboy. This is how I talk to my friend, who is one of the truest, wisest, and most capable people I've ever met."

I sighed. And told him. He listened with his whole being, which is what he always does. I watched his olive skin grow pale. He wears a small silver crucifix under his shirt; it hangs down over his heart. He touched it absently, as he always does when his own worldview changes gears without a clutch.

When I was done he spent a few minutes not looking at me or anything. The distant hospital ICU noises were the only sound.

"Then this is what you have to tell Mr. Church and Joan Holliday," he said at last, his voice hushed. "Junie, too. She'll need to be in on this. God."

"What is it you need to tell me?" said a voice, and we turned to see Mr. Church standing in the doorway.

CHAPTER SEVENTY-TWO

COURTYARD BY MARRIOTT—NEW CARROLLTON LANDOVER, MARYLAND

Valen ditched the stolen motorcycle twenty blocks from where he had recovered the God Machine. As he had worn leather gloves the whole time, there were no prints to worry about.

His rental car was parked near the border of Maryland and he got in and drove through packed traffic to the hotel in Landover that was the rendezvous point for the six members of his team. Ari would no doubt be waiting, having gone for the closest device. The other five were agents supplied by Gadyuka—three men and two women who had lived in America for most of their lives. People who were above suspicion. They would be debriefed and then sent back to their handlers and probably fold back into their affected daily routines.

Valen wondered if they would be given safe passage out of the country before things got really bad. Knowing Gadyuka, he doubted it. A mass exodus of any kind would raise red flags, and from what the viper said about the DMS, a pattern like that would be noticed.

So, they would be left to die, or—best-case scenario—shelter in place until such time as they could be extricated.

He went to his room without haste, and spent a few minutes sweeping the place for bugs. Then he opened a bottle of vodka and poured himself a generous shot, knocked it back, and poured another.

Over the course of the next two hours, five of the agents arrived, knocked discreetly, and were let in. Only one had actually been required to retrieve a damaged machine. The others were in the field to make sure that each of the remaining devices had thoroughly detonated. They had. The thermite AXL compound, coupled with the timer that sent the machines into overload, resulted in a fireball that was intense and effective, though short-lived.

The agents did not know Valen's name and referred to him by the false identity under which he'd checked in. James Wilson, a systems software salesman, which was as vanilla as it got.

The agents came and went and Valen sat alone, waiting for Ari.

Minutes crawled past.

Valen tried calling his friend, but there was no answer. Not even voicemail.

He sank into a chair and thought about the day. The cop and his dog—or government agent, or whatever he was—had been a frightening surprise. Gadyuka and Ari would both likely mock him for using a Taser instead of something more lethal. He could even imagine the shape of that mockery—the God Machines had just slaughtered more than thirteen hundred people, and he could not bring himself to shoot a cop and a dog face-to-face.

Valen understood how silly that seemed. Even he did not understand it. By now his crimes had to place him in the highest levels of mass murderers throughout history. Much as he wanted to, Valen could no longer count the dead.

The flat-screen TV mounted over the dresser was black and he did not dare to turn it on. He'd seen enough.

Enough.

More than enough.

Valen poured himself another vodka, sat facing the door, and waited.

But Ari never came.

CHAPTER SEVENTY-THREE

THE WHITE HOUSE

Jennifer VanOwen checked in with her staff, with the senior advisors, with the chief of staff, and with the president himself. They were all in various degrees of stress, ranging from moderate freak-out to complete panic. That was fine. That was exactly right.

She was the voice of reason, and people throughout the West Wing would remember that. History would remember that Jennifer VanOwen kept her cool. That would play well when she made her move out of the shadows and onto the radar of the power players who were looking for the next face of the party. It was time for a woman to ascend to the American throne.

Such as it was.

For as long as it lasted.

Her contact assured her that there would be six or eight good years before the red, white, and blue lost its value as the currency of global economic power. That was good. She only wanted four years. Not the last four, but the ones coming up. Let someone else sit behind the big desk when it all turned to shit. People would be tripping over themselves to say that it wouldn't have happened on her watch.

VanOwen told her secretary that she was going to go out to see how things were being handled in the streets. The president hadn't budged from the bunker, and frankly everyone seemed okay with that. This wasn't something he was equipped for or capable of handling. The less he got involved and the more he allowed actual experts to make decisions, the better he would look in tomorrow's news cycle. At least that's what VanOwen told him.

For her part, VanOwen needed to be visible. Very visible. She picked the right places to be seen huddled in earnest conversation with firefighters, police officials, doctors, aid workers, and ordinary citizens who had come out of the woodwork to lend willing hands and strong backs. Picking those spots had required a few hours of careful monitoring of reports, and some tips from her spies. Her employer's people had given her some leads, too.

VanOwen spent hours in the field, and she contrived to get smudges of dirt and blood on her expensive suit, her hands, and even her pretty face. Her hair was carefully mussed and she knew that she would look amazing on Fox, CNN, and the BBC news. Her actions were orchestrated to emphasize the power of "us," but it would drive iron rivets into her campaign once it launched. News reporters would make career jumps off their coverage of her, and that was good. When one cable news show ran different pictures of her—holding an IV bag of blood, working with a black teen to pull a Latina from beneath a collapsed storefront, handing coffee to weary EMTs, standing with a hand to her shocked mouth and tears in her eyes as she viewed a long row of sheet-covered corpses, yelling fiercely to direct an impromptu rescue crew to make a human ladder to pull a child from a sinkhole—the anchor dubbed her Hurricane VanOwen. In that instant she went from a relative Beltway nobody to a force of nature.

And then she withdrew, telling reporters that she was going back to fight this on a different front—the donations of money, food, and clothing pouring in from the "wonderful Americans who want to do their part even if they're hundreds of miles away." It was a great sound bite, and once more she contrived to have tears—this time of pride—in her eyes.

She made her way to her car and was driven out of D.C.

During the trip, she made over forty phone calls, doing a lot of what she had just promised to do. Then, when the broken city was behind her and the green of Virginia wrapped itself around her, she told her driver to take her to the Barn. It was the code name for a division of DARPA that had ostensibly been closed down. The official story of its current use was testing flight simulators for a proposed virtual reality training center for drone pilots. Intriguing enough to convince the right people to keep the facility's top-secret clearance in place, but boring enough to keep congressional spooks from nosing around.

The guards at the Barn were repurposed military. Not MPs or anyone who had a propensity for problem-solving or investigation. These were the kind of soldiers who could stand post all day, never ask a question, and be content with that. There were plenty of them in any branch of the service anywhere in the world.

Her driver presented the credentials for someone other than VanOwen. The soldiers barely looked in the back, and if they did, they saw a woman with curly black hair, garish lipstick, and horn-rimmed glasses. Later, when investigators checked this all out, they would match the description and the ID with Gloria Paley, a seasoned representative from Iowa. Ms. Paley would never afterward be found, and any blame would land solidly on her. Her credit card would be used in Guatemala over the next couple of days and then never again. VanOwen did not know, nor care, what would happen to the body. Her employer had people to handle those kinds of details.

The driver parked near the eighth in a row of sixteen Quonset huts that stretched down between stands of trees. VanOwen got out and went inside quickly. Her driver stayed outside. His ID was fake, too, as were the plates on the car.

VanOwen used Paley's ID to access an elevator that went down two levels to a lab that actually ran beneath all of the Quonset huts. The guards did not question her at all, because it was Paley's job to oversee this project. They never looked closer than the wig and glasses and lipstick.

In the rear corner of the massive lab was a row of small aircraft. Eight of them, each with a slightly different configuration, but all following a similar design philosophy. Only three people were in the lab, the rest having gone upstairs to the staff lounges to watch the news. Or home to be with family; or to D.C. in the hopes that they did not have to think about grief and funerals and loss.

The three remaining staff members were in white lab coats. Two were senior techs and one was the project manager. They all turned as VanOwen approached. The techs nodded and turned back to their work. The scientist rose from a chair and came to meet VanOwen, but nearly missed a step as she closed. Confusion clouded her face, and it was clear she realized who it was behind the glasses and fake hair.

"I—" she began, but VanOwen touched a finger to her lips, then took the scientist by the elbow and led her a few paces away.

"I'll explain later," said VanOwen, touching her wig. "Did you prepare everything?"

"Yes," said Yuina Hoshino.

"All of it?"

"Yes."

"You're sure? We will index everything."

Hoshino looked pained. "I told you from the beginning that I will do anything and everything you want. I have all of the designs, the metallurgy, the chemistry, the complete genomes of over forty candidates, everything. It's a complete copy."

"Good."

"But it's still a waste of time," she said. "Without tissue samples from host pilots, none of these will fly. Ever."

They turned and looked at the line of craft. Each of them was much smaller than the machine that Howard Shelton had sent to try and destroy China. They were similar, though. Triangular hulls with no obvious front, a central dome, and round white lights on the undersides of each point. They stood on metal platforms, but VanOwen knew that under the right circumstances they would not need landing struts. They would hover, floating on a cushion of charged air, defying gravity as if it was irrelevant. These T-craft were not intended for combat use, but were instead scaled prototypes that allowed for redesign and modification more quickly than full-sized machines.

"Get the files," ordered VanOwen. Hoshino nodded and went over to her desk, where an oversized metal briefcase stood. VanOwen followed and told her to open it. Hoshino did, revealing that it was crammed with ultra-high-capacity storage drives. "Close and lock it."

As Hoshino did, VanOwen beckoned to the technicians to come over. They obeyed at once, and as soon as they were within range, VanOwen drew a Glock 19 from inside her coat. It was fitted with a sound suppressor. She shot each of the technicians in the face. They dropped at once, and as a horrified Hoshino watched, VanOwen walked over and shot them each again. Three shots in head and heart.

"What . . . what . . . ?" gasped Hoshino.

VanOwen gave her a radiant smile. "Thank you for all of your loyalty and hard work, Doctor. You are really quite amazing."

"But I . . . ?"

VanOwen shot her through the heart and then put two rounds in her head. Brass tinkled and she did not bother to pick it up. There were no prints on the spent cartridges and the gun was unregistered. The driver, stone-faced, walked between the corpses and picked up the case. He took the gun from VanOwen and they left the lab, the building, and the base together without saying a word.

On a deserted road, VanOwen got out of the car, leaving the disguise behind. Her own Lexus GS was parked in the dense shadows of a side road. The driver put the heavy case in the trunk, turned, got back in his car, and drove away. Except for a brief exchange with the gate guards, he had not spoken a word since D.C. Likely he would vanish from all public records and be reassigned by their employer to some other work.

VanOwen got behind the wheel but did not start the engine. Instead she turned on the inside lights and stared at her face in the rearview mirror. The murders in the Barn were easy. Very easy, and she knew it should frighten her. Or sicken her. But there was nothing in her eyes and nothing in her heart.

The lack of feeling was what frightened her. She licked her lips, tasting the last of the garish lipstick.

"Christ," she said. She switched off the light but did not start the car for nearly half an hour, preferring instead to sit in total darkness. Without, and within.

CHAPTER SEVENTY-FOUR

JOHNS HOPKINS UNIVERSITY HOSPITAL
BALTIMORE, MARYLAND

Church closed the door to the solarium, shook hands with us both, allowed Ghost to sniff his black-gloved hand, and then sat.

"Before you start," he said, "I spoke with the doctors. Sam Imura will be in surgery for several hours yet. The injuries he sustained in the explosion are considerable. He has multiple fractures, including his left humerus, both femurs, several ribs, and right cheek; and they've identified forty-three separate pieces of shrapnel. Beyond that he has burns and surface lacerations. He is in critical condition, and the doctors have confided that they are only cautiously optimistic that he will survive the surgery."

"Ay dios mío," breathed Rudy. "I will call his parents. They're in California, I believe."

"Yes. Brick can supply you with their information. And I understand you've already spoken with Agent Ming's family. Thank you for that."

"D.J. and his partner have two adopted children," said Rudy heavily. "Four and seven."

I said nothing but there was a big hollow cavern opening inside my chest.

"Aunt Sallie is another matter," said Church. "She suffered a massive stroke and it is too early for a prognosis. She is alive, and they are working to keep her stable."

"Damn," I said. "Maybe I should have taken her somewhere closer and—"

Church leaned over and clamped a hand around my wrist. He looked me in the eyes, and even through the tinted lenses I could see the intensity of his stare.

"Listen to me and hear me, Captain," he said. "You saved her life.

You defended her and then did exactly what you needed to do in order to get her to the best available medical treatment. There were no better options, and I want that to sink in. Even if she dies, there was nothing else you could have done. For that, I will always be indebted to you. More than you can know. I am not a sentimental man, as you are eminently aware, so this is my truth. Hear me."

I looked into those eyes for as long as I could, then I nodded. He gave me a final squeeze and sat back, brushing invisible lint from his immaculate trouser leg.

"Now," he said calmly, "tell me what it is you think I need to know."

"It's only a theory," I began. "There's a whole bunch of supposition, wild guesses, and maybe just me being crazy."

Church leaned back and folded his hands in his lap. "Please, Captain, don't pull your punches with me. Believe me when I tell you that I've probably heard stranger things."

We studied each other for a moment, then I launched in.

"It's the God Machine that made me think of this," I said. "We know that when it's in idle, it messes with your head. It allows some people to step into the heads of other people and take them over. We know that because they used it on us. Top and Bunny on the gas dock in Oceanside. That wasn't them killing people, it was assassins hijacking their minds and bodies to do that. Same with me. Harcourt Bolton and Rafael Santoro were both inside my skull. They got Rudy, too, made him attack me. So, there's no way we can dismiss mind control as part of this, because we suddenly have hundreds of people going bugfuck nuts and attacking each other or committing suicide. If I hadn't seen a small God Machine firsthand I might have thought this was more of the nanite stuff from last year. Or some kind of rage virus. Or something, but now I'm landing pretty hard on this being those devices. With me so far?"

Church made a twirling motion with a finger, telling me to get on with it. He likes to be informed, not schooled.

"Okay, so we have the Speaker of the House kill himself in a big, flamboyant way. What's the immediate upshot? Suddenly all eyes are on D.C. Bam. Just like that. Everyone is tuned in to TV, Sirius, their online news services, and social media. The bad guys had used that to draw the eyes of the whole country, and as soon as we've all been brought to point, there's an earthquake. And before you say anything, boss, there is nothing you can say that is ever going to convince me that the earthquake was a coincidence."

Church gave me another of his microsmiles. "When have you ever known me to err on the side of coincidence, Captain?"

I grinned. "Fair enough. So, the earthquake hits, and hits hard. Just as everyone is watching D.C., the earthquake destroys the Capitol Building, damages the White House, and fills the streets with what amounts to a riot. Rudy is the expert here, but I'm pretty sure that once the shock wears off we're going to see a nationwide dramatic drop in confidence in the government. It's like what happens when a head of state is assassinated—people panic because there's no mommy or daddy in the room. Have you checked the stock markets? I bet they've dropped like a son of a bitch."

"They have."

"Has POTUS suspended trading?"

"He has not."

Rudy cursed under his breath.

"He should have done that already," I said.

"And I, along with a number of others, have tried to advise him on that point. Our requests have gone unanswered."

"Crap. Okay, getting back to my theory. The government is going to take a credibility hit bigger than what happened with FEMA after Katrina. If POTUS has made a public statement to try and reassure the people, I sure as hell haven't heard it."

"He has not," said Church. "The silence is telling."

"And damaging," added Rudy.

"Okay, whatever. All politicians blow. Back to this crap," I said. "The Secret Service tried to pick me up before the earthquake. Twice. Why? My guess is that someone thought I was in the area for some reason other than why I was actually there."

"And why would they do that, Captain?" asked Church, though I suspected he already knew.

"Because I was the point man for the Kill Switch op, and I was the point man for Extinction Machine. We now know that tech from Kill Switch is in play; and as you pointed out, boss, the two guys Top, Bunny, and I danced with were not rent-a-Closer. They were the real deal. Actual men in black. Maybe that makes them aliens, or weirdos working for E.T., I don't know. But they bugged out of there in a frigging T-craft, and that means that whatever's going on ties in with what we were into during the Extinction Machine case. Two of my biggest cases overlapping, and suddenly the Feds want to put a black bag over my head and whisk me off for some water sports. I don't buy Brierley's theory that this was POTUS flexing his muscles and just screwing with us. The timing is wrong. How would they know I was coming to Baltimore? It wasn't a long-range plan. I grabbed an open spot in my calendar and just went. So, I think someone spotted me in town and thought I was there investigating whatever hinky shit they were planning. And if POTUS isn't being mind-controlled, then there's someone in his circle who is."

"Or," countered Church, "there is someone in his circle of influence who is involved in whatever conspiracy is in play behind the scenes."

"I can buy that, too," I conceded. "Maybe even more so."

"Who would we suspect of that?" asked Rudy.

"I'll put our analysts on it," said Church. "We'll make a list."

"That brings up my next thing," I said, "and it's as obvious as it is scary. If these real-deal Closers are back on the case, then we have to accept the possibility that someone inside our government has gotten their hands on some of what was in the Majestic Black Book."

"That seems likely," admitted Church, and he did not look happy about it.

"Wait for a moment," interrupted Rudy. "The last time that happened, the aliens or whatever they are threatened to cause a megatsunami. Could the earthquake be a warning from them? Or a punishment?"

We considered that, then Church and I began shaking our heads at the same time.

"No," I said. "The earthquake thing works too well with a more political agenda."

"Whose politics, though?" asked Rudy. "I can't see any American political agenda being supported by this kind of damage. It would be like setting fire to a house you wanted to rob."

We hashed it back and forth and, sadly, came up with a very long list. America doesn't have as many friends as we like to think it does. And there are a lot of small groups that are not full-fledged national states that have been doing bad things with technology that can be easily transported. The God Machine I saw was frighteningly portable.

Church looked at his watch and stood. "I have to meet with doctors who I've asked to come here. In the meantime, I would greatly appreciate it if you would come up with a list of search arguments and give them to Bug and Nikki. If you're right about this, Captain, and I believe you are, then there has to be a pattern out there. This is too big to have happened and been planned in a vacuum, even with people who are determined to keep it off the Net. No one is that clean or efficient. Someone somewhere will have made a mistake. Be exhaustive, and check in with Doc Holliday and Junie on this. In fact, Captain, I think you should go to Brooklyn to consult with them."

Rudy and I stood. He said, "Then you don't believe the attack on Washington was the purpose of this conspiracy?"

"You mean I don't believe that 'either,' Doctor? No. To expand on Captain Ledger's metaphor, I think this is a larger and shinier object of distraction. And, Captain, what you said about FEMA disturbs me greatly. After that event, when Hugo Vox was still believed to be on our side, he ran a scenario at his Terror Town facility, focusing on how a natural disaster could be used to maximize the effect of an attack while minimizing the likelihood of an efficient or effective federal response. If someone has developed a way to induce earthquakes, then as bad as D.C. is, there are much more dangerous targets. Here and abroad."

"Like?"

"Like the Long Valley Caldera in California and Yellowstone Caldera in Wyoming. Like the island of Manhattan. Like any of the nuclear power plants, the largest dams. It does not have to be bigger than Washington, Captain. If this process is as portable as it seems, they can play hit-and-run and wear us down like a pack of lions attacking an elephant. Persistence, elusiveness, and intelligence are their weapons. Our own size makes it difficult for us to respond. This is why terrorism has flourished, and why it is so often effective."

With that he left.

Rudy and I stood in the doorway and watched him move down the hall like a man pushing through walls of solid lead.

"Joe," said Rudy softly, "you know that he should have already thought of this."

"He was on the same page," I said.

"No. He was a step behind you. All of this with Auntie, with the DMS being persecuted by the president, Sam . . . Joe, aren't you afraid that it's made him lose more than a step getting to first base?"

Ghost pushed between us and whined a little.

CHAPTER SEVENTY-FIVE

6800 BLOCK OF WEMBERLY WAY
MCLEAN, VIRGINIA

Jennifer VanOwen drove to McLean to meet her employer. It was only the third time they had ever met and VanOwen was nervous. Prying eyes were everywhere, especially in this era of cell phone cameras and social media.

Even so, it was a quiet street and the house had been continually occupied for years by a family whose members actually worked for the U.S. government. That they worked for another government as well was a deeply buried secret, one that had been protected since the early 1980s.

While she was away from D.C., carefully selected people from her employer's organization would seed eyewitness accounts of her being here or there, and always having just left. Photos taken earlier would have their digital time stamp altered and would be sent to the news to keep the story of Hurricane VanOwen going. Those same people fed data to VanOwen so she would know where she was supposed to have been.

As she pulled into the short driveway, the garage door rolled up to let her pull inside. There was no light inside the garage, and no one visible.

She killed the engine and waited. She was not allowed to get out of the car and had never been inside the house. Several minutes passed before a piece of shadow inside the garage detached itself from the blackness and moved toward her. VanOwen opened her car door and the dome light sketched the outline of a woman dressed in a military camouflage uniform with the twin bars of a captain. The face beneath the billed cap was familiar. Pretty, stern, expectant.

"And . . . ?" said the woman.

"I got it all," VanOwen told her.

"Show me."

VanOwen popped the trunk, got out, and walked around to stand beside her employer. VanOwen opened the case.

"Excellent."

"I have to get back to D.C.," said VanOwen. "I'll be missed soon."

"Yes," said the woman, "you will."

VanOwen heard the faint metallic click behind her but did not turn fast enough to see what it was before the knob on the end of a collapsible spring-steel fighting stick struck her at the base of the skull. The blade was angled so precisely that pieces of her shattered skull severed the brain stem and revoked all nerve conduction in a microsecond. She was dead before she knew that it was even a possibility. The next six blows were unnecessary and yet delivered with as much force and precision as the first. Her body slumped, and the other woman caught it, steadied it, and then leaned it forward so that VanOwen's upper torso leaned into the trunk. The woman removed the metal case, set it down, and then hoisted VanOwen into the back with a grunt. VanOwen was not a large woman and she fit easily.

The woman used VanOwen's skirt hem to wipe blood and hair from the fighting stick, then tapped the knob on the floor to reverse the telescoping weapon down to a six-inch tube. Very efficient. The weapon went back into her purse. She closed the trunk, picked up the case, and walked into the house. She made a single call on a disposable cell phone.

"Where are you?"

"Heading back to my hotel," said Valen Oruraka.

"Wait for me there," said Gadyuka, and hung up. Ten minutes later a woman who looked nothing at all like a Marine Corps captain drove toward Maryland in a white Camry. No one took any note of her at all.

It would be days before the smell emanating from the garage spurred a curious letter carrier to make a 9-1-1 call.

CHAPTER SEVENTY-SIX

JOHNS HOPKINS UNIVERSITY HOSPITAL
BALTIMORE, MARYLAND

They call it standing vigil.

Grandiose word for "waiting." I kept hoping that it wasn't a deathwatch, but that's how it felt. Rudy and I had made our lists of keywords and shared them with the teams back at the Hangar. So, first there's panic and hurry, and then there's waiting.

Top and Bunny showed up, looking like they'd both been dragged down flights of stairs by their heels. We hugged and slapped backs—they didn't know how bad mine was until I nearly fainted in Bunny's embrace. Then we sat. And waited.

I still wore the same dirty, stained, and torn clothes I'd put on that morning. Bunny went out to the car and brought in our suitcases and we took turns getting cleaned up in the doctors' lounge. More of Church's influence.

Bunny wore a sleeveless Under Armour tank and board shorts;

Top had on an ancient Atlanta Falcons sweatshirt over jeans. I came back wearing a floral-print Hawaiian shirt and an ancient but comfortable pair of Levi's. The last sets of clean clothes we had after our trip out here were stuff more appropriate to the beaches of San Diego. Only Rudy was different, dressed in a quiet dark suit and polished shoes.

I brought a bag of treats for Ghost, who ate one but then sat looking at the closed door of Auntie's room.

We continued our vigil. Nobody bothered us. There were empty chairs around us, but after taking a look at the four men and the big dog, other folks decided they'd rather sit anywhere else. Or stand. Guess we gave off a vibe.

We talked to Bug and Doc Holliday because Top and Bunny had tweaks to our keyword list. We hashed out my theory. Then Bug told us about the Speaker's family and what was written on the wall. Deep Silence.

"The hell do you think that means?" asked Bunny.

No one had a theory that covered that phrase, though something tickled at the back of my mind. Something I could not see clearly enough to understand. Silence. Deep and profound silence. Yeah, there was something there, but the harder I tried to catch a glimpse of it, the more elusive it became. Exhaustion, pain, and pain meds were not helping.

Hours passed.

The body count on the news was close to thirteen hundred. Thousands more hurt, and scores missing and unaccounted for. Experts kept insisting that this wasn't the worst natural disaster in the United States, but other experts refuted it. Thousands died in the 1906 earthquake in San Francisco. This was the second worst in U.S. history, they insisted. This was the worst of the twenty-first century in the U.S. It was the worst East Coast quake, both in terms of deaths and damage. They kept finding new ways to frame it. Some experts were giving predictions for what the final butcher's bill would be. Others were floating dollar amounts for destruction.

"Bunch of damn ghouls," muttered Bunny.

No one disputed him.

Church joined us and told me that Junie was flying to Brooklyn to bring FreeTech's mojo to bear. My heart did a small skip and jump, though I wondered why she hadn't called me directly. When I looked at my phone I saw that the screen was busted and dark.

"Was working earlier," I said pointlessly, and could not actually remember if that was true or not. I was so goddamn tired.

"Bug is using MindReader and Calpurnia to help facilitate legitimate rescue and support services," said Church. "He's also assigned Nikki to hunt down and destroy any fake donation sites that pop up."

"Thank God," said Rudy. That was a pet peeve of Rudy's and Bug's. They hated when people used catastrophes to scam goodhearted people who tried to help. With MindReader, Bug was not only able to identify bad guys and return the donations to the donors, he also outed the perps to the FBI and did a few other nasty things. Not sure of the details, but I've heard that these scam artists suddenly had very, very unsavory search histories on their computers that they were unable to delete. So sad.

I went through every detail of what happened, and the four of them listened. Top dismantled a ham sandwich and fed it in bits to Ghost as I spoke.

"Designer earthquakes?" said Bunny. "That's weird, even for us, isn't it?"

"We can never be certain where the ceiling is when it comes to malevolent use of technology," observed Church. "Science is evolving faster than our ability to predict its growth."

My earbud suddenly came to life, and it was Bug. "Cowboy, is the Big Man with you? If so, tell him to log in to this channel."

We all tapped our earbuds to get onto the same call.

"Talk to us, Bug," said Church.

"Something's happening, and it's bad," said Bug. "There are tons of cell phone videos showing up on social media and the news. And, Cowboy, it's all you and Aunt Sallie. Ghost, too. All three of you beating the shit out of a bunch of unarmed civilians."

CHAPTER SEVENTY-SEVEN

COURTYARD BY MARRIOTT—NEW CARROLLTON
LANDOVER, MARYLAND

When he heard the knock, Valen fairly leapt to his feet and hurried across the room.

"Ari," he cried as he opened the door, but then he stopped. It was not him. It was her.

Gadyuka pushed him inside and kicked the door shut.

"When did you last sweep the room?" she asked, but before he could answer she removed her own scanner and spent five minutes assuring herself that there were no active or passive listening devices. Only then did she shrug out of her coat, lock the door, and make a beeline to the vodka bottle, skipping the available glasses and taking a deep swig. Then she turned and leaned back against the desk, studying him with her cold, calculating eyes.

"Did everyone report in?" she asked.

"All but Ari. I haven't heard from him yet."

"Ari isn't coming here."

"What do you mean? Where did he go?"

Gadyuka took another, smaller drink, and set the bottle down. "Ari Kostas is dead."

It took three full seconds for her words to make sense to Valen. "What . . . ?"

"The other device exploded. He was killed instantly and a DMS field agent was sent to the hospital."

Valen tried to speak, but could not. Instead he lurched to his feet, blundered past her, and ran for the bathroom.

Later, when he came out, his face tingling from washing after he'd thrown up, he slumped down on the edge of the bed. Gadyuka studied him like he was a display in a museum of oddities.

"You are a difficult man to understand," she said. In his absence she'd gone to fetch ice, and now handed him a glass. He took a sip and his hand shook so badly the ice tinkled against his teeth. "You have worked so long, so hard, with such brilliance to bring us to this moment, and now that we're so close we can taste it, you're losing your nerve?"

"I'm not losing my nerve," he spat, surprised by his own harshness. "I think I'm losing my goddamn *mind*."

She began to say something but Valen cut her off.

"No. Don't. I can't bear any more of your political pep talks. I know that what we are doing will allow the New Soviet to exist. I know that if we carry it out to the end then we will have changed the world forever. I know that America will be both punished for old crimes and removed from the political equation. I know all that, Gadyuka. I know the math and I know the propaganda."

"It's not just propaganda," she insisted, rising and taking the glass from his hands. She looked him in the eyes. "We are saving our country. What we are doing—what you are doing—is no different than what our partisans did to the Germans in World War Two. They blew up trains and factories and airfields, and not everyone who died was a Nazi. There has never been a war fought without civilian casualties. Not once in history."

He sneered at her. "That's hardly an argument in favor of what we are going to do next."

"No, because what they did were half measures. Even the dropping of the atomic bombs on Nagasaki and Hiroshima were half measures. The war was won. That was America threatening the world and forcing its way into becoming the global superpower and corrupt empire that it has become. They nearly dropped a bomb on Moscow at the end of the war. You know that to be true. If they knew we would obtain nuclear weapons technology as quickly as we did, they would have bombed us. They would have done worse to us than we are going to do to them. Much worse. They would have turned Russia into an uninhabitable radioactive wasteland."

"How is that better? America will be uninhabitable when we're done."

"For how long? Three years, at the most? None of the survivors will have radiation sickness. There won't be generations of genetic disorder and rampant cancers. They will bury their dead and, over time, they will become an agrarian culture and never again threaten the world with their nuclear arsenal. We will have not only pulled their fangs but given them no one left to hate. There will be no villain in this, Valen. Russia—the Novyy Sovetskiy—will offer unlimited help. Medical aid, cultural and agricultural aid. We will even offer to protect them against other countries that might seek to exploit their weakness."

He walked to the far side of the room and stared out the window. "Words, Gadyuka. Pretty words to hide the ugliness of what we are doing. What we have done. What we are about to do.

"God almighty," he breathed.

"Stop saying that," she said.

Valen half turned. "What?"

"Lately you keep saying things like that. 'My God,' 'God almighty.' You don't believe in God, Valen, and to use those phrases does nothing more than stick bamboo shoots under your fingernails. Stop it. You're only hurting yourself."

He could not meet her eyes, and after a moment turned back to the window, beyond which was a parking lot and nothing of interest. Certainly nothing he actually saw.

"Now," she said, "we need to move. We're done here. Let the Americans pick up the pieces in Washington. We have bigger fish to fry."

When he did not move, she came over and stood behind him, then bent close and gently—ever so gently—kissed the back of his neck.

"History is calling to you, my love. Let's go save the world."

God help me, he thought.

And meant it.

CHAPTER SEVENTY-EIGHT

JOHNS HOPKINS UNIVERSITY HOSPITAL
BALTIMORE, MARYLAND

Church commandeered an office for us to use, and we all hunkered down around his laptop to watch the news.

I *was* the news. There were feeds from six different cameras. None of them caught all of it, but each caught some, and I was there—smack-dab in the middle, beating the shit out of reporters, unarmed civilians, Secret Service agents, and cops. Auntie was in two of the videos. Ghost was in three.

The panic and the constant shuddering of the ground kept any of the videos from being crystal clear, and even when the networks froze an image and enhanced it, my face was a little blurry. But it was me and everyone knew it.

How did they know it was me?

Because my fucking name was right there on the screen.

Government Agent Joseph Ledger in Violent Attack

And . . .

Son of Baltimore Mayor Attacks Crowd

And . . .

Captain Joseph Ledger and Unnamed Woman
in Unprovoked Attack During Deadly Earthquake

Top Sims blew out his cheeks and sat heavily on the edge of the desk. Rudy groaned softly and put a hand on my shoulder.

Bunny said, "Well, now we're in the shit."

I said nothing.

"This is the gas dock all over again," said Top.

"'Cept Joe's not killing anyone," countered Bunny, but it was a weak riposte.

"I'm not sure that will matter," said Church. He glanced at me. "The fact that they identified you would be manageable. You were, after all, a Baltimore detective, and your father is in a high-profile job. You've been in the news before."

"Never as 'Captain' Ledger," I said.

"No, and that's the most troubling aspect of this. That designation is only ever used within certain levels of the intelligence and justice communities. You hold no verifiable rank. The press should not have been able to tag you in this way."

"Which means what?" asked Bunny. "Did one of those Secret Service goons out him?"

Before Church could ask, a new banner appeared beneath the video footage of Auntie, Ghost, and me fighting together.

Rogue Agents from the Department of Military Sciences

We stared at that.

Church, who had been standing, sat down slowly and heavily in the leather chair behind the desk. He removed his tinted glasses and pinched the bridge of his nose.

"Well," he said slowly, "isn't that interesting."

CHAPTER SEVENTY-NINE

JOHNS HOPKINS UNIVERSITY HOSPITAL
BALTIMORE, MARYLAND

Church put all of the DMS field offices on secure lockdown. So far, no reporters or crowds had materialized at any of them, but this wasn't a time to take chances. Top and Bunny wanted to go out and help with rescue efforts in D.C., but Church nixed the idea.

"Even if you carry false ID," he said, "someone in the Secret Service or other agencies with which you've interacted over the years could recognize you."

"There are people who could use our help," protested Top.

Church wouldn't budge. "And if you are recognized, that will cause enough of a stir to draw resources away from those same people. You could create a distraction that does more harm than any good you might accomplish. I'm sorry, gentlemen, but while I commend your generosity and compassion, you would be of greater use elsewhere."

"Where, exactly, sir?" asked Bunny, his face flushed with anger.

"In San Diego," said Church. "Echo Team is composed of mostly new operators. Two of them have never been in a DMS action; one came in at the end of the Dogs of War event but without real training. And the fourth, Agent Duffy, is new to his role as team sniper. None of them have gone into the field as a DMS team. With everything that is happening, I would be comforted in knowing that they are ready to roll."

"Against who?" growled Top.

"That's always a challenge for us, First Sergeant; but when we come up with that name I want you ready to charge the field. And trust me, gentlemen, we will find out who is behind this."

They didn't like it, but we all knew Church was right. Top and Bunny stood. We don't stand at attention in the DMS, and we don't salute, but they both gave the impression of doing both. Mr. Church rose and offered his hand, nodding to each as they shook. I saw the guys out to the parking lot, and asked them to take Ghost along. The fur-monster wasn't happy about it, and gave me an *I'm going to pee in your shoes* look as he trudged along behind them.

Brick intercepted me on the way back inside and handed me a new cell phone. Same make and model as mine but with a hardened case.

"Bug downloaded all your contacts and apps," he said, "so you're ready to roll."

"Thanks," I said, and began to slip it into my pocket, but he shook his head.

"Joe, when's the last time you spoke with Junie? She's at the Hangar now and would probably take it as a comfort if she heard directly from you that you're all right."

He clapped me on the shoulder and went inside. Brick is one of the good guys. Because he's this huge, battle-scarred old soldier, it's easy to make the wrong assumptions about him, but there are good reasons Church picked him as his aide. Brick is smart, educated, kind, lethal as fuck, subtle, and compassionate. He is the nicest of people most of the time, but you absolutely do not want to get between him and someone he wants to protect.

I stayed outside to call Junie. She answered on the first ring.

"Joe!" she gasped. "Are you okay?"

"I am."

"Thank God. I love you," she said, and there was such heart, such meaning in her words that I felt an actual warm glow in my heart. Don't laugh, it happens; even to cold and cynical freaks like me.

"I love you, too, sweetheart." I closed my eyes and conjured a memory of her. Tall, with wild blond hair that always looked like she'd stepped off a windy moor. The bluest eyes in creation, and splashes of freckles across cheeks and nose, and across her chest. When she wasn't in the field in a third-world country, she tended to wear flowy peasant skirts in floral patterns and sheer white blouses. Her jewelry tended toward silver and crystals and rare stones in irregular shapes. Lots of rings on every finger and jangly ankle bracelets. Recently she'd had the phases of the moon tattooed across her left side so that the full moon was on her back and the new moon under her breast.

"You're in New York?"

"At the Hangar, yes. Toys and I flew out. Joe, it's so awful about Aunt Sallie, D.J., and Sam."

We talked about our fallen friends for a while. Sharing fears, offering mutual comfort. The survival tactics of frail and compassionate human beings. Then Junie shifted gears and said she'd seen me on the news.

"Does that mean they're going to arrest you?" she cried.

"They can try."

"No," she said sharply. "Don't do that. Don't give me that kind of macho bullshit answer, Joe."

I winced because she was right. Junie is way more mature than I'll ever be. Bravado may be good for trash talk and psyching one's self up, but it's often bullshit and it's evasive and she deserved better from me.

"Sorry," I said. "Really. Look, Junie, this scares the piss out of me, too. No joke. But we are the DMS. I'm going back in in a second to talk to Church and Bug about what we can do, and you have to know that we're going to have options on how to spin this."

"Can it be spun?" she asked. "I mean, they mentioned your name and they mentioned the Department of Military Sciences. What's that expression you like so much? You can't unring a bell?"

I leaned against the cold concrete wall next to the ER entrance. An ambulance was parked, engine off but the red and blue lights still turning, slapping me with color as if in silent reminder that the whole country was an active crime scene. Thanks, O subtle genies of the universe, I get the metaphor.

"Yeah," I said to Junie. "And no, you can't. Don't know what's going to happen to us yet. Church is not exactly BFFs with the president these days. Even before all this today we've kind of been expecting something from the White House. Like our charter being run through the shredder."

"Do you think he'll actually do that?"

I leaned my shoulder against the cold cinder block wall. "I don't know, babe. Things have been going south for us these last couple of years. Hell, for almost as long as I've been with the DMS. First Hugo Vox turned out to be a bona fide supervillain, then MindReader gets hacked and hacked again. And on and on."

"Right, but now you have MindReader Q1, or is that closing the barn door . . . ?"

"It might be."

We were quiet for a moment.

"Joe," she said after a while, "I miss you."

"Yeah."

"I've missed you so much lately."

"I know. Me too."

"No," she said, "I mean I think we need to talk."

"Now? About what?"

"Not now," she said, "and not on the phone."

I tensed the way you do when you know a punch is coming but you don't know from which angle or how hard.

"Junie . . . ," I began, but let it fade.

"We've been apart so much these last couple of years," she said. "I feel like we're becoming strangers to each other."

"You know who I am, Junie. I know who you are. Just because we're both busy doesn't change that."

"Doesn't it?"

"No, damn it," I said.

"Don't yell, Joe," begged Junie. "Please. I'm not trying to hurt you."

"What you're doing is scaring me. I love you."

"And I love you," she said. "This isn't about love."

"Then what is it about?"

Her pause was long enough to make my jaw hurt from clenching. "I'm tired, Joe."

"Tired of what? Us?"

"I shouldn't have said anything. I'm sorry. Let's talk some other time."

"Hey, wait, you can't leave me hanging like this."

"It's okay, Joe. It'll keep."

"No, tell me—"

"I love you, Joe," she said, and then the line went dead.

I went inside. The hallway was empty, and so was I.

I nearly called her back. But didn't. My need told me to do the former, but my instincts—faulty as they sometimes were—stayed my hand. Instead I stood there, leaning against the wall, wanting to bash my head against it. I'd have done it if there was even the slightest chance that it would force the world to make sense.

CHAPTER EIGHTY

DRIVING IN MARYLAND

Valen drove at five miles over the road speed, only used the fast lane for passing, and made sure he used his blinkers to lane-change. The car Gadyuka provided was a two-year-old Nissan Ultima, one of the most common cars on American roads. Silver color; the second-most popular hue after white. There were no bumper stickers on it and absolutely nothing to make it stand out. He would never have driven anything that looked sporty, and certainly nothing red, because red cars are pulled over by highway patrol more than any other cars, even when driving at the speed limit.

The credit cards he had belonged to one of the deeply positioned American spies, a third-generation sleeper. The cards were clean and the accounts they drew on were years old and sensibly maintained. He had a driver's license with his face, but the name attached to the account. As he drove, he listened to news radio and tried not to cry.

He turned off of George Washington Memorial Parkway onto the exit for I-495, heading toward Maryland. Heading west. He had more than two thousand miles to drive. Planes and trains weren't safe anymore. Not since he'd let the government agent see his face.

Joe Ledger. The psychopath who worked for the Department of Military Sciences. It had definitely been him, of that Valen had no doubt. He watched the footage on Fox News over and over and over again of the same man and the same dog fighting people on the steps of the Capitol Building.

He hadn't told Gadyuka about the encounter while recovering the machine. All he said was that he recovered the damaged machine without incident. A lie.

Why had he lied? Why hadn't he told her about Tasing the man?

Why hadn't he told her when he'd realized who that man was? Why?

Valen drove.

He kept looking in the rearview mirror. It would be many miles before he realized who he was expecting to see behind him. And it was no comfort at all to see no one.

CHAPTER EIGHTY-ONE

JOHNS HOPKINS UNIVERSITY HOSPITAL
BALTIMORE, MARYLAND

"Bug," I said as calmly as I could, "tell me I am not well and truly screwed."

I was in a borrowed doctor's office with Church, using a wall-mounted Scroll for the teleconference. A Scroll is Doc Holliday's tweak of the flexible computer screen. It looks like a big map on thick paper, but the material is actually a blend of several polymers with flexible circuits built in. Once unrolled it can be attached to any flat surface. The skin acts as a high-resolution screen that made it look like Bug was in the same room with us.

Bug—born Jerome Leroy Williams—is smallish, medium brown, with colored contacts and a perpetual smile. Except now that smile looked fragile. He wore a Wakanda Forever long-sleeved T-shirt and was surrounded by computer monitors and pop-culture action figures of Black Panther, Shuri, Luke Cage, Ant-Man, The Wasp, Falcon, Doctor Strange, and Agent Dana Scully. At least they were the ones I could identify.

"Here's the situation," Bug said, trying to sound upbeat despite the sweat glistening on his face, "your name is out there, Joe. The photo is out there, and so is the video footage. So is the DMS's name. That's the bad news. The good news is that they haven't ID'd Aunt Sallie, and she's registered at Johns Hopkins under an alias no one is ever going to break."

"That's something," I muttered.

I knew Brick always had a professional makeup kit with him, and he could transform me into someone who could ride in an elevator with my own brother without being recognized. That wasn't the problem. The press was tearing themselves apart trying to figure out who and what the DMS was. The story was even competing with the mounting death toll in the nation's second-worst earthquake ever.

"Who outed us?" I asked.

"We don't know for sure," said Bug. "The story broke on Fox and MSNBC within minutes of each other. Anonymous tips that came in on cell phones belonging to key news producers. I hacked both phones and verified that the calls originated from the same cell phone. Before you ask, the cell was a burner bought for cash at a Target in Virginia. I had Nikki go through the store's video records and we have a good image of the man who bought it."

An image flashed onto the screen, showing a man in jeans and a blue windbreaker moving away from a register toward the exit. The image froze and expanded to show his face.

"He looks kind of familiar . . . ," I said.

"He should," said Bug. An overlay of facial recognition software isolating sixty-two unique points on the man's face, head, ears, throat, and shoulders. A second window popped up to show the same man much more clearly. It was from an official ID for the United States Secret Service, and I knew him at once. It was my buddy Lurch from the cemetery.

"When was this video taken?" I asked.

"The day before you beat him and his buddies up," said Bug. "So, this thing was in motion before you ever got to D.C. Oh, and Mr. Church already brought me up to speed with your theory. I wish I could say that it was too weird to be likely, but, dude, this is us." He spread his hands.

"It's fair to say that we are on the outs with the current administration," Church said as he sat and studied the last piece of a cookie. "This is something we've seen coming. They want us gone, for whatever reason. Probably because it's well known that our loyalty is not conditional. What troubles me, though, is the apparent clumsiness of it."

"You'd rather they were sneakier?"

"I admire quality tradecraft, but this may be a mix of ham-fisted clumsiness and very sophisticated subtlety. I think the group behind this agenda—what you and Bug tend to call the 'Big Bad'—has done its work with great skill. So great that we haven't caught a whiff of it and even now only have a theory rather than facts. On the other hand, the task of taking you off the board was handled badly. That suggests that either we are still missing something about the nature of that pickup, or the skill of the Big Bad does not translate as it goes lower on the chain of command."

"Leaning toward that last one," I said, and Bug nodded. "We know for a fact that the Secret Service and some of the other agencies are not playing the same kind of pro ball they used to or should be."

Bug raised his hand. "Um, I think the pickup on Joe was considered scut work, and they only give that stuff to the back-benchers. Look, we've run deep backgrounds on all the agents involved in the two pickup attempts. If we wanted to take the Secret Service apart, we could. They're classic examples of job promotion based on favors rather than merit. Not exactly illegal, but unethical as all get-out. A lot of the better agents have either been transferred to other assignments or encouraged to change jobs. Some of the better ones have gone to work for private security firms. So, if the Big Bad influenced someone in the White House to pick you up, they didn't have the best tools for that job."

"The upshot of that, no matter how it was handled," I said, "is that we, too, had our attention drawn to D.C., and as a result we may be looking in the wrong direction."

"That is almost certainly the case," said Church. He selected another cookie and tapped crumbs off it. "We are a secret organization created during an earlier administration. We've been instrumental in taking down corrupt politicians before, admittedly as side effects of other cases. We have MindReader. Perhaps this Big Bad has, directly or through agents positioned to appear as close and loyal advisors, convinced POTUS that if we lose our charter we will slink away, pull the plug on MindReader, and cease to be a threat."

"But . . . ?"

Church took a bite and munched for a moment. His eyes were steady as lasers. "We have not tried to be a threat. It would be unfortunate if we were forced to make that kind of play."

That hung in the air for a moment. Bug and I exchanged a look. We were on the same side as Church, but he scared us both. That is not an exaggeration.

Bug cleared his throat. "And, there's also the fact that a lot of people in Washington still don't understand how the DMS works. MindReader isn't government property. It belongs to Mr. Church. None of the DMS operations are funded by the United States government. Except for the access and freedom of action we get from the charter, we're entirely separate. So, we could actually just up and leave."

"Sure," I said, "but if we take our dolls and dishes and leave the tea party, then what? It's not like the war ends if we opt out."

Church almost smiled. "No."

"So, what do we do? Starting with the DMS being outed, I mean? And my face on every freaking news feed."

"Bug . . . ?" asked Church mildly.

"Okay, in the short term," said Bug, "I've hacked into all of the news feeds and uploaded every bit of cell phone video data they've received. They've been playing fast and loose with how they're reporting it. Probably based on the biased tip from your Secret Service buddy. If you watch all of the videos you can see that people were fighting in the streets and that you were defending yourself. And, once Auntie collapsed, anyone can see that you and Ghost are protecting her."

"So, why isn't that extra footage out there?"

"It is," said Bug. "I mean, it's out there now. I used a network of a couple thousand servers and fake accounts we have set up to seed the complete video files to YouTube and like a zillion other sites, including BuzzFeed, HuffPost, Politico, Snopes, you name it. It's trending like crazy, and because it's trending so heavily, the twenty-four-hour news services have had to pick it up in order to stay current. Fox and MSNBC started showing the unedited files an hour ago, and now Joe Ledger isn't the bad guy. He's kind of a badass hero."

"Yay me," I said listlessly. "What about the DMS?"

"I, um, tapped a few of Mr. Church's friends in the industry to go on as talking heads. Turn on any news feed and three of the four talking heads are ours. Some of them are talking about the strategic importance of deep-cover covert ops. Some are talking about how the DMS has been key in those stories the general population already know—the Sea of Hope, the drone thing, the pathogen outbreak at the Liberty Bell Center in Philly, and how we're part of the ongoing response to the Dogs of War rabies and nanites thing. We've got endorsements from the last four presidents, the past three secretary-generals of the U.N., and the who's who of Nobel Prize winners. Plus generals, heads of state. We're crushing the whole 'DMS are bad guys' thing."

"Nice to know you still have friends in the industry," I said to Church.

This time he did smile. "Don't ever let yourself believe that political party affiliations, right or left, dictate everyone's actions or inspire everyone to compromise their own ethics. The people it is my pleasure to call friends tend to go deeper into the concept of patriotism than that, and they do not play party politics. Not when that requires that they act against the genuine best interests of the American people."

"Yeah, well, that's pretty frigging great and all," I said, "but doesn't that put us more out than we were?"

"Out is out," said Church. "The DMS is no longer a secret organization and never will be again. We need to accept that and move on."

"Who else's name is out there other than mine?"

"No one," said Bug. "We stopped that in its tracks."

I sat back and sipped my coffee. My hands were shaking, and not all of it was from the caffeine I'd been chugging since getting to the hospital. "Where's the White House in all this? There hasn't even been an official statement about the earthquake other than the usual 'thoughts and prayers' crap."

"Nothing from the Oval Office," said Church. "Though there was a tweet about 'rogue secret organizations' undermining the country."

"I missed that one."

"It was pulled as soon as the full video stories hit the news services," said Bug.

I glared at him. "Can't you just go in and deactivate his social media accounts?"

"Sure, except that I'm under orders not to." He glanced at Church, who shrugged.

"The DMS is not a bully," said Church, "and it is not our policy to interfere with the First Amendment. What Bug did with the cell phone videos is providing more information, not editing what is being put out there."

"And our talking heads?"

Church locked me in the eye. "Find one who has uttered a single untruth."

I sighed. "Guess I've become too conditioned to false narratives."

"Sign of the times," said Bug. "Oh, hey, on a totally different topic . . . when are you coming up here, Joe?"

"I . . . um . . . well, with Auntie and all . . ."

"Captain," said Church, "I don't think there's anything else you can accomplish here. Doc Holliday has been in discussions with Junie about the incident on the road with the Closers and the T-craft. And Nikki Bloom will likely have useful information based on the keywords you provided. Take my jet to Brooklyn. Listen to the presentation and then we'll talk again."

And that was the end of the conversation. He stood up and tapped the Scroll to end the videoconference. His expressions are always hard to read but I knew enough not to push the matter now. He wanted me in New York and I think he wanted to use the time it would take me to get there to allow him some quiet time to think things through. Pushing him on it wasn't going to get me anywhere.

So I went to Brooklyn.

CHAPTER EIGHTY-TWO

JOHNS HOPKINS UNIVERSITY HOSPITAL
BALTIMORE, MARYLAND

After Captain Ledger left, Mr. Church spent two hours sitting beside Aunt Sallie's bed, holding one limp hand. He ignored the constant noise of the ICU and instead listened to his own thoughts. Auntie slept on, probably unaware that he was there. Parts of frowns and splinters of winces tried to manifest on her features—conjured no doubt by her dreams—but the muscles were too slack and the emotions melted away.

He felt his phone vibrate in his pocket, and when he looked at the display he felt a wince form on his own mouth. Church rose and walked into the hall and stepped into a quiet corner as he answered.

"Good evening, Mr. President," he said. "I'm glad you and your family are safe."

"Is that supposed to be a joke?"

"A joke, sir?"

"Oh, like I'm supposed to believe you're happy the White House didn't fall down on our heads."

Church closed his eyes. "Why would I make a joke in a time like this? My concern is genuine. And again, I extend the offer for any assistance myself or my department can offer."

"Assistance? That's a laugh. You're lucky I don't have you and everyone who works for the DSM arrested. Your boy Ledger is a terrorist and belongs in Guantanamo. I've spoken with the director of Homeland Security and the attorney general, and don't be surprised if you hear from them."

"Mr. President," said Church patiently, "I would caution you against taking such an action. I understand that you are upset, but I can assure you that Captain Ledger is—"

"He's a psychopath and a criminal and he's going to jail. I've requested that Congress establish a committee to review all DSM cases and actions, and as soon as things settle down here you can expect that to happen. Don't think it won't. You've been a rogue organization for too long and I will shut you down."

"Mr. President, it would be a mistake to cross that line."

"Is that a threat?"

"It is a statement of fact. The DMS exists to be a first line of defense against terrorist threats involving radical technologies. We are uniquely qualified to handle such threats, and we are structured to be a rapid-response unit. There is no other organization within the United States government that can do what we do. Not in the intelligence community nor the military. To remove us would be to expose this nation to grave threats."

"Wow. I'm not sure I've ever encountered this level of arrogance before," said the president. "Who exactly do you think you are?"

Church said nothing.

"I'm going to take you down," warned the president. "You and every single one of the traitors who works for you. That's a promise. Want to make another threat now? Is that what you want to do? Go ahead, see what happens."

"No, Mr. President," said Church evenly, "I believe we understand each other."

The president began to say something else, but Church ended the call. He leaned on the wall for almost a full minute, looking down the hallway at the door to Aunt Sallie's room. He pushed off the wall and began walking away when his phone vibrated again. Despite the stress he was feeling, Church smiled when he saw who it was.

"Lilith," he said gently. "It's good to hear your—"

"Listen to me," barked Lilith, "it's Violin. . . ."

CHAPTER EIGHTY-THREE

OVER PENNSYLVANIA AIRSPACE

While I flew to Brooklyn I spent some quality time with the DMS version of an Identikit, which is a utility cops all over the world use to make composite drawings of suspects. Like all cops—or in my case, former cops—I'm a trained observer who knows how to spot unique details. The MindReader version is intuitive and offered a lot of suggestions based on the architecture of similar kinds of faces to the one I was building. It took about an hour and two glasses of Church's very expensive Teeling Vintage Reserve, thirty-year-old Irish single malt, but when I was done I stared down at the face of the man who'd Tased Ghost and me.

It was not a killer's face. There was none of the vacuous stupidity of the street criminal or the hardened soullessness of the professional assassin about him. There was no fanatical gleam in his eyes. It was a face. In my reconstruction I'd even managed to put some of the emotion I'd seen on his features. Regret. I was sure of that. And fear. Maybe even panic.

I hit the keys to enter the image into the MindReader facial recognition and pattern search utilities. They not only matched the photo to indices of mug shots, but also the millions of snapshots taken by traffic cams, airport cams, CCTV, and social media. The collective database was massive and I leaned back with my whiskey and figured that I'd get some kind of hit within the next twenty-four hours.

The system pinged me in eight minutes, and that reminded me that MindReader Q1 was a quantum computer. It did not search or process like any other system on Earth. It was faster by orders of magnitude.

Several photos popped up on the screen, each tagged with source data. There were versions of the man with different haircuts and hair colors, varying degrees of tan, shifting eye color, and a variety of facial hair styles. But they were all the same man. MindReader kicked out seventeen aliases, but one name began showing up over and over again. I leaned close to study this man.

"Valen Oruraka," I said. "Now who in the wide blue fuck are you?"

As if in answer, the system began chunking out data in bulk. The name was clearly phony, and even though this cat had used a number of false names, Valen Oruraka had become a kind of default personality. The first official record of it was prior to his enrollment at MIT for graduate work. When I checked for his undergraduate records, they all cracked open to reveal phony shit. Whoever had built the Oruraka personality had been pretty good at it, but they hadn't counted on MindReader.

There was nothing before that, though. No facial recognition pics, no trace. That told me he was not American. Q1 can reverse-engineer photos to show us what adults might have looked like as kids, just as it can age pictures. There were no school photos in any database of that face, and he was young enough to have been in school when all such pictures were digitally archived.

So, I told the system to go wider, and there he was.

I made a call to Church, but couldn't get through, so I called Bug, who answered. "Look at what I just sent you."

"Got it," said Bug, and began giving me the highlights. "Valen Oruraka, aka Oleg Sokolov. Born in Novosibirsk, Russia. Thirty-nine. Unmarried. No children. No living relatives. Parents died when he was young, lived for a while in Ukraine with his aunt and uncle and . . . wow."

"Wow, what?"

"His uncle was Dr. Abram Golovin."

"Who's he?"

"He's dead, but he was the chief structural engineer at Chernobyl."

"Hm. What else?"

"Went into the military and, bang, that's it. Officially he died in a car crash on base. Buried in a family plot in Novosibirsk. Then he shows up in America under the name Valen Oruraka and enrolls in MIT and studied . . . oh, damn, Joe, you're going to love this."

"When you say that I never love it," I said. "What did you find?"

"Joe, he studied seismology and geophysics."

"Bingo," I said, and pointed my finger like a gun at the face on my screen. "Bug, I need you to find this son of a bitch. Put as many people as you need on it. We know he was in D.C. today. My guess is that he's taking his little God Machine and getting the hell out of Dodge. He knows I saw his face, so I don't think he'll be stupid enough to go through airport security. Find him anyway. You hear me? *Find* him."

"Yeah," said Bug. "Count on it."

CHAPTER EIGHTY-FOUR

OVER PENNSYLVANIA AIRSPACE

The plane hadn't logged very many miles before Bug was back on the line.

"You found him already?" I asked.

"No, no, you got to give me some time," he said quickly. "But I got something else. Jerry Spencer and his team worked the crime scene where Sam was hurt. They've been scraping up pieces of the other biker, and they hit gold. Jerry found the man's left hand and one intact eye."

"Okay. Disgusting, but useful. Tell me what he got."

"Jerry lifted fingerprints and also ran a recognition program off the retina. We got no joy on the prints, but the retina print got a hit. It was in a database of high rollers we, um, borrowed, from a casino in Dubai. The eye belonged to a Greek national named Aristotle Kostas."

"Wait . . . I've heard that name somewhere. At least the Kostas name. Black market, maybe . . . ?"

"Right. The Kostas family pretty much own the Mediterranean black market, and serious points in illegal trading in the Middle East and Africa. Guns, art, stuff supposedly destroyed by ISIL. He got on our radar as a possible person of interest when we started looking at the Turkish guy, Ohan, who was tied to Rafael Santoro's search for the Unlearnable Truths."

"Right. Kostas is the dead guy? How's a power player like him tied to earthquakes in D.C.?"

"That's the interesting part," said Bug. "He went to MIT. Want to guess who his roommate was?"

"Son of a bitch."

"Some of the images Q1 pulled of Oruraka were from street and hotel cameras in Greece. We can put those two together at like fifty different places in the U.S. and abroad."

"This is great stuff, Bug. You're a genius."

"I am. It's true," he said.

"Put it all together and upload it to my computer. And call me the second you find Oruraka."

"Will do." And he was gone.

I poured myself another whiskey and felt a knot of tension in my chest ease by one small increment. We had names now. We had a major player who studied seismology and geophysics. We had ties to black marketers, though I didn't yet know how that played into things. Maybe Ari Kostas was the guy who smuggled the God Machines into the country.

The fact that Kostas and Oruraka were both doing fieldwork on this was interesting. Either their group was so small that everyone had to get their hands dirty; or they were working for someone else. If so, who was upper management?

I was making inroads into my third glass of Irish whiskey when Church called.

"Glad to hear from you," I said. "I have something to—"

"Captain, listen to me first," he cut in, and the tone of his voice instantly chilled me to the bone. "I received a call from Lilith. She said that Violin has been injured while on a mission."

"How bad?"

"She was shot and has suffered severe blood loss, shock, and internal bleeding. Her status is critical and trauma surgeons are working on her at a United Nations field hospital in Syria."

"Who shot her?" I demanded. "I am going to fucking kill them."

Church paused for a moment too long before he answered, and I knew that he was going to say something neither of us wanted to hear.

"It appears that Harry Bolt shot her."

I nearly threw the expensive whiskey across the cabin. "Tell me."

He did, about how Violin and her pet idiot had gone on a covert op in Syria. Both of them were fitted with RFID chips, but their signals had abruptly stopped minutes before an earthquake rocked the region.

"Whoa," I said, "wait a minute. An *earthquake*?"

"Yes," said Church.

"Another freaking earthquake? Oh, come on."

"Yes. Two days ago. It was not particularly large and did no damage to any civilian population, which is why it did not make the news. Bear in mind, Captain, that there are thousands of earthquakes felt around the world. On average, fourteen hundred per year, which averages to about forty per day. Usually only those above magnitude six are reported, and of those, only the ones occurring in industrialized nations or near population centers. Earthquakes are not at all rare, but where they occur along the plate boundaries strongly influences whether anyone notices."

"Thank you, Bill Nye."

"This one, though, is suspicious because of the nature of Violin's mission. She was tracking agents of the black marketer Ohan."

"Ohan? That piece of shit?"

Ohan, a non-Muslim Turk, was one of the most effective and dangerous dealers in stolen technologies, weapons, and other items that "fell off a truck" in the Middle East. Because the CIA sometimes used him, Ohan's designation was "hands off." I had him on my personal list because he was involved in the Kill Switch case.

His sideline was obtained items looted from libraries, tombs, sacred sites, and university museums in areas overrun by ISIL.

"It gets worse, Captain," said Church. "Lilith confirmed that Ohan's team was searching for another book from the *Index Librorum Prohibitorum*."

My heart jolted to a painful halt in my chest.

"He's after one of the Unlearnable Truths?"

"Yes," said Church. "Lilith sent Violin to secure the book before Ohan's men could obtain it. Her last report was that she and Harry Bolt had tracked them to the Citadel of Salah Ed-Din, near Al-Haffah. They apparently entered the citadel, there is evidence of several fights, and then the earthquake hit. The Arklight team entered less than a day later and found Violin clinging to life."

"Why did Harry do it? Why'd he shoot her? Did he out himself as being just like his asshole traitor father?"

"Harry was in a deep state of shock," said Church. "He had a deep laceration on his scalp and some cranial damage consistent with having tried to shoot himself in the head at the wrong angle. The bullet crazed him and rendered him unconscious."

"So, what's that? Guilt? Remorse?"

"I think it may be something more relevant to this case, Captain. Please take your emotions out of gear for a moment and think it through. Harry, who we all trust, shot Violin during a mission to find one of the books Prospero Bell said were relevant to the creation of a God Machine. He then turned his gun on himself. What does that sound like?"

"Jesus Christ," I said.

"Lilith has dispatched a team to find Ohan. I imagine they will," he said. "They are highly motivated, as you might imagine. And Lilith herself is coming here, because the connection to what's happening in America is undeniable."

"Was there a God Machine there in the citadel?"

"None that was found," said Church, "but many of the underground vaults have collapsed in. However, they did find the book. And the Arklight team also found some pieces of green crystal."

"So?"

"Junie insists that is important. She'll brief you."

Before I could ask more, the line went dead. The plane carved a hole in the air on its way to Brooklyn.

CHAPTER EIGHTY-FIVE

DAYS INN
LISBON, OHIO

Valen checked into an inexpensive motel, slipped out to buy take-out Chinese food, bottled water, and a bottle of vodka. He ate the food, washed it down with a third of the vodka, and spent half the night throwing up.

His cell phone rang eight times. All from blocked numbers. Gadyuka, probably going crazy wondering what was happening to him. She probably had a tracking device in his car, but his not answering the calls had to piss her off.

Fine.

He tried to go back to bed, got sick again, and eventually fell asleep on the floor of the bathroom, curled up between the toilet and the tub.

In the morning he woke, showered for nearly an hour, standing under the spray, scrubbing at his skin until it was red and raw, rinsing.

Weeping.

The death toll kept rising. Collateral damage. The unfortunate civilian casualties of any war.

He still had a long way to drive. And then . . .

Millions would die.

Millions.

Thinking that made him vomit again, though by then all that was in his stomach was half a cup of water.

He dropped onto his knees in the tub and pounded the porcelain until his hands began to swell.

"My God," he whispered. "My God."

An hour later he was back on the road. Heading west.

CHAPTER EIGHTY-SIX

OVER PENNSYLVANIA AIRSPACE

I never got to Brooklyn.

The pilot came back to tell me that he'd been ordered to land at a private airfield in Eastern Pennsylvania.

"Why?" I demanded.

"Doc Holliday wants me to activate an ORB for you," said the captain. "Doc said the team has intelligence for you."

"Where are we heading?"

"Vancouver," he said. "That's all I know."

He returned to the cabin and locked himself in. Immediately the lights dimmed and a series of two hundred small lights blinked on, which made me feel like I was floating in outer space. This was one of Doc Holliday's favorite inventions, and rumor has it that she'd cooked up the first prototype while in high school and watching *Star Trek: The Next Generation*. It was her attempt to create a holodeck, where people could step into another place that looked entirely real, but which was illusion. Unlike in the *Star Trek* version, I couldn't pick up the objects I saw. This was the twenty-first century, after all. But the 3-D holography was absolutely state of the art. It's like wearing virtual reality glasses except that you aren't wearing any goggles. The cabin of the jet became a conference room. Just like that. The name, ORB, means "Operational Resource Bay," and personally I think the acronym came first and they retrofitted it because it sounded cool. This is teleconferencing taken to a weird new level.

The ORB flared for a moment and there was Doc Holliday in all her glory. Beneath the white coat she wore boot-cut jeans that looked to be a thousand years old and a silk blouse that was the same unnatural Maxfield Parrish sky blue as her eyes. Shocking red lipstick, too much eyeliner, and mountains of blond curls. I do not know how much of her is real or comes from surgery, makeup, and special effects; and I don't much care. Doc Holliday looked exactly like she wanted to look, and was therefore the perfect example of herself.

"Howdy, Cowboy," she said. If you tried to take the temperature of the day based on her exuberance and radiance you'd think all was right with the world and we'd all just stepped into the last, happy minutes of a Disney film filled with songbirds and bunnies. The truth is that she is at her happiest when the door to hell has fallen off its hinges and the demons are running wild. "Well, hoss, they did warn me that weird clings to you like flies on tree sap. What you're not is boring."

"Thanks?" I said.

"How's your Russian?"

"Good enough," I said. "Why?"

"'Cause you've won an all-expenses-paid, fun-filled trip to sunny Moscow."

Doc raised a small clicker, pressed it, and suddenly Nikki Bloom was in the ORB with us. Not sure you could find anyone who is a more startling contrast to Doc. Nikki is a tiny woman, barely five feet tall, which made her a foot shorter than the scientist. She is built on a delicate frame and the only thing that seems to give her mass is a lot of wavy black hair. She wears shapeless sweatshirts without logos, and nondescript pants. Her one nod to color are Keds, which she has in every color they make. Currently, orange plaid.

"Um . . . hi . . . ," she said meekly.

"Oh, come on now, don't be shy, sugar-lumps," laughed Doc. "Tell Joe what you found, you being so gol-durned clever and all."

Nikki, now the color of a ripe tomato, cleared her throat and said, "I, um, have been going over the keywords you gave me, but I also added a bunch of my own, and I've been getting a lot of different kinds of hits. We're putting together a profile on this Valen Oruraka, aka Oleg Sokolov. We think he is some kind of Russian agent."

"Kind of figured that, Niks," I said.

"No, I mean something special. Do you know anything about the Novyy Sovetskiy?"

"Sure," I said. "The New Soviet. It's a fringe group that thinks they can rebuild the Communist Party in Russia. They've been fumbling around for years, but no one's been taking them very seriously. Why?"

"We've unlocked some of his e-mails sent from a server when he was at MIT, and there's loads of political stuff on there. Long, rambling e-mails with friends back in Russia about how Stalin derailed the Communist ideal and corrupted it, and how a new pure Party would save Russia from itself."

"Hate to break it to you, Nikki, but long and rambling political discussions are part of what college students do. I ranted a bit myself."

"Sure, but what's important is who he was ranting to." Nikki raised her hands and spread them, and as if by magic a list of names appeared in the air. Holograms are kind of cool.

The names were all Russian. "Valen—and I'm calling him that because it's what he's calling himself now, okay?—swapped e-mails with eleven different people in Russia, and a few Russians living in Ukraine. Over a period of months, his e-mails got more intense, and it's pretty clear that he was completely sold on the idea of this New Soviet thing. If he'd been in America we would have put him on a watch list because of the things he said. About how old structures needed to be torn down and how this was a war. That was the key right there, Joe, because it's clear that he saw the Cold War as a real, declared war, and that the fall of the Soviet Union did not end that war. He makes references to partisans and how their fight was never recognized as a declared war, but it was all the more honest because it was from the true heart of loyal Russians."

"Yeah," I said. "So where does that take us?"

"The names on the list are actually people he knew," she said, but then she swept four names away. "We checked some out and dismissed them as 'talkers.' People who love to argue and wrangle about politics but really aren't all that genuinely political. Not enough to try and bring something like the New Soviet into being if it meant pulling triggers."

"Right. And the rest?"

"That's where this gets really fascinating," said Nikki, warming to the topic. "Of the remaining names, all but one are friends of his who were studying computer sciences in various schools. They all went into different related fields, including IT, information services, code writing, and public relations. I had a feeling, though, and kept drilling down into their lives. And . . . do you remember the list of Russians indicted a while back? The ones accused of hacking into voting records and also waging a disinformation campaign on social media? Well, all of Valen's friends, the ones we didn't eliminate from our list, were part of that."

"Well . . . holy shit."

"It gets better," she said, and now Nikki was grinning as broadly as Doc Holliday. "The last name on the list was an old girlfriend of Valen's who was probably the one who got him into politics in the first place. She was the granddaughter of a senior Party member during the old Soviet days and was in that group of very vocal radicals who were very open about rebuilding the Party and getting it right. By reading back through the e-mails, it's pretty clear that she's helped shape his thinking from when he was in high school. Maybe earlier, but that stuff isn't on e-mails. There are references to 'conversations' they had, so it was probably in person. She and Valen stayed in touch for years even though they did not actually physically meet after he enrolled as a freshman in college; and then it all ended when she died in a skiing accident."

"And . . . ?" I asked, waiting for the other shoe to drop.

"We deconstructed this girl's life, and I think the person Valen was talking to via e-mails all those years was not that girl. Sure, she did die in an accident, but that happened right after high school.

The e-mails went on all through college and then Valen's graduate studies at MIT. Nearly seven years of constant e-mails."

I frowned. "Okay . . . so if this girl died young, then who the hell has he been talking to?"

"I ran a syntax algorithm, and even though the fake friend did a pretty good job of pretending to be the old girlfriend, there are unique identifiers. Everyone has them. And I've found some hits that back me up on this. There are nine other people, kind of like Valen, who talk politics with 'old friends,' both male and female. All in cases where they aren't able to see those old friends. Clever photo-manipulated pics are sent, but there aren't any real-world encounters. I think they've all been talking to the same person. Maybe it's a recruiter for the Novyy Sovetskiy. Certainly someone who understands psychological manipulation to an ultrasophisticated degree. Some of the verbiage from her political comments was cut and pasted into e-mails to the other nine."

"So, this guy is cultivating talent?"

"I don't think it's a guy. Sometimes she pretends to be one, but the language structure is female."

"You can tell that from e-mails?"

Nikki shrugged. "Of course I can."

I did not ask how, because the explanation would take hours and I would sink beneath minute detail never to be seen again. I know this from experience.

"I also think I have an idea about who this woman is," said Nikki. "Have you ever heard about a spy code-named Gadyuka?"

"The viper," I said. "Sure. But she's a myth."

"More like a ghost. There's a lot of crazy stuff about her floating around the intelligence communities. Like Professor Moriarty from Sherlock Holmes. Gadyuka's supposed to be behind all sorts of crazy stuff, but there's never any evidence that points back directly to her."

"I know," I said, "but I read a Barrier report that theorized that Gadyuka was a cover name for a whole bunch of different agents. A shared cover."

"What if it's not, Joe? What if there really is a master spy, and this is her? I mean, what if she's really behind the earthquakes and all of this?"

"I'd be more enthused about that possibility if we had even a smidge of evidence. That Barrier report gave eight or nine different physical descriptions of her, including one that said she was a slim man pretending to be a woman. No one has any idea who she really is, what she looks like, or . . . well . . . anything."

Nikki did not look frustrated by that. If anything, she seemed intrigued. A new puzzle to untangle. "Mr. Church asked that everything we have on Gadyuka be sent to Lilith via the Oracle uplink. I think that means Arklight is hunting for her."

"Sucks to be Gadyuka, then," I said. "I wouldn't want Lilith dogging me. Not after what happened to Violin."

Doc spoke up. "Whoever this Jezebel is, I think our mystery woman is cultivating the zeal for the next generation of New Soviet party members. Valen is one, and he's a geophysicist and seismologist. The others are specialists, too. Epidemiologist, meteorologist, botanist, geneticist. Like that. All very dangerous professions. All very skilled experts in those fields. Frankly it's making my ass itch, and whenever my ass itches there's trouble in the tall grass."

Nikki nodded. "When we widened the search we found that, like Valen, some of the friends of each of these experts have likely been recruited, too, with a bias toward anyone with deep social media or hacking skills."

"The new battlefield," observed Doc, "isn't tanks and bombs. It's weird science and the Internet. Anyone who says different isn't paying attention."

"Well, this is scary as all hell," I said, "but it doesn't tell me why I'm flying to Russia. Valen is here."

"Yeah," said Nikki, "I haven't gotten to the scary part yet."

CHAPTER EIGHTY-SEVEN

OFFICE OF INTERNATIONAL EXPORTS, LTD
ISTANBUL, REPUBLIC OF TURKEY

"Pull the blinds, Adina," said the older woman.

This was done, and the lights in the small reception area were turned out. Adina followed Qadira and the other Arklight women into the back room. She was careful to step around the bodies instead of over them. A superstition that persisted among the sisterhood. She was also careful not to step in the pools of blood.

The women gathered in a half circle around the man seated on the chair in the middle of the room. He was short, fat, hairy, trembling, and naked. His arms and legs were lashed to the chair with many turns of strong electrician's tape. He was not gagged, but one woman stood with the tip of a long-bladed knife resting on his flaccid penis. The man kept his mouth shut, though terror sweat coursed down his body.

Qadira pulled over another chair so that it faced him. She sat down, crossed her legs, and rested her hands in her lap.

"Tell me," she asked mildly, "do you know who I am? Who we are?"

"You are insane, is who you are," gasped the man. "Do you know who I am?"

"Yes," said the old woman. "Your name is Volken Çalhanoğlu. You own this business, and many other businesses. You are very rich, very powerful, and very influential."

"Then you know what will happen to you if you hurt me," he snarled.

Qadira smiled. "You haven't answered my question. Do you know who we are?"

The man did not answer, clearly afraid of what the consequence of a wrong answer might be.

"My name is Qadira. This girl is Adina. Isn't she lovely? Very smart, too. Very tough. These other women are my sisters. Not blood kin, but sisters all the same."

"What is this all about? What do you want with me? Why did you attack my people? Are you insane?"

"It is very likely that I am insane. At least by certain standards. Adina is quite mad in her way. She would have to be, considering what she's been through in her life. What we've all been through."

The man looked suspicious. "I . . . I don't have anything to do with that."

"With what? With slavery and sexual subjugation? Oh, please, we both know that you do. Oddly, though, that's not why we're here. Mind you, we would have paid you a visit eventually. Your name is on our list, and has been for some time."

"List? What are you talking about? What list? Who are you?"

"I'm sure you've heard of us, Mr. Ohan."

The name seemed to burst in the air, and it made the man recoil. "O-Ohan? I do not know this name. You . . . you have the wrong man."

Qadira flicked a tiny glance at the woman with the knife, who made the slightest motion. Not to destroy, but to draw a thin bead of blood from the helpless man's penis.

"That was the only lie we will allow you, Ohan," said the old woman. "Lie again and my sister will do more than *prick* you."

Ohan's jaws were locked shut with terror.

"Now," said Qadira, leaning slightly forward, "you sent a team to Syria to recover a book. One of the Unlearnable Truths. No . . . shhh . . . don't speak yet, because you don't know what I'm going to ask, and you really do not want to give the wrong answer, do you?"

The man glanced around at the faces of the women. He saw no flicker of pity or compassion or mercy. He looked at the girl and tried to appeal to her with his eyes.

Adina smiled at him, which made Ohan return the smile. An ally. A friend. A hope.

Then she held out her hand to the woman with the knife. That woman glanced at Qadira, who nodded; then she handed the blade to Adina, who took it and slid the flat of it under Ohan's testicles with such delicacy and skill that the scrotum was lifted but not cut. The steel was so cold it felt like a burning brand, and Ohan had to bite back his own scream. Adina's smile never faded, never even flickered.

"We are the Mothers of the Fallen," said Qadira, and when that did not register on Ohan or break through his terror, she added, "but you will know us as Arklight."

Ohan's eyes went wide and his bladder released, splashing on the knife.

The old woman nodded. "Yes, you *have* heard of us. Good. Then you will know what we will do if you do not tell us everything we want to know."

"You . . . you'll . . . kill me anyway?"

"Everyone dies, Ohan. The question is whether you want to die screaming as a eunuch or quickly as a man? The choice is entirely yours. However, you'll tell us either way. Everyone does."

CHAPTER EIGHTY-EIGHT

OVER PENNSYLVANIA AIRSPACE

I stood in the ORB, arms folded across my chest. Nikki's eyes glittered with all the things she wanted to tell me.

"Okay," I said, "hit me."

An image flashed on that showed a bloody crime scene, and I recognized it from the news. This one was uncensored, with nothing pixilated. There were body parts all over and everything was awash in blood. That wasn't what Nikki wanted me to see, though. On the wall above the couch were two words written in what I had no doubt was blood.

Deep Silence

"Mr. Howell wasn't the first person to use that phrase. Or, at least something like it," she said. "'Suicide' and 'suicide note,' along with a lot of variations, were among the keywords we added to the general pattern search. And since you had the idea that God Machines might be somehow connected, I accessed the Gateway incident reports prior to you, um . . . blowing the place up."

Doc snorted. I ignored them both.

"Not everyone who committed suicide left a note, and not all of the notes had anything to do with what Howell wrote," said Nikki, "but there were a few that talked about the 'silence' or the 'quiet' or the 'big nothing.' There were five out of nineteen suicides. The likelihood of that, even for a base in Antarctica, is too much."

"Yeah," I said.

"Then I added those phrases to my search and started looking for suicide notes left in areas where there has been some kind of seismic activity. I went back ten years, but we didn't start getting hits until the earthquake in Valparaiso two years ago. The big one that knocked down the hotels, remember?"

"Sure. It was horrible."

"In the weeks leading up to the earthquake, there was a sixteen percent jump in suicides, and a lot of them were people who had not sought therapy or treatment for depression. Neither, by the way, had the Speaker of the House. In Valparaiso there were suicide notes of different kinds. One of the victims wrote: 'I can't hear my own thoughts.' I think that would qualify as a 'deep silence,' don't you think?"

"Sure as shootin' sounds like it to me," agreed Doc. "You're even smarter than you are pretty."

Through her second round of furious blushing, Nikki said, "And we're looking into police incident reports and crime scene files for hundreds of other suicides in areas where there have been quakes. All over the world, too, with translations of words and phrases slowing us down just a little. Not enough to keep us from seeing a pattern."

"Deep silence," I murmured. "When we were being attacked outside of the Capitol Building people were saying stuff about silence. One woman kept asking why she couldn't hear her own head.

Someone else, a reporter I think, kept screaming and asking if people could hear him. There were others, too."

"Yes," said Nikki. "Whatever this is, however it works, this is a symptom."

"You got any answers, Doc?" I asked.

"Without having a God Machine to tinker with," she said, "no. Best I can do is make horseback guesses, but that's all they'd be. I need you to get one of those doohickeys for me, Cowboy."

"Deep silence," I said again. "This is great, Nikki. Where does this leave us though? Are we thinking that Valen and his New Soviet study group are causing earthquakes all over the world? Why? Is there a pattern to where those quakes took place?"

"I've been putting that together, but I'm nowhere near done yet. We've been looking at anything related to seismic activity, with a bias toward unusual or unexpected activity, and we got a bunch of stuff, including one in January in Vrancea in Romania. Remember that one? Did a load of damage there and in Moldova, Bulgaria, and Ukraine."

"Yeah, but I read that they had a history of earthquakes there."

"Sure, sure," said Doc, "but the timing and some other stuff about it were kind of weird. Even though the epicenter was in Romania, the fault line running straight into Ukraine was suddenly much wider and did more damage than in any of the previous quakes in 1940, 1977, 1986, and 1990. A lot more."

"Where's the timing weirdness in that?"

Doc winked. She is the only person I know who can pull off a wink in this kind of circumstance and really make it work. "Two weeks before the quake, the Ukrainians moved a significant number of tanks onto a base there. A refitting base where those tanks were being upgraded with new targeting systems purchased from the United States. The quake destroyed most of that base, and many of the tanks were badly damaged. Estimates are that it set the Ukraine resistance to Russian invasion back by six months."

"Hunh," I grunted.

"There's more, Joe," said Nikki. "There's been a slew of small earthquakes around the world over the last four years. I looked at all of them and isolated eleven that were in geologically stable areas. And another six that were in areas near a dormant volcano that suddenly went active. And in each of those places there was an uptick in suicides. Anywhere from three to nineteen percent above normal."

"Oh," I said. "Shit. Are any of those other sites strategically useful to Russia? Or to a new Soviet Union?"

"Not really," conceded Nikki. "Actually, most of them aren't strategically useful to anyone for anything."

"Unless they are," said Doc, and I nodded, seeing where she was going with that.

"Testing sites for the earthquake tech?" I suggested. She blew me a kiss.

The pilot's voice filled the air to tell me we were beginning our descent to the airfield.

"Okay," I said, "so that still doesn't tell me why I'm flying to Moscow. This is State Department stuff. I'm not sanctioned for ops on foreign soil without some kind of approval. Even black ops have to be approved by someone."

"You think *this* president is going to give you his blessing to carry out a mission to Russia that's tied to election rigging?"

"That earthquake nearly killed him," I said. "I think the honeymoon's over. I mean, as wake-up calls go, this is one for the history books."

"Thirteen hundred and eighty-four dead," said Nikki.

The numbers hurt. They hurt real damn bad.

"Moscow," I said to Nikki.

"Okay," she said, and I could see that her eyes were wet, "one of Valen's pen pals is a Yuri Rolgavitch. His family owns a big import-export business that deals mostly with electronics. Radios, speakers, headphones. Like that. Yuri recently took over the company when his father had to retire because of diabetes. He sometimes uses his company e-mail server for private correspondence."

"That's thin."

"No, it gets better," she said quickly. "We picked apart Yuri

Rolgavitch's e-mails. Not just the ones to Valen, but some other stuff that he sent out as encrypted. There were e-mails to e-mail accounts here in the States, and in a couple of them I found several coded references to something that is scaring the living crap out of me. I don't have full context because it was only a couple of oblique references to '*zemletryaseniye*.' That's Russian for—"

"Earthquake," I said quietly. "Holy rat shit."

The floor seemed to tilt under me, and I didn't think it was because the jet was landing.

"That e-mail is dated eight months ago," said Nikki. "And there's more. There are other mentions of *zemletryaseniye*, and the corresponding dates are close to other earthquakes, like the big one in Valparaiso two years ago. But the timing's weird. Every reference predates the actual events. We tried to go deeper, but Bug thinks that their office mainframes aren't connected to the Internet. We can't get anything more than that. But . . . well, what do you think?"

I took a deep breath. "I think I'd like to go to Moscow. Better call Top and Bunny and have them tell the rest of Echo Team that we're going hunting."

CHAPTER EIGHTY-NINE

JOHNS HOPKINS UNIVERSITY HOSPITAL
BALTIMORE, MARYLAND

Church and Brick sat on opposite sides of a borrowed desk, both of them making calls, taking calls, and responding to intelligence reports via their laptops. On the Scroll, various DMS heads popped up to provide more data.

Information was flooding in.

"This is starting to make some sense," said Brick. "But it feels like we're a little farther back behind the eight ball than usual. How'd these bastards get this far without us catching a whiff?"

"Because of betrayals and loose lips, there are too many people in too many places who know about the DMS and what we can do. They know about MindReader and its potential, and they plan accordingly."

Brick sighed and took a sip of Diet Dr Pepper. "Really makes me long for the old days when we were an actual *secret* secret organization."

It was meant as a joke, but Brick saw the look in Church's eyes.

"What?" he asked.

"Let's just say that we're very much on the same page."

CHAPTER NINETY

ROLGAVITCH TECHNOLOGIES
KOTELNICHESKAYA EMBANKMENT
MOSCOW, RUSSIA

Friendship is a fickle and fragile ol' thing. Especially when we're talking the friendship between nations.

Case in point . . .

The relationship between Russia and the United States has always been a little weird. Maybe more than a little, actually. At the beginning of World War II we were not pals because Russia was part of the grouchy little Kaffeeklatsch that was the Axis powers. Then when Hitler stepped on his own dick and invaded Russia, suddenly we were chums standing shoulder to shoulder to save the world from evil. I remember history-book photos of Stalin, Roosevelt, and Churchill looking like frat brothers at the Yalta Conference. Smiles all around. The enemy of my enemy. That sort of thing. Political exigencies can often be embarrassing to students of history, or, say, truth.

At the end of the war, General George Patton wanted to roll his tanks into Russia because he was positive they were going to be the next big threat. He was talked out of it, or maybe assassinated. Opinions differ. There was some discussion about dropping an atomic bomb on the Kremlin. I'm no political philosopher, so I don't know if that would have been a good move or a bad one. One view is that it would have stopped the spread of Communism right there, prevented the Cold War, and the phrase "mutually assured destruction" would not have entered the global lexicon. Maybe that would have ensured that no one ever developed a competing nuclear program. On the other hand, there would have been hundreds of thousands of innocent dead and we would have taken the third step on the pathway to establishing an American Empire with a proven track record for using atomic bombs as policy statements. That's scary no matter from which direction it's viewed.

For a lot of years, the Cold War was all the evidence anyone needed that Russia and the U.S. of A were not BFFs. Then the Berlin Wall fell, and the Soviet Union became an interesting historical oddity that was not even much of a part of my life growing up. There was trade, cultural exchanges, and even some reasonable reductions in nuclear and bioweapons development. There was also an explosion of crime and corruption—the Russian Mafiya was largely composed of former military people who brought their battlefield coldness along with dangerous skill sets.

And then along came Vladimir Putin, who, I'm reasonably certain, has a Joseph Stalin plushy toy that he sleeps with. With Putin came a kind of neo-Soviet state, complete with reinvigorated secret police, assassinations, suppression of the media, and all the fun stuff. With Putin, we also got a new kind of weapon of mass destruction in the form of cyber hacking. The last American and French elections pretty much proved that there was a new kind of warfare and, for a while, Putin's geek squad had the biggest bombs.

Now we have this Novyy Sovetskiy thing, which I'd been naïve enough to think was a splinter group that lacked the support or resources to do more than raise hopes among those old duffers nostalgic for the good old days of the Party.

That was before Valen Oruraka and Ari Kostas wrecked Washington, D.C., and killed thirteen hundred people. I had a brand-new take on the New Soviet now. They were real, they were dangerous, and I was going to dismantle them in very ugly ways.

Which explains why I was sitting in the office of a Russian shipping mogul, dressed all in black, armed to the teeth, and kind of pissed off. On the upside, they had a coffee maker in the office and some really superb Turkish blend. I was on my third cup, and it had so much caffeine that my eyes were twitching and I was starting to hear colors. Ghost had spent some time licking his balls, then when they were clean and shiny he went to sleep. I sat for a while behind a big oak desk and looked at a bunch of framed photos of the manager's wife and kids. Nice-looking wife; adorable kids.

When the door opened and a man came in, I said, "Well, it's about goddamn time."

I said it in Russian.

The man stopped dead in his tracks, one hand on the knob, the other clutching the key he'd just taken from the lock. His heavy topcoat was damp with melting snow. He stared at me. Gaped, really. After all, I was in his locked office, which means I'd gotten through three levels of pretty sophisticated security without alerting the team of guards downstairs. And I was dressed all in black.

He said, *"Tchyo za ga `lima—?"*

Basically, *What the fuck.*

I pointed a pistol at him and held a finger to my lips. "Shhhh."

CHAPTER NINETY-ONE

ROLGAVITCH TECHNOLOGIES
KOTELNICHESKAYA EMBANKMENT
MOSCOW, RUSSIA

The Russian guy shushed. As one would, all things considered.

Actually, he pretty much turned to a statue. Eyes bugged, mouth open in a silent O, skin becoming a lovely shade of gray-green. The barrel of my gun was pointing at his crotch, so there's that. I prefer to be eloquent and articulate whenever possible. Or, maybe he turned that color because a big white shepherd rose from behind a guest chair, his body covered in Kevlar and lamplight gleaming off his six titanium teeth, as he stood snarling in ghastly silence at him. That'll do it, too.

Ghost is a nice dog, some of the time. When he's home. When he's catching Frisbees on the beach. When Junie and I are in bed on a Sunday morning reading the paper and watching TV. The rest of the time, like when we're on foreign soil and bad things are very likely on the dance card . . . eh, not so much. The metal teeth were replacements for the six he'd lost fighting genetically enhanced killers in Iran. Ghost likes showing those teeth almost as much as he likes using them.

"Yuri Rolgavitch," I said quietly, and he flinched at my use of his name. Continuing to speak in Russian, I said, "Step into the room. Drop the key right there. Go on, you won't need it."

Rolgavitch did. I could actually see beads of sweat burst from his pores and run down his cheeks.

"Place your hands on your head, lace your fingers. Good. Turn around and don't move. If you do anything stupid I'm going to let my dog play with you. He'll enjoy it a lot more than you will."

Rolgavitch did as he was told, though he kept cutting glances at my gun, trying to figure out what it was. Good luck. I carried a snubby little Snellig A-220 gas dart pistol. The company that manufactured it no longer exists because we shut them down and stole all their toys. They were making weapons for bad people and now all of those people are dead and we have the toys. The A-220 fires little gelatin darts filled with an amped-up version of the veterinary drug ketamine, along with a powerful hallucinatory compound. We call it "horsey." One shot and you drop like a rock and dream of purple jitterbugging penguins. When you wake up you'll have only a vague recollection that something untoward happened but will remember only two things about the last hour or so: jack and shit. You'll also be prone to explosive diarrhea for the rest of the day, but I'm pretty sure that was designed into it for pure entertainment purposes. We have some deeply troubled people working for the D of MS.

"Ghost," I said, "watch."

He watched very closely.

I pressed the barrel of the pistol against the base of Rolgavitch's spine and held it there while I patted him down with my free hand. Took a sweet little MP-443 Grach automatic from a belt clip and an equally spiffy Samozaryadny Malogabaritny compact pistol from an ankle holster. I tossed both onto the guest chair. I pocketed his cell phone and looked at his wallet to confirm that this was indeed Yuri Rolgavitch. Imagine my embarrassment if he hadn't been.

"Now, *tovarisch,*" I said, "let's have us a chat. If I get the answers I want, then I'll zip-cuff your wrists and ankles and won't hurt a hair on your head. Your people will find you sitting at your desk, there will be evidence of a common burglary that will corroborate any story you want to tell. You'll never see me again. If I *don't* get what I want, and if you make me do anything to aggravate my achy back muscles, then it's going to get weird around here. I don't mean frat party weird, either. More like psycho beach party weird."

Rolgavitch was late thirties but fat and unfit, with a thick mustache and the largest nose I've ever seen on a human face. Made him look like a frightened puffin. He was not going to try anything. We both knew that. Ghost knew it, too, and I could read the disappointment in his brown doggy eyes.

"Who . . . who are you?" he stammered.

"C'mon, Yuri," I said agreeably, "you know that's not the conversation we're going to have. What's important here is that I know who *you* are."

Sweat glistened on his cheeks. His lips and eyes were wet, too. "Wh-why are you here?"

"I'm here," I said, "because you are doing something very sneaky and very dangerous, but you're not as slick about it as you seem to think."

"I'm not—" Rolgavitch began, but I cut him off by raising the barrel to point at his nose. Impossible target to miss.

"Do not under any circumstances waste my time by saying that you aren't a bad guy. I know you are. This is not up for discussion."

Rolgavitch said nothing. He couldn't know what or how much I knew, or that I was largely bluffing. I mean, sure, Nikki had found the earthquake references and that Yuri was a pen pal of Valen Oruraka, but that's all we really had. No actual details. Quite frankly I didn't know how deep he was into Valen's activities.

"What do you think I know?" he asked with a confused smile, trying to sound innocent and even contriving to come off as aggrieved. Nice try, but I wiped that smile off his face with what I said next.

"Tell me about Valen Oruraka."

I watched his eyes when I dropped that name. They widened until I could see whites all around the irises. His mouth sagged open, too. Yeah, he knew.

"Or should we call him Oleg Sokolov?" I asked.

In a hollow voice filled with equal parts shock and dread, Rolgavitch gasped, "How do you know this name . . . ?"

"How about we accept that I *do* know it and go from there?" I said. "What's really on the front burner here is what you can tell me about him."

"No! No, I can't," he protested. "They will kill me."

I gave him a wide, white, toothy smile. The kind of smile I never show to people who I care even a little bit about. The kind of smile I'd never show to my lover, Junie Flynn. I've been told that it is not a very sane smile. Fair enough.

"*They're* not here right now, Yuri," I said quietly. "*I* am."

Ghost gave a soft *whuff*.

When he sat there and stubbornly shook his head, I reached over to the row of framed photos on his desk and turned them around, one by one. Wife. Teenage son. Preteen daughter. Baby. I angled the pictures so that their faces were looking at him. I sat down on the edge of the desk and laid the pistol on my thighs.

"Go on," I said quietly, "tell me how badly you want me to have to insist?"

CHAPTER NINETY-TWO

BALTIMORE MARRIOTT INNER HARBOR AT CAMDEN YARDS
BALTIMORE, MARYLAND

Lilith sat at the small desk in a far corner of the hotel. Her travel bag lay open but unpacked on the bed and she was methodically strip-cleaning the two unregistered handguns left for her by the local Arklight team.

Her laptop, a small Oracle remote unit in a hardened case, stood ready on the desk. The beatific face of Mona Lisa smiled benignly at her for hours. Then, suddenly, a voice spoke.

"You have a call from your sister Qadira," said the voice of Oracle.

Lilith set down the bottle of gun oil and tapped a key. The wizened face of the field team leader filled the screen.

"Tell me you found something," said Lilith.

"Ohan was working for a group of Russians. He said they claimed to be a private organization, but when I, um, *pressed* him, Ohan said that he believed that some or all of them may have ties to the Kremlin."

"Did he give you a name?"

"He only knew one of them. A woman who calls herself Gadyuka."

"Ah," said Lilith. "So, she's real, then?"

"Yes."

"What did he say about her?"

"More than he wanted to. He was very afraid of her."

Lilith nodded. "Which makes sense if Gadyuka's reputation is to be believed. The viper is supposed to be very dangerous. Highly skilled. An assassin who is making the move into management. Does he know her real name?"

"He did," said Qadira, emphasizing the past tense. "Ohan trusted no one and put his own spies on her. They've been keeping her under surveillance for him. Ohan even allowed Gadyuka to capture and kill two of them to make her think she had cleaned up the surveillance. The two sacrificial lambs were fed information that implicated a different person, so she never suspected who was tracking her. But Ohan's network is huge and subtle and very practiced. In the end, though, he gave me everything."

"Then give it to me."

"I'm transferring it all to you through Oracle," said Qadira, then added, "Lilith, this Gadyuka is in the United States. In Washington, D.C."

Lilith hissed. It sounded like she was in pain, but it was something else entirely.

CHAPTER NINETY-THREE

ROLGAVITCH TECHNOLOGIES
KOTELNICHESKAYA EMBANKMENT
MOSCOW, RUSSIA

We had a very nice talk, Yuri Rolgavitch and me.

He kept looking at the pictures of his family. He ugly cried. I handed him the box of tissues from his desk. He sat on the leather visitor chair and I sat on the edge of his desk, swinging a foot. Chatting. Ghost came over and began sniffing at Yuri's naughty bits. The dog has a theatrical flair at times.

Rolgavitch gave me what he had. Every other sentence out of his mouth, though, was him begging me not to hurt his family. He peed his pants. Tears and snot ran down his face. He told me absolutely everything he knew.

The bad news was that he didn't actually know what Valen was up to. They were friends from high school and he swore he'd tried to talk Valen out of changing his name. The story his friend gave him was that he was reinventing himself because there was a lingering stink on the family. His uncle, Dr. Abram Golovin, had been the structural engineer at Chernobyl and was blamed for that catastrophe. It was a good story, because I'd encountered enough former Soviets who had also re-created their lives and identities as a way of distancing themselves from things they may have done for the Party. Rolgavitch sold it hard, too. He said he kept in touch because Valen was a friend.

I sat for a while just smiling at him. Letting him wonder how much of it I believed.

"Why did Valen study seismology?" I asked.

"Because he did not believe Dr. Golovin was really at fault. It always hurt Valen that everyone blamed his uncle. Valen went to great lengths to obtain his uncle's design plans and bulk research. He even got materials that had been classified above top secret during the old Soviet Union days. Valen studied seismology but also geophysics and structural engineering. He reconstructed the landscape and geology of the area around Chernobyl to an incredible degree. Three-D models, spreadsheets, deep data analysis. He wanted to prove that the accident was because of a fluke earthquake or something else that a standard geological survey would not have predicted. He learned everything he could about random earthquakes and plate tectonics. He surpassed many of his teachers. Valen is a genius."

"Uh-huh. So, tell me, what has your genius friend been doing with all that knowledge about earthquakes?"

"I . . . well, I really don't know. We haven't spoken in quite some time."

"Uh-huh."

The last e-mail between him and Valen that Nikki found was six years old, but I didn't for a minute believe they were no longer connected.

"You know something about it, though," I prompted.

"I really don't know," he insisted, fresh sweat rolling down his flushed cheeks. "I asked once but he told me that I wasn't *allowed* to know. People have been killed for asking about these things."

"That's not my problem," I said. "Maybe you saw the news

yesterday about what happened in the United States. Yeah, I can see you have, so tell me something that will keep me from doing very bad things. What's Valen up to?"

"I don't know," he said quickly. "I'm not on that level, and was warned never to ask more than I was told."

"Warned by who?"

He hesitated. I made a subtle finger movement that was a cue for Ghost to growl and show his teeth. Yes, I trained Ghost to do that. What can I say?

Rolgavitch flinched. "A woman. I don't know her real name. No one associated with this uses real names. She is called Gadyuka."

I wanted to close my eyes and say *Ahhhhhh,* but did not. I am, after all, a professional.

"Tell me about her," I said, giving him more of that smile.

None of Yuri's communication with Gadyuka was ever done via the Net or over a phone. That's what we thought. In a high-tech world, some security protocols are going very low-tech. There was no footprint at all, no trail to follow. These people were, after all, world-class cyber warriors who were fully cognizant of all ways the CIA, the NSA, and shady organizations like the Department of Military Sciences could follow even small threads and counterattack. It was a sensible blend of caution, paranoia, and plausible deniability that left us nothing actionable, nothing we could bring to the U.N. or a world court.

Rolgavitch's involvement was clearly on a pretty low level, and it corresponded with what Nikki had learned. His company handled the logistics of shipping items manufactured at a number of companies. Most of the materials he shipped for Gadyuka came from a company called Pushkin Dynamics. Rolgavitch said that he had never visited that factory, and knew the contents only through the manifests which he was provided. He was notified when a "special order" was ready. He never called Gadyuka and had no numbers with which to do so, anyway. When she needed to talk to him she showed up. Never at the office. She might suddenly be standing next to him on a train platform or walk up to him on the street. She always looked different, too. Sometimes very tall, other times average height. Heavy or thin. Well dressed or shabby, looking fifty or forty or thirty. A real chameleon. Even the timbre of her voice changed, as well as her accent. Bottom line, Rolgavitch couldn't tell me anything about her except her gender and code name.

So, I asked the obvious question. "How can you be sure it wasn't a bunch of different women using the same code name?"

He looked at me and shivered. "No," he said quickly. "If you ever saw her, you'd know it was her. She's . . . she's . . ."

"Pick an adjective," I suggested.

"She's not *human*. She's a snake. Like her name. No matter how she's described, the feeling is the same." He shivered again.

"What kind of orders does Gadyuka give you?"

He gave his lips a nervous lick. "Mostly she contacts me about when and where to ship materials . . . and before you ask again, no, I really don't know what kind of materials. Everything is boxed and sealed with the kind of tape that changes color if it's been tampered with. I make arrangements and that's all. I'm not important enough to know more. I'm a middleman."

I slid off the desk, nudged Ghost out of the way, and squatted down in front of Rolgavitch. I smiled my best blue-eyed smile. "Here's the problem, *tovarisch*. I'm running out of time and I don't think you're telling me everything you know."

"I have answered all of your questions," he said. "Please, please, don't hurt my wife, my kids. . . ."

"Yeah, I know," I said, "but you see, our problem is that maybe I don't know the right questions to unlock you. I'm admitting that. I'm up front about that. But it kind of pisses me off. It's frustrating and it makes me feel bad. Cranky. That's an English word. Cranky. It means that I'm getting out of sorts and I'm about to go all peevish and petulant."

He said nothing.

"My instincts tell me two things, Yuri," I told him. "Want to know what they are? The first is that you probably know something really useful that would put a happy smile back on my face. No need to say anything, because we both know it's true. And the second thing my gut tells me is that if I put a bullet through one of your kneecaps, you'll tell me. It's what we call a 'come to Jesus moment.' If I put bullets through *both* of your kneecaps you'll *beg* to tell me. But then there will be all that blood, all that screaming, and it would spoil this happy moment we're currently having, am I right?"

He stared at me like I was a complete monster.

Still holding the gas dart gun in my right hand, I used my left to remove his own automatic from my belt. I placed the barrel against the front of his right knee.

"This will really hurt, Yuri. I can assure you that even with a total knee replacement you'll never walk right again. From this angle, the bullet will take off a chunk of the femur and maybe furrow all the way up and clip your femoral artery. Depending on the load in the bullet, it might even punch a big red hole through one of your nuts. Bet that would hurt."

He was crying now. And his nose was running. His whole face looked like it was going to disintegrate. I pressed the barrel harder against his knee.

"Now . . . tell me something that will put a smile back on both our faces."

He sobbed. A bigger, heavier, deeper sob than before. It shook his body. I did not blink or change my expression. If he saw madness and horror in my eyes, then he was seeing into a part of me where the Killer lived. Of the three people in my head, the Modern Man was a civilized and compassionate person; the Cop was the rational and pragmatic aspect that usually drove the bus. The Killer was neither civilized nor compassionate. He was in that dark evolutionary space between lizard brain and monkey mind. He was ugly and vicious, utterly pragmatic, and uncompromising. I seldom let him out to play, because when I did, very, very bad things happened. Each time I let him out he was more reluctant to go back to his cave. I could feel him behind my eyes and, worse, behind my smile. That is not a smile I would ever show to my Junie, or even to my best friend, Rudy. It is not a smile I ever show to anyone whose life I care about.

Yuri Rolgavitch saw the Killer, and when his eyes cut toward Ghost he saw something behind my dog's eyes as well. He saw the wolf. A primitive version, maybe a dire wolf; old and patient and merciless.

I said, "Tell me about the things you ship. From where, to where? All of it."

He started talking Pushkin Dynamics. That was where the shipments came from. He said he'd once heard one of the technicians there use the phrase "deep silence." It wasn't said to him, but was part of a whispered conversation he overheard. It made him believe that whatever was being manufactured and shipped from that place was connected to that project.

Rolgavitch sold all of this to me hard. He kept looking into my eyes, kept catching glimpses of the Killer. That was good. It kept him honest. It loosened his tongue.

But . . . he just did not know enough. Finally, he sagged back, shaking his head, begging me to believe that it was all he could tell me.

"What do you know about what Valen did in the United States?" I asked, purposefully not mentioning D.C. Rolgavitch frowned and looked genuinely confused. "I did not know he was in America. The last time I heard from him he was in Greece." He paused, reading my face. "You must believe me. This is all I know."

I studied him, read his eyes, and saw the truth.

"I believe you," I said.

And shot him.

CHAPTER NINETY-FOUR

JOHNS HOPKINS UNIVERSITY HOSPITAL
BALTIMORE, MARYLAND

Church visited Sam Imura and lingered for a while, carefully reading the postsurgical reports that had been prepared for him. The doctors were not optimistic, but that was to be expected.

Church placed his hand flat over Sam's heart and felt the beat.

He closed his eyes and was like that for a long time. Brick stood outside and made sure no one came in.

"Peace, little brother," said Church as he withdrew his hand.

He turned and left the room. He and Brick walked four rooms down, to where Aunt Sallie lay.

"Give me a moment," he said. Brick touched Church's arm and they shared a long look. One of the silent conversations they had come to have over the last few years. Church smiled and nodded, and Brick stepped back and took up a station outside the room.

Once inside, Church stood for a long time saying nothing, because the woman in the bed could not hear him. She was deep down in a dark place.

Instead, because he was alone and because he cared, Church bent and kissed her very gently on the forehead.

"If you have to go," he murmured, "then go. My love and blessings go with you."

There was no answer but the steady beep of her heart monitor.

"If you choose to stay, then you will always have a place with me. You are my sister and my family, Alexandria Sally Peters. Knowing you has made me a better man."

He kissed her again and straightened.

Brick entered the room and offered Church a paper napkin. Church nodded and dried his eyes. They both cast a last look at Aunt Sallie, then they left, heading for the elevator and the waiting car, and the jet that was already fueled. Neither spoke. They understood each other so very well.

The war was waiting.

CHAPTER NINETY-FIVE

ROLGAVITCH TECHNOLOGIES
KOTELNICHESKAYA EMBANKMENT
MOSCOW, RUSSIA

I shot Rolgavitch with the gas dart.

I mean, c'mon . . . I'm not *actually* a monster. Mind you, if I thought for a second that he was complicit in the attack on Washington, it wouldn't have been a gas dart. Might not even have been a bullet. The Killer in my head had very specific ways of dealing with his enemies.

He went instantly limp and slid out of the chair onto the floor. The chemical cocktail in the darts works that fast. When he woke up he wouldn't remember much, and would probably pee in his pants, but he'd be alive. The horsey would break down in his bloodstream, too, so there would be nothing for anyone to find except a poor schlep who got blindsided and robbed. I'd even given him a very precise and careful rap on the back of his head so he'd have physical proof to sell the whole robbery thing.

Oh, and for the record, I had no intention of laying a finger on anyone in his family. Sure, I'd mind-fuck him all day, but I'm not evil.

I tapped my earbud and Bug was right there. "You get all that?"

"Got it, Cowboy," Bug said.

"So, Gadyuka is either the Big Bad, or she's the shop foreman for the Big Bad. In either case, Valen, dangerous as he is, works for them. What's that tell us?"

"Nikki's still tearing Valen's life apart for more clues. And she has three people on Gadyuka. There are so many theories about her that it's hard to tell if any of them are accurate or if all of them are crap. But, you know Nikki . . . if there's something to find, she'll find it."

"What do we know about Pushkin Dynamics?" I asked. "We have anything on them?"

"Looking at it now," said Bug. "At first glance it looks pretty normal. Ships to dozens of international markets. Legit on the surface, but I'll drill down to see what's really going on. Hey . . . it's already getting interesting. They have some impressive firewalls, though. Way, way, *way* above the industrial level for companies like that. This is Russian military stuff."

"Gosh, that's a surprise."

"Might take a minute to punch through it but, hey, this is me. I'll upload everything to your tactical computer."

"Make it fast."

"I was going to go out for a sandwich and coffee first," he said.

"Don't make me hurt you, nerd boy."

"Don't make me create a Tinder profile for you that'll put you on watch lists," he countered.

I laughed. "Touché."

While I waited, I worked the room. I plugged a MindReader uplink into Rolgavitch's computer and the little lights began flashing as the Q1 drive began gobbling up every scrap of data. Once finished, it would exit and rewrite the security software on the target computer to erase all traces of having been hacked. It would, however, leave behind some truly nasty Trojan horses that would, in a very real sense, turn my friend Yuri's computer into MindReader's yard bitch. Doing this stuff is so much fun it gave me a tingle in my happy place.

Next, I used a scanner to locate Rolgavitch's hidden office safe behind a section of false paneling. The safe was protected by eight levels of ultrasophisticated security software. A top-grade professional thief might walk away from that kind of protection; however, I came armed with lots of nifty toys. These included a Tick, which is a proprietary intrusion device designed by Doc Holliday. The Tick was something she'd put together in an afternoon while—she insists—binge-watching the first two seasons of *Stranger Things*. It combines the comprehensive ass-kickery of MindReader's new quantum computer system and decryption software with some of her own devious tweaks. I swear I could hear the little Tick snicker as it bypassed all the security levels in a microsecond. High-tech, baby, it's the only way to fly.

Did I hum the *Mission: Impossible* theme while I worked? Why yes. Yes, I did.

I opened the safe and removed over four million rubles—roughly eight hundred grand—as well as some flash drives, another pistol, and a Patek Philippe Henry Graves wristwatch that was probably worth as much or more than the cash. The money and watch went into a bag I'd brought along for that purpose. Then I plugged the flash drives into a handheld uplink, stole the data, and tossed them onto the floor like they were of no value to a common burglar.

I was about to turn away when I glanced at the screen on the Tick and saw that it was displaying readings for a second security system. I bent close to the safe and peered inside and the Tick chittered and beeped and then the back wall of the safe *clicked* and opened inward as hidden locks were disengaged. Immediately a green glow leaked out around the edges of the small door. From across the room, Ghost gave a nervous *whuff.*

Just to be safe, I ran a radiation scanner over it, but the rad scanner blipped. Seriously. It made a tiny *blip* sound and the needle twitched and then it settled back.

"Bug . . . ?" I said quietly. "Assure me this isn't something weird and that my nuts are not going to shrivel up and fall off."

"Everything's in the green, Cowboy."

"I can *see* that it's green," I said, eyeing the glow with unease. "Literally green."

"No, I mean it's all good," Bug insisted. "Telemetry says there's no source of dangerous radiation in there."

"You better be right. If I die, I'm going to haunt your ass and yell *Boo* every time you take a shit."

"Funny," he said, not meaning it.

I put that scanner away and tried my BAMS unit—more formally a bio-aerosol mass spectrometer—but found no traces of viruses, bacteria, spores, or fungi.

I took a breath and opened the little door the rest of the way, not sure what I thought I'd find. A big stack of emeralds, maybe, or a vial of the Incredible Hulk's urine. It was neither. Instead I found something that looked like a novelty water pistol carved out of a chunk of green crystal. When I picked it up I was surprised how little it weighed. More like plastic than stone, but it was very dense to the touch and definitely crystal of some kind. The handle was curved and half again as wide as my palm, like something made for a bigger hand. And there was a ridged button instead of a trigger. The barrel, though, was broken off and ended in a jagged stump, and some chips were missing from various places as if it had been roughly handled. There were smaller chips and granules of the same material in the safe, but they looked too small to matter, so I left them there.

The gun was translucent, and I could see the internal workings, but it wasn't a water reservoir and pump, nor was there the standard machinery of either a pistol or a dart gun. I bent close to examine it and saw what looked like circuitry. The whole thing was immaculate and looked to have been highly polished, and yet I had a weird feeling that I was holding something very old. There was nothing at all to hang that feeling on, though. It was rock. All rocks are old. Even so, the feeling persisted.

"Okay," I said, addressing Bug and anyone else in the TOC—the tactical operations center back at the Hangar in Brooklyn. "I'm open to suggestions as to what I'm holding."

"No idea. Looks like a ray gun from a video game. Hold on, here's Doc."

"Cowboy," said Doc Holliday, "what can you tell me about that weapon?"

"I was hoping you'd tell me something." I described the weight of it and turned it at different angles so she could see every part of it. I knew cameras were recording it all. "It's broken in a couple of places. This make any sense to you?"

"Maybe," she said slowly. "I need to check some things. In the meantime, don't pull the trigger."

"There is not one chance in holy hell that I would do that," I said.

"Good." And she was gone. I slipped it carefully into my pocket.

"It's okay, fuzzball," I told Ghost, and now that the gun was out of sight he relaxed by maybe one tenth of a percent. Even so, he kept cutting looks at the pocket. Very reassuring.

The clock in my head was ticking, so I decided to get the hell out of Dodge. I stood up and stretched, feeling the bruised muscles in my back protest. I'd popped as many painkillers as I could on the way to Russia, and they were wearing off. Fun.

I wanted to leave the right impression in the office for whomever found my snoring buddy. I went through his office and smashed a bunch of stuff, slashed chairs, flipped over the area rug, and dumped desk drawers onto the floor to set the stage. Then I tore a bunch of paintings from the walls to sell the idea that I'd had to search for the safe. I used a felt-tip marker to write crude graffiti on the walls in Russian slang. I even encouraged Ghost to pee on the rug because thieves sometimes do that, and Ghost was happy to oblige. Then, as promised, I bound Rolgavitch's wrists and ankles, and wrapped his tie around his eyes. I left behind no traces of anything that didn't look like the fiction I knew my pal Yuri would earnestly want to sell, if he even remembered the conversation, which was unlikely. Horsey tramples all over short-term memory.

Then Ghost and I got the fuck out of there. A black sedan was waiting for us two blocks away.

CHAPTER NINETY-SIX

THE HANGAR
FLOYD BENNETT FIELD
BROOKLYN, NEW YORK

Doc Holliday and Junie Flynn sat on chairs in the Playroom—the massive, sprawling complex of labs that formed the inner sanctum of the DMS Integrated Sciences Division. Scientists and technicians moved like silent robots around them, each of them pretending not to listen to the conversation the two women were having.

"I'm not going to sugarcoat this, sweetie," said Doc, a smile lighting up her face, "but there's a pretty darn good chance that you're completely out of your mind. You know that, right?"

Junie's smile was all freckles and light. "Sure, but that doesn't mean I'm wrong."

Doc looked down at the thick file on her lap. It was a sub-report of the Extinction Machine case, and it was currently open to Junie's account of her own complex heredity.

"Alien DNA? Bug told me that, but I thought I was being pranked."

"Really?"

Doc looked away and studied the middle of the air for a long moment. Her shoulders rose and fell. "No," she said.

"No," agreed Junie.

"But I guess I don't want to believe it, and that's a hell of a thing for me to admit out loud to anyone. I'm a scientist. I'm a damn good top-five-in-the-blessed-world scientist, and I don't want to believe it."

"Yeah? Try looking at it from inside my head. I grew up with this."

"So, we're talking what, here?" asked Doc, still smiling. "Little green men?"

"I have no idea if they're little," said Junie, "but I doubt it. The pilot seats on the original T-craft were built for very tall beings."

"Bipeds?"

"Yes. And, I think, reptilian."

"As in *the* Reptilians? 'Cause I've read a lot of wacko conspiracy theory stuff about aliens called that. Big, nasty green guys."

Junie shrugged. "Reptilians, Draconians, reptoids . . . there are a lot of names. Some of them going back to antiquity. The idea of reptile people interacting with humans is not exactly new. Most people think the idea started with a short story, 'The Shadow Kingdom,' written by Robert E. Howard, the author of *Conan the Barbarian* and *King Kull*."

"Right," agreed Doc. "In pulp fiction."

"There's a theory—one I agree with—that the pulp fiction

movement, with all of its fantastic imagery, otherworldly and metaphysical story elements, were the result of the firing of an early prototype God Machine."

"Right," said Doc cautiously. She set down the report, picked up a cup of tea, and tried to take a sip, but it was empty. "You also said that the surrealist movement was caused by the same thing. And the same for parts of the hippie acid rock stuff of the sixties."

"I can give you a lot of evidence to support that supposition," said Junie with a thin smile. "And I can give you the pharmacology, the psychology, the social culturalism, and a lot more to support it." She paused. "Besides, we know that the T-craft exist. We know that whoever designed the original machines threatened us to acquire and turn over the Black Book. This isn't science fiction, Doc. It's science fact."

Doc Holliday stared into the empty cup. She was no longer smiling. "I know," she said. "It's just that I don't *want* to believe it."

Junie put her hand on Doc's knee. "I know. Believe me . . . I know."

CHAPTER NINETY-SEVEN

ROLGAVITCH TECHNOLOGIES
KOTELNICHESKAYA EMBANKMENT
MOSCOW, RUSSIA

I climbed into the passenger seat of the sedan. Bunny was behind the wheel, huddled in a fur-trimmed anorak and shivering his Southern California cojones off.

"How'd it go, boss?" he asked as I fished in the glove box for my bottle of painkillers.

"It went well," I said, removing a packet of pain pills from an inner pocket and dry-swallowing two of them. "We have a new target."

"Something good?"

"To be determined. But it's a better lead than any we've had." I gave him the address of Pushkin Dynamics and forwarded the same info to Top, who was waiting with Echo Team somewhere discreet. Bunny put the car in gear. While we drove, I filled him in on what happened in Rolgavitch's office. He seemed amused by it until I got to the part about the green gun. When we stopped at a traffic light I showed it to him. Bunny started to touch it but withdrew his hand.

"What's wrong?" I asked.

He shook his head and either didn't want to answer, or couldn't. The green glow made him look ill. I put the crystal gun back into my pocket and we drove in silence. I caught him glancing at me in the rearview mirror, looking troubled and uncertain.

CHAPTER NINETY-EIGHT

PUSHKIN DYNAMICS
VOSTOCHNY DISTRICT
RUSSIA

"Here we are," said Bunny. He pulled off the street into the parking lot of a big factory that was shrouded in shadows.

Pushkin Dynamics looked exactly like the fiction they were trying to sell. A big, sprawling, old, two-story weather-stained brick factory. It should have had "nondescript" painted over the door. There were a few cars in the lot, clustered together as if for warmth.

I tapped my earbud. "Bug, we're at the second location. Where are we with the security cameras?"

"Their external camera system is connected via Wi-Fi to the security office," said Bug, "and there's a hardline backup. So, naturally I hijacked it. Recorded a ten-minute loop, and it's on continuous playback. You're good."

"Owe you a case of Red Bull."

"Yeah, you do."

Another vehicle that was parked in deep shadows flashed its lights and Bunny parked beside it. I got out and shook Top's hand, nodded to the others.

"Gear up fast," I said. "Full kits. Lethal and nonlethal guns, the Toybox, all of it. Mission briefing starts now."

I was the only one in civvies, and I stripped down to thermal underwear and pulled on DMS versions of ACUs—the all-black army combat uniforms we wore for gigs like this. Nonreflective, without insignias or patches of any kind, and made from a special blend that made virtually no rustling sounds even when running. We all put on utility belts with plenty of gadgets and gewgaws, as well as lots of extra magazines. I still had my gas dart pistol, but now I also wore a shoulder rig with a Croatian HS2000, one of the handguns favored by ISIL. All of the weapons we carried were of the kind favored by those guys. If it came to a gunfight, we wouldn't stop to pick up our brass. Let the Russians get pissed off at ISIL for any damage we did. Oh, what tangled webs we weave when first we practice to deceive.

I watched the team covertly as I shrugged into body armor. I saw Top checking the gear of the only woman on the team, Tracy Cole, a former soldier-turned-cop from South Carolina. Cole had signed on during the Dogs of War gig and had, in the short time she'd run with us, been through the storm lands enough times to have the souvenir key chain. And some scars. She was practical, tough, smart, and reliable. Couldn't ask for a better combination. We'd had one DMS candidate who thought women couldn't handle the rigors of combat as well as men. Notice I said "had." That boy is still working through physical therapy, after which he'll likely go off in search of a clue. Cole's combat call sign was Gorgon, and like her namesake, you wouldn't want to try and stare her down.

Standing by himself was Steve Duffy, call sign Spartan; a sturdy guy with an Irish face and cold eyes. He'd been attached to the Warehouse in Baltimore, and I arranged his transfer to Echo Team last year. Duffy had been personally trained by Sam Imura and earned his hard-won seal of approval as an expert with any long gun. Second best in the DMS, which put him in the top three or four worldwide. Unlike most snipers I've known, Duffy was not a laconic loner with questionable social skills. He was the hammer of God with a rifle, but off the clock he was hilarious and affable and . . . well, normal. Not sure why I found that mildly disturbing.

To his right were the two newest DMS members, Brendan Tate and Pete Smith. Tate's combat call sign was Coffey, because he looked like the huge black guy from that old Stephen King movie, *The Green Mile*. He wasn't as tall as that actor had been, or even as tall as Bunny, for that matter, but Tate had the kind of stocky build that gave his enemies serious pause. Duffy once remarked that Tate looked "like he could bench-press North Dakota while getting a blow job." Now . . . why or how oral sex factored into, or indeed validated, that observation is one of those things about military humor that makes sense without making sense. You have to understand how soldiers think for it to be funny. We all thought it was hilarious. Tate was our team's tech geek, and he had a lot of Doc Holliday's nasty toys with him.

Pete Smith, call sign Darth Sidious, was Tate's former patrol partner from their cop days in Durham, North Carolina. He didn't look like a soldier at all, or even a cop. Looked more like a high school gym teacher or Little League coach. He was easygoing, eager to please, and served as our utility infielder. Pete was the kind of cat who could play any position and never got ruffled.

For Smith and Tate, this was their first field op. It was Duffy's first time on a gig outside of the continental U.S. Cole had been on a short thing in Mexico, but that was it. So, the nervous Nellie part of me wasn't all that happy about taking a mostly green team into a mission as covert and critical as this.

On the other hand, Top had trained Cole, Tate, and Smith, and that meant I had no doubts at all about how they would handle themselves. Top is a nice guy, except when he's running team exercises or under live fire. Actually, I think he's at his meanest and most inflexible when he's teaching. A lot of people get booted by him, and even more quit to do something easier. Like giving rectal thermometers to cranky honey badgers. The candidates who make it all the way through and earn Top's grudging seal of approval are the kind you can genuinely trust to have your back no matter how much shit is raining down.

That said, the stakes were high.

We worked in silence and got as ready as it is possible to get for facing the unknown. Ghost sat watching me, and it was odd because he sat a little farther away than he normally would. And he watched me with a steadiness that was borderline creepy. Like he expected *me* to do something wrong. I smiled at him, but his expression and body language did not change a bit.

I told them everything I'd learned from Yuri Rolgavitch and made sure they were all keyed into the mission intel channel. We all wore Google Scout glasses, which were something developed exclusively for the DMS by one of Church's friends in the industry. They were several steps above standard night-vision. We could switch to thermal scans and cycle through ultraviolet and infrared. And we could get hard data projected onto one lens. We all still wore small tactical computers strapped to our forearms. Especially for a job like this where we are making it up as we go, there's never "too much" when it comes to access to fresh intel. I was about to begin mapping out our approach when Bug contacted us.

"Cowboy," he said quickly, sounding stressed, "we picked up a police call for Rolgavitch Technologies."

"Yuri woke up pretty quick," I said.

"No," said Bug. "Yuri Rolgavitch is dead."

"Bullshit. I darted him with horsey, and we checked ahead of time to make sure he wasn't allergic to any of the components. No way that killed—"

"Cowboy," Bug cut in, "Rolgavitch called the police to say he'd been robbed, but when they arrived he *attacked* them with a golf club. Beat one cop's head in. Killed him . . . and then another officer shot him."

"What?" I demanded.

"Yeah, death by cop. He also started a fire in his office and half the building is burning."

CHAPTER NINETY-NINE

THE HANGAR
FLOYD BENNETT FIELD
BROOKLYN, NEW YORK

"So what do these Reptilians want?" asked Doc.

Junie was busy refilling their teacups and took a moment with that. She brought the cups back and sat again. "Here's the central problem with the UFO conspiracy world. A lot of people—the majority of all people on Earth, by the way—believe that we have been visited by alien races. Now, most reasonable people, when they see a strange light in the sky, may think 'Okay, that's a UFO,' but their default opinion is that it is precisely that. An unidentified flying object. A smaller percentage will assume that any UFO is automatically of alien origin. An even smaller group will make snap judgments—based on whatever underpins their own belief systems—that they may be from this world or that. Often that depends on the shape or movements of the observed craft. And then we get down to those people who see a UFO, decide it is alien, and then purport to know the planet of origin, the nature of the species, and the details of their agenda."

"The aluminum-foil-hat crowd," suggested Doc, but Junie shook her head.

"You'll be on safer ground," she said, "if you don't leap to dismissive judgments. Some of them may be right. We don't know for sure that they're wrong. After all, some of them were right about aliens when the scientific world tended to dismiss it out of hand. I am proof that some of those people were right, can we agree on that?"

"Very reluctantly," sighed Doc.

"Okay, but here's the thing—I have proof. My DNA has been sequenced, as has that of Prospero Bell and Erasmus Tull, the only two people we have definitively established to have come from the same breeding program as me. Tull worked as a Closer for M3 and Prospero built God Machines."

Doc sipped the hot tea and winced, but it was likely not because of any burn.

"So, given that I am actually part alien, and was raised by people who were building craft based on recovered alien technology, yet none of them—not one—knew who actually built the machines, where they came from, or why they came at all. We are completely in the dark. In fact, I've never seen a photograph of any of the original crew of the crashed vehicles. If Howard Shelton or the other governors of M3 ever did, it was not recorded in the Majestic Black Book."

"So . . . they could have been reptiles?"

"Yes," said Junie. "And the Closers who Joe and his guys dealt with on the road in Maryland bled green."

Doc drank her tea and stared at Junie for a long, long time.

"Okay," she said weakly, "what else can you tell me?"

Junie thought about it. "Well . . . I read the field report Top filed. He said there was a distinct green color in the explosion on the road. And we know from Washington that the God Machines exploded with a green fireball."

"Yes. So?"

Junie blew across her cup and peered at Doc. "What do you know about Lemurian crystal?"

CHAPTER ONE HUNDRED

PUSHKIN DYNAMICS
VOSTOCHNY DISTRICT
RUSSIA

Bug shifted to the mission at hand.

"Well," he said, "it looks pretty ordinary from the outside, but it's not. First off, they have too large a facility for the amount of product they sell, at least according to their balance sheets. Maybe forty percent of the factory and staff would be needed for what they pay taxes on. I can back that up with utility usage, too. They're using way too much electricity and water, so figure they have at least double the staff running twice as many machines, and they have too many trucks going in and out. And there is a big shipping bay on one side, but in back there's a garage for buses. Why have buses unless they're bringing in more staff than they have on the books?"

"Understood. So, what else are they making?"

"We still don't know that," admitted Bug. "Companies in the competitive electronics market are usually filing patents every five minutes. Pushkin was, too, but there's been a slowdown on that recently, which is weird, because everyone else in their field is speeding up that process. Tech changes so fast that you have to innovate and rush new models or products into production in order to survive. Pushkin is doing well financially, but I don't like the fact that they're not filing enough patents. And they're sure as heck being cagey with internal discussions on new R and D. They're being really, really careful, Cowboy, because there's nothing about what they are really doing stored on their company hard drives. Probably using intranet computers with no exterior hardlines. So, what we need are samples, photos, scans, and anything on their computers."

"Hooah," I said, and everyone nodded.

"Oh, and since we don't know what's in there, Doc wants you to use rad scan and BAMS."

"Copy that," I said. "Do we have an eye in the sky yet?"

"We haven't had enough time to retask a satellite," said Bug, "so you have to use your drones. I arranged for a couple of the big eagle drones to do a flyover, and they picked up ten thermals. Pushkin's pay records account for that many nighttime security guards, so that's kosher at least."

"Ten guards are a lot for overnight security," said Tate. "Place this size would only need two, maybe three."

"Right," agreed Bug, "so why they need ten guys is one more

oddball thing. The total effect is giving me the wiggins. Anyway, I sent a basic floor plan of the building and security data to your team. I suggest you put some pigeons on the roof to watch the parking lot. I hacked local law enforcement and sent you patrol patterns. They never seem to enter the parking lot of the place, though, so they must have been told not to. That says something."

"Okay, Bug. Thanks. Keep digging."

The news about Rolgavitch twisted inside my head, and I could feel the depression gnawing at the edges of my mind. Maybe it was Auntie and D.J. and Sam. Maybe it was all the dead Americans in D.C. Maybe it was the fact that the DMS and I had been outed on the news. I don't know, but I felt like I needed a week of extra-long sessions on Rudy's couch. Or maybe to go skydiving without a chute.

I stopped when that thought flitted past. Ghost growled very softly, but no one else except me heard it.

"It's okay, boy," I said to him, and offered my hand for him to sniff. He did, but that still didn't change the way he looked at me. Top gave me a curious look, too, as if he read my mood. Wouldn't surprise me if he could. He was that sharp.

"Huddle up," I said, and as they gathered around I opened my laptop and called up a schematic of the building. "Two-story building with basement. No windows, no skylight. What we know about the insides are only what was on the original construction blueprints and reports from city inspectors."

"Can we count on any of that being accurate?" asked Cole.

"Doubtful. We'll bring a bunch of houseflies and let them map the place once we're inside."

Houseflies were small sensor drones closer in size to bumblebees. They could travel solo or in swarms, transmitting telemetry to the computers we all wore on our wrists. Those, in turn, fed the data to the TOC.

"Bottom line is that we're not sure of anything," I said. "We're here to gather intel, get all possible information, and get out without making a fuss. Top, you and Cole go in through the loading bay. Tate and Bunny, go in through the east-side door, which looks like offices. Ghost and I will take the front and see if we can find the computer room. Smith, you walk the perimeter. Stay out of sight and be ready to come in if any team needs extra muscle. Duffy, find an elevated shooting position that covers the parking lot and front door. Combat call signs from here out. This is a soft infil, so we go in quiet as church mice. Don't break anything unless you have to."

"Rules of engagement if things go south?" asked Top; mostly asking because he wanted the team to hear it and have those rules reinforced. He never stopped teaching.

"Weapons slung except for dart guns. Even so, we don't fire first," I said. "Those guards may be innocent working stiffs and, if so, they don't need to get hurt. But if you are fired upon and cannot retreat without engaging, then do what you need to do in order to save your lives and the lives of the rest of the team. We all go in and we all come out."

"Hooah," they said softly.

I looked at their faces. Seeing strength, resolve, and confidence, but also some fear and uncertainty. It is a mistake to forget that soldiers, even top-flight special operators, are human. Just as it's a mistake for them to forget it, too.

"Now hear this," I said, "Coffey and Darth Sidious, this is your first field op, but it's not the first time you've been in the shit. You were cops and your records speak to your courage and professionalism under fire. You're here because you've both demonstrated superior skills. You got gold stars from Top Sims, and believe me when I tell you that he is a hard sell. Remember your training, trust your instincts, trust to knowledge rather than assumptions, and be the elite operators I know you are."

Tate and Smith said, "Hooah." There was no high-fiving or trash talk. This was a moment for sober understanding, clearheadedness, and resolve

"Then let's roll," I said.

And so we rolled.

CHAPTER ONE HUNDRED ONE

THE HANGAR
FLOYD BENNETT FIELD
BROOKLYN, NEW YORK

"Lemurian crystal?" echoed Doc. "Never heard of it. But don't tell me you want me to believe in the lost continent of Lemuria. What's next? Atlantis?"

"No," said Junie. "Look, Atlantis was almost certainly the Minoan culture, and what's left of it is probably Santorini and some smaller islands. That's not where I'm going with this. In the areas where Atlantis and Lemuria were thought—by some—to have existed, there have been artifacts found made from a very specific kind of green quartz crystal."

"From Lemuria?"

"No. Just listen, okay?" Junie explained about the two types of quartz labeled as Lemurian crystal, and how the much rarer green variety was tied to the ancient Roman festival of Lumeralia. "The Romans performed rites on the fetish items they carved, and these rites were intended to activate some kind of power. In the texts they called it summoning or invoking, and they believed the activation called a demon or god to inhabit the stones. Now, I don't believe that's what happened, but there may be a hint in there, an echo of what really happened. The story has it that these Lemurian crystals were part of an altar, and if the pieces were assembled the correct way it opened a doorway to the realm of gods. Opened the wrong way, it opened to a world of demons and evil."

Doc Holliday tried to keep a disbelieving smile on her face, but as Junie spoke, it cracked and fell away. "Lordy, I see where you're going with this," conceded Doc. "Kind of like what Prospero Bell's dadgum God Machine was supposed to do."

"Right. From what I've been able to piece together, the ancients knew how to assemble a completely crystalline version of the God Machine. Maybe it's an older technology from before the earliest machine ages, or maybe it's simply a similar design with a different purpose. We don't know."

"The machine Joe saw was metal."

"Right, but with green crystals inlaid. Possibly a third design, possibly a Russian redesign . . . I don't know. What I do know is that in all of the old legends and histories, those crystals are not natural to our world, but were part of some kind of technology brought here by—"

"Let me guess . . . little green men."

"*Big* green men. Yes. The Reptilians," said Junie.

Doc suddenly stiffened, squeezed her eyes shut, and slapped her own forehead. "Junie, you may be as crazy as a box of frogs, but here I am being one fry short of a Happy Meal. Why didn't I see it when you said it?"

"What?"

"You done said it yourself, about how the Romans who were exposed to the activated green crystals ran wild? Ran wild . . . *how*?"

Junie's eyes were filled with strange lights. "If the rituals of proper handling were not followed to the letter, some people would run mad and kill their own families, slaughter whole villages, and often kill themselves."

"Riiiiight. Now . . . what does *that* sound like?"

CHAPTER ONE HUNDRED TWO

PUSHKIN DYNAMICS
VOSTOCHNY DISTRICT
RUSSIA

Once Duffy was in place, and Smith was spooking his way around the perimeter, the rest of Echo Team moved out, running low and fast. The fact that all the video cameras were hacked was not an invitation to be clumsy or incautious.

The first two teams split off and vanished. I knelt in place and covered them until everyone was in position, then Ghost and I ran for the front door. The lock was expensive and trustworthy by ordinary standards, with a keypad and a card-swipe. I smiled, feeling almost nostalgic for quaint stuff like that. It's adorable. I tapped my earbud.

"Bug—"

"On it." Without me having to touch anything, the little red lights on the keypad flicked to green and I heard the door click open.

"Thank you, Thing," I said in my best Gomez Addams voice. Bug laughed, because Gomez sounds a lot like Rudy Sanchez.

There was a short entrance hall inside, with an umbrella stand, time clock, various official certificates on the wall, and doors leading to an empty conference room, a broom closet, a secretary's office, and a set of stairs. I swept the area for motion sensors, found none, and shook a bunch of housefly drones out and let them buzz their merry way throughout the building. A built-in reconnaissance program coordinated the swarm's dispersal pattern with the floor plan of the building. Got to love twenty-first-century mad science.

The new DMS policy was that if anyone else had the same toys, Mr. Church made sure to give us *next* year's stuff. He had a lot of "friends in the industry" dedicated to making sure we would never be outfoxed again. At least not by technology. And Doc Holliday was right there with him, upping the game in a lot of truly disturbing ways. Disturbing for people we don't like, I mean. Personally, I found it all on the comforting side of creepy.

Ghost and I took the stairs, moving without sound in the empty building. The lack of noise bothered me on a weird level and I had to fight to keep myself focused. Made me wonder if I wasn't beginning to manifest a little PTSD. If so, the timing really blew.

"Bug to Cowboy," came the quiet voice in my ear. "I'm still picking up the energetic signature from that green crystal gun. Have you found more of it or is that thing still with you?"

The hall was empty, so I risked a response. "With me."

"It's messing with your suit's telemetry."

The new combat rig for Echo Team includes a fully integrated tactical telemetric netting sewn into our clothes. What that means in human language is that there are hundreds of tiny sensors in every part of our clothing and equipment. It hot-links to all of the other sensors and to our forearm computers so that we are both gathering information through those sensors and being fed real-time data. And we each wore special contact lenses that gave us a virtual reality display of information that ranged from facial recognition to a mission clock to technical readouts. It's all very science fictiony and I felt a bit like a horse's ass with it running. The trick is to not let yourself be distracted by the available data.

"Messing with the telemetry how?" I asked.

"Weakening the signal on your vitals. Suggest using a Faraday bag."

"Why? It's broken and it doesn't have any electronics that I can see."

"The interference started when you took it from the safe, and it's getting stronger, so humor me, okay?"

"Yes, mother," I said with bad grace. "Wait one."

Faraday bags were an invention by the late Dr. William Hu, former director of the DMS Integrated Sciences Division and Doc Holliday's predecessor. The one into which I placed the green crystal gun was a heavy plastic envelope veined with a wire mesh that nullified all electronic signals. I mostly used them to disguise my own electronic gizmos when traveling commercial, because they won't register at all, even in a metal detector; but the bag also kept high-tech surveillance devices from transmitting signals. As I sealed the bag I felt a shiver whip through me. It was so fast and intense that I nearly cried out. Ghost came to point and stared fixedly at me, then he came closer and pushed his head against my hand. It surprised me, but I ran my fingers through his white fur.

"Okay," said Bug almost at once, "the signal's clearing up."

"Copy that." Beneath my balaclava and helmet I was sweating like a pig. "I'm going to want to have Huckleberry explain how a piece of quartz with no wires in it can do this to our gear. She said her new stuff was top of the line, and this is a perfect 'put up or shut up' opportunity."

"Huckleberry" was Doc Holliday's call sign.

"Um, you know she's actually in the TOC, Cowboy," said Bug nervously. "Standing right next to me. She can actually hear you."

"Good," I growled, and I thought I heard a female voice in the background say something very specific about me getting frisky with livestock.

"You're good to go. Everything's in the green," Bug said, then he quickly added, "Not that crystal green, I mean, I—"

"Yeah, yeah, got it," I said.

I clicked my tongue for Ghost and we began moving along the empty second-floor hallway. We paused near the top of the steps and I touched a dial to send some houseflies up there and then along the hall. The lights were low and the tiny drones would be virtually invisible. They whipped down the hall to a T-junction and cut left and right. The left side was empty, but on the right I saw a guy dressed in a drab gray security company uniform standing guard outside of a locked room. The logo stitched onto his jacket read: *Sluzhby Zashchity,* which translates as "Protection Services." Appropriately nondescript. Ghost ran to the end of our hall and stopped out of sight of the guard, crouching, waiting for me to give the word. I ran to catch up.

Ghost looked at me as if to say, *I'm good to kill this guy, boss.*

I winked at him. Not really sure if dogs get the whole winking thing, but Ghost shifted and tensed for a rush. I gave him a hand sign to signal him to be ready, but not attack. He gave me a mildly disapproving look. I holstered my pistol, drew the Snellig dart gun, leaned around the corner, and shot the faux guard in the thigh.

Horsey works on everyone. Even brutes as big as this guy. I ran and caught the guard before he hit the floor, then stretched him out. A quick pat-down produced nothing of use. A packet of tissues, a roll of mints, and that was it. No ID of any kind and no cell phone. However, he wore what looked like a high school ring—you know, the kind with the big, fake jewel. Except that there was a metal cap over it. Something about the ring bothered me, so I jiggered around and finally forced a hidden release and the cap flipped open to reveal a stone that shone with a very familiar green radiance.

"Cowboy," said Bug, "I'm beginning to get more of that interference."

I angled my bodycam to show the ring. "Check it out."

"If you take it," said Bug, "Huckleberry wants you to put it in the Faraday bag." I did that, and was told that the interference was now gone.

"Curiouser and curiouser," I murmured, then dragged the guard around the corner and into a women's bathroom. That hurt my back, but I ate the pain because now was not a time to go all whiny.

I went to the security door and bypassed the locks. Inside, there were rows of computer workstations, each with a desk-model computer. Everything looked new, and all of the hardware I saw was state of the art.

"Bug . . . ?" I asked quietly.

"Seeing it, Cowboy," he said. "This is all high-end stuff. Mostly Russian manufacture, but there are some Chinese and Japanese computers, too. Hey, the one on the end of the left-hand row. See it? The one with three monitors? That's probably a supervisor's desk. Find a USB port and plug me in."

I hurried over and did as he suggested, socketing an uplink device into the side of the central monitor. "Done."

"Okay," said Bug after a moment, "couple things. First, there's a command log-in program installed on that computer. Looks like everyone has to log in through the supervisor and get the day code."

"Shit. Can you bypass it?"

Bug's snort of derision was eloquent.

"Sorry," I said.

"They are definitely using intranet instead of Internet. Nothing goes outside of this room. Computer access here isn't even connected to the rest of the building. I see a link to a multi-disc DVD burner, so they must use that when they need to take bulk data to another site. Otherwise, just the twenty-three computers in that room. I'm not detecting any landline or Wi-Fi at all."

"Got you covered," I said, and produced a compact but very powerful portable router and attached it to the uplink. Screens all through the room suddenly winked on.

"Perfect," said Bug. "Let me see what I can—" He stopped. "Oh, shit."

"What?" I demanded.

"I just pulled up a building floor plan from their internal computers, and it doesn't match at all with the one I already gave you. They totally redesigned the place, and they didn't build out or up, they went down. I'm seeing three levels of subbasement. Looks like they installed some of the most sophisticated security equipment I've ever seen. The second subbasement ceiling is titanium-sheathed lead with a ceramic core. Nothing on Earth can scan through that. There could be a hundred people down there for all we know. Makes me think more about those buses, you know? There are also delivery receipts for tons of materials and sixteen big-ass generators."

"What the hell are they building down there?" I asked.

"I don't know," said Bug, "but Doc wants you to go down there and find out."

CHAPTER ONE HUNDRED THREE

PUSHKIN DYNAMICS
VOSTOCHNY DISTRICT
RUSSIA

Tracy Cole loved watching Top Sims move. Not for any sexual or romantic reasons—he was too old for her and she was too professional—but because he moved like a cat. Quick, quiet, efficient; able to go from stillness into rapid motion and then freeze on a dime and vanish into the background.

Tracy had read about soldiers who were like that, but she'd never met one. Not really. Not even during her time in Afghanistan, Iraq, and Syria with a U.S. Army detail attached working as United Nations peacekeepers. She'd met SEALs who moved with less grace, and even Delta shooters who were younger and stronger but who didn't have the same gift. It reinforced why Top was Captain Ledger's right hand; and why he was the one who trained the top fighters in the DMS.

She wondered if there was anyone other than the captain who could take Top in a fight. Sure, Duffy was a better shot and Bunny was stronger than the Hulk, but . . .

Top reached the door and dropped down onto one knee, his weapon and eyes moving to cover the area around him. Then he gave her a single wave and covered her as she broke from cover and dashed across the parking lot, trying to mimic the sleek grace of the older man. Cole knew she was good, but she never accepted good as enough. Not when she was in the army, not as a cop in South Carolina, and sure as hell not now that she was running with the big dogs.

She reached the wall and crouched down on the opposite side of the loading bay doors. There were four big roll-down doors and one smaller service entrance. Top gave her the nod and she slung her rifle and dug out the high-tech equipment that allowed her to bypass the locks. A device the size and shape of a nickel was pressed to the underside of the keycard reader and gave her a soft go-ahead ping in her earbud. Cole swiped a blank card through the slot once, waited for two seconds, and then again. The second time the red light on the security card reader flicked from red to green. It took MindReader only two seconds to hack the system, own it, and add the right code to the blank card. The same codes would be sent to identical cards carried by everyone. Each time they encountered a similar lock, two swipes would share the right codes with everyone. Smooth. Almost scary, but comforting, too.

"Go," murmured Top, and Cole pulled the door open. He rose and moved past her as she covered, and then he faded to one side and covered for her as she followed.

The loading bay was huge, with mountains of crates stacked

nearly to the ceiling. Hundreds, perhaps thousands of them, each coded with different symbols. They moved together to clear the room first, making sure there were no guards. When it was clear they were alone, they went along the fronts of several rows, making sure their bodycams recorded the data stenciled on each. Bug was Captain Ledger's live intel guy, so they had Zero, one of the other field support specialists.

"Are those bar codes?" asked Zero. "Scan one for me."

Each crate had a lot of numerical codes written either in black, red, or green ink, but every crate had a similar black bar code on the bottom front. Cole slipped a hand scanner over her glove. It was about as thick as a pencil though half as long, and fitted over the glove with an elastic band. Ultra-high-res lasers scanned the data and her combat suit's telemetry uploaded it to the drones, which in turn relayed it to a MindReader burst-transfer substation in the car they'd come in. All of that happened in a microsecond as Cole waved her hand over a dozen different crates, making sure to get some of each of the three color codes.

"These are destination codes," said Zero.

"Where are they going?" asked Cole, and Top nodded his approval.

"A lot of places. Scan more of them."

As Cole did that, Zero began reading off the destinations. The crates marked in red seemed to be going to cities all over the world, without any immediate pattern.

"Got to be something in common," said Top.

"I'll find it," promised Zero. Prior to becoming a field support specialist, he'd worked for two years with Nikki's pattern recognition group.

"What about the others?"

"All the green boxes so far seem to be addressed to Ukraine—that's weird. Since when are they engaging in friendly commerce? And Lithuania, Bulgaria, Croatia . . ."

"All Europe?" asked Cole.

Zero took a moment on that. "No. Those last two you did, do more in that stack. Yeah . . . looks like they're all for China. No,

I'm wrong. There's a couple for . . . hey, that's really weird. North Korea?"

Another voice came on the line. The stern voice of Doc Holliday. "When y'all are done pulling your puds, maybe you could open some of those darn crates."

Top and Cole removed small pry bars from their packs and jimmied open a lid, then sifted through foam popcorn. Top lifted out two identical parcels, set one down, and removed plastic wrapping from the other.

"Some kind of machine part," he said, turning it over in his hands. The object was lightweight, silver in color, and wrapped with coils of copper wire. "Think it's aluminum or magnesium. Weighs hardly anything."

Cole went fishing through the crate. "All the same thing. Identical. But what is it?"

"Don't know," said Zero. "We need to find a shipping manifest."

"Open some of the other boxes," directed Doc.

They did, moving quickly from one stack to another. It soon became apparent that there were forty different pieces in the various crates on each stack. The same forty pieces in each stack.

"Okay," said Cole, "but what do these things assemble into?"

Zero said, "I got a bad feeling we already know the answer to that, guys."

CHAPTER ONE HUNDRED FOUR

PUSHKIN DYNAMICS
VOSTOCHNY DISTRICT
RUSSIA

The new schematics Bug pulled from the hard drives gave me a clear route to a concealed set of stairs leading down into the basement. The entrance was behind a large set of double file drawers that slid sideways on concealed tracks. Behind that was a handprint and retina scanner, but Bug owned the system now, so he accessed the records tied to the security office and transferred a high-density overlay to my right contact lens and a pattern to the pads of my gloves. Suddenly I was Sergei Alexandrovich, deputy director of research. The door opened as if happy to see me.

Ghost and I crept inside. I had an Anteater bug detector attached to each sleeve, so as I stepped inside I gave it time to search for secondary security. All clean. Stairs zigzagged down, so down we went. There was an elevator, too, but they come with all sorts of possible complications, and there are plenty of very nasty security systems that can turn an elevator car into a temporary prison or a gas chamber. No thanks.

Down and down we went, passing through more security. Apparently Dr. Alexandrovich had a free pass everywhere. Nice. With each flight downward, though, I could tell that Ghost was becoming more uneasy. His fur rippled with tension and he often paused to bare his teeth at empty corners. I didn't scold him or tell him that there was nothing to be afraid of. He had sharper senses than I did, and I've learned from experience that electronics aren't always superior to a dog's perceptions. When Ghost reacted to something, I respected that, and made sure I always looked, my hand ready on my weapon.

Always.

The schematics indicated that the subbasements had high ceilings, and from the number of flights of stairs that was true enough. It felt like we were descending into the underworld.

Ghost stopped again at the bottom of the second-to-last landing and he stood with tail straight out behind him and head lowered, the way he does when he perceives a human presence. I took a horsefly from my pocket and sent it buzzing. It landed on the wall and crawled the rest of the way as I watched its video feed on my wrist computer. There was a last—and damned impressive—airlock, guarded by two sentries who looked tough, fit, and competent. These men were not dressed in the same security company uniform as the one upstairs; they were actual soldiers. However, they wore no unit insignia or rank, but they were in steel gray and mist white fatigues and gear. They were armed with SR-2 Veresk submachine guns. Very nasty guns that fired proprietary 9×21mm SP-10 rounds designed to penetrate most body armor. Maybe even the spider-silk-and-carbon-fiber stuff I was wearing. I wasn't sure, and didn't want to find out.

My Anteater flashed at me, and when I checked the screen it told me that the bottom six steps had all kinds of motion and pressure sensors. No way I could sneak close enough to fire the Snellig.

It was a crisis moment. If I did nothing and just spooked my way out of there, then the mystery of the earthquake and the suicides might never be solved. If I moved forward there was no way to do it without killing them. The gas dart gun just wasn't reliable enough if I had to move fast. If the arms race shifted to weapons that could drive people crazy and induce earthquakes, how could we compete? We'd either have to throw nukes at Russia to make a statement, or get shaken and stirred into rubble.

On one hand, if I forced my way in and they were making something totally benign and unrelated to what happened in Washington, then that would make me a murderer. On the other hand, if I shot my way in and there was proof that Valen Oruraka's devices were tied to an official Russian agenda, then Washington was an indisputable act of war. And there would *be* a war. Some kind of war. Cold or hot. My pulse was racing and I felt trapped by colliding realities and possibilities. And I couldn't really fall back and ask for advice. I was the director of the Special Projects office. I was the guy who any other DMS field agent would contact to make his call.

I looked down at Ghost and he looked up for the pack leader to actually lead.

The two guards stood between me and some kind of answer. The Modern Man inside of me pleaded for mercy. The Cop told me that we needed those answers, and I could feel that part of me hardening his heart. The Killer's heart was already hardened. Not against feeling, but against failing to act because of those feelings. It reminded me of a Navajo guy I knew in college. We'd go deer hunting and before he even loaded his gun he would pray to the deer, honoring it, thanking it, becoming somehow in alignment with it. There was never disrespect, even when, later, he sighted and pulled the trigger. There was never a loss of his compassion and humanity, even as he dressed his kill. That is the difference between a warrior and a soldier. The warrior never loses sight of his humanity and his place in the completeness of the natural world.

So I said a silent prayer in my own head, then ran down the last steps and killed both of them.

CHAPTER ONE HUNDRED FIVE

PUSHKIN DYNAMICS
VOSTOCHNY DISTRICT
RUSSIA

Bunny and Tate moved quietly through several rooms filled with machinery for manufacturing sound equipment.

They were the two biggest men on the team, but each knew how to work within the skin of silence, leaving no mark on the air to signal their presence. Twice guards strolled by within easy arm's reach of them. Bunny could have reached out of the shadows and taken the men, ended them right there; but this wasn't that kind of day, and he was glad of it. Like all good soldiers he could kill with professional efficiency and natural diligence, but never for fun. He never got a thrill from it, even when taking down the worst of the worst. To give in to that kind of pleasure was a long step down a very bad road.

Tate, he suspected, was much the same. And Bunny was wise enough to know that it was more typical with large men to be brutal at need but gentle by nature. Rudy had explained it to him once, saying that since they did not have the fears of being physically inadequate because of size and strength, they felt no juvenile desire to demonstrate their strength.

He was curious to see how Tate would be if this went south on them. Top had given his nod, but Bunny had his own standards. He looked for the emotional connection between soldier and action. Between the person and what that person was called upon to do; and how that manifested in the visible emotions. He'd given red cards to a few shooters over the years, sending them off the field if they looked like they were getting high from spilling blood.

Tate was cool, though. There was no flicker in his eye, no twitch in his fingers as if he wanted to grab and hurt. Bunny nodded to himself.

The second guard reached the far side of the room they were in and then used a keycard to exit. When the door closed, Bunny and Tate stepped out from their places of concealment between hulking machines. They moved off, staying close but maximizing their time by looking at different machines, opening different cabinets and desks. Tate understood technology better than Bunny and he took point when giving details to the TOC, and occasionally directed Bunny's bodycam to help him get a full picture of each large machine, which Doc Holliday quickly identified. Machines to shape and mold plastic or metal; machines to attach component parts; machines to weld and seal.

"Gorgon and Sergeant Rock found crates of the stuff these machines make," explained Doc. "Leave chameleon sensors and move on."

Tate removed a bag of nickel-sized devices and they went to work. The sensors had plastic strips on each side. Once the top strip was removed, the sensor was placed against the surface where it would be left. The photosensitive chemicals adapted to the color of the surface within seconds; then the sensor would be removed, the back strip torn off to expose adhesive, and then the device would be set in place. Once placed, they would blend in perfectly and, unless you knew where to look, they would vanish from notice. It took several minutes to tag all of the machines, but the effect would be a constant feed of data back to the Hangar.

They moved on. Snugged into one corner they found a large cabinet that, when opened, proved to be a false front, behind which was a very large industrial safe. Bunny stepped back and kept guard while Tate took a set of electronic devices from a pouch on his web belt and set to work bypassing the security.

"This is freaky," said Tate quietly. "Most dial-type safe locks are three-, four-, or five-digit combinations. This is twelve. Screws the math up something fierce."

"Shit," complained Bunny. "How long's it going to take you to—?"

Tate pulled the door open.

"Oh," grunted Bunny. "Well, okay then."

As the massive door swung open, the darkness was suffused with an intense green light so bright that it made both men throw arms across their faces and wince as they backed away.

Bunny had to squint to see through the glare. He felt strangely sick and gagged as he stared inside. There were a dozen shelves and each was stacked with pieces of glowing green crystal. Bars and disks, milled tubes and uncut chunks. Hundreds, maybe thousands of pounds of the stuff.

"Close it," he gasped.

"What?" asked Tate, but it wasn't a response to his statement. Instead he stood there, eyes wide and mouth open, looking like a sleepwalker.

"Close it," Bunny growled, and when Tate still didn't move he stepped forward and kicked the door shut. It slammed and there was an audible *click,* and the green light vanished all at once. Bunny sagged back and caught himself with a hand on the edge of a machine. He swayed, dizzy and sick.

Tate dropped to his knees, his big body convulsing, and then he tore off his balaclava and vomited all over the front of the safe. Bunny tried to say something to comfort the new guy, but when he opened his mouth he threw up, too. The thought that ran through his head, though, made no immediate sense.

I can't hear myself think.

Over and over again, while his stomach heaved.

CHAPTER ONE HUNDRED SIX

PUSHKIN DYNAMICS
VOSTOCHNY DISTRICT
RUSSIA

The sentries dropped where they stood, their weapons clattering to the floor. Ghost swarmed past me to check up and down the hall, then he came back and sniffed at the bodies. Maybe he could hear the silence in their chests. Maybe there is some canine way of knowing wounded from dead. Probably. They had a dead look to me, too. Inside my head the Modern Man flinched and turned away, ashamed of being part of me, repelled by my actions.

I removed the magazine from my gun and replaced the four bullets I'd used and rammed it back in place. Then I dragged the bodies out of the way and used my gizmos to bypass the security. It took time, and I felt my face go stiff and wooden as I worked. A defense mechanism. The clinical term for my psychological condition is, I believe, bugfuck nuts.

As I turned away from the corpses, something caught my eye and I knelt between the dead soldiers. Both of them wore identical rings to the one I'd taken from the guard upstairs. I worked one off a slack hand and peered at it. The ring was heavy, and I figured it was metal around something dense, like lead. There was a cap over what I assumed was another chunk of green crystal. So the cap was what? Protective shielding? Maybe, but there was no actual way for the wearer to open the cap. When I ran the Anteater over them, though, I found that there was a spring trigger activated by a radio receiver. That was odd, but it wasn't what I had time to think about right then, so I added the two rings to the Faraday bag.

The massive airlock clicked and then hissed as it swung outward on hydraulic hinges. It exhaled chilled air that smelled of rotting meat. It was like a punch in the stomach and I staggered back, glad that the balaclava was some kind of filter. Ghost growled at the smell and the hairs on his back stood up.

I braced myself and stepped over the threshold, raising my weapon because every time I've smelled something that bad in a lab, things went south. Very far south. This particular stench had a vaguely familiar tang to it, but I could not grab the attached memory.

Ghost and I moved inside and shifted away to keep from being silhouetted against the open door. There were only a few security lights on. Huge pieces of machinery crouched there in the shadows, their shapes and purposes indistinct. I tapped my earbud for Bug but got nothing at all, and when I checked my wrist computer it told me there was no signal and no chance of one. Bug warned me about the shielding. It was strange for a grown man and a practiced killer like me to suddenly feel insecure about being in what was essentially an empty room.

On the other hand, I'd been in underground labs before, so it's not like my fears were totally unfounded.

Ghost was spooked, too.

We moved through along the wall and found no switches, so I darted to the other side of the door and there they were. I kept my gun in one hand while I turned them on.

The overhead lights flared bright, burning off all the shadows, revealing every single detail of where I was and what was in there with me.

If it had been vampires, demons, hobgoblins, berserkers, or genetically engineered werewolf supersoldiers I would have been less terrified than by what I saw.

Nothing alive. Not really.

It was a machine, surrounded by other lesser machines. It was built like the mouth of a tunnel, thirty feet high, with a series of inner rings that stepped back at irregular intervals. The primary structure looked to be made of steel, but there were other metals, too. Lots of exposed copper, some crude iron bands, gleaming alloy bolts, and long circular strips of what looked like gold. Heavy black rubber-coated cables were entwined with the rings of metal, and coaxial cables as thick as my thigh snaked along the ground and ran farther down the slope to where a series of heavy industrial generators were positioned on a flat stone pad. Sixteen generators. Lots of power. The tunnel stretched back so far it disappeared into darkness.

It looked like the mouth of the big hadron collider at CERN.

It wasn't

I think my heart stopped in my chest. I had seen two of these machines before. Two this size. One down at Gateway in the Antarctic. The other in the basement of Harcourt Bolton's mansion.

And now this one.

The rotting meat stink came at me in waves from the open mouth of the machine, like some dragon was breathing in a troubled slumber. All around the opening were round slots into which carefully carved stones could be placed. I knew this, even though those slots were currently empty. I knew, without knowing how, that the stones for this machine were not going to be diamonds and rubies and sapphires. Not like the Gateway machine. Not like Prospero Bell's. No. The stones for this one would be green crystal.

I stood and stared, wide-eyed, dry-mouthed, terrified at the gigantic God Machine.

CHAPTER ONE HUNDRED SEVEN

PUSHKIN DYNAMICS
VOSTOCHNY DISTRICT
RUSSIA

I had no radio, and no way to even contact my team.

So I did what I could. I took out a small digital camera and took as many pictures as I could. All angles of the machine. And everything else in the lab. I also went to each computer workstation and plugged in high-capacity flash drives to download as much data as possible. My regrets over killing the two guards were diminishing. Wished right then I had all the scientists working on the project there, along with Gadyuka, Valen, and every damn person they ever met.

This wasn't a work in progress. This was a completed machine. In the back of the lab I found a vault that actually had a printed sign: *SVOD KRISTALL*. Crystal vault. I had to really talk myself into opening it, and my hands were slick with sweat by the time the locks clicked. But then I took another look at the heavy radiation suits hanging on hooks beside the vault, and pushed the door shut again.

Was there time to put one of the suits on?

There wasn't one that fit Ghost. What would that much green crystal radiation do to him? Did I need to risk finding out?

"Yeah, goddamn it," I muttered. To Ghost I said, "Ghost, back. Out. Post."

It was our shorthand to tell him to go back the way we'd come and stand guard outside of the lab. He gave me a lingering look in which I could read doubt and fear in his brown eyes. But he obeyed and moved off, casting looks over his shoulder as he went.

As soon as he went out I moved fast. The radiation suits were oversized and went on easily. I unslung the Faraday bag and set it aside until I was sure all the seals were secured, then I reopened the vault, picked up the bag, and stepped inside. There was no immediate splash of green luminescence. They were too careful about that, and I should probably have thought it through better. They had to keep the rest of the lab staff safe.

Inside there were rows of file cabinets with shallow drawers, much like those used in jewelers' warehouses. Each drawer was marked by a numerical code, which I ignored. I opened one and there they were. Row upon row of green stones, each cut like a faceted emerald, but of the wrong color. These matched the crystal gun in my pocket and the stone in the guards' rings. When I picked one up I again noticed how light the stones were; unlike any crystals I'd handled before.

Every file drawer was filled with them. Most were the same size, but then I found raw and uncut stones of various sizes. I didn't hesitate and began cramming both kinds of crystal into the Faraday bag. I couldn't take all of them, but I took a lot. It bothered me that I was leaving a significant number of them behind, so I went outside, closed the vault, unzipped my radiation suit, and removed three large blaster plasters. These are self-adhering high-yield explosives. Once applied they can be triggered by, say, a door opening and tearing them apart, thereby mixing the chemicals inside; or via a small timer the size of a quarter. I used those, went back inside, dumped all of the stones into a metal trash can I brought in with me, and then wrapped them in the blaster plasters. There were enough high explosives in there to blow up half the lab. Not enough, alas, to destroy the God Machine. But I had photographic proof it existed, and it was too big to pack up and cart off. Maybe an airstrike would handle it. Maybe the State Department. Who knows. That was above my pay grade.

I set the timers, closed the vault door and sprinted across the lab, slammed the big airlock door behind me, and shucked off the radiation suit.

"Ghost," I yelled as I ran for the stairs. We got halfway up when thunder boomed and chased us. The whole basement shook, and I hoped that I'd underestimated the explosive power of the plasters. Maybe they'd have vaporized the crystals and done some serious damage to the God Machine, too. From the rumble, I didn't think many of the computers would survive, either.

We ran up and up until I found a signal.

Then I called it in.

CHAPTER ONE HUNDRED EIGHT

THE HANGAR
FLOYD BENNETT FIELD
BROOKLYN, NEW YORK

Bug sat in his sealed computer clean room, listening as Joe Ledger made his field report. The details punched him back against the cushions of his chair.

"Damn," he said aloud, even though he was alone, "I kind of hate it when I'm right."

CHAPTER ONE HUNDRED NINE

PUSHKIN DYNAMICS
VOSTOCHNY DISTRICT
RUSSIA

"Okay," I said to Doc Holliday, "what in the wide blue fuck is up with these green crystals?"

I didn't exactly yell, but Ghost gave me a reproving *whuff* and cut a significant glance at the doorway.

"Answer my two questions first," she said. "Are the crystals unusually light in weight? And do they glow at all? Not when you shine light on them, but as if they are lit from inside."

"Both. Why?"

"Shit," she said. "Listen, Cowboy, we are putting together a field briefing for you on that."

"Don't be coy, Doc," I said. "If you know something, then tell me right now."

"I can't. There's too much to go into. Bookworm will brief you shortly," she said.

"Bookworm?" I yelped. That was Junie's call sign, for those rare times she was in the field or advising a field team.

"It is absolutely critical that you avoid *all* physical contact with the green crystal, particularly if they glow and are lighter than they should be. It means they have been activated. Don't ask me what that means, because this is Bookworm's territory. I'm as much a tourist as you are on this. Follow my orders, though. If the crystals are not in a Faraday bag, then retreat from them immediately. No exceptions."

"Copy that," I said, and then verified that my telemetry was working properly. It was, and so was the rest of Echo Team's. "Then I think we're done here. Initiating soft exfil now. Huckleberry, stay with me. I'm going to bring the team up to speed."

I tapped over to the team channel and gave them the bullet points. Doc told them again about the dangers of direct exposure to the activated green crystals.

"Now, listen closely," said Doc, repeating the same instructions she gave me, then adding, "You need to work the buddy system more than you ever have. If anyone—*anyone*—begins acting strangely or erratically, you need to get them out of that building. If they begin to exhibit violent behavior, use horsey on them and carry them out. The green crystal affects mood and behavior. We think that's part of what happened in Washington. You need to evacuate that building right now. Is that understood?"

There was a beat before we all agreed. And I thought back to how my mood, and Bunny's, shifted into low gear after I left Rolgavitch's office.

"I want everyone to confirm Huckleberry's orders right damn now," I growled.

There was a chorus of emphatic *Hooahs*. Bunny hit it a little harder than the others, which meant his thoughts had gone in the same direction as mine. We'd both felt it in the car on the way here.

"Okay," I said once Doc dropped off the call. "Gather all samples, upload all data and photos. You have ten minutes and drop and go. Evac by teams and converge on the vehicles."

That got a much more enthusiastic reply.

"Cowboy," said Top, "we still going soft in here?"

"When possible," I said. "Mission priority is to get out with evidence. If we can do that without additional casualties, then we play it that way. However—and everyone hear me on this—the future of our country may depend on us getting this evidence back home. Nothing prevents that from happening. Hooah?"

"Hooah!"

Ghost whuffed. There was some edge in it, just as there was in the agreement from my team. The day was sliding downhill and we all knew it.

CHAPTER ONE HUNDRED TEN

PUSHKIN DYNAMICS
VOSTOCHNY DISTRICT
RUSSIA

Sometimes they start off bad and then the universe decides to really up its game and show you just how truly nasty and weird it can all get when it doesn't like you.

Ghost and I made our way along the corridors, doing quick-checks in the various rooms, and suddenly my wrist computer pinged that one of the doors was not the standard metal-covered oak but a solid piece of reinforced steel. When I bypassed the locks I found another high-tech door behind it. Not as intimidating as the airlock downstairs, but clearly intended to keep everyone out who wasn't authorized to be there. MindReader laughs at that kind of thing, and the door yielded to me.

Suddenly Ghost went into a tense crouch, and a split second later I heard voices inside the room. Two men speaking in Russian. Saying something about a girl one of them was dating who he thought might be sleeping with a guy who lived in the flat above her. They were strategizing on whether to brace the guy and beat the shit out of him. Or maybe kill him. Or maybe kill the girl, too. Every option seemed to be on the table. A couple of real pillars of society. This, for the record, is part of the reason I have rage issues. Besides, most of my buttons had already been pushed, so I was profoundly cranky.

I listened from the doorway. There was a short corridor inside that led to a T-junction. Light and the voices were coming from the left-hand side; only shadows from the right. I sent a couple of houseflies to check it out and they sent back a livestream of two guys dressed like the guards I'd killed downstairs. Tough, with cold eyes and automatic weapons. On the wall against which they stood was a symbol I know way too well: a plain trefoil, with three circles overlapping each other equally like in a triple Venn diagram with the overlapping parts erased. The international symbol for biohazard.

We moved to the very edge of the T-junction, and I signaled Ghost to stay. I took a breath, wheeled around the corner, and shot each guard in the head twice. They went right down, and I pivoted to make sure there wasn't anyone else at this party. There wasn't. Pushkin seemed to have a pattern. Two special nighttime guards at each of their higher-security labs, and the cookie-cutter guards patrolling the hallways in ones or twos.

A glance showed me that these guards also wore heavy rings.

I holstered my gun and used the BAMS unit to sniff the air. The lights glowed a reassuring green. When Top, Bunny, and I had encountered our first God Machine, it had belched out a witch's brew of toxins, including a hitherto unknown strain of the Spanish flu. We all got sick and I nearly died. I was planning on lighting a candle to whichever saint was in charge of keeping idiots like me safe. Or, safe-ish, anyway. There were no obvious microscopic monsters here. Did that mean they hadn't turned it on yet? Or had found a way to prevent those sorts of things from happening? No way to tell until Bug and Nikki tore apart the data I'd sent, and there was a whole damn lot of it to sort through.

I wondered how they were doing with the hunt for Valen Oruraka and Gadyuka. I hoped like hell there would be a clear scent to follow once we got back from Russia. Shooting the guards hadn't resolved my anger management issues.

The room with the two dead guys held nothing of interest, so I moved down the right-hand side of the T-junction. I switched the BAMS to my left hand and drew my gun with my right. The other room was a large lab with rows of computers, workstations, locked file cabinets, and a massive glass-enclosed hot room in the center fitted with a revolving-door airlock complete with steam and disinfectant spray jets. There was a medium-sized vault inside the hot room, but I was not wearing a hazmat suit. There were plenty on hooks by the entrance, but that was going to take more time than I had.

Ghost came up beside me. Dogs react mostly to smell and hearing; slightly less so to sight. There was no sound or odor, but he came to point and stared at what lay on the table. I glanced down and saw that once more all the hair stood up on his neck. His low growl of anger and defiance was laced with fear. The hairs on the back of *my* neck stood up, too. Any thoughts I might have entertained about the rest of the day making more sense died right there. I touched my bodycam to make sure it was on.

There, against the far wall, was a second secure chamber, also glass-fronted. It was forty feet long and ten feet high, and inside there were stainless steel dissecting tables and heavy-duty shelves above them on which were huge clear specimen jars.

The world seemed to dwindle down to that chamber and what it held. My mouth went dry, but I tapped my earbud to get the TOC and managed to croak out a few words.

"Tell me you're seeing this."

I heard Doc Holliday say, "What the hell is *that*?"

"Kind of hoping you'd be able to tell me."

At a glance, from across the room and on the other side of the glassed-in hot room, it looked like a tentacle. Now, standing five feet away, with a crystal-clear wall between me and it, I was positive no marine biologist would hang that label on it. It was at least fifteen feet long, and had been torn off at the thick end. Torn, not cut. The flesh looked . . . chewed. A shark, maybe? If so, it had a hell of a big bite.

The thing was enormous. Easily four feet thick at the tear, tapering only a little to about two-thirds that thickness at the undamaged end. There were rows of huge suckers on it. But, unlike an octopus, the suckers were not all on one side. They covered the entire thing. A little bit of high school biology crept back to me, telling me that this was actually an arm, not a tentacle, because tentacles have suckers only near the end, while a cephalopod's arms have suckers the whole length. But not on all sides. I was sure of that.

And the suckers themselves were . . . *wrong*. Octopus, squid, and cuttlefish suckers are round, with an outer rim and a hollow cavity inside. These are all made of muscle and covered with something like a cuticle to protect the flesh. It's the flexing of powerful muscles in the suckers that crushes prey and tears it apart.

That's not what I was seeing here. The suckers were round, yes, but the inner cavities were not hollow. Fuck no. They were lined all around with row upon row upon row of small, sharp teeth. Actual teeth. Or, maybe fangs was the right word.

The end of the tentacle was worse, though. It did not end in blunt flesh like an octopus's or even a paddle like a squid's. Instead it terminated with a clutch of bony, hooked things that looked like claws. I stood there and stared at it. And I'm sure everyone back at the TOC was staring, too. No one said a word.

I glanced up at the specimen jars. There were parts of the thing that corresponded with surgical gouges in the flesh. But there were other things, too. Creatures that looked like deformed crabs or lobsters. They floated—dead, I hoped—in liquid.

The crustaceans and the cephalopod—if those words even applied—were similar in one regard, though. They were mottled and armored like the back of a Louisiana alligator; and they were colored in a hundred different shades of green. And not merely green . . . buried between the knobs and bumps on the strange skin I saw tiny glints of something else. I risked a closer look, bending toward the glass, peering to see what I did not want to see. Light was sparkling off the sharp tips and edges of pieces of green crystal. Without going inside the tank I couldn't tell if the pieces had been forced into place or whether they were in some way a part of this thing. Maybe they were like barnacles. But they looked so orderly in their placement that it was almost as if they had grown *out* through the mottled flesh.

When I could speak I said, "Doc? What. The *fuck*. Am I looking at?"

"God almighty," was her only coherent reply.

Then there was another voice on the line. Junie. "Don't touch it, for God's sake, Joe. I mean Cowboy. Don't go near it."

"There is not one chance in *hell,*" I said, backing away. "I wouldn't go in there at gunpoint."

Before anyone could gather herself to say anything more, a situation alert bell *bing-bonged* in my ear and then Duffy broke into the call.

"Spartan to Cowboy," he said in a fierce whisper, "be advised, we got company. Three big SUVs just pulled into the parking lot and a whole team has deployed. Count eighteen hostiles. Civilian clothes, but they're all locked and loaded. Automatic weapons. Six heading for the front door, six each heading to the side door and the rear loading bay. Looks like a raid. We must have tripped an alarm somewhere."

"Copy that," I said, then cycled over to the full team channel and repeated what Duffy had said. "Echo Team, abort mission. Retrieve all gear that you can. Burn what you can't take with you. Do it now."

I stood for a long moment looking at the thing on the table, at the specimens in the jars. Something about this triggered a memory that was either too deep to grab, or one that did not want me to pull it into the light. Things from dreams, from nightmares. Images from the fevered hallucinations I'd had while the Spanish flu was burning me alive. Ghost stood up and placed his front paws on the glass and snarled with unfiltered hate. He was so upset, so angry, so *scared*, that his whole body trembled with it and he was panting.

"Ghost . . . ," I said gently, and he turned his head and gave me a werewolf growl. I patted my thigh and he looked at me without a trace of recognition, still wrapped up in whatever complex emotions were tearing at him. I called his name again, but his eyes were glassy and strange.

So, I tried it another way. I straightened and snapped my fingers, loud as a gunshot. "Ghost. *Come*." I put all of my voice of command into it. He flinched and blinked and the feral look in his eyes flickered. All those thousands of hours of training him ever since he was young; the combat simulations and then the missions. All of the hell we'd run through together. All of the blood and smoke and gunfire. All of the times we limped off the field when damn near everyone else was dead. All of that was hardwired into him on a deep, deep level. It went deeper than his fear, the way it does with all good soldiers.

He dropped to all fours and trotted over to me, turned, and sat down by my side. Ready. In position. *With* me. We both took a lingering look at the horrors and mysteries behind the glass. Then we looked at each other.

Then we got the hell out of there.

CHAPTER ONE HUNDRED ELEVEN

THE HANGAR
FLOYD BENNETT FIELD
BROOKLYN, NEW YORK

Doc Holliday pointed to the picture of the tentacle that still filled one of the big viewscreens in the TOC. Her finger trembled visibly.

"What in hell is that?"

When no one answered, she swung the finger around and pointed to one of her lab techs. "You. Get to a terminal, call up image recognition, and cross-reference with the fossil record database and any other source you can access. I want to know everything about that thing, all the way down to the size of its dick, and I want it in the next ten minutes."

The tech literally broke into a dead run.

She pivoted and speared another tech with her glare. "You, I want a different search. Go into art files and other image sources. If someone so much as doodled that thing on a cocktail napkin, I want a full report. *Move!*"

She kept rattling orders. Junie stood and watched, finally impressed by Doc Holliday. Until now she had been getting very frustrated by the woman's reluctance to think outside of the box. That had been a flaw in Dr. Hu's makeup; Bill Hu had flatly refused to believe in the possibility of extraterrestrial life until the unfolding Extinction Machine case forced him to. Foot-dragging was always tedious to Junie, but ten times more so when Joe's life was on the line.

When Doc paused to gasp in a breath, Junie asked, "How can I help?"

Doc looked around, clearly seeing no one else that she needed to make jump. She turned back to Junie. "If there's more I need to know, then damn well tell me. I am officially open for business in every possible way. We got big green Reptilians, madness-inducing green crystals, interdimensional gateways, and giant alien tentacles. I think we can declare my skepticism dead and damn well buried. So . . . as Joe is so fond of saying . . . *hit me*."

CHAPTER ONE HUNDRED TWELVE

PUSHKIN DYNAMICS
VOSTOCHNY DISTRICT
RUSSIA

There is a popular military acronym: SNAFU. It stands for "situation normal, all fucked up." Some people will insist it's "fouled" up, but it's not. It's fucked. As we pretty much were.

Duffy said that the newcomers were massing at the doors but had not yet breached. "Not sure what they're waiting for, Cowboy. No breaching tools that I can see, but they haven't touched the hand scanner or keycard box. Wait. One guy in the front has his hand to his ear. Think he's talking to someone, maybe getting orders. I'll send a bird drone over to try and eavesdrop."

"Bug," I asked, "can you hack the transmission on the new players?"

"Working on it, Cowboy," he said, and I could hear him hammering on his keyboard. "It's some kind of cyclical scrambler. Something new and spiffy."

"Ticktock," said Top. "I've got guards coming."

"Me, too," said Bunny, "but they're still on slow foot patrol. No one seems to be running. No alarms going off inside. What gives? Are the jokers outside on their side or did someone else just buy into this poker game?"

"Unknown," I said. "Don't even know if the rent-a-cops up there knew about the pro ballers I ran into."

"Guys outside look like serious players," warned Duffy.

"Call the play," suggested Top.

"I—"

That was all I got out, because suddenly there was a sound. Very loud, very odd, impossible to really describe. Kind of a gigantic *whoooooomp!*

It shook the entire building with such force that my immediate reaction was: *Bomb*. But it wasn't. I've heard thousands of explosions, from firecrackers up to fuel-air cluster bombs. This wasn't like any blast I'd ever heard. It was softer, more compressed. Close to the sound of something very large and flat being forcibly slammed down on a flat table, with the sound of impact softened by the air as it is forced to escape. Like that, but not like that. It was also something that vibrated everything. I felt it like a punch to the breastbone. It hurt my heart and buckled my legs, and I went down into a duck walk that ended with me on my knees, crammed up against the corridor wall. Ghost belly flopped and skidded past me. We both froze there, gasping. Feeling momentarily battered and sick. All of the alarms in the entire building went off at once.

Smith, outside, was the first to call in. "Cowboy, was that an explosion? It looked like the whole damn building shook."

"I . . . I don't—" But again I was interrupted.

"Spartan to Cowboy," yelled Duffy. "Be advised, you have hostiles coming in all three doors."

In the distance, I could hear gunfire. And screams.

So many screams.

CHAPTER ONE HUNDRED THIRTEEN

PUSHKIN DYNAMICS
VOSTOCHNY DISTRICT
RUSSIA

Soft exfil my shiny white ass.

"Cowboy to Echo Team," I yelled as I struggled back to my feet. "Cleared to go weapons hot. Hard exfil. Repeat, *hard* exfil."

I whipped the door open and ran into the hall with Ghost at my heels. There was no one in sight, but in the distance, coming from several other parts of the building, I could hear the gunfire. Various calibers. Shouts in Russian, some in English, all too muffled to understand. The screams were not the high-pitched shrieks of pain. Not exactly. I've heard enough battlefield injury cries to know them in their various intensities, and this wasn't that. This was more like madhouse screeching. Filled with power and raw emotion.

I heard one voice shouting *"Zatknis! Zatknis!"* Over and over again. *Shut up.* No one seemed to be responding to him, though. His voice was rising to a hysterical pitch and sounded odd. Wrong.

Then there was another, louder voice bellowing at my men to stand down. From the barrage of responding gunfire it was clear my guys weren't all that much in a stand-down kind of mood.

"Ghost," I said, "find Sergeant Rock. *Shield. Shield. Shield.*"

My dog was trained to locate my team by real names or combat call signs, and he bounded forward toward the left end of the corridor and I raced after. We were halfway down the hall toward our intended exit route when a door opened and two men stepped out of a stairwell. Both were dressed in identical black suits, both carried automatic rifles. Soldiers, not guards. They immediately swung their barrels toward us and began shooting. What happened next occurred all inside the bubble of a cracked half second.

A bullet punched into my hip and slammed me halfway around.

White-hot pain exploded in every nerve—but even with its intensity I knew that the round hadn't penetrated. The Kevlar and spider silk had done their job, and the impact-dampeners had sloughed off some of the force. There was impact pain but not the hot burning agony of a bullet passing through.

I used the impact to spin me all the way around and came out of it shooting. The two soldiers split left and right and my rounds chased them. Ghost was already moving, having launched himself at them before their fingers had squeezed the triggers. He was a white missile; all teeth and claws and savage intent. The closest man went crashing back against the wall. I corrected my aim and used my pistol to put two center mass in the other guy. He was not wearing the most advanced shock-absorbing, bullet-stopping body armor currently available, and I was firing armor-piercing rounds. He sat down and died, his gun hitting the polished floor and sliding ten feet.

All of that. Done in a heartbeat.

I wheeled to see if Ghost needed help.

He didn't.

It takes a little bit of time for him to wrestle a guy down and subdue him if the command was to "own." Killing is always quicker. It simplifies the math.

I limped forward, feeling for damage. My hip hurt like a bastard, but it held. Nothing broken, I thought, then heard a glassy rattle. When I checked the pouch on my upper thigh, I found that the round had smashed the green crystal gun I'd taken from Yuri's safe. It was in a hundred pieces and some jagged ends had slashed through the Faraday bag. None had sliced through my trousers, though, so there was that. I debated throwing it the hell away because—let's face it—green crystals in any form were beginning to freak me the fuck out. But before I could do that, there was noise from inside the stairwell and I did a quick-look around the doorway to see a third man coming up fast, gun socketed into his shoulder. I shot him twice in the face and he tumbled back down.

The moment became instantly still as I listened for more immediate threats. Nothing close to hand; all of the weird screams and sounds of battle were downstairs and in remote parts of the building. Even so, there was an odd little flicker inside my head and heart as I looked at the three dead men, and for the strangest moment I saw my own face superimposed over theirs. And in that fragment of a second, I wished it *was* me lying there with my brains blown out. With all of my bad memories splattered across the floor. An ugly little voice seemed to whisper to me.

That's how the pain ends. Miss the next shot. Pause for a heartbeat and all of this goes away. Helen and Grace and your mom . . . they're all waiting for you.

It stopped me. Chilled me. Horrified me.

Because that inner voice was mine. Or . . . *one* of my voices. It was the Modern Man aspect of my fractured personality. The civilized part of me. The one who would have been dominant if Helen and I had never been attacked. Maybe the real me. The Modern Man was not a killer, not a soldier, not a cop. He wasn't part of anything that happened in my life after Helen. Nothing. He was stalled at the ending point of my innocence, standing on that cliff edge.

Never once in all my life had he ever spoken so harshly, so savagely, to me. Never once in my life had he made so goddamn much sense.

Let it end and be free, he told me.

The Cop part of my mind rose up and began to talk, to reason, to construct arguments against that kind of insane thinking, but he was howled down by the Killer. Guilt, heartbreak, despair were all as foreign to him as the kind of weariness of spirit I heard in the Modern Man's voice. The Killer threw back his head and roared an inarticulate challenge. In hatred and defiance.

And then I heard Ghost bark. Once. Twice. Not at another threat heading our way. He was barking at me. Sharp, angry, frightened barks.

I flinched away from those barks and toppled back against the wall, gasping as if I'd run up a flight of stairs.

That fast, it was all over. I was back in complete control and there was no inner argument. It was so sudden and so total that I had a very hard time accepting that I'd heard the Modern Man say those things. Looking inward, even he seemed surprised.

Ghost barked once more. Low and mean and urgent.

"I'm okay," I said, gasping it out. "I'm good."

The wolf eyed me without tolerance or mercy. I straightened and I could feel the Killer looking out through my eyes. In the presence of his true pack leader, Ghost sat down and even wagged his bushy tail.

My life is a freak show. Ask anyone.

CHAPTER ONE HUNDRED FOURTEEN

PUSHKIN DYNAMICS
VOSTOCHNY DISTRICT
RUSSIA

"Area," I said to Ghost. It was the command to use his canine ears and nose to assess the stairwell the two soldiers had come out of. He whuffed quietly. All clear. We went down fast. I cleared each corner and made sure, though, because even a dog as well trained and experienced as Ghost can be wrong.

We went down three flights, and with each step the sounds of battle grew louder. We moved out into an empty hall. As we ran along it, I tapped my earbud to the team channel and left the signal open.

"Sergeant Rock," I said quietly, "sit-rep."

I wasn't sure if he'd be able to answer, but his gruff voice was in my ear, breathless and tense.

"Got some weird shit coming down, Cowboy," he said. "The new hostiles are soldiers, no doubt about. No rank or insignia, but they move like SpecOps. But the security guards are queering the math. Those assholes have suddenly gone totally ape shit. They're shooting up the place. Not really aiming, but throwing a lot of ordnance downrange, aiming at anything that moves, *including* the soldiers. Don't make sense to me, but that's the situation."

"Sergeant Rock," I said, "confirm that the Pushkin guards are shooting at *everyone*?"

"Confirmed, Cowboy, it's like they're drunk or something. But there's a shit-ton more of them than we thought. Not just more guards, but a bunch of guys dressed like factory workers, too. At least thirty. Some guys in white lab coats, too. Coming out of everywhere."

Bunny came onto the call. "Got that here, too. Couple of doors opened to a lab or something. These assholes are streaming out. Most do not have firearms. Repeat, most civilians are not carrying guns. They're coming at us with broom handles and fire extinguishers. They're not even organized."

"Green Giant, have you engaged the soldiers yet?"

"Negative. Coffey and I are moving through a suite of offices. Only encountering some guards and civilian staff."

Smith chimed in, "You're about to have a lot of company, Green Giant. Count ten hostiles. Possibly more."

"Three more SUVs just pulled in on the far side of the lot," called Duffy.

Well, I thought, *isn't that just peachy?*

"Keep them entertained, Spartan," I ordered, and he actually chuckled. Fruitcake. "Green Giant and Coffey, open the Toybox."

"Hooah," said an enthusiastic Tate. The Toybox was a satchel of really nasty booby traps and urban-warfare limited-area mines developed by Doc Holliday. Tate, who was the techiest of us, loved all that shit. While Top and Cole had been investigating the loading bay and I'd been visiting the damn Twilight Zone, Bunny and Tate spent their time preparing for a worst-case scenario with Doc's gruesome gizmos.

"Everybody turn your Tinglers on," said Bunny. We all did. Tinglers are a real-time warning system hardwired into our suits that let us know where the booby traps were, what they were, and which routes were safe for us to use.

"Sergeant Rock," I called, "what's your twenty?"

"We're still in the loading bay, rear exit," said Top. "But we're boxed. I have shooters between me and the exit and behind us firing from cover, and a lot of those crazy-ass guards and lab techs running everywhere. We're going to have to start dropping civilians if we're going to get clear of this."

"Coming to you," I said.

Duffy chimed in. "Echo Team, be advised you kids better haul ass or hide, 'cause there's a shit-ton of them about to storm the castle. We're not getting out of this without a gunfight."

Top said "This is going south on us, Cowboy."

And Bunny was back, yelling in near panic. "Fuck, I just had two lab guys try to bite me."

"Confirm . . . *bite*?" I demanded. A chill raced through me nonetheless. We'd encountered biters before. The living dead infected from Seif al Din, the genetically enhanced Berserkers, and the bloodthirsty Red Knights. I could feel terror boiling in my gut.

"Roger that," Bunny said, sounding out of breath. "It's cool, it's cool. I don't think we're dealing with Seif al Din. These guys had heartbeats. When they couldn't bite me, they began punching each other. I banged their heads together and they went out for a nap. But there's more chasing us. We're heading to the lobby. No other route possible, but there's a shitload of these assholes on our six. Coffey's leaving some parting gifts on our back-trail."

"Green Giant, are you able to confirm if the hostiles are wearing heavy rings? White metal."

There was a rustling sound and then he said, "Yeah. Both of them. And . . . oh shit. The rings have a little cap on them and they're open. I can see some of that green crystal stuff."

"Get away from them," I roared. "Do it right now."

"Okay," whispered Bunny, "we've moved to an alcove. We're good."

"Echo Team, listen to me," I said tersely, "all of the hostiles are wearing rings with green quartz chips. The rings are activated by an electronic signal, and it's somehow been sent. Assume that everyone else in this building is under the influence of crystal energy."

It sounded stupid to say that, but no one laughed. We'd gone past that point.

"We need to just end this," I said. "Eat your gun. Whatever. End it."

And then I froze as the echo of my own words came back to me. I tried to fix it, take it back, change it. I yelled at them to disregard, but the wrong words came out of my mouth.

"It's too damn quiet in here," I heard myself say. "I can't hear my own damn thoughts. I can't take it."

There was a weird sensation in my arm and I looked down to see my hand raising the pistol toward my own face.

CHAPTER ONE HUNDRED FIFTEEN

PUSHKIN DYNAMICS
VOSTOCHNY DISTRICT
RUSSIA

Ghost attacked me.

He launched himself into the air and slammed into me with both front paws, knocking me back, ramming me against the wall. I hit my head and the point of one elbow, and my trigger finger jerked and the blast blinded and deafened me. Fresh pain flared through the bruised muscles of my shoulders and lower back. I slid down and Ghost came at me again, standing on my chest and snarling, his gleaming teeth inches from my face. Beyond those teeth, though, I did not see anger. I saw total, mad panic.

I shook my head, trying to make sense of my own thoughts. The gun. Jesus Christ. The gun. My cheek stung from powder burns and there was a terrible ringing in both ears.

Ghost barked at me, but I couldn't hear him.

Somehow that scared me more than anything so far. It was like watching a movie with the sound turned all the way down. The only noise was the ringing in my ears and . . . something else. It was like wind, but distant, faint. Like the breeze you can hear in parts of the Grand Canyon. Far away and ghostly.

There was darkness at the edge of my vision.

Let me fall, I said.

Or thought I said.

Ghost kept barking in total silence. The fear in his eyes was like a fist that punched me in the face. It was one of the worst things I'd ever seen in my life.

I pushed him back with palsied hands. And then I slapped my own face. Hard. Really fucking hard. Again. And again.

Ghost barked again and this time I heard it. Faint. But there. And in my mind I ran toward that sound. Fleeing from those distant, empty winds, running from my own thoughts. He kept barking. Drawing me out of the deep and silent darkness, and he was the light. That bright white fur. Those desperate eyes.

Then I heard voices. I turned, fumbling for my gun, but immediately realized the voices were in my head. In my ear.

My team.

They were yelling. There were other sounds. Snarls and screams and gunfire. But my mind fought me, trying to wash the sounds away again. So I belted myself across the face again and again. I punched myself in the stomach, and then pounded a fist against my bruised hip.

It helped. The pain was specific, it was tangible, and it helped.

Top was yelling for me, but I had no voice and did not trust what I would say. So, he took command of the situation. "Okay, Echo Team," he roared, "we ain't playing no more. Let's light these motherfuckers up."

I fell over and it took forever for me to get to my hands and knees. The torn Faraday bag was there, with the spilled pieces of broken green crystal. I wanted to pick them up, take them. Eat them. Push them into my skin. Put them into my eyes.

Ghost shifted to stand over them. Growling again. I heard it now, and when I looked at him I knew that he would tear me apart to keep me from those stones. I hated him. I wanted to kill the damn mutt. I wanted to stab him to death and wear his skin and . . .

I screamed.

It bubbled up from deep inside of me and I screamed so loud that I could feel my throat ripping raw. And I flung myself away, falling, crawling like a baby, scrabbling, kicking my way along the floor, away from that green glow. Ghost stood his ground and watched me, his sides heaving, drool dripping from his lips.

Suddenly an explosion rocked the whole building.

It wasn't the soft *whump* of earlier, but something much bigger, much worse. And it seemed to come from everywhere, rippling out in waves of destructive force that made the floor under our feet writhe as if we were on the back of some living thing. The poured linoleum cracked underfoot. I tried to stand but fell at once. Ghost went skittering and sliding away from me. As I reached for the wall to steady myself, jagged cracks whipsawed from ceiling to floor, snorting out plumes of brick dust. Framed art fell from its anchors and crashed to the floor and I could hear pipes inside the walls groaning as they were twisted out of shape.

I gasped, "What the—?"

And then there was a second massive *crunch* as if a towering giant had swung a pile-driver punch into the very heart of the building. The shock wave plucked me off the ground like I was nothing and slammed me into the wall. I tucked my chin to save my neck and skull, but the impact drove the air from my lungs and stabbed me with daggers of pain. I heard Ghost utter a sharp cry as he crashed into the opposite wall. We both fell hard onto the juddering floor. He scrambled to his feet but stood quivering, his hair standing on end, eyes wild with terror.

I lay there, dazed, my eyes filled with bright and painful lights. I spat brick dust, coughed too hard, and felt something burning in my chest. My ribs and shoulders were mashed and each square inch felt like a separate volcano spewing red-hot lava. When I tried to get up, the next aftershock punched me into the wall so hard that my head chunked against the cracked plaster. All the lights winked out for a moment and I fought my way back to consciousness, blinking a paste of dust and tears from my eyes. There was a high-pitched ringing in my ears. I lifted the ten thousand pounds of cracked block that was my head.

And that's when the whole fucking day went sideways.

The wall ten feet in front of me seemed to shimmer and lose solidity and for a moment I thought I was seeing the structural integrity disintegrate as vibrations turned brick and plaster to powder.

That would have been bad enough.

Yeah. That would have been bad.

What I saw was worse.

CHAPTER ONE HUNDRED SIXTEEN

PUSHKIN DYNAMICS
VOSTOCHNY DISTRICT
RUSSIA

The shimmer seemed to be shaped like an irregular crack, but it was clearly not part of the wall.

Actually, that's wrong—I could *see* the regular wall pushed back like a curtain. It was as if the wall was nothing more than an image painted on cloth and something was parting it. The cracks that had been there before were still visible, but rippled and pushed aside. And, yes, I know how that sounds. I know how crazy it sounds.

The shimmer was green, and as I watched, it became a deeper and more vibrant green. Luminescent, as if there was a powerful light beyond it and someone was turning a rheostat to make it brighter. Understand me, there was no light hanging on that wall, and I don't think this was light shining through it from another room. The hue was exactly like that of the broken gun and the guard's ring. It was exactly like the spikes in the tentacle—or whatever it was—in the lab. The same. An alien hue, like a shade of green that doesn't really fit into this world.

My bruised head could not make sense of it, failing even to select the right adjectives to describe it internally. My heart began racing and I sat there, so startled that I did not even think of getting away. Ghost got to his feet and stood trembling, but then he began barking furiously at the green glow as he backed nervously away.

Then there was a shadow within the shimmer. It was a figure and it seemed to be moving inside the distortion, and in my semi-delirium I wondered if maybe whatever was happening had indeed punched a hole into the next room and this was one of the Russians trying to get out.

That, you see, would make some sense.

Panic flared and I thought for a twisted moment that it was the rest of whatever that tentacle had belonged to.

It wasn't either of those things.

The moment, you see, was heading in a completely different direction, because the figure that stepped through the crack in the wall was not a Russian soldier, or one of the guys in dark suits, or a lab technician, or even a security guard. Nor was he one of Echo Team come looking for me. Not a tentacular sea beast, either.

The figure that stepped through the wall was tall. Very tall. At least seven feet. It was dressed in some kind of strange and weirdly stylized body armor. It was as green as the shimmering light but painted to look like scales. Darker green on its massive shoulders, arms, and legs; paler with yellowish horizontal plates across its chest and abdomen. The figure wore bizarre boots and gloves that were scaly and oversized, and each toe and finger ended in a thick, dark nail. Or, maybe . . . *claw*?

The intruder stopped and looked down at me. It wore a mask and helmet that, like the rest of its armor, was designed to look like the horned, knobbed, ridged face and skull of some kind of unnatural reptile. Instead of eyes there were large goggles with lenses painted to resemble a lizard's slit-pupiled eyes. The mask had two slits for nostrils and a lipless slash of a mouth. It had on what looked like an old Apache breechclout made from tooled leather and covered with symbols I could not identify. Belts crisscrossed its hips and there were objects in holsters whose nature and purpose were beyond my failing mind.

Lying there, dazed and concussed while the building shook itself to pieces around me, I stared up at the intruder and tried to understand what I was seeing. Clearly this was someone in a costume, in exotic body armor. I mean . . . really, what *else* could it be?

Ghost kept barking and backing away, his tail tucked under its hip, and eyes wild. The tension in his taut muscles told me that he wanted to run, to flee, but his need to protect his pack leader kept him there. He was losing it, though, and any second he was going to cross the line of pack mentality into pure survival mode. He'd flee, and I would be left staring at the man—if it was a man—who towered over me.

I fumbled for my sidearm, but my holster was empty, the gun lost when Ghost attacked to keep me from blowing my own brains out.

The big stranger looked down at the pieces of crystal on the floor. The tremor had scattered them around. If someone wearing a Halloween mask could frown, then that's what it looked like he did. He took a device from his belt and squatted down. I heard a whir of a small motor and stared in frank astonishment as he vacuumed the green crystals up. He nodded to himself, stood, hung the vacuum on his belt, and drew an object from a holster and pointed it at me. It was unlike any gun I'd ever seen, if gun it was; it looked more like a flashlight with a pistol grip. The whole thing, body, handle, and bulb, was not made of metal or glass but instead seemed to be made of some kind of that same green quartz. However, his device did not glow like the pistol had. Did that mean it was of a slightly different material, or was it not, as Junie put it, *activated*? I had no way to know, no way to even properly theorize.

The intruder thumbed a lever and the gun suddenly glowed with a yellow-green light so intense that I winced and half turned away. Again, the light was not the same hue as before. He did not fire at me, but instead raised his weapon and aimed at the far wall. For one terrible moment I thought he was going to shoot Ghost, and that snapped me halfway out of my daze. I snatched my Wilson rapid-release folding knife from its pocket, snapped the blade into place, and lunged at him. The blade flicked across his calf as he dodged away, but only the tip made contact, drawing a thin cut through his armor.

He hissed like an iguana and I froze, gaping at his leg.

The body armor was bleeding.

Green liquid, thick as blood, beaded up and ran in lines down his leg. That slammed me into absolute stillness. It was the same color as the green substance I'd seen on the injured Closer in Maryland.

Not paint.

Blood.

The intruder rattled off something in a language I'd never heard before, wheeled, pointed his gun at the far wall, and pulled the trigger. There was another massive rumble and once more the building seemed to shudder as if struck by some titanic fist. Overhead lights snapped loose and crashed to the floor, showering me with fragments of glass from the fluorescent tubes. I didn't care. I couldn't care, because all my attention was fixed on the opposite wall. A new crack appeared and it shimmered like the other one had, and once more the wall seemed to open and part like curtains on a stage. The intruder kept his gun pointed at it, the trigger pulled back until the crack widened enough for him to step through.

I watched him go.

I could see that the wavering crack was not really in the physical structure of the wall, but rather imposed upon it. Don't ask me how, because I was way beyond the capacity for rational thought.

As the intruder vanished inside I caught a glimpse—just the merest glimpse—of a different place. Not another room, not even the darkened parking lot outside. This was a rocky slope painted by bright sunlight that was the wrong color. More of a sickly sea green than yellow. Plants and flowers bloomed between the rocks and I did not recognize a single one of them. They were towering ferns with leaves as long and sharp as swords; and something like a three-headed rose, its petals the color of fresh blood. Weeds lined with seedpods swayed in a wind that I did not feel. At the top of the slope was a building, a tower made from what looked like carnelian and red jasper, that rose into the sky. And the sky. Dear God, *that sky.* There were two large moons and a dozen smaller ones partly obscured by wisps of clouds, and beyond all of them was the monstrous curve of a gas giant that swirled with storms, like Jupiter, only more violent.

Something flashed—a burst of green light that snapped like lightning from that alien sky and struck my chest with such force that I was picked up and smashed once more against the far wall. I managed to duck my head this time, but it didn't matter. The world went black then green then red. I dropped to my knees and felt like my head was cracking into a hundred tiny pieces. Little bursts of color, like crimson poppies, blossomed in the air in front of my eyes. And when I looked down at my hands I could see tendrils of electricity writhing and twisting on my gloves and up my arms.

When I raised my head toward the impossible crack in the wall, it was gone.

Bang.

Just like that. The crack on that wall and, when I turned my aching head to look, the other one as well. Leaving no trace at all of what I'd seen. I shook my head, trying to clear away the debris inside my skull. There were other cracks from the explosion or earthquake, or whatever it was that was destroying the building, but no trace of the two cracks that had allowed the man in reptile-painted body armor to pass.

If the armor was armor at all.

If the man was a *man* at all.

The last of the electricity faded out from my arms and I sagged back, gasping, my head hurting, my heart hammering. I dug into my pocket and pulled out the torn Faraday bag. The green crystal gun and the guard's ring lay there, shattered into fragments and dust. I peered close and saw that each piece was glowing as brightly as the wall had done a moment ago. Then it faded, faded, faded . . . and went dark.

No. Almost dark. Deep inside of it there was a tiny spark of the green shimmer, but it looked strange. Like it wasn't so much small as very far away. Which was, of course, impossible.

Impossible.

What in the holy hell just happened?

What had I seen?

What?

CHAPTER ONE HUNDRED SEVENTEEN

PUSHKIN DYNAMICS
VOSTOCHNY DISTRICT
RUSSIA

I got shakily to my feet. My balance was for shit and I felt sick and stupid and strange. The committee of three in my head was silent for a change, as if they, too, were dazed and battered. Sounds were weird, too. I could hear the gunfire and yells from different parts of the building, but they sounded too far away. Miles away. Or . . . or maybe it was that my mind kept not wanting to hear them, or care about them.

My instincts kept yelling at me to pay attention to that. Not to disregard what was going on, but to start damn well *caring* about it. There was a big trench opening up in the gulf between mind and heart, and too damn much of me wanted to lean so far over the edge that I'd fall.

Then, as if from all the way at the far end of a football field, I heard Doc Holliday's words come echoing back.

If anyone—anyone—*begins acting strangely or erratically, you need to get them out of the building.*

"Jesus Christ . . . ," I breathed. My head felt like a cracked egg, my nerves were shot, and I had no idea if I'd actually experienced and witnessed any of that, or if my brains were scrambled by trauma. The tremors were subsiding, but the building was a mess. Ghost came over and leaned against me, whining, needing comfort, as if

I had any to give. I squatted down and wrapped my arms around him, sharing my reality with his. It was maybe cold comfort, but it was what we had. I felt tears burning in my eyes. My dog had saved me. He'd somehow understood what I was going to do, and he attacked me to save me. It was the smartest, bravest, most heartbreaking thing I've ever experienced. I hugged him and kissed his fur and wept as he whined and tried to lick me.

Then, slowly . . . slowly . . . I got to my feet. The floor was buckled and cracked, but it was solid. There were no dark winds blowing, no shadows in my mind. They had gone when the green man had taken the crystals away. Junie was right, as she was often right. Doc Holliday might be a hard-core scientist, but she was going to have to embrace a wider definition of things now that she was working with the DMS. The stuff we encountered was often outside the box of science as she knew it. Sometimes way outside, and Junie was likely to be her guide. After all, Junie's DNA was proof that we are not alone.

No. Not alone.

The green man could have killed me.

He did not. And as I thought about that, the memory of what the Closers on the road in Maryland said came back with a lot more force and clarity.

We are not your enemy.

I licked brick dust and tears from my lips and nodded as I walked over to the far wall. There was a slender crack caused by the explosion—if it was an explosion, and I had my doubts; but it was less than a finger's width apart. Everything around it was solid and showed no other evidence of what I'd seen. The opposite wall was the same—only a crack that a baby mouse couldn't squeeze through.

Then there was another rumble way down deep beneath my feet, and I could feel the vibration through the soles of my shoes. It was distant, though; farther away. More explosions?

No, I didn't think so. Not explosions. The God Machine was down there and the earth was trembling. That wasn't difficult math for me to understand.

I tapped my earbud. "Echo T-team," I said, tripping over it, "r-report."

Top came on the line and used an executive code to isolate the call. "Where's your head at, Cowboy?"

"Exposed to green quartz," I said. "I'm clear now."

"How sure are you?"

"Sure."

"Okay then," he said slowly, and put the whole team on the call. "Listen up. Cowboy got dosed by the green quartz shit. He says he's clear, but nobody takes chances with *anybody,* do you copy?"

He said it harsh and hard and they all responded with passion. No one offered sympathy or support for me, because that's not how it's done. Later, maybe, we'd all get drunk over it. Now we had to survive.

"Give me a sit-rep," I said, fighting to keep the shakes out of my voice. There was a jumble of responses, and I heard pain in every voice. Every single one of them checked in. A few dents but no real injuries. No casualties; at least on our side. Thank God for that.

"Cowboy," demanded Cole, "what happened to the building? Was that a bomb?"

"I think it was another goddamn earthquake," I answered. "There's a God Machine in the subbasement and I think it somehow went active. Continue exfiltration," I ordered. Then I closed out of the team channel and got Bug on the line. "Kid, tell me you guys all saw what just happened."

"Cowboy, I—" he began, but stalled. The fact that his first question wasn't "Saw what?" was a total gut-punch.

Before he could say more, another voice broke into the call. "Cowboy, this is the Deacon. We saw everything your bodycam showed us. Are you in immediate danger from the person you just encountered?"

"No . . . no, I don't think so," I said uncertainly. "But I don't know what the hell it was."

Instead of answering, Church said, "Get your team out of that building. By any means necessary. Do it right now."

A new rumble shook the building, and the floor canted under

me. I grabbed the doorknob and jerked it open just as yet another massive jolt shook the whole building. Bigger than the first two. Ghost went skidding past me, his nails scraping lines all the way to the wall. He barked angrily, but at what? The building? The Earth? God?

I heard Duffy yelling over the shared line. "Echo Team, part of the south wall just collapsed. I think part of the parking lot's collapsing. Oh . . . *shit*! A fucking sinkhole just opened up in the parking lot. Everyone get out of the building *right now*."

Right now was a problem, though, because the building may have been falling the hell down, but it was also filled with a bunch of guys trying to shoot us. Christ. Ghost and I, weak and battered and sick as we were, ran down the stairs to join the fight.

CHAPTER ONE HUNDRED EIGHTEEN

THE ORB AT THE HANGAR
FLOYD BENNETT FIELD
BROOKLYN, NEW YORK

Doc Holliday and Junie Flynn stood in a factory in Russia without ever leaving New York. On one of the big screens they watched the feeds from Echo Team's bodycams as they moved through the shipping warehouse and rooms filled with manufacturing machines. The individual pieces were absorbed by a MindReader engineering program that applied design logic software and assembled the pieces. The software relied as much on its deep database of existing machinery as the imperative logic of a computer. The pieces could only fit together in so many possible ways, and the quantum system calculated hundreds of thousands of possibilities.

Junie watched holograms of the various pieces turn this way and that and then fly together, and moment by moment she could feel her heart race faster and faster, and her blood turn to ice. She knew what was coming. When she cut a look at Doc, it was clear the scientist did, too. Neither of them liked it. Both of them were terrified at the possibility. At the reality.

Calpurnia, speaking for MindReader, spoke so calmly as to be intensely unnerving. “Assembly complete,” said the soft, feminine AI voice. “Pushkin Dynamics is manufacturing and shipping God Machines.”

CHAPTER ONE HUNDRED NINETEEN

PUSHKIN DYNAMICS
VOSTOCHNY DISTRICT
RUSSIA

Doc called and told me the bad news. The scary news. The more she told me, the scarier it got.

“How many?” I asked, not really wanting an answer. I was working my way along a hallway that was cracked and choked with debris. Clouds of dust filled the air.

“It’s bad. Estimating the contents of the crates in the shipping bay . . . ? Maybe six hundred.”

I closed my eyes.

“These are the small ones,” she said, trying to sound hopeful. And failing. The small ones were what they used in D.C.

“How many were sent to the States? More than were used in D.C.?”

“We can’t tell yet.”

“Try harder,” I snarled, and disconnected from the call. *Six hundred God Machines in the shipping bay.* Good lord. So many questions caught fire in my head. How many had they already made? How many had been shipped? And . . . to where? Was D.C. only the first of a series of attacks?

“Yes,” I said aloud, and my voice echoed eerily.

I looked around and saw only damage. That felt like a statement about life in general. Whatever was happening here—an earthquake, a God machine coming to life, or maybe something as mundane and comforting as a fricking bomb—the building had taken a real beating. The walls and floor were crisscrossed with cracks and there was nothing left in the windows but broken teeth of glass. Cold wind blew in from outside, turning the swirling dust into frigid ghosts. The rumbling stopped again and now there was a heavy silence, but I did not buy the implied lie that it was over.

That orderly process was getting its ass kicked by memories of a guy dressed like a reptile walking out of walls and walking into walls. That was seriously scrambling my head, and I had no idea in hell what I was going to do with that.

There was sporadic gunfire from several different parts of the building, and then Bunny called, "Green Giant to Spartan, be advised Bravo Squad's coming out, but we don't want to walk into a shooting gallery. We could use some covering fire."

Duffy's reply was, "Yeah, yeah, don't tell your grandma how to suck eggs." Despite everything, he was trying to sound normal. Cool and confident. It was a soldier's trick; a battlefield version of fake it 'til you make it. But the cracks in his voice were as evident as those in the walls. Even so, I heard two spaced shots accompanied by the sound of shattering glass. Then a third shot.

"No one's waiting outside the door, kids," he said dryly.

"What about the parking lot?" asked Bunny.

"They left four men outside to guard the vehicles," said Duffy. "Mind you step over the bodies."

"A team is pinned down in the loading bay," called Cole. "Count twenty-plus hostiles between us and the door. Guards and staff, and all of them acting crazy."

"B team is in the same shit, boss," said Bunny. "We're about to get swarmed. No way we're getting through this without putting civilians down."

I took a breath in through my flaring nostrils and ground my teeth. "There are no civilians in here. This is a target-rich environment.

You are free to go weapons hot, weapons all. Get out of the building by any means necessary."

I heard Tate's bass thunder of laugh. "Then hold on to your nutsacks, kids, because it's about to get loud in here."

And by that we all knew he was about to unlock Doc Holliday's Toybox.

Bunny and Tate hunkered down behind a row of file cabinets as a bunch of Russians ran through the darkened office suite. There was no plan or coordination to the movement of the hostiles, and Bunny could see three distinct types of enemy: men and women in lab coats, upper-floor security personnel, and soldiers.

"Where are all the lab guys coming from?" murmured Tate. "Thermals said there were only guards in here."

"Got to be shielded labs like the ones Cowboy found," said Bunny. "No way to know how many cockroaches are going to come out of the woodwork." He shifted around to look into Tate's eyes. "You ready to do this?"

The bravado Tate had used when on the team channel was just that. The reality of using deadly force against people who were clearly under the influence of some kind of strange technology, and many of them civilians, was the kind of thing that could cripple a soldier. It could also make a soldier freeze, or hesitate. Or it could go the other way and turn a horror show into something approaching entertainment. None of those outcomes was good.

The balaclava hid Tate's mouth, but from the way the material moved it was clear Tate was licking his lips. Dry mouth. Fear. Yeah.

"I'm good to go, Green Giant," said the big former cop.

"You sure?"

"I'm good," Tate said. They studied each other for a moment longer, and then Bunny gave him a single, slow nod.

"Then let's do this and go home."

Tate pivoted on the balls of his feet and peered around the edge of their shelter. A pack of the madmen were coming their way.

"Fire in the hole," said Tate as he reached for the buttons on his wrist computer. He didn't yell it, though. It was like he was telling himself to brace for what was coming.

The blast and fire chased all shadows from the room.

"Sergeant Rock," cried Cole, "on your six!"

Top ducked, spun, and fired as a bearded man in a lab coat swung a heavy fire ax. The blade whistled three inches over his head as three rounds from Top's gun punched neat red holes in the attacker's chest. The ax, released from dying fingers, thumped hard between Top's shoulder blades and drove him down hard on his knees.

"Stay down," Cole yelled as she fired over him at two other attackers, catching them dead center in the sternum. Then she caught Top under the shoulder and hauled him to his feet. "Are you hurt?"

"Who cares?" he growled as he turned to cut down a pair of soldiers with submachine guns.

I heard Bug in my ear as I ran toward the sounds of battle.

"Cowboy, the building's coming apart."

"No shit," I said as I jumped across a four-foot-wide split in the floor that widened further as I cleared it. Ghost barked furiously and then ran and leaped across. I snaked out a hand and caught his harness and hauled him to safety.

"Listen," said Bug urgently, "the cracks in the structure are allowing the thermal scans to get a better picture of the sublevels. There are five big rooms, labs or machine shops or something. There are more than a hundred new thermal signatures. There are a lot of people down there."

The screams and gunfire that spiraled out of the closest stairwell made it sound like a war zone.

"No shit," I said again.

Pete Smith ran through shadows, moving from one parked car to the other, working his way around to a covering position on the back door.

He froze as one of the SUVs came rolling up and stopped outside, blocking the exit. Six heavily armed men piled out, each of them dressed in nondescript black. They left the engine running and closed on the door.

Peter could hear them talking in Russian, but he did not much understand the language, and it was too far away for his Mind-Reader link to capture and translate it. So Smith edged forward, staying low and out of sight. One of the newcomers spoke to the others with a clear voice of authority. He caught a terse order given by the leader in a clear voice.

"Ubit' vsekh."

Kill them all.

"Well, boys," murmured Pete to himself, "you called this play."

He took a fragmentation grenade from a pouch on his belt, pulled the pin, counted, and threw. He had done this a thousand times playing *Call of Duty.* He'd done this in training countless times—M69 practice grenades in nonlethal drills; live ones on a throwing range. He'd tossed stun grenades on the job working SWAT in North Carolina.

This was the first time he had ever thrown a real grenade at real people.

He twisted down and back behind the vehicle. There was a thump. Two men shouted warnings at once. Too late. And then the blast. His grenade landed in the middle of the tight knot of soldiers. The man most distant from it was no more than six feet away. From the time the spoon was released there were five seconds before it exploded. The men tried to scatter.

The injury radius of the M67 is forty-nine feet. The fatality radius is sixteen feet. All of the men were too close for any chance at all. They were blown apart, lifted, scattered, flash-burned. Ruined.

When Smith leaned out and looked through the smoke, what he saw did not resemble anything that had ever been human. It was the first time in his life he had killed. He knew—even as he moved out of cover and ran for the door—that he had just been marked. He knew he had crossed a line for which there was no going back, no do-overs, no absolution. He was now, and always would be, a killer.

He could feel his heart shift inside his chest as he ran.

"I'm sorry," he said as he ran through blood and stepped over torn legs and shredded skin. "I'm sorry."

The blast had punched the door inward, half tearing it from the hinges. Smith raised his leg and kicked. Once, twice, three times, and then the hinges snapped and it canted in and then fell with a monstrous clang.

Smith paused for one moment, and almost looked down at the blood on the ground and at the parts around him. He almost made that mistake. He did not, though. That marked him, too; but in a different way.

Steve Duffy had a perfect elevated shooting position, from which he could see most of the parking lot and nearly all of the arriving hostiles. Nine of them lay still on the ground and the rest had scattered. Duffy's rifle had a flash suppressor and a high-tech silencer to make tracking him difficult. And he could control the pigeon drones to emit flashes and digital recordings of gunshots from various points in the area. It was easy enough to time them so they flashed and banged as he pulled his trigger. That made the bad guys keep looking in the wrong direction. Duffy had suggested this to Doc Holliday and was delighted when she made it happen and implemented it for all field team snipers. There were rabbit drones that could do the same thing. In order to accommodate a speaker with enough fidelity for a loud bang, the drone had to be at least that big. Horseflies were too small.

All he had to do to trigger a distraction was tap a sensor with the little finger of his left hand, leaving the other fingers to steady his rifle and keeping his right hand completely free. Easy as pie.

Duffy believed himself to be a good man. Even-tempered, easy to get along with, generally happy. He held very little animosity in his soul, and did not even particularly hate the men who were pouring in to try and kill his colleagues. They were a problem to be solved. Angle and elevation, tactics and strategy, cause and effect. He was not a philosopher and tended not to brood. As he saw it, these guys put on targets when they put on their uniforms, and they made those targets glow in the dark when they rolled in here. Sucked to be them.

The newcomers had stayed outside since arriving, but now they raced for the doors, opening them and pouring inside.

"Oh, crap," murmured Duffy. He triggered another drone and fired at just the right time. His bullet punched through the chest of one man in black and blew a hole the size of an apple out of his back. The shot had been placed slightly off center so as to spin the target. Duffy triggered another flash and bang at once but did not fire, letting the noise and light turn every eye that way. The men in black opened up on a patch of empty darkness.

Duffy called in to Echo Team to tell them that there were new hostiles in the building. "I don't think they're affected by that green crystal shit, guys. Heads up. I'll see if I can thin the herd."

Duffy killed another of them. And another. He triggered four drones at once and the men scattered, thinking there was a kill team in the bushes on the wrong side of the parking lot.

In his head the Queen song "Another One Bites the Dust" played over and over again on a continuous loop.

The Toybox had a cute name, but it was a monster.

Bunny and Tate shifted around to watch what happened. Hardened as Bunny was, what he saw chilled him to the bone.

Two of the soldiers in black—the ones Duffy warned them about—charged into the room, yelling in Russian for everyone to stand down and throw down their weapons. One of the wild scientists rushed at them with a knife in his raised fist, but the soldiers cut him down without hesitation. Then they opened fire on everyone else. More of the soldiers came into the room, guns ready. The room was dark and they never saw the fishing line strung across the passage between a row of desks and a file cabinet. It broke easily and there was a flash of tiny silver flechettes whipping through the air and then three soldiers went down, their faces slashed to red ruin. They landed hard and their screams stopped all at once. The flechettes were smeared with Botulinum toxin type H, the deadliest neurotoxin available. You do not get clumsy-fingered around that stuff. The soldiers were probably dead before they landed.

One Russian who'd seen them fall waved off a second man and

they backpedaled and cut to their right to skirt the area . . . and ran straight into a spiderweb—an ultrathin filament that is nearly invisible even in good light. It wrapped around their torsos and the explosive chemicals in the woven strands combined and detonated, blowing one man in half and setting the other one's clothes on fire. The modified thermite burned into his chest and groin and thighs, and what was left of him collapsed in a fiery heap, arteries exploding in geysers of red. It was ugly, but it was fast.

Five men in three seconds.

Bunny and Tate crabbed sideways to the end of a row of cabinets, then broke for the door. The soldiers spun toward their movement, but Tate twisted as he ran and hurled what looked like a string of popcorn behind him. The kernels exploded with a white light so intense that the soldiers screamed and staggered and blundered through more of the trip wires. Bunny grabbed Tate and shoved him through the door as fire and screams filled the room.

Then someone came out of nowhere and tried to take Bunny with a burst of automatic gunfire, but the big young man had been ready. He jagged right and opened up with his heavy MPS AA-12 drum-fed combat shotgun loaded with explosive pellets. The first round hit the attacker center mass and blew him apart, Kevlar notwithstanding.

Bunny spun as three more of the Russians swarmed him from close range. They hadn't fired because their man had been between them and Bunny, but as that guy fell, the first Russian slammed shoulder-first into Bunny. The attacker was a brute who looked like he could bench-press a grizzly, but Bunny twisted and sloughed the impact off, and used the chunky stock of his shotgun to crush the back of the Russian's head. Bunny whirled as the other two brought their rifles up, but suddenly Pete Smith was there. He carried guns, but he preferred knives for close work, and had a matched set of marine KA-BARs in his gloved fists. The seven-inch blades whipped across arms and faces and throats and Smith walked between the falling bodies to check on Bunny and Tate.

"Lead the way, brother," said Tate, relieved to see his friend.

"Can't," said Smith, moving off to the left, "I got outlaws on my back-trail. We need to find Alpha Team and get out through the loading bay."

"This is going south on us fast," Tate grumbled.

"Welcome to Echo Team," said Bunny, and fell in behind the others, walking backward fast, his shotgun ready. There was the sound of running feet from the direction Smith had come, and he did not think it was the cavalry. "Go, go, go!"

CHAPTER ONE HUNDRED TWENTY

PUSHKIN DYNAMICS
VOSTOCHNY DISTRICT
RUSSIA

I paused at the entrance to the stairwell and watched the drama play out on my wrist computer. All of my team were fighting for their lives. I felt pride for the way they handled themselves; for their efficiency and skill and courage. I felt fear in an equal measure.

Alpha and Bravo Squads both needed my help, but Bravo had the Toybox and Alpha did not. So, I ran for the loading bay.

Ghost barked a warning that was immediately drowned out as a huge chunk of the ceiling in the stairwell dropped down with a murderous thud. Then I heard and felt the grumble of protesting timbers and the cough of shattering concrete as another tremor—heavier than the others—punched and kicked its way through the building. It rose up from beneath me and tried to pull the whole building down.

The tremor ended but there was a tension buzzing in the air and I did not for a minute believe this was over.

I tapped to the command channel. "Bug, kill the lights. Sergeant Rock, I'm on my way. Be there ASAP. Watch for me on your six."

A second later the whole place went absolutely dark.

I slipped on a pair of the Google Tactical Military Scout glasses that had been designed by one of Mr. Church's "friends in the industry" expressly for covert special ops use. I set the controls to night vision, and then Ghost and I went hunting in the dark.

The shadows were filled with wild gunfire, but the bad guys didn't know where to look or who was in there with them. Top and Cole immediately shifted position per our training patterns. They would have their night vision on, too.

I saw them moving from behind cover. Security lights flashed on, but Cole punched them out with three fast, precise shots. It seemed like there was an army of killers between me, Top, and Cole, and the door. We could see in the dark, though. They could not.

Bunny, Tate, and Smith came in from a side door, and then it was all of Echo Team against five times our number.

Long story short, we killed them all.

CHAPTER ONE HUNDRED TWENTY-ONE

PUSHKIN DYNAMICS
VOSTOCHNY DISTRICT
RUSSIA

Duffy stared through the scope and tried to understand what he was seeing.

The sky was growing intensely dark, as it often did right before dawn, but there were stars up there.

Except the stars were moving.

They weren't shooting stars, either. They moved with an eerie grace just above the horizon. Three of them in a perfect geometric formation. A triangle.

"No," breathed Duffy as he realized what he was seeing.

There had been training videos and photos in DMS case files, but he had never actually seen a T-craft before. He didn't want to see one now.

It came closer, lower.

It was wrong, somehow. It was too big, for one thing. The machines Howard Shelton had built were only a little larger than F-16s. This one was five times as big.

And the three lights, one on each wingtip, which he had mistaken for the last stars of a fading night, were no longer white. No, they cycled through white to yellow and now they burned with a brilliant, luminous green.

The T-craft moved toward the building in a dreadful silence. That twisted Duffy's brain, because it seemed impossible for something so large to be so quiet. It was like something in a dream.

Or a nightmare.

The green lights pulsed once, twice . . . and then every car in the parking lot seemed to judder and dance as if they were somehow coming alive. They were not. Duffy knew that because he, too, was trembling.

It was the ground.

It was another earthquake, and Duffy knew with absolute clarity that it wasn't the God Machine Captain Ledger saw in the basement causing this destruction.

It was the T-craft.

CHAPTER ONE HUNDRED TWENTY-TWO

PUSHKIN DYNAMICS
VOSTOCHNY DISTRICT
RUSSIA

"Spartan to Cowboy," Duffy yelled in a voice that had risen past alarm to actual panic, "you need to get out of there *right fucking now.* Half the damn building's coming down."

He was wrong about that.

It was the *whole* damn building.

The rumble swelled to thunder and suddenly the walls seemed

to shiver, shedding pieces of masonry and plaster like a dog shaking water off its coat. I heard a sharp sound within that roar and saw a massive chunk of the ceiling tear loose.

"Top!" I screamed, but Cole was already in motion, hurling herself at Top with a flying tackle that caught the older man around the waist and drove him backward. They fell together and rolled, bumping the ground with elbows and knees as ten tons of wood, steel, and debris whumped down exactly where Top had been. I saw Tate push Bunny and Smith away as a stack of wooden crates toppled and fell. The crates exploded on impact and pieces of God Machines went skittering across the floor.

"Out, out!" I yelled, but everyone was already running for the loading bay door as more cracks snapped their way across the ceiling. Behind me, Ghost gave a sharp bark of alarm and warning, and I spun to see him leap forward as the floor gaped like the mouth of some hungry monster. Gas and dust belched upward and for a moment I couldn't tell whether Ghost got clear or was swallowed whole. Panic flared in my chest, but then a white bulk sprang through the veil of dust and landed beside me, nails skittering on the broken floor.

"Cowboy," bellowed Top, "side door."

I spun to see him and Cole at the exit. She was fighting the lock. "There's something wrong with the lock," she said. "Give me a second. . ."

Top pushed her aside, tensed, and gave the door a savage kick. Top is as experienced a martial artist as I am, and he put every ounce of his considerable muscular mass and power, along with a metric ton of fear, into that kick. The door, however, barely budged. As I ran toward them I saw Top assess the frame, and I could see what he saw. The earthquake had twisted the frame out of true and the metal security door was wedged there. He turned and looked at the other exits, but debris was raining down in front of them. And there was no time for a blaster plaster. It was kick the door or get buried alive.

"Well fuck you and your mama, too," he roared as he gave the door a second kick. A third. Then I was there and we kicked it together. Once, twice, three times. On the fourth kick the door did not open, instead the whole wall simply cracked apart and collapsed backward away from us in huge chunks.

"Jesus Christ," said Cole. "You boys sure know how to impress a lady."

Top and I exchanged a wild grin. We knew we hadn't done it. The building was dying. But it was funny in the way things are funny to soldiers in the heat of battle. Cole ran past us, with Ghost at her heels. Top and I leaped after her, and not a moment too soon, because the rest of the ceiling came down with such a tremendous clap of thunder that the force picked us all up and hurled us into the parking lot. I tucked and rolled as I landed, but there was so much impetus that I rolled three times before I could get to my feet, and even then I pitched into a stumbling run. Ghost flew like an overgrown Underdog past me, yelped on impact, but did not fall. When I turned to see how Top and Cole were, they ran past me and skidded to a stop. We stared in horror as Pushkin Dynamics collapsed amid clouds of dust that was peppered with debris. I looked around but could not see anyone else.

Bunny and Tate came staggering and coughing out of the smoke to our left. Smith came running around from the right, his weapon up and ready. Then other figures emerged. Five of the Russians who had been inside the building. Two of them raised weapons. Smith put one down and a bullet from Duffy exploded the other one's head. The three remaining Russians bolted and ran. One of them looked up in the sky and screamed.

We looked up, too.

I heard Cole and Tate cry out. Smith hissed like he'd been burned and Ghost began barking wildly. Top, Bunny, and I merely stared.

There, hovering in ghastly silence above the building, was the largest T-craft I'd ever seen. It was massive, and the three glowing lights on its wings pulsed with that awful, familiar green. In the first hint of dawn I could see a faint shimmer in the air beneath the craft. At first I thought it was the antigravity drive, but then I understood.

"Run!" I yelled.

We ran.

We ran likes maniacs.

The deepest, loudest rumble yet made me turn back just in time to see what was left of Pushkin Dynamics crumble and fall into a massive sinkhole that kicked up a towering whirlwind of dust. Huge chunks of the parking lot snapped off and dropped down, too, and as I turned to run I caught the faintest hint of a glow from deep inside the cloud. Not the red or orange of fire and not the blue of burning gas. No, this was that same eerie green glow. It was there and then it was gone, totally obscured by the dust clouds.

We ran so hard and so fast, but the ground seemed intent on devouring us.

SUVs tilted and rolled down. Trees snapped off and fell. The air was filled with thunder and dust and death. A great geyser of water shot up from a ruptured main and hammered down on us.

There was a different kind of roar and I saw one of the SUVs—the one Echo Team had arrived in—racing toward us. It spun into a skidding, screeching turn and stopped and I could see a wild-eyed Duffy behind the wheel. We piled in and Duffy was moving before the doors were closed, his foot welding the gas pedal to the floor. We blew past the other Russian SUVs and Tate whipped an arm out of the window to deliver some going-away presents. As our car sped away I craned my neck to see a ball of black-veined orange lift the cars and hurl them at the trees, which immediately burst into flame.

The earthquake tried to kill us.

It tried.

But we erupted from the lot and onto the street and fled into the dawn.

CHAPTER ONE HUNDRED TWENTY-THREE

DMS SAFE HOUSE
UNDISCLOSED LOCATION
NEAR MOSCOW

Duffy parked behind the safe house and left the key in the ignition. Someone would come and take the SUV away to be sanitized, repainted, and sold in a legitimate used car lot. Two new cars were parked nearby and the keys for those were on the kitchen table.

We closed all the curtains, made coffee, made food, and sat in the kitchen without touching any of it. Lots of staring. Lots of eyes not making contact. Except for Bunny and Top, who glanced significantly at each other and covertly at me.

Eventually the others looked my way, too. It was a weird moment. We all had what felt like gallons of adrenaline supercharging our blood, and if they were anything like me, it was triggering more of the flight than fight response.

And it was Duffy who broke the silence. He held his hand up to his head, little finger and thumb splayed to mimic talking on the phone. "Hi, Mom? How was my day? Oh, you know, the usual. Alien lizard guys and spaceships."

We all cracked up. Fist-thumping, eyes running with tears, coughing and choking laughter. It happens like that sometimes. When it faded, it left us giddy, which was all nerves. Smith raised his hand like a schoolboy.

"Ask it," I said.

"Can I be excused and go back to the real world?"

"No. Next question."

"Then, okay," said Tate, "we got all this weird shit going on, and I'm going to need therapy for like ten years. But what does it mean? How's it all fit together? Does it even make sense?"

I turned my chair around backward and leaned my forearms on the back splat.

"It makes sense," I said. "Let me fill in the blanks of what you don't know, and then I want *you* to explain it back to *me*."

I went over every detail, starting from the Secret Service coming after me at the cemetery. I backtracked to hit the highlights of the Extinction Machine and Kill Switch cases. I told them what Doc and Junie told me. I gave them everything I had from Bug and Nikki. I told them about Violin and Harry. All of it.

It took a while. We ate scrambled eggs and toast and drank three pots of coffee. The morning burned on, chasing away the Moscow chill. Birds sang in the trees and the world turned as if everything was normal. When I was done, we had another long time of silence. I could see their eyes shifting to look inward at their own thoughts; I could hear gears turning. They were professionals, even the newbies. This was what the DMS was all about, and they were each members of Echo Team for a reason, and that meant it ran much deeper than their skills in a firefight. They were all smart and they possessed insight and intuition. Useful tools for this kind of work.

"So," I said, "talk to me."

"We need to get home," said Cole. "They shipped a lot more God Machines than they used in D.C."

"Yeah," said Tate, nodding, "if they hit us once, they're going to hit us again."

"It's more than that," said Top, and everyone looked at him. "Those guys in the T-craft ain't joking. These God Machines belong to them every bit as much as the Majestic Black Book did. Valen and the Russians may have trashed Washington, but it was the *original* owners of that tech who shoved Pushkin down the drain. One of them saw you, Cap'n, and if they're the same cats we saw on the road in Maryland, then they're trying to make a point. They told us they weren't our enemies, but they aren't our friends, neither. They *let* us get out of the building. That was them making a point."

Smith frowned. "What point?"

"Give us back our toys and do it right damn quick," I said. "Don't think they're going to give us a *third* chance."

Top nodded. So, after a moment, did everyone else.

CHAPTER ONE HUNDRED TWENTY-FOUR

THE HANGAR
FLOYD BENNETT FIELD
BROOKLYN, NEW YORK

Bug had a large team, one that grew faster than any other department within the DMS. Cyberterrorism and cybercrime were the greatest threat to governments around the world since the creation of atomic weapons—and far more insidious. They could cause incredible destruction without scorching the earth or irradiating the air. And the weapon of choice in the twenty-first century was a laptop with good Wi-Fi.

Bug was on the other side of that battlefield. He—like many of his employees—had begun his career as a gray-hat hacker. Some of his people had actually been black hats, though when faced with a choice of using their skills to help rather than harm, had made sensible choices. Others Bug had tried to recruit hadn't made the right call, and they were in prison cells, denied any access to computers.

This did not mean that Bug and his people respected laws. That was hardly the case. They routinely committed felonies of all kinds. The difference was the reason. For Bug and his department, it was very much a philosophy of the ends justifying the means.

When he forwarded requests through proper channels to initiate a nationwide search for the male identified as Valen Oruraka, a suspected Russian agent, his request was denied. The refusal came down from the highest office in the land, and was front-loaded with a blistering reprimand and all manner of threats should the Department of Military Sciences try to hijack already overtaxed systems for a wild-goose hunt. And various words to that effect. The doors of free and unfettered access to the various databases of the American intelligence networks were slammed in his face.

"Fine," said Bug, "be that way."

He called a brief meeting with his department heads and told them what he wanted them to do. None of the people in the meeting looked particularly dangerous. An outsider might label them geeks or nerds. Those labels were fair enough; however, they were very dangerous geeks and nerds. They were, in their way, every bit as dangerous as Joe Ledger, Top, Bunny, or any of the shooters who went into the field. None of Bug's team carried a gun; most wouldn't know how to even load one. They didn't need to. They had MindReader Q1

"Find Valen Oruraka," said Bug. "No mercy."

The "no mercy" thing was an unwritten in-house protocol. It meant that the full power of the world's most powerful, sophisticated, and subtle computer system, with all of its super-intrusion software, would be aimed at those closed doors and the trigger pulled.

The vast databases of the FBI and the Department of Homeland Security never saw them coming. They did, however, brace for an attack, because the White House told them to expect some kind of trickery from the DMS. They looked, but they did not see the bullet. Neither did the CIA, the DIA, the Secret Service, or any of the dozens of other departments and agencies in the collective law enforcement, intelligence, and investigative community. MindReader Q1 walked past all of their watchdog programs, invisible and unfelt It accessed trillions of files and rewrote the host software to erase even the slightest trace of its presence. No footprint was left, no echo, no scar.

Bug's intercom buzzed and he punched the button. "Thrill me," he said.

"On your screen," said Delilah, one of his best gunslingers.

An image appeared, showing a man with black hair, a goatee, Wayfarer sunglasses, and a cowboy hat walking into a convenience store attached to a gas station across from the Econo Lodge in Livingston, Montana. The black-and-white surveillance cameras got good views of him from three different angles. He wore boot-cut jeans and a Western-style shirt. The boots had thick soles and thicker heels. He did not look remotely like the man they were hunting.

Bug smiled anyway. He bent close and looked at a dozen pop-up windows that overlaid the video feed. Minute measurements of ears, cheekbones, nose, and other features flashed as they lined up with the college identification photo of Valen Oruraka.

"Got you, you son of a bitch," murmured Bug.

PART THREE

HOT TIME IN THE OLD TOWN TONIGHT

The darkness drops again; but now I know
That twenty centuries of stony sleep
Were vexed to nightmare by a rocking cradle,
And what rough beast, its hour come round at last,
Slouches towards Bethlehem to be born?
—"The Second Coming"
William Butler Yeats

CHAPTER ONE HUNDRED TWENTY-FIVE

IN FLIGHT
OVER CANADIAN AIRSPACE

"Cowboy," said Bug via the command channel, "the pilot says you're not going to Montana."

"No," I said, "I'm going hunting for Valen Oruraka."

"But Valen's in Montana," insisted Bug.

"Maybe," I said, "but that's not where he's going."

Doc Holliday said, "Activating the ORB. I think we need to have us a little powwow."

Suddenly she was there, with Junie, Church, and Bug, along with my whole team.

"Before I explain where I'm going, I want to go over some things. Let's take this one piece at a time. Honest opinion, guys . . . is Valen our Big Bad?"

"No," said Bug. "It's Gadyuka."

"I agree," said Junie. "Valen is a scientist and an idealist. He's fighting for a cause. Two causes, really. This New Soviet thing, and family. He thinks his uncle was unfairly blamed for Chernobyl. It's been the focus of his whole life to learn enough to be able to prove what he believes."

"He's still a bad guy, though," said Bunny. "Heartbreak or not, he's just killed nearly two thousand people."

"Two thousand one hundred and nine, as of this morning," corrected Doc. That hurt. It really goddamn hurt. I saw Top wince; Cole turned away, unable to look at anyone for a moment.

"Let me change the question," I said. "Is Gadyuka the Big Bad?"

"Yes," said Bug.

"Yes," said Doc and Junie.

"No," said Church. "Gadyuka is a spymaster and, possibly, an assassin, but the setup at Pushkin Dynamics could not exist without substantial political juice. Someone had to authorize the money for it, make sure it was left alone, guarantee that the tax returns would not be looked at too closely, and grease the wheels for the exports. That takes an infrastructure of considerable size. Gadyuka seems more likely as the director of field operations, but I can't buy her as being senior management. It would be too risky to run an op of that size from the field. That, for the record, is why I do not go into the field anymore. Any chain of command needs to be solidly anchored."

Doc frowned for a moment. "When you say 'infrastructure,' you're not talking about Russian Mafiya? Do you mean a ghost organization within the Russian government?"

Church shrugged. "That, or something bigger."

"What's bigger . . . ?" began Bunny, then he stopped and goggled. "Wait . . . you're talking about all the way big, aren't you? Like the *actual* Russian government. Are we talking Uncle Vladimir as the Big Bad?"

"Anything is possible, Master Sergeant."

I said, "No way something like this was happening without key people at the very top being involved. The risk is too big, for one thing. If a single shred of proof ever gets out connecting Russia to D.C., then it's an act of war. Such an event would splinter all global alliances. Countries would have to decide if they wanted to move fast to help crush Russia completely to prevent the use of the earthquake weapon; or they might align themselves with the New Soviet for fear of devastating retaliation. We have proof that Pushkin was shipping, or planning to ship, those machines to China, England, and other countries."

"Well, we have the shipping records from a building that no longer exists," corrected Bug. "That's not going to be enough for declarations of war. We're going to have to be careful how we break this."

"I agree," said Junie. "This news is like a nuclear bomb. Last thing we want is politicians overreacting and demanding that we put missiles in the air."

"For the record, guys," said Bug, "I'm not a fan of that whole mutually assured destruction thing. I've seen those movies. First bombs, then giant radioactive cockroaches and gorillas on horseback with carbines. No thanks."

"He's right," said Junie. "As much as I'm usually for full disclosure, there is no way to spin this that wouldn't result in a panic or a war. Or both."

"Can't let it go unanswered," said Top.

"No," agreed Church.

"Who do we tell?" asked Doc. "Last I heard everyone in Washington was hanging up on you."

"First things first," I said. "Valen is still out there. Bug, have you been able to decrypt the shipping records? How many God Machines were sent to America?"

"Well," Bug said, "some of it is still rough guesses, and not all of the shipments went to the United States. But if you include Canada, to places where there's a lot of interstate trucking heading down to the States, then it's a lot of them. Possibly as few as eighty and as many as two hundred."

"Two *hundred*?" cried Cole.

"Maybe more," said Bug. "It breaks down like this. Fifty of them were sent to Baltimore via container ships. The dockyard records show them coming in from three different points of origin, none of which are Russia. The shipments were moved around a lot. Any customs computer whiz would have missed it, because the guys at Pushkin were very smart about it. But . . . y'know . . . MindReader and all. So that accounts for all of the D.C. machines, and maybe some others as backups, or defective. There are no records at all after they were picked up by local trucking companies and delivered to a warehouse in Baltimore. They were probably picked up from there by Valen and his crew. The warehouse has been swept and is clean."

"Big question," said Doc, "but where'd the rest of the gol-dang machines go?"

"Five different ports in Western Canada. Coming from all sorts of fake destinations, but I can prove they started at Pushkin. The cargo was picked up by truckers and came into the U.S. via the standard routes through Canada Route 99, to Route 5 in Washington, and then west along 90, and probably south on 15."

"That means we can track them," said Duffy. "Good. Let's roadblock these sons of bitches."

"Bug, tell them the complications."

Bug sighed. "First thing is that most of the parts shipments were sent to their destinations months ago. Not sure how long it takes to assemble one of these God Machines, but from our experience with Gateway and Prospero Bell, it's tricky. There are all sorts of alignment issues, and you really don't want to get the math wrong."

"Assuming they know how to build them," said Top, "what's the timetable?"

"I think the clock's ticking down to boom," I said. "Bug spotted Valen in Montana. I think he's out there to oversee the next phase. But before we get to that, let's backtrack and add the other big piece of the puzzle. The *why*."

"About that," said Cole, "what's his beef with us? Unless I skipped that day in history class, we didn't sabotage Chernobyl." She glanced at Church. "Did we?"

"No," said Church. "We did not sabotage Chernobyl."

"Then why did he wreck Washington? And why's he out there maybe setting up some other attack?"

"Why did the Soviet Union collapse?" asked Church.

Cole thought about it. "It was economics, wasn't it? Trying to keep up with us, building up their military and all that. We have more natural resources and a stronger economy."

"Top marks," said Church. I'm sure if he'd actually been in the same room with us he'd have given her a cookie. "There were other elements, but as is often the case, it comes down to money. We have more of it, and we used it more effectively. There was tremendous economic turmoil, poverty, corruption, and internal strife in the aftermath of the fall of the Soviet Union. We prospered and even offered financial aid, which seemed like compassion and forgiveness, but wasn't. It never is in such circumstances. The ideal outcome for America would have been to turn Russia into another postwar Japan or Germany. That nearly happened, too, but there was too much resentment and it lasted much longer than the tensions between America and its enemies during World War Two. The Cold War never truly ended, at least for key players in Russia."

"There's a conspiracy theory," said Junie, "that the influx of Russian Mafiya to America was a deliberate tactic. After all, so many of them were former Soviet military."

"There may be a great deal of truth in that, Miss Flynn," conceded Church. "Which supports the view that the Cold War hasn't ended. When the Wall fell, the Cold War went dark, but it is still being fought as a long-game special operation. There are hawks on both sides, and in times when those hawks were not in open political power, they worked tirelessly behind the scenes. It's only been more recently that the hawkish views in Russia have become less well hidden. Maybe because they knew that they were going to finally win that war."

"So, wrecking D.C. was what? Their opening move?" asked Duffy. "Are they going to hit New York next? If so, why aren't we going there? That's where the money is. That's the heart of the economy, unless I'm reading *Forbes* magazine wrong."

"Money passes through there," said Church. "It's the brains of the national economy, just as Washington is the center of the infrastructure. But it's not the heart of the economy."

"Then what is?"

I bent and tapped some keys on my laptop, and some pictures I'd preloaded popped onto the virtual walls of the ORB. Oceans of wheat blowing in the wind; thousands of acres of corn and barley and soy; groves of fruit trees. "This is America," I said. "This is what Valen is going to destroy."

Duffy shook his head. "How? He'd need a million God Machines to cause that many earthquakes."

"No," said Doc Holliday, her face draining of all color, "he won't. He could do it with the machines they've already sent to America."

"But . . . *how*?"

"Tell them, Cowboy," said Doc.

I could see the precise moment when Junie got where I was going.

She went pale as death. Doc, too. They looked like they wanted to flee. As if that was even possible.

I pushed another key and one more image came up. It was of Yellowstone National Park in Wyoming. "Beneath the park is the Yellowstone Caldera," I said. "Church, you even listed it as a possible target when we were at the hospital. One of our own analysts put together a paper on this a few years ago when we were tracking that Apocalypse Cult in Montana, the ones we thought might have brought in some old Soviet nukes bought on the Chechnyan black market. Because Montana's just north of there, the analyst put the caldera at the top of our worry list, and for a good goddamn reason."

"Maybe I wasn't in school that day," said Smith, "but what the hell is a caldera?"

"It's a large volcanic crater," Doc explained. "There's a huge one beneath Yellowstone National Park. Between thirty-five to forty-five miles across. Absolutely massive. There is a nasty geological hot spot. Very similar to the Hawaiian Islands, actually, but this one's on continental crust rather than oceanic crust. Geologic hot spots are when molten rock or magma continuously upwells from the mantle, burning a hole in the lithospheric plate above. That's what causes eruptions on the surface of the Earth. What makes this one so bad is its size and location. Unlike in Hawaii, this one is not surrounded by ocean. It's surrounded by America's agricultural states. Shorthand answer is that we're talking about a supervolcano."

"Well . . . shit," breathed Smith. "Sorry I asked."

"Buckle up, because here's more bad news. Each of the past three Yellowstone eruptions occurred between six hundred thousand to eight hundred thousand years ago. The last one was six hundred and thirty thousand years ago, so we're technically due. By best geological guesses, though, there is only a small chance it will erupt in our lifetimes."

"Unless Valen uses his freaking machines," said Tate.

"Yes."

Duffy looked around. "Okay, but we had Mount St. Helens, right? I mean, bad, sure, but—"

Doc looked sick. "Kids, if the Yellowstone Caldera blew, we'd be looking at a force twenty-five hundred times that of Mount St. Helens. That's a blast equal to twenty-seven thousand Hiroshima-sized atomic bombs."

No one spoke. No one could.

Doc nodded and turned the knife. "The last one laid down a layer of ash over most of the western central United States that is estimated to have been six hundred and sixty feet thick. That means the ash bed would have been thick enough to bury modern skyscrapers. And that doesn't even count the ash released into the atmosphere. A supervolcano would change the climate, cooling the Earth. Maybe not into another ice age, but enough to affect crops."

"*How* bad?" asked Bunny.

Doc Holliday turned to him, and for once she was not wearing that perpetual smile. Maybe things had to get this bad for her to lose the jackal grin.

"How bad?" she echoed. "Let's see. There would be about anywhere from three hundred to a thousand inches of ash over everything from Missoula to Denver and Boise to Rapid City. Gone. As much as thirty inches of it on the next ring outward, from Seattle to Chicago. Beyond that? Maybe as little as a couple of inches in New York. But all across the country's fields and farms, there would be destructive hot ash; which would also choke the streams and rivers. We would lose years' worth of crops, probably see a die-off of over ninety percent of animals like pigs, cows, and chickens. Timber and mining would stop. And you wouldn't have enough people left to bury the millions of dead."

"And," I said into the absolute silence, "we may be out of time to stop it."

CHAPTER ONE HUNDRED TWENTY-SIX

GRAND HYATT HOTEL
NEW YORK CITY, NEW YORK

Gadyuka sat cross-legged on the bed with three laptops around her. Her flight to Paris was scheduled to depart in six hours, which gave her plenty of time to watch it all start. Plenty of time before planes departing New York would be affected. She would be eating in a sidewalk café near the Louvre before it all fell apart. After that? She would take her time making her way back home. Three or four weeks, with plenty of time to sightsee and watch history change via the media.

The news from Washington was stunning, and all of the coded messages from back home were filled with congratulations and praise. The ones from the highest offices hinted at promotion, medals, and some more substantial rewards.

The prudent part of her mind would have had her halfway back to Moscow by now, but where would the fun be in that?

Fun.

She thought about that. The word, the concept. Was this fun?

Gadyuka reached over to the bedside table for the glass of vodka and took a thoughtful sip. The effect would be fun. The New Soviet. A new party. Bigger and stronger than the one that had fallen when she was a little girl. Something that would outlive her, and would both dominate and stabilize the world. Yes, that would be fun.

But getting there . . .

Well, that was something else. Valen was falling apart, and her people on the ground out West told her that he was looking stressed and a little manic. Gadyuka was more than a little certain that her pet mad scientist did not necessarily want to live in the new world he was creating. That was something she could understand. It would be a problem for the New Soviet to have so many sleeper agents and others who had spent so much time in the West return to live in a true Communist society. Could they ever really adapt? And how could some, like Valen, reconcile what they had done with the peacefulness needed to be good citizens?

Could she do it? When she'd read the e-mails and those hints at substantial rewards, was that a clue of some kind? A warning? Were they testing her to see if she was motivated by financial gain rather than the good of the Party? In the old days many millions had died to try and erase that hunger from the hearts and minds of the people.

She sipped the vodka. It was Van Gogh. Not even a Russian brand. The stuff was made in Holland, for God's sake. It was her favorite, and her next three favorite brands were Belvedere from Poland, 1.C.1 Vodka from California, and 42 Below, which came up from Australia. Gadyuka could not actually remember the last time she drank Russian vodka.

She would have to give all of that up. Her fine clothes, the freedom to buy anything she wanted anywhere she wanted. The food. Good lord, she would miss American food. And all these lovely vodkas. Gadyuka drained her glass and shimmied off the bed to get the bottle out of the ice bucket. She was halfway there when the door to her hotel room blew inward off its hinges. It slammed into her, lifted her, smashed her against the bureau. The TV leaned forward and fell, exploding in sparks as it landed, partly on the door and partly on her.

At first Gadyuka was too stunned to even understand what just happened. There was the smell of burned wood and plastic explosives in her nostrils and blood in her mouth. A fire alarm began screeching and the overhead sprinklers kicked on with a venomous hiss.

She looked up and there, moving slowly through the smoke, was a figure. A woman she did not recognize. Tall, slender, in her late fifties or early sixties, with a face like a fierce and unforgiving queen in an old painting. She was dressed all in black—pants, a formfitting top, gloves. The woman tossed a small detonator onto the floor and drew a slender, double-edged blade from a sheath behind her back.

"Get up," said the woman in a heavily accented voice. It was not a Russian accent, not a Russian face.

"Wh-what . . . ?" stammered Gadyuka as she reached into her thigh holster for her gun. The door completely hid the action.

"I said get up," said the older woman.

Gadyuka fired four shots through the door.

CHAPTER ONE HUNDRED TWENTY-SEVEN

THE HANGAR
FLOYD BENNETT FIELD
BROOKLYN, NEW YORK

"The real question," said Junie Flynn, "is what would cause the Yellowstone Caldera to erupt?"

She and Doc Holliday were in the ORB alone now, with Bug on the screen. Echo Team had signed to try and cobble together a mission directive. Nevertheless, the holographic conference room was crammed with hundreds of images and lists of data and other information. Some of it swirling as MindReader made connections; others stable and as fixed in place as a bullet hole.

"The last eruption at Yellowstone was about six hundred and thirty thousand years ago," said Doc. "To get things rolling now, if it was all left up to Mother Nature, and if she was in a bitchy mood, then you'd need the underground magma chambers to fill up and build pressure before it blows."

"What can Valen do with his damn machines?"

"Well, since I haven't had a chance to actually study the machines, I guess he'd have to use it to open conduits—cracks, in other words—from depth to allow magma to flow upward beneath Yellowstone. That happened around the Long Valley Caldera in California in the 1980s. Lots of earthquakes and dome-like swelling were thought to indicate an imminent eruption. They evacuated people, but luckily it never blew."

"I saw the green reptile guy do something that folded the stone walls in the hallway at Pushkin like they were shower curtains. If that's how the technology works, then Valen can use them to open channels to the magma chambers."

Bug asked, "If they could do this, then why hit Washington?"

Doc Holliday walked around the hologram of the God Machine, then turned to look at a series of photos of Valparaiso, the military base in Ukraine, and newer pictures of Washington.

Junie fielded that. "Joe once tried to explain boxing to me. He said some boxers like to batter their opponents' arms to make them too sore and achy to lift, which makes them too slow to block a solid punch to the face. Other boxers go a different route and try to hit their opponent on the nose early on. Especially if it looks like the other boxer's nose hasn't been broken before. It's a psychological and physiological thing. I mean, what happens when someone gets a broken nose?"

Doc shrugged. "Intense pain. Bleeding. Externally, of course, from torn tissue, and internally. Blood in the throat and Eustachian tubes. The eyes water. If the punch is heavy enough there's even a chance of whiplash. And there's possible disorientation and loss of balance if the synovial fluids in the inner ear are disturbed."

"Right. All of that is disorienting and distracting. Joe says that he's won more fights by punching the nose than by any fancy martial arts moves. Plus, he says that we tend to ascribe emotional meaning to physiological effects. Break a nose and the boxer's eyes tear. For an experienced boxer that's nothing; but to someone far less experienced, the tears are equated with crying, with weakness or fear."

"Which then becomes an internal and therefore greater distraction," said Bug. "Okay, I get it. It's what boxers call 'taking the enemy's heart.' They lose the fight because they are too distracted, too emotional, too confused, and no longer confident in their own strength."

Doc gave him a dazzling smile. "Well, well, you're more than a sexy mind and clever fingers, aren't you. I'll text you my private number."

"Behave," said Junie.

"Where are you going with this?" asked Cole, steering the conversation back to the point.

Junie spread her hands over the satellite image of Washington, D.C. "This is America's broken nose. We have a new administration, a president who isn't a politician and hasn't handled a major crisis, fractured infrastructure, political infighting, and party polarization. Then the earthquake hits. Now we have pain, distraction, indecision, the practical—or perhaps *im*practical effects of party politics, disorientation, and too much raw emotion."

Cole's eyes went very round as the full impact of this hit her. "God almighty. If Yellowstone blows, we're not going to be able to react or respond in any way except badly. Jesus H. Christ, Esquire. If we can't stop this, we're going to lose the whole damn country. Not just the crops . . . we'll lose *everything,* including any chance we have of protecting the survivors."

Duffy gave a weird little smile. "But, hey, no pressure."

CHAPTER ONE HUNDRED TWENTY-EIGHT

GRAND HYATT HOTEL
NEW YORK CITY, NEW YORK

The hotel door was heavy and it took effort to shove it off of herself, but as soon as it thumped away, Gadyuka scrambled to her knees, raising the gun, aiming it through the falling sprinkler water.

At nothing.

The older woman was not there.

Water splatted down on the carpet, making bloody droplets dance. Then there was movement coming from her right, from the wrong side of the room. Gadyuka snarled and spun and fired at the same time a foot lashed out and caught her in the hip. Gadyuka whirled and tried to use the impact to spin her all the way around so she could slam her attacker with the butt of the pistol. She put all her fear and anger into it, but the gun whistled through empty air as the woman ducked and punched her hard in the ribs. Gadyuka coughed and staggered, and then the woman chopped down with an elbow, nearly breaking her hand and sending the gun spinning away.

Gadyuka struck with her left hand, landing a brutal blow over the attacker's heart that sent her staggering back. They paused for a moment, taking each other's measure. The woman was bleeding from a gunshot wound to the lower left side, though based on the speed with which she moved she was either not badly hurt or insane. Maybe both.

"Who the fuck are you?" demanded Gadyuka.

The woman smiled a killer's smile and there was blood on her teeth. "Call me Lilith."

Gadyuka could actually feel her blood turn to icy slush. *Lilith.* Dear God.

The savage smile brightened. "Good. You've heard of me. *I've* heard of you. Your pet toad, Ohan, told us so many interesting things about you before we skinned him alive and cut his throat. He was only a lackey, but you actually gave the order. Imagine what I am going to do to you."

Gadyuka dove for the bed, bounced onto and over it, and snatched up her purse. She dug something out, flung the purse at Lilith, and rose into a fighting crouch, snapping her wrist to release a telescoping spring-metal fighting stick.

"Come and take me, you old hag."

Lilith reached into an inner pocket and drew out a knife with a blade so long and slender it looked like a needle. A boning knife.

"If you insist," she murmured.

CHAPTER ONE HUNDRED TWENTY-NINE

IN FLIGHT OVER WYOMING AIRSPACE

Bug called me just as we were dipping toward the runway.

"I think I have something," he cried, sounding agitated to the point of near hysteria.

"Hit me."

"It was you mentioning the Chechnya thing during the ORB conference. About the Apocalypse Cult? Well, a bunch of the members of that cult came from prepper groups. Not the normal survivalists, but the lunatic fringe. The ones who *want* the world to end so they can be proven right. The ones who seem to think it'll solve their problems, cancel their debt, and get the government off their back."

"Yup. So what?"

"We ran backgrounds on them and have kept tabs on the scarier ones. Some are dead now, some are in jail, and a few dropped off the grid to the point of no Wi-Fi or cell phones and no utility bills in their names. But there's a bunch of them—just over forty—who are very much on the grid because they work for one of two big trucking companies based in Washington state."

"Ah," I said. "And now you're going to make me happy by telling me that these are the same companies Pushkin Dynamics sent their boxes of God Machine parts to, aren't you?"

"Yes, I am," he said, and almost giggled. "It gets better, though. When I hacked the records for the companies, I found shipping records for a last batch coming from one of Pushkin's dummy companies. The trucks carrying those shipments arrived this morning."

"Arrived *where*?"

"That's what I'm trying to tell you. Their cargo is listed as parts and equipment to install a thermal venting system intended to regulate pressure buildup at the Yellowstone Caldera. Cowboy . . . they're right there, right now."

CHAPTER ONE HUNDRED THIRTY

GRAND HYATT HOTEL
NEW YORK CITY, NEW YORK

People were running and yelling; alarms howled and the sprinklers hissed. A hotel assistant manager, responding to the crisis, reached room number 2301 and skidded to a sloshy stop in the doorway. The entire frame was ruined and the door lay inside, the dense wood splintered and pocked with holes. The whole room was in ruins. TV shattered, mattress torn and bloody, sheets scattered around, coffee maker crushed as if stepped on, and the big reinforced glass window completely smashed. The only consolation—and it was a small one—was that there was no fire.

He yelled at someone to shut the sprinklers down, but they twitched and sputtered and died anyway, the heat sensors failing to find cause. Water dripped heavily onto the soaked carpet. His boss, a stern-faced Asian woman of fifty, came hurrying into the room and stopped beside him.

"What happened?" she demanded. "Where's the guest?"

All he could do was shake his head. They stared at the window and walked numbly toward it in complete silence, terrified of what they might see splashed far below. They leaned carefully out over the jagged teeth remaining in the frame.

A few people stood on the pavement, glancing down at the glittering shards of glass and then up to see where it had come from.

"Where's the body?" asked the manager.

Six floors lower, in a junior suite with the blackout drapes closed and opera playing very loud, two women had a conversation in the bathroom.

One was dressed only in blood. The other wore white, disposable coveralls of the kind used by crime scene forensics technicians.

It was a corner suite, chosen because there was no one on the other side of the bathroom wall. The soprano arias sounded enough like screams to convince passersby in the hallway, should other screams get too loud.

Lilith sat on the closed lid of the toilet, forearms resting on her thighs. She held the boning knife loosely between the thumb and index finger of her left hand.

"You disappoint me," she said in a voice that almost sounded gentle. "From your reputation I expected more. But . . . I suppose it does not require much to stab from a shadow or fire a gun through a window. A pity."

Gadyuka cringed in the tub. She was able to breathe, and weep, and talk. So many other things were beyond her now.

"You still have a chance, my pet," said Lilith. "You have to make a very important decision now. What means more to you—your cause or your skin? And I am not speaking in the abstract."

"Please . . . ," begged Gadyuka. "I . . . I . . . can't . . ."

The head of Arklight cocked her head to one side. "Is that really true? I wonder."

The aria playing was Maria Callas singing "Suicidio!" from *La Gioconda*. Very appropriate.

CHAPTER ONE HUNDRED THIRTY-ONE

THE HANGAR
FLOYD BENNETT FIELD
BROOKLYN, NEW YORK

Church stepped away from Doc Holliday and Junie to take the call.

"Lilith," he said. "How is Violin?"

"Alive. But that's not why I'm calling. Do you know the name 'Gadyuka'?"

Church stiffened. "Yes. Why?"

"We had a long conversation," said Lilith as casually as if she were discussing yesterday's news. "About earthquakes and green crystals and God Machines and destroying America. In any other circumstance I would think she was lying, but trust me when I say she was very earnest in convincing me of the truth of everything she said."

"I believe you," said Church. "We already know quite a bit and have made some guesses about more. Did she say anything about Wyoming?"

"Yes," she said. "Tell me you have a team there already."

"They are on the way."

"Then they may already be too late."

CHAPTER ONE HUNDRED THIRTY-TWO

YELLOWSTONE AIRPORT
WEST YELLOWSTONE, MONTANA

"How we going to get there?" asked Bunny as he bent over a map. "Map says that you have to go all the way around the damn thing to get there by road. Four and a half damn hours."

Top and I leaned down next to him. I grunted. "There's got to be another way if they're bringing in parts. A service road somewhere."

"There," said Cole. She tapped the glass on one of the windows. There, a few thousand feet below us, we could see a semi creeping along a dirt road through the rocky terrain.

"Not on the map," said Bunny. "They must have put it in for the venting job."

Since Nikki had found out about the truckers, she backtracked into state and federal records to find the details on the venting project. It was there, but it was hidden. Not under top-secret labels, but behind veils of what had to be deliberate obfuscation. Someone did not want it found, and by the time we were wheels down, Nikki came back to us with the name of the official go-to person in Washington.

"Who's Jennifer VanOwen?" asked Smith.

"You've seen her," said Tate. "Blond chick who stands behind POTUS and nods a lot."

Smith shrugged. "She one of our bad guys?"

"I'm not liking her much right now," said Top.

"She had the road built," said Bunny.

"Jesus, Farm Boy, you took a nap on the plane and woke up stupid. Yeah, that road'll get us there, but it's how these motherfuckers have been getting their God Machine parts out there in the first place."

"Just trying to make lemonade, old man."

"Fuck you and your lemonade."

The jet thumped down, jostling us all since none of us had bothered to buckle up for safety. By the time it was done rolling, we were locked and loaded. Tate disarmed and opened the door and deployed the collapsible stairs.

"Wheels?" asked Duffy, but the answer was rolling right toward us. A huge Toyota Sequoia painted in the colors of the National Park Service. "Well, there *is* a God."

Shorthand is, we commandeered the truck, crammed enough weapons and ammo to storm the gates of hell, and squeezed all of Echo Team into the SUV. Top drove like the world was on fire.

CHAPTER ONE HUNDRED THIRTY-THREE

THE HANGAR
FLOYD BENNETT FIELD
BROOKLYN, NEW YORK

It took too long for a call of this kind to make it through channels. In previous years, and even in the early days of this administration, the call would have gone straight through. Ultimately, he had to fudge the math and have Bug force it through the cell towers and security barriers and make it damn well ring in the president's hand. While he waited for POTUS to answer, Church calculated the number of laws that call broke. Seven, he concluded.

"How in the hell did you call me?" demanded the president. "I blocked your number."

"Mr. President," said Church, "I need to inform you of a grave threat to national security."

There was a beat and for a moment Church expected the line to go dead.

"You have one minute," said the president.

Church told him of the conspiracy involving Russia, Gadyuka, Valen Oruraka, and Pushkin Dynamics. He named all the right names and offered to provide substantial evidence to back it all up. It took more than a minute, and the president was still listening at the end of ten minutes. The ensuing silence was a great deal longer.

Then, "And you can prove this?"

"I can, Mr. President."

"Do you understand that you're asking me to declare this an act of war?"

"Yes, sir."

"And that I'll have to respond by declaring war."

"There may be other strategies to deal with that," said Church.

"This is a hell of a lot to ask me to believe. Wyoming? Since when is there a volcano in Wyoming?"

"For quite a long time now."

"Well. I've never heard about it."

Church found it difficult not to smash the phone against the wall. Brick, standing a few feet away, his big arms folded across his chest, raised one eyebrow. Church shook his head.

"And," continued the president, "you want me to believe that Jennifer VanOwen is involved?"

"It would appear so. At least as far as facilitating deliveries to our chief suspect, Mr. Oruraka."

"Jennifer's been here in Washington. She's all over the news. She's a damn American hero. Hurricane VanOwen."

"I've seen the coverage, Mr. President," Church said with forced patience. "It does not change the facts. And it does not alter the timetable. In the short term we need to evacuate Wyoming, Montana, and Idaho for a start. I have a team on the ground, but we need to be proactive to protect as many American lives as possible."

"What do you mean by a 'team'? What team? Who's running the ground operation? It had better not be that criminal Ledger."

"He is my finest field team operative, and he is the one who I trust most to run point on this. His team is on the ground in Wyoming and we have National Guard converging to provide support and containment."

"No."

"Sir?"

"No damn way. I didn't authorize that."

"Not to be indelicate, sir, but the DMS charter allows for necessary shortcuts like this in order to get ahead of any threat of this kind."

"Did you hear me? I said I didn't authorize the National Guard."

"I heard you, Mr. President."

"When I get off this call I am going to call the governors of Wyoming, Montana, and Idaho and tell them that you do not have my approval for this operation."

"Mr. President, we need to act together and with a great deal of urgency in case my team is unable to—"

The line went dead.

Church looked at the phone, wondering if it would feel good to smash his phone to bits. He did not, but it was close.

CHAPTER ONE HUNDRED THIRTY-FOUR

YELLOWSTONE NATIONAL PARK

The semi had a forty-minute lead on us and the driver had the pedal down. It was a rough grade, though, and the sheer mass of the truck kept its top speed down around fifty.

Top Sims went a hell of a lot faster than that.

This time we all buckled up, or there wouldn't have been enough of us left to pour onto the ground. My aching back felt every goddamn rock and divot along every goddamn inch of that goddamn road. It hurt, but more than that, it made me mad. The truth is that if you eat enough pain you want to vomit fury.

Even so, even with Top racing at full speed, every second seemed to take an hour.

"Hey," yelled Smith over the roar of the engine, "I think we're good. I mean, think about it, these guys aren't going to set off the volcano while they're here, right? They're not stupid; they don't want to die. Right?"

Tracy Cole turned her head and gave him a long, withering stare.

"What?" he demanded.

"During that whole conversation about those doomsday prepper truckers being part of an Apocalypse Cult, were there any words in particular that stood out?"

He started to say something. Didn't. Turned tomato red, avoided her eyes, and checked that the magazine in his gun was properly loaded. I thought I could hear Top chuckling.

There was no actual way to get there straight as the crow flies. Hills, slopes, craters, thermal vents, and downright dreadful terrain made even the access truck route a snakelike fifty miles. Ghost yelped a few times. I could sympathize.

The truck was in sight now, though mostly veiled by a drifting wall of brown dust. I turned to look at the team. They were all tense. None of us had gotten enough sleep on the plane. They—well, *we*—were all wired and scared. Angry, too, but that was as much resentment as it was animosity toward this country's enemies. When someone is trying to kill *most* of the population of the nation in which you live, it actually stops being purely patriotic and gets very personal.

Let's face it, true patriotism is personal. It's connected to more than the physical substance or a land, and a hell of a lot more than a piece of cloth, no matter how symbolic it was. We did not pledge allegiance to the flag. Not really. Anyone who did was missing the point. It was always a love of who we were, and what our country represented. Not when it stumbled or erred, and there are a lot of times it did that, from slavery through its attacks on civil and human rights; but for what we all aspired to. We all wanted the country to live up to the best ideals implied by our Declaration and Constitution. All the rah-rah "America first" and "my country right or wrong" histrionics is so much bullshit unless it's built on a foundation of deep love for what truly made America great in the first place. A desire for freedom, diversity, democracy, and as a machinery for making positive change.

Tate took some pigeon drones out of a case, synced them with his tactical computer, and hurled them out of the window. They rose high and flew away. They were faster than either vehicle, but they had to circle around the dust cloud or risk having grit clog their engine intakes.

"Wish I was driving a Betty damn Boop," groused Top. "Could use me some rocket pods right up in here."

"Chain guns'd be nice," agreed Bunny almost wistfully.

"I'd be okay with a couple gunships in the air," said Duffy. "Some recreational hellfire missiles. You know, just to start a conversation. A minigun on rock 'n' roll."

"We have air support on the way," I said. "Wyoming and Montana National Guard are both sending air and ground forces. We got here first, so we get to be the opening act."

"We know how many of these truckers are here?" asked Smith.

"Depends on how many were in each truck," I said. "And how

many of them stayed. If Valen needs them to help him finish assembling the machines, and if there are as many machines as we think, it could be upwards of forty and as many as ninety."

"Not enough," said Tate.

"Captain said we have backup on the way," said Cole.

"No," replied Tate, "there won't be enough of *them*."

She studied him a moment, and at first I thought she was going to blast him for trash talk. She didn't. Instead, Cole held her fist out for a bump. "Hooah," she said.

"Hooah," he replied. And we all echoed it.

"Getting a live feed, boss," said Tate, and I opened the same screen on my wrist computer. There were eight big rigs parked haphazardly around a small prefab structure. Great mounds of dirt and rock were heaped near a couple of heavy-duty front-end loaders and a massive bulldozer. There were a dozen men there, some looking through binoculars at the approaching truck. One of them, though, stood on the roof of the structure and was looking *past* the truck.

"We're made," I yelled, but at that moment a man walked out from between two mounds of dirt with an AK-47 in his hands, stood wide-legged in the center of the road, and opened fire. We all ducked down, the windshield blew apart, and hot rounds tore into the car.

CHAPTER ONE HUNDRED THIRTY-FIVE

YELLOWSTONE CALDERA
YELLOWSTONE NATIONAL PARK, WYOMING

Top turned the wheel hard and skidded off of the road. The SUV bounced horribly over ancient lava rock. He stamped down on the gas, crashed through some withered brush, and crunched against a jagged ridge.

"Out!" I bellowed, but Bunny was already shoving people toward the doors. Cole jerked up the handle and fell onto the hard-packed dirt and rock, with Smith nearly crashing down on her. They slithered like snakes to the crest of the ridge as more bullets punched chips of stone out of the irregular shelter. The others got out, too, but the two big men, Tate and Bunny, risked death to drag out the equipment bags and boxes. The metal boxes were lined with plate steel sheathed in Kevlar, so the others took them and built a stronger shelter. Duffy immediately opened his rifle case and took out his weapon. Top slid out of the seat and stumbled, pawing at his face, which was smeared with blood.

"Are you hit?" cried Bunny, beginning to crawl toward him, but Top waved him off.

"Glass cuts. Shit. Get your big white ass under cover, Farm Boy, before they shoot your dick off."

"Watch your own ass, Old Man," grumbled Bunny.

"How many shooters?" asked Smith.

Tate was studying the video feeds from the drones. "Count three. Guy in the road, one on either side. And, shit, there's two guys going around the truck, heading into the hill south of us. One of them has a scoped rifle."

"They brought a sniper," complained Smith. "That's just—"

There was a *crack* and his head whipped around to see Duffy raise his head from the scope of his rifle. "*Had* a sniper."

"Nice damn shot," said Top.

"What was that?" asked Cole. "A thousand yards."

"Give or take," said Duffy as he worked the bolt on his CheyTac M200. "Hold on."

Another *crack*.

Tate snorted. "Other guy's down. Tried to pick up the hunting rifle."

"Of course he did," said Duffy. "That's why he was with their sniper. Two hunters."

"Should have sent four," said Smith.

Duffy shrugged. "I brought more than two bullets."

"We get out of this," said Bunny with a grin, "I'm going to get you drunk and laid in the town of your choice."

"Sexist asshole," murmured Cole, but she was grinning, too. Then we all stopped grinning as the other shooters opened up with a new fusillade. From the drone video feed, it was clear there were five shooters now, and they had all taken cover.

"I don't have a good line on any of them," said Duffy. "They're shooting over stuff and around corners. Putting a lot of ordnance downrange to keep us pinned. Figure they got some other play."

Top met my eye and gave me a hard look. We both knew what that play was. Bunny caught on, too.

"We need those damn helos," he said.

I tapped my earbud to get an ETA and got the news. The National Guard had been recalled. Instead, state police were coming to arrest us, with the job to hold us until the FBI could take custody. My team all heard it. It was insane news. It was the kind of thing that could steal the fire from a dragon's heart. We were seven people up against an army of survivalists, pinned down behind a nonarmored vehicle with sketchy ground cover. We were a handful of soldiers trying to save our entire country. We had every right to expect to see the cavalry come galloping over the hill, flags flying and guns a-blazing.

There was a special *bing-bing* in my ear that I knew was the private line between Church and me. I held my hand up for silence. They nodded, understanding. They turned away and screwed their game faces on and looked for opportunities to return fire.

"Captain Ledger," said Mr. Church, "I'm sorry that it's come to this. I spoke with the president and outlined the entire case. He believes that we are taking actions outside of our jurisdiction."

"Is he insane? Doesn't he understand what's going to happen?"

"I would like to think that it is the devastation in Washington that has shaken him so badly that he can't think clearly. That and the fact that he doesn't have enough experienced professionals around him to keep things going if he loses a step. That isn't what we have here. He either does not believe me or can't afford to, because accepting the truth means having to address other issues within his administration, his career, and his life. I don't think he can afford to spend that coin."

There was a lot of gunfire and I didn't know if the others could hear me. Our mics are tiny dots beside our mouths and they have incredibly sensitive pickup. A whisper, a murmur, and that's enough.

I said, "We're fucked."

"Are we, Captain?" he asked calmly. "This is the war. This is the job. We are in place because we are the select few who can think outside the box enough, act quickly enough, hesitate less often, and act more determinedly than anyone. I formed the DMS to be exactly that. Without ego or distortion of our own capabilities. We are our own backup. And if the situation is so dire that we lose faith, then there is no plan B. So, tell me, Captain, where does that leave us? Tell me if we are out of options. Tell me if we have already lost."

I looked at my team. They were already fighting. They were doing their jobs even though they'd heard the same news, that we were out here alone. It was a humbling thing to see. As if he could feel my eyes on him, Top looked over his shoulder at me. He gave me a single nod.

I gave it back.

To Church I said, "The sun's going down. That will help us more than them. But I think that also means the clock is ticking down. It would do more harm to have the volcano erupt at night. Rush hour in some places, diminished workforce at hospitals and with first responders. I think that's Valen's timetable."

"I agree. It coincides with the last shipments arriving now. What is your plan?"

I smiled. "My plan is to kill every last one of these evil sons of bitches."

I heard a sound. A rare laugh from Church. We were both standing on the edge of the abyss and I'd just told him I was going to jump. "Then good hunting, Captain," he said.

CHAPTER ONE HUNDRED THIRTY-SIX

YELLOWSTONE CALDERA
YELLOWSTONE NATIONAL PARK, WYOMING

We huddled together and I told them my plan.

They grinned like a bunch of ghouls. And, if there was fear in their eyes too, and a little panic, then they kept it locked down and tightly secured.

We had to dismantle some of our wall in order to get to the right equipment, and as each box was emptied it was put back into place but angled to give us loopholes for counterfire.

Included in our gear were six pigeon drones, a hundred horseflies, grenades, night-vision goggles, more body armor, and more of Doc Holliday's Toybox. Most of the latter, though, required application. They were booby traps to prevent pursuit rather than tools for a frontal assault. Didn't matter. Smart soldiers improvise, and Tate was proving himself to be a devious bastard. Cole, Smith, and Bunny maintained a steady return fire. Not wasting bullets, but making sure we didn't get rushed. Duffy still couldn't get a good kill shot, but he punched holes in whatever the shooters were hiding behind, delivering eloquent warnings about what would happen if they got sloppy. One of them did, in fact, lean too far out, and Duffy blew his arm off in a very loud and messy way. The screams resulted in a shocked pause and then a new barrage of outraged automatic weapons fire. That was fine. Let *them* waste bullets.

The sun was a tiny yellow ball that was rolling fast off the edge of the world. There were no clouds, nothing to reflect the sun and maintain the illusion of light. When the sun went down, it dragged the rest of the day with it.

In combat, the largest force owned the daytime, because that's when their numbers allowed them to dominate the landscape. Small and more mobile forces owned the night.

"Do it," I said, and Tate launched all six drones at once, steering them low so they flew no more than five feet above the ground. Four of us opened up with heavy fire and then two of the drones made their flash-bang faux gunfire as they moved out at right angles from our position. The incoming gunfire immediately split, firing into the dark to catch runners. That was the fiction we were selling, and anyone who'd had military or paramilitary training would buy it for what it seemed to be: shooters giving cover fire while runners broke cover and ran to flank the enemy.

We reinforced it by sending two more drones and reducing our central fire to a pair of guns. The flash-bang effects now seemed to be coming from all over the landscape. It scattered the enemy fire, thinning what was aimed at us.

Tate sent a swarm of horseflies out and I watched their infrared video feeds. The shooters were breaking up and spreading out to intercept us, not knowing that they were hunting ghosts.

While Duffy was hunting them. He had his sound and flash suppressors in place, and as the truckers ran to cut off flanking attacks they were pinned against the darkness through his night vision. Duffy fired and fired and fired. Single shots, and any chance of them tracing it back to him was confused by Top firing straight up the pipe with a noisy Heckler & Koch 416. He'd even risked a magazine with tracer rounds as a dangerous way to reinforce our fake-out. When that mag was dry he swapped in one without tracers and shifted to the far end of our shooting blind, letting return fire pound a spot where no one was standing.

Tate shifted the drones to our left as if we were running in a widely staggered line to try and claim the high ground. The incoming fire shifted that way, with a greatly diminished attack on where we actually were.

"Time to go, Cap'n," called Top.

I slipped on my Google Scout glasses, switched them to night vision with a geodetic survey overlay, thermal scan, and distance meter. The others did the same, checked that they were carrying as much ammo as possible, and buddy-checked each other's armor. The horseflies gave us a clear picture of the best route. It was tight and we had to move fast, but we'd scattered their focus. One by one Echo Team broke right and vanished into the darkness until only Top remained. He emptied a full magazine into the dark, paused to make sure it was clear he was reloading, then fired another, and during this pause he ran to catch up.

We scattered as we ran, with Duffy and Smith heading uphill to establish an elevated shooting position at a distance that would, for most people, be too far away to do any good. Duffy wasn't most people; and sharp-eyed Smith would be his spotter and bodyguard.

Top and Cole split to circle the shed from the far side, while Bunny and Tate cut sharply left to come in tight on the blind side of where the knot of shooters were by the trucks. I sent Ghost ahead of me to scout the best path, and I followed his RFID chip signal on the glasses lens.

Sure, the bad guys had numbers and position, they had some training, and they knew the terrain. But no matter how many times they'd chased each other around in the woods playing soldier, they were *not* soldiers. And even if they'd worn uniforms once upon a time, we were way the hell out on the cutting edge of military tech. It was going to suck to be them.

No, let me go a step further with that. These were militiamen who hid behind Second Amendment protections and then tried to use those same laws to hurt their countrymen. They were traitors to everything they claimed to stand for. It didn't matter if they knew they were working with the Russians or thought they were somehow defending their own skewed view of America. The truth was that they were the enemy and Echo Team was going to war with them under a black flag.

CHAPTER ONE HUNDRED THIRTY-SEVEN

YELLOWSTONE CALDERA
YELLOWSTONE NATIONAL PARK, WYOMING

The drones kept popping their fake rounds and there was scattered return fire as the truckers chased phantoms through the night-black landscape. Ghost led the way and I followed through a weird green world. Night vision always turns the world into something from a science fiction or horror movie. Intense blacks and whites, and a thousand shades of green. Of all the colors that I did not want to see, it was that one. My imagination kept populating the darkness with green-scaled giants, writhing tentacles, and creatures too bizarre to even comprehend, let alone describe.

When I saw an actual shape detach itself from the dense shadows I felt a brief but intense flash of irrational fear. But it wasn't a lizard man or even a Closer. It was a burly trucker with an AR-15, and he was swinging the barrel to track movement. Ghost, probably, but my dog knows the game. I saw Ghost circle fast and come up behind the shooter and then stop because I had not given a command to kill. It was dark and quiet and I needed to get to the shed without raising an alarm. I knelt and went still and let the trucker chase movement that wasn't there. He came within six feet of me, and if he'd turned toward me I'd have shot him. I carried a Sig Sauer with a Trinity sound suppressor and he was in my kill zone the whole time.

"What you see?" called another trucker.

"Nothing. Deer maybe," called the guy near me. "Coming down to you. I think those pricks are up on the east ridge."

He moved away and for now that meant he got to stay alive. For now.

I rose and moved, and Ghost moved with me.

The shed was close, and I came in from a corner angle, keeping my eyes on two sides of it. There were four guards out front and two more standing at a distance. I could see light streaming out from under the shed's door, but there were no windows. It looked like the kind of simple structure they placed at the top of mines, betraying a much more complex facility below.

I knelt again and tapped my earbud. "Cowboy to Spartan, what's your twenty?"

"About seventy yards upslope and to your right," said Duffy. "I can see you and the pooch. Got a good view of the shed. Count six targets."

"I'll take the four out front as soon as you drop the others."

I never heard the shots, but the two men standing farthest from the shed spun away and fell. Then I was moving, yelling, "Ghost, *hit, hit, hit!*"

Even as Ghost surged forward I began firing as I ran. The truckers were looking at their fallen comrades and turning to look for the shooter. They expected him to be coming from where they thought we were. I came at them from the side and slightly behind, firing, firing. Two of them went down right away and Ghost did as ordered and hit a third, snapping his metal teeth down on the wrist of his gun hand. The fourth swung his gun at me and I jagged right and shot him in the chest, but all it did was stagger him. Must be body armor under his coat. Fine. I put the next round through the bridge of his nose and his head snapped back on a broken neck as blood splashed on the shed door.

I pivoted to see if Ghost needed help. He didn't. There was a severed hand on the ground and a savaged throat gaping beneath a face filled with profound surprise. As I watched there was a final, feeble spurt of blood from his carotids and then the man slumped over.

The whole thing had taken about three seconds.

There are a lot of myths about the bite strength of dogs. Sure, wolves can chomp down at 400 pounds per square inch on average and up to 1,200 PSI when defending themselves, but dogs can't. For dogs, the common American breeds with the strongest bites are Rottweilers, who have the strongest bites at 328 PSI, and bull terriers at 235; but shepherds are in the number-two slot with average bites at 238. Now, add a lot of combat training designed to teach Ghost how to destroy bone and tendon with six titanium teeth, and the math gets ugly.

"Good doggy," murmured Duffy in my ear. "Coast is clear, Cowboy, but you better haul ass. Pigeon drones are picking up a shitload of thermals coming your way."

I ran to the shed door and amped up the thermal imaging, but it bloomed way too hot, from the lava down deep. Thermals were going to be useless in there; so was night vision. I took off the glasses, swapped in a full magazine, cautioned Ghost to be as silent as his name, and eased the door open.

The space inside was built to allow access to an elevator and a set of spiraling stairs. It was hot as hell in there and my clothes were instantly soaked, despite the whole "but it's a dry heat" thing. It felt like every drop of moisture in my flesh was being leached out. Every other spare inch of floor was crammed with stacks of equipment, and along the walls were racks of black coveralls of a kind I'd never seen before. They looked like rubber but when I touched them the material felt more like a flexible plastic. Thick, though, and a quick examination revealed that each was double-lined to allow for tubes and wiring. Small harnesses and rows of tanks gave me the answer. These were some kind of advanced coolant suits to allow Valen and his team to work down near the thermal vents.

I wasted no time and put one on. As I did, it occurred to me that Ghost could not go with me, and he couldn't stay in the shed because there would be nowhere for him to run if the truckers came in. So I told him to go find Top. As usual, Ghost didn't like it, but he gave the soft *whuff* that's his version of "hooah." He ran out into the night. It bothered me to see him vanish into so deadly a darkness, and I had a horrible feeling that I might never see him again.

"Sergeant Rock," I said quietly, "Ghost is coming to you. Can't take him down with me."

"Roger that, Cowboy," he said, then added, as if reading my mind, "We'll keep him safe."

I finished sealing the suit and as the last zipper pull locked into place, the internal works activated. Cool air flooded through the outfit, but it did not blow up like a hot-room hazmat and instead kept a normal shape. That made sense, since Valen and his team needed to be able to assemble the God Machines. One precaution I'd taken was to remove my combat harness, and I buckled it on over the suit, allowing me access to extra magazines, grenades, and fighting knives.

The suit's cowl came complete with goggles with orange-tinted lenses that reduced glare but were nonetheless sharp. It was nice tech and I hoped I lived long enough to steal it for the DMS. Junie could probably find a use for it, too, maybe for firefighters battling California forest blazes.

I removed the sound suppressor from my gun, ignored the elevator as a damn death trap, and started down the stairs. I had an unnerving flashback to my college days, when a comparative lit teacher had us read Dante's *Inferno.* As the narrator passes through the gates of hell he sees an inscription:

LASCIATE OGNI SPERANZA, VOI CH'ENTRATE

It amused me at the time, but absolutely chilled me now to reflect on the translation: *Abandon all hope, ye who enter here.*

CHAPTER ONE HUNDRED THIRTY-EIGHT

YELLOWSTONE CALDERA
YELLOWSTONE NATIONAL PARK, WYOMING

Top Sims moved through the night like a murderous specter from some old folktale. That's how Tracy Cole saw it.

There were a lot of truckers out now, using flashlights mounted on rifles or shooting flares into the sky. Echo Team cycled its Scout glasses to compensate for the flashes of light and instead of being blinded used them to pick their targets. Tate and Bunny were down among the trucks now, wiring everything with nasty items from the Toybox. Duffy was the finger of God, flicking people off the planet one bullet at a time. Cole had taken two of the militiamen out so far, both with double-taps from her Glock. She preferred handguns for night fighting.

Top went another direction, using stealth and speed to bring him close and personal, and then he used vicious kicks and a bayonet to drop and kill. He never used a wide variety of techniques; instead, like most expert fighters, relied on a few simple moves over which he had great mastery. No one saw him coming, and he killed them. It was unadorned and frank, devoid of emotion or complication. It was strange to see it, because she knew that emotional fires had to be burning in Top's head and heart. He was a passionate man beneath all that control. Maybe that was why he never hesitated and showed no mercy at all. There was too much at stake.

They moved through the nightmare landscape of volcanic rock, twisted shrubs, and brutal death.

Bunny and Tate reached the truck that they'd followed here. Only three of the truckers were still using it to fire on the wrecked SUV. Those men were intent on their work and did not see the two hulking figures that came up behind them. They did not even hear the silenced shots that killed them.

"Open the truck," ordered Bunny, and when they'd swung back the doors they found crates of parts identical to what had been found at Pushkin. The truck was only a quarter full, though.

"There's not enough stuff here," said Tate. "Shit. I think they have most of the parts already."

"Yeah, damn it," growled Bunny, and he called it in. There was no answer from Captain Ledger. "He must have gone down to find Valen," he said to Tate.

"Want me to blow this stuff up?"

"No. Rig it so it blows up whoever comes looking for it. Then we'll go set up a playground between here and the shed."

Tate nodded and set to work. He heard footsteps and a man call out in inquiry, but didn't turn to see what was happening because there was a sudden muffled cry of pain that ended in a wet gurgle.

"Work fast," murmured Bunny as he lowered a dead man to the ground.

"Jesus, man, I'm working as fast as I can."

Tate cut a look behind him in time to see Bunny fire three shots with a silenced pistol. A running man suddenly lost all coordination and fell badly. Bunny put a foot on his throat and shot him once more in the head.

"Work faster."

"Christ," murmured Smith, "they're coming out of everywhere. How many of them are there? I thought there was supposed to be like . . . forty, tops."

Duffy looked up from his scope at the shadowy figures swarming across the landscape. He stopped counting at sixty.

"No National Guard," said Smith. "No backup coming at all."

The two men looked at each other, and some truth passed between them. An understanding of the reality of this mission.

"Then we take as many of them with us as we can," said Duffy. "We buy the captain enough time."

Smith licked his lips and he could feel something within him change. It was something he'd read about and heard about from other soldiers. When you think you are going to make it out of a fight, you cling to the hope of survival, and sometimes that keeps you alive, and sometimes it shines a light by which the bad guys can take aim. But if hope dies in you because you know—without a shred of doubt—that you aren't going to walk off the playing field, then you become a different person. It is no longer about winning in order to go home. The fight becomes a hunt, where all that matters is clearing as many of the enemies off the board as you can so you can be laid to rest on a mountain of their corpses. It was old thinking, maybe going back to the Vikings or the Romans or the Celts or whomever. It was the battle madness they used to write about in old epics.

So be it, thought Smith. *If they want me, then they'll have to earn it.*

He set aside the night-vision binoculars he was using to spot for Duffy and picked up his own rifle.

"Hooah," he said.

Duffy grinned. "Hoo-fucking-ah."

They opened fire at the swarming figures.

CHAPTER ONE HUNDRED THIRTY-NINE

YELLOWSTONE CALDERA
YELLOWSTONE NATIONAL PARK, WYOMING

The stairs went down and down and down. Through long patches of darkness and into a light that seemed to come from the burning heart of the Earth herself.

Great coils of steam rose from below, and when I looked over the edge of the railing I could see the work platform far below. A dozen men milling like ants around something that gleamed like silver. A God Machine, I had no doubt. A big one. Bigger than the one in D.C. And around it were smaller ones that the workers were lifting and carrying away with them. From what I could make out, they had finished the construction of the devices, or at least all the ones down there. But they were still placing them.

My heart lifted and perched on a fragile branch of hopefulness. There was still time.

The stairs were metal, so I had to move slowly enough to stay silent, and it was a long way down. The elevator looked like it opened right behind the big machine, so taking that would definitely have been suicide.

I moved down and down, and I could feel the rising heat even through the suit's cooling system. Sweat stung my eyes but I blinked them clear.

Down and down.

When I was two flights up from the bottom I paused again and gave my earbud the tap-pattern to let them know I could hear but not speak. I wanted confirmation that they were seeing this, too.

There was absolutely nothing. Not from the TOC, the ORB, or my team. I glanced around. Down here, deep inside the caldera, this close to a trillion tons of lava and gas, yeah . . . no signal of any kind was getting out without a cable running up to the surface.

Fair enough. It meant the assholes down there weren't speaking to anyone, either. I crouched and watched, letting what I saw teach me.

The big God Machine was maybe six times larger than the smaller ones, though less than a fifth the size of the massive one at Pushkin. It had a line of green crystals in slots on its side, but they were covered with a thicker slab of glass that was veined with wires. Some kind of signal blocker, I guessed, to keep the effects of the activated crystals from affecting the workers. Okay, that made me unclench a little. And I thought about the wires in the coverall I was wearing. Maybe a backup to that? I hoped so.

The God Machine was already on. I could see it vibrate and the air around it shimmer. The effect made the stone wall against which it was set look insubstantial. Hard to say whether that was an accurate assessment or merely a distortion effect, like a heat haze. No green men stepped through, though; nor did I catch any glimpses of alien worlds.

The smaller machines were not active, it seemed. The workers picked them up and placed them on carts before pushing them down side tunnels. When I leaned to look into the tunnels it appeared as if they curled around, and my guess was they formed a ring around what I assumed was a rock-lined thermal vent. I'm no scientist, but I've blown enough things up to be able to make an assessment. If the vent was as big as it looked, based on the arc of the tunnels, then it seemed likely Valen was going to use his machines to drastically destabilize it once all of the devices were on. The big machine already running had probably set the groundwork—literally—by tampering with the fault lines running through the whole caldera. I would have bet a shiny nickel that there were more of the big ones somewhere. Running. Getting the whole thing ready to blow.

I saw something odd—well, something in keeping with the general and pervasive oddness of the scene. The tunnels themselves seemed to shimmer, very much like the walls had in the hallway at Pushkin. What did that mean? Were they real tunnels, or some kind of matter disturbance effect of the God Machine?

The big question remained . . . what next? I had a whole bunch of grenades as well as some blaster plasters. I could blow the big God Machine halfway into orbit. What, though, would be the effect? Did those machines just turn to rubble when they blew? The ones in D.C. exploded with real force. What would happen to the big vent if I destroyed this one?

Would destroying it be enough? What if the machine needed to be adjusted and dialed down, like cooling a nuclear reactor? The more complex the machine, the greater the forces within it, the more complex it gets to turn it off.

I mean, sure, I could try and force Valen to do it, but how would I know if he was doing that or turning it so high it overloaded? I already half suspected he was out of his mind and maybe suicidal, because he was here instead of fleeing the country before it blew.

Which meant . . . what? Was our race against the clock not as down to the wire as it seemed? If so, damn, that would make a really nice change and I would promise to devote my life to good works and Jesus. Hell, I'd get a sex change and become a nun if this was all next week's doomsday clock.

But I didn't think so. Too many loose ends. Too many of these militiaman flunkies who could get drunk and talk big and ruin the whole thing. No, I thought the clock was ticking and boom time was close.

Real damn close.

But how to stop it? I was pretty sure the tallest of the three men nearest to the big machine was Valen Oruraka, because he was giving orders to two others.

Well, as my old math teacher tried to explain to me once, when faced with a complex problem, begin by solving those parts you understand.

Okay.

I crept down to the ground level, picked up a clipboard that was resting on the edge of a cart, walked over to the men loading a God Machine onto another cart, and shot them in the head. Another man cried out and tried to unsling a rifle. He died, too.

First part of the problem solved.

The tall man whirled and stared at me through the orange lenses of his goggles. Yeah, the same eyes I'd seen in D.C. looking down the barrel of a Taser, except now I had the only gun.

"Hello, Valen," I said.

CHAPTER ONE HUNDRED FORTY

YELLOWSTONE CALDERA
YELLOWSTONE NATIONAL PARK, WYOMING

He stared at me with eyes filled with strange lights. Not madness, exactly, but definitely a profound surprise, horror, and something else. Relief? No, that was wishful thinking on my part.

"Ledger," he said hoarsely.

I touched the barrel of the gun to his face, right between his goggle lenses.

"Turn it off," I said.

Valen reached up a gentle hand and moved my gun barrel. Not to the side, but down, placing it over his heart. Making a statement about his acceptance of what I could do, but also creating an easier line of communication between us. It was a strangely intimate act.

"I can't," he said.

"You can," I said.

"Go ahead and kill me, Captain Ledger. I've already accepted that I'm dying today."

"Yeah, well, hoorah for you. This isn't about you making a grand sacrifice to usher in the Novyy Sovetskiy."

He looked surprised for maybe half a second, then nodded. "She told me you were smart."

"You mean Gadyuka?"

I couldn't see his mouth, but his eyes crinkled. He was smiling. "Very smart."

"She's dead," I told him.

"Oh."

"You're not surprised?"

"A little. She seemed like the kind of person who would be hard to kill," said Valen.

"Do you want to know how she died?"

He shook his head. "You're trying to rattle me. But it's a little late for that." He gestured to the machine. "You see, I really *can't* turn it off. That was a design requirement from Gadyuka. She was the only one who had the code. Did the person who killed her bother to ask? No. I can see it in your eyes. They didn't, which means the code died with her." He paused. "Do you know why Gadyuka had them build that into the machine? Because of me."

He looked down at the gun, shook his head, and stepped away from me, walking over to the rows of green crystals.

"She said it was because of them. The Lemurian quartz. We were all afraid of the effect . . . which you've seen. If you spoke with Gadyuka then you know that the activated crystals drive people crazy. Murder. Suicide. Mass hysteria. You saw it in Washington. I've seen it many times. Gadyuka was afraid that the men working with me here—and I—would go crazy and damage it. So they built in safeguards, a locking mechanism that freezes the controls once they're set. I couldn't stop it even if I wanted to."

"Mr. Valen," called a voice, "I . . . holy shit!"

Another pair of truckers had come back with an empty cart, and had seen the dead bodies on the floor. They went for their guns. I already had mine out. I shot them both and all Valen did was stand there and watch. I swapped out my magazines and pointed the barrel at him again.

"How far did you idiots think this through?" I asked. "You're going to kill a hundred million or more people in America. Maybe half the population of Canada and a big chunk of Mexico. If this thing blows really big, then you have nuclear winter and then there's famine everywhere. Including your New Soviet."

"I know," he said, and his eyes glistened. "God help me, I know."

"So why do it? Is wrecking half the world really going to bring about the future you want?"

"Yes," he said. "Prevailing winds will sweep the ash to parts of Europe, some of Africa, and across Asia. We've run the computer models a thousand times. Of all the superpowers, Russia will be the least damaged. When the skies clear and the snows melt, we will be the last powerful nation left standing. We will be able to control the smaller agricultural nations. Easily. We have a nuclear arsenal and they do not. The United States, the United Kingdom, France, Israel, and China will be crippled. They will *need* our help, and we will give it."

"You mean you'll sell them wheat and corn as long as they pay for it by becoming good little Communists."

Valen shrugged. "The projections say that after a time of turmoil there will be one world. Fewer people, less of a strain on resources, and a strong central government. A world government." He paused and again I saw his eyes crinkle. "You think I'm insane, of course." He shrugged. "You're probably right."

I lowered my pistol and stepped closer. "How is it worth it? How is any of this worth it?"

Valen shook his head. "I love my country, Captain Ledger. I would do anything to save it."

"Even this?"

Tears fell from his eyes. "If I could stop the machine, Captain, I would. I think. I . . . I don't know. I drove all the way here from Washington, listening to the news as they counted the dead." He stopped and shook his head like a dog trying to shake off fleas. "I went to church, you know."

"You what?"

"I went to church. To ten of them, all through Washington.

Every night before we turned on the machines, I went to church. I talked to the priests. I'm an atheist, Captain. I don't believe in God. Not a Catholic God or any god. I only believe in my country, and yet . . . I went to church. I talked about sin and redemption. I asked the priests how the church reconciles the sin of killing with the Ten Commandments, with scripture. With Jesus. I couldn't understand it, you see, and I wanted to. I wanted to know that I wasn't going to hell."

"You're an atheist and you believe in hell?"

He laughed. "Maybe it proves I'm insane. I had to ask the questions, Captain, because I felt that I was confronting a crisis of faith. Not in God, but in my purpose. You see, my group, my party, does not accept that the Cold War ever ended. The war goes on. It is complex and hard to explain, but it persists."

"The war is the war," I said, and he looked surprised.

"Then you understand."

"I understand devotion to country. I understand raising a gun to defend those you love."

"And do you love your country?"

"Yes," I said.

"Right or wrong? No matter which direction it takes?"

"I'm not on the policy level."

He shook his head. "You have an opinion."

"I'm sworn to protect my country, even when some of the people running it make the wrong call or do the wrong thing. When I want to affect policy, I go and vote. I don't blow up half the world. And you want to talk about sin? Sure, the history books your new Communist Party will allow people to write about this will probably paint you as a hero. But you're a monster. If this machine goes off then you will be the biggest monster in the history of the world. Nothing is worth that. No cause, no religion, no politics can ever justify this. Never. And I think you know it."

He turned and looked at the machine. "When I came down here, Captain, I thought about what would happen if I could somehow switch it off. But I can't. To do that would be to betray more than my party. It would mean betraying my people. It would mean abandoning them to greater hardship than they have ever known. Within a hundred years, Russia, as we know it now, will be gone. Bankrupt, torn apart, broken beyond repair. I can prevent that and help usher in an era of genuine abundance. America will fall, yes, and other nations will be hurt, but Russia will enter a golden age of prosperity." He looked at me, tears streaming down his face. "How can I turn aside from that? What choice do I have left?"

"None, I guess," I said as I raised my pistol.

And that's when someone shot me in the back.

CHAPTER ONE HUNDRED FORTY-ONE

YELLOWSTONE CALDERA
YELLOWSTONE NATIONAL PARK, WYOMING

Top Sims saw Tracy Cole fall.

He was reloading when the shot rang out and her cry rose like a tortured gull into the night. He pivoted and fired, catching the shooter in the upper chest, just above the line of his body armor. The man went down, but by then Top was running to where Cole had dropped. He went down on his knees, trying to see how bad it was.

Her face and throat were painted with black, which is the color blood looks through night vision. He felt for a pulse and found it, but it was too light and too fast. Then he saw the hole. It was in her upper right side, and it had to have been made by an armor-piercing round. It was big and red and had tunneled through her upper chest and out through her shoulder bone, doing dreadful damage.

"I got you," he said as he tore open his pouch for sterile packing to stanch the blood flow. "I got you."

"I know," she said, but her voice was very far away.

Ghost came running toward them. Top tried to ward the dog away. There was a sharp scream and suddenly Ghost was falling, his white fur turning the same slick, oily black.

* * *

Everything went perfect. Until it didn't.

The truckers and militiamen came thundering along the road, racing toward the shed with the ferocity of men answering a call. Bunny knew that it had to mean Captain Ledger was in the middle of it. They were coming from the hills, though. Only a few were going to pass between the trucks, which was where the majority of the traps were set.

"Shit," cried Tate.

"I know," growled Bunny as he snatched up his drum-fed combat shotgun. "Guess we do this old school."

They opened fire. Seven militiamen went down in the first barrage, but the rest turned and the sounds of gunfire—booms and bangs and cracks and pops—filled the night. Bunny and Tate ran for cover, but there were simply too many hostiles and they covered too wide an area. There was no safe place left.

Behind them the first of the smaller band of truckers kicked their way through the Toybox trip wires and the world turned from dark night to fiery day.

From his shooting spot, Duffy did not have the challenge of finding a target, but of having too many targets. He fired and fired, killing or at least dropping someone with every shot. More kept coming.

A dozen yards to his left, Smith was lobbing grenades with great force, sending them arcing down into the mass of shooters. The blasts blew apart the truckers, but more ran forward over the dying and the dead.

Smith screamed and fell back, and when Duffy looked he saw his friend sprawled like a starfish, mouth gasping like a fish, eyes white and staring upward at the night.

Duffy reloaded and fired. And fired.

CHAPTER ONE HUNDRED FORTY-TWO

YELLOWSTONE CALDERA
YELLOWSTONE NATIONAL PARK, WYOMING

The bullet hit me between the shoulder blades and knocked me against Valen. The punch was so hard my gun went flying and the barrel cracked one of the Russian's goggle lenses before falling out of sight.

I dropped, trying to breathe. The spider-silk-laced body armor stopped the round and sloughed off some of the impact, but I still felt torn in half. I flung myself down and rolled toward the God Machine. The next rounds missed me and struck the device. Metal wires burst apart and the reinforced glass over the green crystals shattered.

"Stop! Stop!" cried Valen, waving his arms and throwing himself between the shooter and me. He backed up and stood with his shoulders against the panel, arms wide, screaming. "For God's sake—*stop*!"

Three militiamen came running out of a side tunnel, guns up, ready to kill. I had no gun and no damn chance at all.

And then there was a sound. A huge, deep, bass *hooooom* sound that shook the whole cavern. Massive chunks of rock cracked and fell from the walls, smashing themselves to pieces all around me. I rolled all the way against the machine and curled up, trying to use its structure to protect myself.

Another earsplitting *hoooooooom!*

The floor split and jets of steam and gas shot upward. One of the shooters was caught by one and instantly burst into flame. The other two skidded to a stop, then turned and ran for the stairs, but a piece of rock the size of a Greyhound bus leaned out from the wall and smashed down on the stairs, crushing them like soda straws and obliterating the two men as if they'd never existed.

There was one more *hooooom* sound and the whole world seemed to shiver. I saw sparks burst from the damaged circuitry on the God Machine. Valen, who still stood with his back to it, began to turn. I was on my belly, leaning against the base of the thing. There was a burst of green light so intense that its brightness stabbed me through the head. I screamed and reeled back.

And then I was falling as the world vanished beneath me.

I fell and fell.

And Valen Oruraka fell with me; and the Italian words kept running through my head. *Lasciate ogni speranza, voi ch'entrate.*

CHAPTER ONE HUNDRED FORTY-THREE

THE VESTIBULE OF HELL

I woke up nowhere.

A nameless place. Empty and colorless and unreal.

I'm in hell, I thought. But that wasn't right. There was no heat. No fire. Nothing. *I'm dead.*

But that was wrong, too. I hurt too much to be dead. So I sat up. My protective suit was ruined, torn, hanging in shreds. How it had been so thoroughly slashed and my skin beneath untouched is something I'll never know.

I stood and stripped it off. My clothes were soaked with sweat and felt cold in the wind.

Wind? I realized that it wasn't that there was nothing to see, but that my eyes could not penetrate the thick and cloying mist that surrounded me. Almost at once I realized that the mist was not empty. Something *moved* in it. There was a clumsy, heavy thump as if the bare foot of something vast stepped down a few yards away. I crouched and tore the fighting knife from the combat harness I'd shucked. It was a double-edged British Commando-style weapon, but it felt absurdly small in my hand.

Stupidly I called, "Valen . . . ?"

Another soft thump. A little closer, and with it was a rasping breath, but if it came from the mouth of some animal, then that mouth was forty feet above my own.

I turned then and ran away. Something buzzed past me and I caught a mere glimpse of it. It was like a moth or dragonfly, but the size of it was impossible. The wings were easily five feet across, and the head of the creature was a deformed nightmare mask.

I fled into the mist. . . .

Hoooooooooom!

I tripped on something in the sand. There hadn't *been* sand beneath my feet a moment before. Or light. I fell and rolled and came up onto fingers and toes, the knife still held in the loop of thumb and index finger. In front of me was a beach. Vast, stretching to either side of me until it vanished in the distance. There was something wrong about it, though.

Two things. One, the sand on which I crouched was not tan or white, or even Hawaiian black. It was green. *That* green. Miles of it. The other problem was the horizon. I've been on beaches all over the world. I've seen bare ones and mountainous one, dunes and flats and rippled sand. This one was green with traces of mud, but it was wrong. There didn't seem to be enough curve to it. Same with the ocean when I looked at it. I could see an impossible distance, even from sea level. The curvature of the Earth was wrong. Not flattened out, but warped, as if I had shrunk down or the world was so much larger that the anticipated and familiar curves were changed.

"No," I said.

A voice said, "You see it, too?"

I turned, and there was Valen. He had also shucked out of his protective garment and wore a plain T-shirt and jeans. His face was different, though, and it jolted me every bit as badly as the horizon line. Instead of the face I'd seen back in Washington, a man of roughly my own age, this Valen was older. Years older. Decades. He wore a heavy, unkempt beard and his hair hung down to his shoulders. His clothes were filthy and threadbare.

Then my brain played back what he'd said. I'd heard it wrong. What he said was, "You see *me,* too?"

I licked a salty dryness from my lips. "I see you."

The man smiled, shook his head, and touched his ear. "I can't hear. Speak slowly so I can read your lips."

I did.

"You're Joe Ledger, aren't you?" he asked in a voice that was cracked from disuse, and badly pronounced the way deaf people sometimes speak.

"Yes," I said. "I'm Ledger. Which means you know why I'm here."

"I had to do it," he said, and tears rolled from the corners of his eyes. "You understand that, right? I had to. I had to."

"No," I said, "you didn't. You made a choice to do it."

"It was for my country. . . ."

I hit him. Not a punch, not a killing blow. I hit him across the face with my open palm. I didn't want him to die. I wanted somehow, impossibly, to literally knock sense into him. He staggered, his cheek turning a livid red. Then he began to cry.

"Did you stop it?" he begged. "Did you find a way to stop the machine?" His weeping suddenly changed to a high-pitched laughter that was so fractured it scared me. He laughed and wept, and tears and snot ran down his face.

"God damn you to hell," I said.

"I prayed to him every night that you stopped it," he replied, eyes wild.

That's what I heard. That's what I understood. But the actual words that came out of his mouth were: *"Y' vulgtlagln h' nilgh'ri n'ghftyar cahf ymg' h' mgepmgah."*

It was a language that I'd heard before. In dreams. In nightmares. A language not spoken by human tongues. A language never meant for us to speak. I'd heard it in the mad wastelands of Antarctica and when I was dying of that impossible version of the flu. And in my dreams at the Warehouse. I'd heard it when Rafael Santoro and I got lost in the God Machine in the laboratory of Prospero Bell.

It was the language of another world. Of *this* world in which we both stood.

A cloud shadow passed over the beach and I turned, knowing that it was not a cloud at all. Valen fell to his knees and buried his face in the sand, weeping and praying and beating his head with his knotted fists. I looked up at the thing that rose from the vast sea. A shape cut of nightmares or the prayers of the damned. A body that was only vaguely humanoid, topped by an octopus head and whose face was a mass of writhing tentacles. Monstrous wings and claws that could tear apart mountains. Behind it I saw ships slashing their way through the sky. T-craft. Sleeker and faster than anything man could ever build.

"Ymg' ngepah h' mgah?" cried Valen.

Did you stop it? He screamed it into the sand as the god of this world threw back its head and howled.

Hooooooooom.

Valen Oruraka and I stood on the slope of a long valley. He was my age again. We were stripped to the waist and we both held knives in our hands made from gleaming crystal.

Both of us were crisscrossed by dozens of shallow cuts, and on some of them the blood had already crusted over. We were both running with sweat, our chests heaving. It was as if we had been fighting here for hours. Days.

Forever.

Valen was weeping but he raised the knife and slashed at me. I parried him easily. He cut again and I parried again. I don't know how he'd managed to injure me so easily, but he was no bladesman, and I was. I could have killed him outright, but I didn't.

I stepped back.

"Stop this," I said.

A voice spoke and I turned to see two figures standing higher up the slope. Both of them dressed in the same lizard-skin armor. Except that I knew it wasn't armor.

"Fahf ah ahf' ymg' ah," said the taller of the two. My mind could still understand the language. I heard it as, "This is who you are."

Those words hurt me more than I could explain. Worse than any of the cuts that had been sliced into my skin.

"No," I said.

"Ymg' ah h' mgathg?"

Do you deny it?

I looked at the knife and the blood smeared along its length. I looked at Valen, who was panting and wild and terrified. Then I turned back to the Reptilians.

"I know who you are," I said.

They studied me.

"In Maryland, on the road, you tried to tell me something. You told me that I was making a mistake."

They said nothing.

"You told me that you were not my enemy. I didn't listen. I didn't understand."

They said nothing.

"I was the one who got the Majestic Black Book for you. I stopped Howard Shelton from using it to build those." I pointed to T-craft that scraped the ceiling of the world. The two creatures did not look up. "I thought we'd given all of it to you. I believed that. That's why you tried to talk with me in Maryland. You knew that there was more of it and that someone was using it. You wanted me to stop them again."

They said nothing.

"I *can't* stop it. The machine is running. It's going to blow up the volcano under Yellowstone and everyone I love and care about is going to die. I can't win this for you and I can't win it for me."

I held out the knife, opened my hand, and let it fall, then pointed at Valen.

"He already won. I'm done."

The taller of the two took three steps down the slope, stopping inches from me. When he spoke, though, he and the shorter one both opened their mouths. They both spoke at the same time, with the same voice, even though their lips did not move. They spoke in my language. In English.

"You are a hunter. You hunted. We followed. You found the machine that was hidden from us."

"Yeah, well goody for me. I got there too late. Now you can take your toys and go home and let me die."

The two creatures glanced at one another, then at Valen, then at me.

"We are not your enemy," they said. "We are not your friends. Your world is your world. Ours is ours."

The shorter one reached into a pouch on his belt and removed a slender piece of that damn green crystal. He showed it to me and nodded. I nodded back, though I don't know why.

Then the son of a bitch stabbed me with it.

CHAPTER ONE HUNDRED FORTY-FOUR

YELLOWSTONE NATIONAL PARK

Top Sims knelt on the ground with Tracy Cole's head in his lap and a pistol in his hand, the slide locked back. He had no more bullets. Cole was alive, but fading. Going away from him, just as hope was leaving him. Ghost lay where he'd fallen and Top couldn't tell if the dog was dead or not. Probably dead.

They'd all be dead soon. He looked at his empty pistol and let it fall. No soldier wins every battle. Top eased Cole's head down onto the ground and rose, drawing his knife. The old joke about never bringing a knife to a gunfight occurred to him and he actually laughed. Militiamen closed in from all sides. Grinning, raising rifles to their shoulders, fingers slipping into trigger guards.

Bunny crawled along the ground, fat drops of blood hanging from his slack lips and falling to mark his slow passage.

Tate was behind him somewhere with a sucking chest wound that was going to kill him as surely as Bunny's injuries would end his own run. Duffy's rifle fire had stopped and all the brush up on the slope where he'd been was burning. Smith was down, too.

It was over. The militia had won from sheer force of numbers, even though more than half of them were dead. The rest would punish what was left of Echo Team. Maybe they would make it quick. Maybe the fucking volcano would blow and burn them all.

Bunny stopped crawling when he reached the AK-47 he'd seen lying by a burning truck. He leaned back on his knees, hissing with pain, checking the gun. Half a magazine. Shapes moved toward him.

"Come and get it, you cocksuckers." He put the rifle to his shoulder and took aim.

Gunfire ripped along the ground and the man he was aiming at danced and twitched and screamed as the rounds tore the life from him. Then the men with him spun and raised their weapons. Not toward Bunny, but up. But a hail of bullets tore them down and they fell like dolls. It was only then that Bunny heard the sound of the heavy rotors as a wave of National Guard helicopters came sweeping over the camp.

Top knelt there and watched the militiamen scatter and run and try to hide and try to fight. And die. M134 Miniguns roared, their six rotating barrels spitting thousands of rounds, tearing apart any hope of cover, ripping through body armor. Missiles streaked like falling stars through the night and lifted escaping vehicles high on plumes of fire.

Suddenly the whole landscape was swarming with soldiers, their guns chewing up the fleeing truckers. Armored Humvees leapt over the crests and slammed down, jouncing and then accelerating as their gunners opened up with heavy machine guns. Top smiled despite his pain and weariness. The militiamen had trained for war, had dared to wage it against their own country, and were now learning what it meant to fight that kind of war, against that kind of foe. How Mr. Church had managed it was beyond him. It didn't even matter. The cavalry had arrived.

He closed his eyes and bent over Tracy Cole, begging her, willing her to keep breathing. Then he threw back his head and in his leather-throated sergeant's voice roared for a medic.

CHAPTER ONE HUNDRED FORTY-FIVE

YELLOWSTONE NATIONAL PARK

When I woke up the first thing I realized was that I wasn't dead.

"God," I breathed.

Then I realized that I was in the chamber by the vent. The heat was incredible. I rolled over onto my hands and knees and then pushed off, raising the ten trillion tons of me onto my feet. The room swayed, or I swayed, or the world swayed. All the same to me. I put a hand out to steady myself on the God Machine.

And fell over because there was no God Machine. It was gone. Totally and completely gone. I scrambled back to my feet and looked right and left, trying to reorient myself, but I was in the right place. It was the machine that had gone.

So, too, had the tunnels. The walls had dropped like curtains and solidified into place. Which sounds as impossible as it looked.

The men I'd killed lay where they'd fallen. My gun was there, too, and I bent to pick it up.

I saw a figure in the shadows a few feet away and walked over to it. Valen Cruraka lay there. Ancient, wizened, dried out as if he had lived a long, hard, bad life and withered into a mummy. I knew it was him because of the knife cuts all over him.

Beneath my feet the Yellowstone supervolcano grumbled. Once. Like a giant turning over in his sleep. That one rumble, and then nothing.

Nothing at all.

EPILOGUE

1.

So, yeah, they found me.

Stairs were gone, radio reception was for shit, but they knew where to look. National Guardsmen rappelled down and got me out. They asked a whole lot of questions for which I had no answers that made sense to anyone.

When I got upstairs I didn't find any of Echo Team. Not one. Not even Ghost. My heart started to break and I think what's left of my mind wanted to snap. Then a colonel was there, coming at me, pushing me down onto an equipment case, pushing a cup of coffee into my hands.

"How many?" I asked through the blackness in my mind.

"All of them," he said. "All of them are alive."

I dropped the coffee, put my face in my hands, and wept.

2.

"Alive" is a relative term. It is often coupled with "well." Not this time.

I sat vigil in another hospital.

Tracy Cole and Pete Smith circled the drain for a long time. Circled and circled, as surgeons worked. I know surgeons get a lot of flak for being hotshots and egotists. Not from me. They are heroes in their own way. They worked all through the night and into the next day.

Tracy Cole lost part of her lung and a lot of useful bone and tissue. Pete Smith lost his spleen. Neither of them were going to walk through the valley of the shadow with us anymore. But the shadows wouldn't own them, either. They were on this side of the dirt, and we all have to put that in the win column.

Duffy had nine broken ribs and a cracked sternum, all from bullets that hit him but didn't penetrate his body armor. The company that made that armor made him a seven-figure offer to be their spokesman. He told them to stick the offer where the sun won't shine. He told me that he'll be back.

Same with Tate. Concussion, seventy-three stitches, and some burns. He looks like Frankenstein, but he doesn't care.

Top took two bullets in the belly. Both were oddball ricochets that hit the lava rock and bounced up under his body armor. They cut him, but the angle was in his favor and both rounds lodged in the plate steel he calls an abdomen. He's already walking around and telling the hospital staff how to do their business. Bunny, on the other hand, had a through-and-through of the thigh. Took a lot of meat with it, but missed the bone and it missed the arteries. His fiancée, Lydia Ruiz, flew out from San Diego and was alternately giving him hell and giving him kisses.

That left me.

I had a bunch of cuts on my body I couldn't explain. I had some burns and I had a moderately nasty skull fracture. They shaved my head, did some weird shit to me, and told me not to drink any booze for a month.

Yeah, we'll see how that plays out.

Ghost had a rough time of it. His Kevlar saved him from bullet wounds, but the incoming rounds had kicked up a spray of jagged stone chips. The doctors removed eleven of them and put in forty-seven stitches. There was some muscle damage, and he would need rest and rehab and lots of TLC. Which he would get. He was already milking it with the practiced ease of a professional scam artist.

3.

Aliens.

Junie came and sat by my bedside, and we talked. Doc Holliday called me twenty times a day, and we talked. Rudy was there, and we talked.

Aliens.

Where do you go with that?

Were they gone? Why were they ever here in the first place? Would we ever really know the meaning of it all?

A lot of Junie's friends in the conspiracy community have always had a lot of answers. Or, theories. Some of them are dingbat nonsense. But some make a lot more sense to me than they did before. When Junie talks about these things, when she plays video interviews with people claiming to be experiencers, with people claiming to be channels for alien beings, I don't laugh or turn away or dismiss it out of hand.

And, weirdly, unexpectedly, it's brought us closer. The truth of what's in her DNA and what I saw firsthand has burned away a lot of ephemeral relationship angst and bullshit. Sometimes at night, when I think about the scaly monsters on the hill in that other world, I give them a nod of thanks.

Does that make me a little crazy? Ha. That ship sailed a long, long time ago.

4.

Mr. Church came out to see me. We sat in the garden of the hospital, drinking coffee and eating cookies.

I told him everything, and he listened without comment. When I was finished he took off his tinted glasses and rubbed his eyes and nodded. He didn't say a thing about what I told him.

Instead, he told me about what the rest of the DMS had been doing while Echo Team was being put back together.

Bug and his team used MindReader Q1 to hack their way through Gadyuka's laptops, which had been obtained by Lilith. Tracing e-mails to servers and decrypting the hell out of all of it gave them the names of everyone involved in the New Soviet. This data was offered to the president and top officials in the State Department, but there has been no response at all.

"Nothing?" I asked.

"Not a word," he said.

Vladimir Putin was clearly behind all of it. We knew it, but could not prove it. Uncle Vlad never sent e-mails, but all references to the "Party Leader" in other New Soviet correspondence had to be referring to him. There was no one else who had the authority to make sure the whole project moved forward unhindered within the Russian bureaucracy. Our government seemed unwilling to touch him, and the DMS could not carry out an assassination. That was extreme even for us.

"So, what do we do?" I demanded. "We just leave him?"

"Not exactly," said Church.

Church had Bug hack into each of Putin's many private bank accounts, where he had tens of billions of dollars squirrelled away. Bug proved how truly devious and dangerous he could be by draining every last penny from those accounts. A full third of it was transferred to charities set up to deal with the families of earthquake victims, and the charitable organizations that worked tirelessly to help in the aftermath of the disaster. Another third was given to Lilith to fund Arklight's expanding global activities.

"Sweet," I said. "And the rest of the cash? What did you do with that?"

Church didn't answer that question. Instead he told me about the other fallen members of our family. Violin was recovering in a private hospital in Switzerland. She was expected to make a complete recovery, though it would take some time.

"What about Harry Bolt?"

"He is steadfast," said Church. "From what I've been told, he hasn't left her side."

"I'm surprised Lilith hasn't had him skinned alive."

"Lilith is a realist," said Church, and left it there.

Sam Imura was also recovering and was in California with his parents.

"Will he be able to come back?" I asked.

"Able? Yes," said Church, "but he doesn't want to. He tendered his resignation via e-mail."

"Damn," I said. That one hurt. "What about Auntie?"

Some of the light went out of Church's face. "She's alive," he said. And that was all he would say.

5.

There were a couple of other things.

The body of Jennifer VanOwen was found in the trunk of a car in a house in Virginia. The owner of that house was determined to be a Russian spy, and had since vanished.

The body of Yuina Hoshino was found, along with two lab techs, in a testing lab, also in Virginia. The bodies were identified by dental records because the lab had burned down. All of the computers and equipment inside were utterly destroyed.

Coincidentally, UFO online clubs widely reported triangular-shaped craft of unknown origin in the area the night of the blaze. The authorities, when contacted by the local news services, declined to comment.

6.

Two months after the events we'd all come to refer to as the Deep Silence case, Church called the senior staff, team leaders, and department heads to the Hangar.

We were asked to assemble at eleven thirty at night. We met in the TOC, the tactical operations center. Standing, sitting on chairs by computer workstations, leaning against walls. The huge multiscreen display wall had been channeled so that all of the screens became one, showing a single image—that of the round symbol of the Department of Military Sciences. A digital clock ticked away the minutes and seconds as we shuffled in and stood waiting for whatever announcement this was going to be. It wasn't Christmas and it didn't feel like anyone's birthday party. Ghost stood beside me, too nervous to sit or lay down. I felt pretty anxious, too.

There were fewer of us than there had been a year ago. The absences were conspicuous. I'm pretty sure everyone felt, as I did, that the others were there, standing unseen beside us. The DMS was a smaller, tighter, closer organization than it had been since I'd first joined, and we were more than merely survivors. We were family.

I stood with Top and Bunny. We were battered and bandaged, but still on our feet. Bug sat cross-legged on the floor below the multiscreen. Doc Holliday stood slightly apart from everyone else, and there were odd lights in her eyes and a strange little smile on her face. Church stood alone in the front of the room, and the fact that Aunt Sallie was not there actually hurt. From what Church had told me privately, she would not return to work once she got out of the hospital. If she got out of the hospital. The stroke had done what guns, bullets, and legions of professional killers had failed to do. The level of grief I felt surprised me. It hurt. It hurt one hell of a lot.

Maybe it ran deeper than compassion for a fallen soldier in this war. Maybe it was a more atavistic dread, because if someone as powerful as Aunt Sallie could fall, then how were any of us safe? I cut a look at my guys and saw identical expressions on the faces of Top and Bunny, who were looking to where Auntie should be standing. Top caught my eye and he gave me a tiny nod, acknowledging that the telepathy people like us sometimes have was running on all cylinders. I returned the nod, but there was probably no reassurance in it.

And then there was Sam Imura. He was done with the DMS. Maybe he'd never pull a trigger for anyone again. Maybe he'd become a different kind of person doing a different kind of work. Impossible to say, but I could feel the universe pushing us in different directions. That hurt, too.

We waited through the ticks of the clock and it was getting close to midnight.

Rudy came in last of all, spotted me, and moved to stand with us. He looked tired and gray.

"How you doing, brother?" I asked.

"Uneasy," Rudy confided. He glanced around. "No one looks happy."

"Nope. You have any idea what's coming down?"

"I—" he began, but then Mr. Church stepped forward and spoke.

"Thank you all for coming out here on such short notice." Church spoke quietly but his presence, his energy dominated the TOC. He wore a dark black suit and quiet tie and I had to push away the thought that he looked like he was dressed for a funeral. "Over the last years we have stood together to fight an extraordinary number of threats, and I am proud to say that each and every one of you has risen to that challenge. *Those* challenges. Over and over again. As did those of our brothers and sisters who were consumed by the fires of this war."

The room was silent as a tomb. Church looked down at his black-gloved hands and for a moment there was a small, sad smile on his lips.

"We've each been marked by the battles we've fought," continued Church. "As our own Dr. Sanchez so often says, violence leaves a mark. Some of those marks are obvious; they are like sigils cut into our skin. Other scars, other wounds, run deeper, and are visible only to others like ourselves; the chosen few who have walked through the storm lands. That is how it is for such as we. The war is the war."

I heard several people around the room repeat it like a litany. The war is the war.

The clock ticked away the seconds.

Church nodded. "Now we are at a crossroads. As of midnight tonight, our charter will no longer be in effect."

I nearly staggered. It was like a punch to the throat.

"Again?" growled someone, and there was even a ripple of laughter. Aggressive laughter. We'd had our charter canceled twice before. However, Church shook his head.

"The DMS charter was not rescinded by the president," he said. "I have canceled it."

We gaped at him. I heard gasps and hisses and even a cry of alarm.

Church held up a calming hand. "Most of you know that we have not always enjoyed the full support of Congress or the White House. That position has slipped several notches in recent years. Some of it was the direct result of hacking and manipulation by the Seven Kings, Zephyr Bain, Nicodemus, and others. Some of it was our own humanity being caught under the wheels of threats bigger than anyone has ever faced before. The fact that we have rebuilt ourselves, strengthened our resolve, and risen to a new high mark of efficiency is a testament to all of you and to the people in your teams and departments. You are remarkable. You are heroes, and that is a word I never use lightly."

There was total silence in the room.

"There have been political threats made against our organization," he said, "and it was only a matter of time before our charter was officially revoked. I, for one, do not care to be a victim of a political culture of power over patriotism, of personal agenda over the common good. So, I have sent a courier to deliver our withdrawal from any official connection to the government of the United States. That person is ready to hand that document to the president's chief of staff."

If we were all stunned before, we were now in actual physical shock. Church gave us a moment. However, seconds kept falling off that clock behind him. I felt cold inside. My hands and feet were numb.

"Those of you with active military rank will be given the option of returning to your branches of service or receiving an honorable discharge," said Church. "That has been arranged with trusted friends of mine within the various armed services." He paused. "No one is being abandoned. No one's record will be adversely affected. Rather, the reverse. Commendations for your excellent service have been added to your files, and anyone who chooses to return to the army, navy, coast guard, air force, or marines will likely receive a promotion and choice of station or assignment. The same goes for those who have transferred here from the FBI, DEA, ATF, or any other law enforcement, investigative, or covert group."

Silence. I don't think any of us were capable of speech.

"For those who choose to take this as an opportunity to retire, I think you will find that the retirement packages will be adequate to your needs. You will receive full pensions and a benefits package that includes full medical coverage for you and your families, as well as other tokens of my personal gratitude. A trust has been set up so that all of your needs will be provided for. You have served your country and served the world, and that service will not be trodden upon once you step down."

Silence.

Church took a breath. It was impossible to read his mood or gauge his expression. He's a spooky old bastard and has the best poker face in the world. Behind me I heard someone sob.

It was Bunny who raised a hand to ask a question. Church gave him a sober nod. Bunny licked his lips. "Sir," he said, "we've been fighting this war for a long time. Just because the assholes in Washington turned their backs on us doesn't mean the war's over."

"Farm Boy's right," agreed Top. "Seems like now we're going to be needed more than ever. Not sure I understand how going home to sit on a porch or stepping back into all that bullshit bureaucratic red tape's going to do anybody any damn good."

Church studied him for a silent moment. He gave another nod. Behind him the clock was getting dangerously close to midnight. It was like looking at the timer on a nuclear bomb. We all feared midnight's strike.

"I could not agree more," said Church. "The war is the war. The war will always be the war. We are in an age of new and greater threats than anything humanity has ever faced. Cyberterrorism, rampant religious hatred, bioweapons, drones, secret cabals, and other terrors are still out there. But it is no longer the job of the DMS to fight that war."

The clock ticked down.

11:57.

11:58.

11:59.

Midnight.

The screens behind Church went black. The symbol of the DMS vanished and was gone. We could feel it leave. It was like having our blood sucked out of our veins. My knees wanted to buckle. I felt that weak. That shattered.

Rudy snaked out a hand and grabbed my wrist with crushing force. Ghost howled. Actually howled. Like a wolf.

I looked around. People were hugging each other, sobbing openly. They were devastated. Church stood apart, his face grave, hands clasped behind his back. Bug looked up at him.

And smiled.

I stared.

Why the fuck was he smiling? Had this pushed him over the edge? The DMS, after all, was the only family he had left. This was his home and MindReader was his god.

Church raised one hand and snapped his fingers. Loud as a gunshot, and we all jumped. Every single one of us.

"Listen to me," he said in a voice that was deadly cold. "The DMS is gone. In my last conversation with the president, he accused us of acting with too much independence, of being a rogue organization."

Mr. Church looked at us and, like Bug, he smiled, too.

"That seemed to be the only worthwhile idea that has come out of a politician's mouth in more years than I can count."

Silence dropped back over the whole crowd.

"I won't speak for each of you," said Church, "but I am tired of fighting the wrong war. I am weary of fighting against our own government, against red tape, against fear of action and restraint born of greed. I am tired of being on a leash. When I formed the DMS it was with the idea that we would have total independence of action and the freedom to pick our own cases and react with our best speed. We were as good as our word for a while, but politics and personal agendas hobbled us. Crippled us. Weakened us."

He was still smiling.

"That ended at midnight," he said. "It's a new day. The war is the war, and it cannot be won by half measures. If going rogue is what it will take, then so be it."

He snapped his fingers again and the screen behind him lit up. A new graphic flooded us with its light. It was not the biohazard code of the DMS. Not anymore. Never again. This was something else. Something new.

I looked around and saw people—Top, Bunny, Rudy, Doc Holliday, and others—mouthing the words that were worked into the new logo. The new symbol.

I spoke those words aloud.

"Rogue Team International," I said.

A side door opened and I saw people enter the room. Junie and Toys. Violin and Lilith. Others I did not know, but who wore the same predatory smiles and looked at us with hunters' eyes. They came and stood with us.

With us.

"Rogue Team International," said Church, and his smile became colder and more deadly than any I've ever seen on a human face. "Self-governing, fully autonomous, independently funded. A global rapid-response strike team endorsed but not answerable to the United Nations."

Beside me, Rudy said, *"Ay dios mío."*

Top and Bunny had tears in their eyes, but they stood straight and tall. Junie flashed me a brilliant smile, and even Lilith gave me a nod. One warrior to another.

Mr. Church turned slowly to look at the sea of faces.

"Welcome to the war," he said.